Retribution

WHAT READERS ARE SAYING

"This is the first book I have ever read by this author and I have to say I couldn't put it down till I finished it. What a ride I got! Love, action, excitement, crime families—heck, what more could you ask??"
—Amazon reader "cedarblue," 5 stars (on *Malavita*)

"This story truly exceeded my expectations. *Revenge* is action-packed, and when the pace picks up, it does not slow down.... Pick up this book today; it will grab your attention from the beginning. I cannot wait to read the next book."
—*The Romance Reviews (TRR)* site, 5 stars, Top Pick (on *Revenge*)

"Here is to a WHOOPING 5 Stars. If I had to describe this book in about four words, it would be action-packed, sexy, romantic, and adrenaline-rushing.... This would make a kick-butt movie! There were times when I was fanning myself, sitting on the edge of my seat, and so mad I had to put it down. The steamy scenes were oh so delicious!"
—*Bengal Reads* blog, 5 stars (on *Revenge*)

"Dana weaves such a wonderful story of love, passion, treachery…, and lies that I stayed up 'til after midnight reading.... The end of the book left me wanting to read the next novel.... It's a book I know I'll read again."
—*Steph's Book Retreat* blog, 5 stars (on *Revenge*)

"The suspense keeps the pages moving quickly in book two of the Blood and Honor series. A fast pace, credible characters and a complex plot guarantee hours of entertainment."
—*RT Book Reviews* magazine, 4 stars (on *Retribution*)

"Not one sentence was wasted filling word count, every word was relevant to the story, keeping it moving and exciting from page one right to the end.... I have just found myself a new series to follow and can't wait for book 3."
—*Lindsay and Jane's Views and Reviews* blog, 5 stars (on *Retribution*)

"This series is awesome!!! If this series was ever made into a movie, it would put *The Godfather* to shame! I am always pulled into the lives that Dana creates in her books, heart beating so fast it is like I am part of the story line!!! ...I VERY HIGHLY RECOMMEND THIS BOOK. I WANT TO GIVE IT MORE THAN 5 STARS."
—Julie's Book Reviews blog, 5 stars (on *Redemption*)

ALSO BY DANA DELAMAR

Blood and Honor Series: Mafia Romance

Malavita (Prequel)
Revenge (Book One)
Retribution (Book Two)
Redemption (Book Three)
Reckoning (Book Four)

Writing with Kristine Cayne

Total Indulgence Series: MMF Ménage Romance

Her Two Men in London (Book One)
Her Two Men in Tahiti (Book Two)
Her Two Men in Sonoma (Book Three) – coming 2018

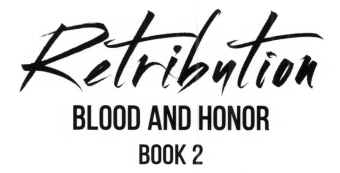

Retribution

BLOOD AND HONOR

BOOK 2

DANA DELAMAR

Book cover design by Dana Delamar © 2018

Cover photo: © Depositphotos.com/feedough

Title page logo design by Scarlett Rugers © 2012

Author image courtesy of LGImages

Ebook formatting: LK Ebook Formatting

Editing, proofreading, and print formatting:
By Your Side Self-Publishing
www.ByYourSideSelfPub.com

ACKNOWLEDGMENTS

Many people contributed to the creation of this book. No writer goes it alone, and I am certainly no exception.

I can never adequately thank my wonderful critique partner, Kristine Cayne. She buoyed me up when the going got tough, gave this book scads of her time and attention, and asked many hard questions. Kristine, I truly couldn't have done this without you. You continually push me to up my game.

Once again, Ann Charles and Wendy Delaney came to the rescue when I was floundering about and needed help replotting this book. Thank you, thank you, thank you for giving up part of another weekend to help me.

I'd also like to thank my beta readers, Kim and Ninia, for their insights, comments, and catches. You made this book better than it was!

I owe a great debt to Romance Writers of America® and specifically my hometown RWA® chapters, Eastside RWA and Greater Seattle RWA, for providing inspiration, support, guidance, friendship, real-world craft advice, industry contacts, and knowledge that proved invaluable. Thank you all.

Last but not least, I'd like to thank my family, my friends, and most of all my real-life hero, James Davis, for bearing with me during the madness. You will always be my honey bunny.

CAST OF CHARACTERS

The Lucchesis

Enrico Lucchesi (LOO kay zee) – *capo* (head) of the Lucchesi *cosca* (crime family)

Kate Lucchesi – wife of Enrico Lucchesi

Nick Clarkston – illegitimate son of Enrico Lucchesi; Interpol agent

Fedele (feh DAY lay) **Lucchesi, Alessandro (Sandro) Lucchesi, Matteo Lucchesi** – sons of Domenico Lucchesi, Enrico Lucchesi's first cousin

Rinaldo Lucchesi – deceased; Enrico Lucchesi's father; former *capo*

Domenico (Dom) Lucchesi – deceased; first cousin to Enrico Lucchesi and former *capo di società* (second in command) of the Lucchesi *cosca*

Antonella (Toni) Lucchesi (née Andretti) – deceased; Enrico's first wife; daughter to Carlo Andretti and sister to Dario Andretti

The Andrettis

Dario Andretti – *capo* of the Andretti *cosca* (Milan branch)

Ilaria (ee LAR ee ah) **Andretti** – wife to Dario Andretti

Delfina Andretti – daughter of Dario Andretti; aspiring fashion designer

Cristoforo (Cris) Andretti – son of Dario Andretti and *capo di società* of the Andretti *cosca* (Milan branch)

Benedetto Andretti – son of Lorenzo Andretti; *capo di società* of the Andretti *cosca* (Calabrian branch); head of La Provincia (quasi-ruling commission of the 'Ndrangheta, the Calabrian Mafia)

Lorenzo Andretti – father to Benedetto Andretti; *capo* of the Andretti *cosca* (Calabrian branch)

Carlo Andretti – deceased; former *capo* of the Andretti *cosca* (Milan branch)

CAST OF CHARACTERS (cont.)

Other Characters

Antonio Legato – *capo di società* of the Lucchesi *cosca*

Ruggero (rooj JAIR oh) **Vela** – bodyguard to Enrico Lucchesi

Giovanna (joh VAN ah) **(Gio)** (Joh) **d'Imperio** – best friend to Delfina Andretti; daughter of Gianluca d'Imperio

Gianluca (jon LOO kah) **d'Imperio** – *capo* of the d'Imperio *cosca*

Leandro (lay AHN droh) **d'Imperio** – *capo di società* of the d'Imperio *cosca*

Jacopo (jah COH poh) **Bossi** – co-worker and friend of Delfina Andretti

Silvio Fuente – officer of the *carabinieri*

Émile Delacourt – Nick Clarkston's superior at Interpol

Flavio (FLAH vee oh) – bodyguard to Dario Andretti

Eusebio (yoo SAY bee oh) – bodyguard to Benedetto Andretti

GLOSSARY OF TERMS

arrivederci (ah ree vah DAIRT chee) – goodbye (formal)

attacca (ah TAHK ah) – attack

basta (BAHS tah) – enough (as in "I've had enough!" or "Stop!")

bella, bellissima (BEHL lah, behl LEE see mah) – beautiful

bene (BEN ay) – good

bisnonno (beez NOH noh) – great-grandfather

buona sera (BWOH nah SAIR ah) – good evening

capisci (KAH pee shee) – you see, you understand

capo (KAH poh) – head (don) of a crime family (*cosca*); plural *capi* (KAH pee)

capo di società (KAH poh DEE so cheh TAH) – second in command of a *cosca*

cara (CAR ah), *caro* (CAR oh) – dear, sweetheart

carabinieri (car ah bin YAIR ee) – Italy's national police force; a single member of this force is a *carabiniere* (car ah bin YAIR ay)

casinò (cah zee NOH) – casino. In Italian, *casino* (cah SEE noh) means "brothel" and *casinò* is a gambling house.

ciao (CHOW) – informal hello and goodbye

come stai (COH may STY) – how are you

comparaggio (cohm pah RAH joe) – the Southern Italian institution of co-parenthood, whereby the person making this vow swears to be as a parent to the child. A co-father is referred to as *compare*; the "parent" and "child" are *compari*. The vow is thought of as indissoluble and incorruptible. Within the Mafia, *compari* will not betray each other.

contabile (cone TAH bee lay) – accountant; treasurer for a *cosca*

cosca (KOHS kah) – a crime family; plural is *cosche* (KOHS kay)

Cristo (KREES toe) – Christ

davvero (dahv VAIR oh) – really, seriously

Dio mio (DEE oh MEE oh) – my God

dottore (dote TOR ay) – doctor; the "e" is dropped when used with a last name

faida (FEYE dah) – blood feud

figlio (FEEL yoh) – son

finocchio (fee NOHK kee oh) – derogatory slang term for a homosexual

fortunato (for too NAH toh) – lucky

fratelli di sangue (frah TELL ee DEE SAHN gway) – blood brothers

grazie (GRAHTZ yeh) – thanks. *Mille* (MEE lay) *grazie* means "Many thanks."

idiota (ee dee OH tah) – idiot

ladro (LAH droh) – thief

Madonna (ma DOEN nah) – the Virgin Mary; Mother of God

magnifico (mah NIF eh coh) – wonderful, magnificent

malavita (mah lah VEE tah) – the criminal underworld, the criminal life

merda (MARE dah) – shit

molto (MOLE toe) – very, a great deal, a lot

'Ndrangheta (en DRAHNG eh tah) – the Calabrian Mafia, or "the Honored Society." Members are *'Ndranghetisti* (en DRAHNG eh tees tee), or "men of honor." A single member is an *'Ndranghetista.*

nonna (NOHN nah), *nonnina* (nohn NEE nah) – grandmother, granny

nonno (NOHN noh) – grandfather

padrino (pah DREE noh) – godfather

paesano (pie ZAH noh) – villager, peasant

papà (pah PAH) – dad

pentito, pentiti (pen TEE toh, pen TEE tee) – penitent, repentant; in the Mafia, *pentiti* refers to Mafiosi who have turned state's evidence

per favore (PAIR fah VOR ay) – please

perfetto (pair FEHT toe) – perfect

polizia (poh leet TZEE ah) – Italian police

porco Dio (POR koh DEE oh) – literally "pig God;" *very* vulgar religious curse

porca miseria (POR kah mee ZAIR ee ah) – literally "pig misery"; means "damn" or "bloody hell"

prego (PRAY go) – welcome

GLOSSARY OF TERMS (cont.)

principessa (prin chee PESS ah) – princess

prozio (proht TZEE oh) – great-uncle

puttana (poot TAH nah) – whore, prostitute

ragazzo (rah GAHTZ oh) – boyfriend

raggazi (rah GAHTZ ee) – people, friends, guys

salute (sah LOO tay) – to your health; cheers!

sangue del mio sangue (SAHN gway del MEE oh SAHN gway) – blood of my blood

scusa (SKOOZ ah) – excuse me

sì (cee) – yes

signore, signora, signorina (seen YOR ay, seen YOR ah, seen yor REEN ah) – sir, madam, miss; the "e" is dropped from *signore* when used with a last name

Sottotenente (soh toh teh NEN tay) – Second Lieutenant

strega (STRAY gah) – witch

stronzo (STRON tzoh) – shit, turd, bastard

ti amo (tee AH moe) – I love you

troia (TROY ah) – slut

vaffanculo (vahf fahn COO loh) – go fuck yourself

vincolo di sangue (VIN coh loh DEE SAHN gway) – blood bond

zio (TZEE oh) – uncle

PROLOGUE

Nineteen years ago
London, England

Nick listened hard for her voice, for some indication that she was all right, but all he heard was water running. He knocked on the bathroom door, a tentative rap. His tight throat strangled his voice. "Mummy?"

No answer. His stomach rolled over, and the supper he'd eaten hours ago seemed ready to come back up. *Why isn't she answering?*

His mum had been in there for ages, weeping at first, then eerily silent for some time now. He'd sat hunched over, hugging his knees, across from the door for hours, praying that she'd come out, smile at him, and make his world right again. But she hadn't.

Nick shifted his weight, and his feet squished unpleasantly in the carpet. He looked down at his white socks, only they weren't white anymore. They were pink. The water seeping under the door was tinged with blood. Had she fallen and cut herself? "Mummy!" he cried, this time smacking the door—*wham, wham, wham*—with an open palm. He tried the knob, but it wouldn't open. The sick feeling in his stomach expanded, grew. *Mummy, answer me.*

He shoved on the door, then put his shoulder into it. In his panic, he forgot that the door had always been sticky. He wasn't that big for an eight-year-old, but his weight was more than enough to do the job.

The door swung inside, bashing into the wall to his left. Nick overbalanced and skittered into the bathroom, arms pinwheeling, his feet slipping on the wet tiles.

His gaze bounced from surface to surface in shock—red, red, it was all so red.

Dangling over the edge of the tub, his mother's left arm oozed blood from a deep gash. The tap was on, cold water cascading onto the floor.

"Mummy!" He slipped and fell in his haste to reach her, bloody water splashing all over his face and hair, soaking his pajamas. Horrified, he wiped the blood out of his eyes. He scrambled up and went to her, the shock of the fall

1

scaring up the sob he'd been holding back. His choked breathing echoed in the room, sounding harsh in his ears. "Mummy? Wake up," he pleaded, touching her shoulder. Beneath his fingers, her skin was icy. "Wake up!"

Her eyes were closed, her blonde hair floating on the dark, dark water, stained nearly black with her blood. A wild cry tore out of him and he shook her hard, praying that she'd open her eyes, that she'd say something.

But she was gone.

She'd left him. Just as his father had left them earlier that day.

It was all his father's fault. If only he'd stayed when Nick had begged him, when his mother had begged him. If only he'd cared.

CHAPTER 1

Present day
London, England

Nick Clarkston trudged up the stone steps to his flat, his rolling suitcase bumping along behind him. Three weeks wasted. He'd chased through every backwater of Sicily, followed every lead, researched every whisper. And ended up with nothing. No drug bust, no Mafiosos in jail. His first big assignment as an Interpol agent, and he'd blown it.

He'd been pleased when his superior, Émile Delacourt, had chosen him. Still he'd wondered why, why him. He was too bloody new to Interpol. And something wasn't right with this case; he'd known it for at least a fortnight. But Delacourt hadn't let him give up on it, had insisted he stay in Italy, had insisted he keep following the leads given by their informant. Leads that led nowhere, that dissolved in wisps of smoke. Why had Delacourt been so insistent? And why had he then abruptly called a halt to the investigation that morning, a full week after Nick had told him it was futile?

Patting his pockets, Nick fished out his keys, fumbling for the right one. He was so bleary eyed that he shoved the key in the lock the wrong way. Jerking it out, he slammed the door with the flat of his hand, then let his arm fall to his side. He was behaving irrationally. *Focus, mate, for just a little while longer. Then you can sleep.*

Finally he unlocked the door and shoved against it with his shoulder, annoyed when it wouldn't open more than a couple feet. Peering around the edge, he discovered the culprit: three weeks' worth of post that had been shoved through the slot and was now jammed under the door. *Bloody fantastic. Now I'm late on my bills too.*

In his excitement about the assignment, he'd forgotten to ask his grandparents to pop by and go through the post.

Sighing, he scooped up the pile of envelopes, catalogs, and magazines, yanking on the items wedged under the door. He ripped the cover of the latest *Maxim*, tearing it in half, then forced himself to slow down, to push the door back into its frame.

He glanced at the torn cover, almost not looking at the girl. *Hold up. Nick Clarkston,* the *Nick Clarkston, former terror of Cambridge, too tired to admire a pretty girl?* That was definitely not normal. He needed a bloody holiday.

Leaving his suitcase by the door, Nick carried the hodgepodge of post into the tiny kitchen and dumped it on the two-person table pressed up against the wall. He sat down and pawed through the stack, hastily sorting: bills, bills, bills, adverts, a wedding invitation, catalogs for products he'd never buy, *British GQ, National Geographic Traveler,* the torn *Maxim.*

Then he saw something that made his heart somersault: a cream-colored envelope postmarked Cernobbio, Italy, his name and address handwritten in black ink.

His pulse tripping, he tore the heavy paper open and pulled out a crisp sheet covered in dark handwriting. Could this be related to his investigation?

"Signor Clarkston,

I beg your pardon for contacting you like this, but I did not have a telephone number for you."

Nick smirked. *Of course you didn't.* He had only a mobile phone. And he rarely gave that number out. Cut way down on the number of advertisers calling him. And he could turn it off whenever he wanted. He didn't much fancy being interrupted at someone else's convenience.

The letter continued, and what he read next made his heart burst into a gallop.

"I know you work for Interpol. And I know you do not have contact with your father. Do you know who he is, I wonder?"

Nick stopped reading. The simple question pierced him. No, he didn't know who his father was. Not in any true sense.

He almost hadn't passed the background check for Interpol because they couldn't verify his father's identity. He'd tried tracing the man himself, but had turned up nothing that made sense. The only Enrico Franchetti he'd found had been an elderly man, far too old to be his father. *What did this person know?* Nick turned back to the page.

"My name is Franco Trucco. I work for your father. And he has done me a grievous wrong. He killed my daughter while driving drunk. He must be brought to justice, he must be held to account, but my hands are tied. Your father is a powerful man who operates outside the law. Given your position at Interpol, I write to you in the hope that you can accomplish what I cannot."

So his father had been at it again, and another woman was dead by his hands. Another woman—maybe a woman in love with him, like his mother had been. Before his father had driven her to desperation. Before he had driven her mad with grief. And of course, his father didn't care about the outcome. He hadn't come to see Nick afterward, hadn't attended the funeral. Hadn't even sent flowers. His father had acted as if they hadn't existed, as if once Veronica was dead, he had no connection to Nick.

Had it not been for the monthly checks sent to his grandparents, Nick would have thought his father had forgotten him entirely. Oh yes, his father had supported

4

him financially. But he'd never visited, never spoken to Nick, never held him in his arms again. Never offered to take him to Italy, never offered to raise him. *Bloody bastard, why do I care?*

Nick heard the crackle and felt the crunch as the heavy paper crumpled in his fist before he stopped himself and smoothed it back out. The letter was a clue. The first clue to finding out who his father really was. The first clue to finally bringing his father to justice.

The only thing Nick knew for certain was that the man who called himself Enrico Franchetti, the man who claimed to be his father, didn't officially exist.

Signor Trucco closed with his phone number, urging Nick to call him at his soonest convenience. Nick picked up his mobile and started to dial the number, then hit the End button. It was just after one in the morning, too late to call. And he ought to sleep first, get some rest. In his current state, it wasn't wise to talk to anyone, much less to a man who worked for his father.

Nick set the phone down and paced around the kitchen, his eyes straying back to his mobile. He wanted to know. *Now.* As much as he needed it, sleep was out of the question. Shoving his hands in his trouser pockets, he debated. Call or wait? He ought to check out this Trucco first, see if he was legitimate. Maybe this was some cruel joke. Not many people knew the story, but one of his mates could have gotten roaring drunk on holiday in Italy and decided to take the piss out of him.

Pulling his laptop out of its padded case, he set it up on the kitchen table, then drummed his fingers on the table's edge, waiting for the machine to boot. At last the Windows startup music chimed, and he entered his password. A few more clicks and he was finally able to log in to the Interpol databases.

His fingers flew across the keys as he hunted for information about Trucco. Nothing, nothing, nothing. Then he looked in open investigations. And there Trucco was—or wasn't.

Franco Giorgio Trucco, aged 62. Found tortured, his throat slashed, in Milan two weeks ago. The murder was listed as a possible Mafia execution. A glass of ice water splashed down Nick's spine. He searched for known associates, but none were documented. Under Profession, the file said Trucco worked as an accountant for Falcone Enterprises.

Nick pulled up the company's website; it was privately held and registered in Switzerland. Which meant the trail had run cold. The airtight Swiss privacy laws would yield him nothing.

But it was a clue, nevertheless. Many Italian firms that incorporated in Switzerland did so to hide from taxes or to cover illegal activity. And many of those firms had Mafia ties. A tingle of excitement sizzled in his chest. He was onto something.

He picked up the letter again, studying the postmark. It was dated just a few days before Trucco's death. Had someone found out about the letter and killed Trucco over it?

Nick tapped his fingers on his lips. Could his father have had something to do with Trucco's murder? Who else wouldn't want Nick to talk this man?

This wasn't the first time Nick had suspected his father of having criminal ties. The most likely false name, the way the checks came—always through a local solicitor's office, always written on the solicitor's account. Never once from his father directly.

Nick had questioned the lawyer before, Edmund Tyrell. But Tyrell had given him nothing, had known Nick had no right to question him, no jurisdiction. He'd calmly listened to Nick threaten him and then just as calmly ushered him out of his office each time.

Well this time, Nick had something. Trucco was dead, but perhaps there was someone at the number he'd left who'd give Nick some answers. And if there wasn't, then by God, Tyrell was going to do some talking. Nick would be at the man's office first thing, right after he called Trucco's number. And he wouldn't leave until Tyrell gave him something.

Something he deserved to know: his father's real name.

———◆———

Nick woke repeatedly through the night, memories of his mother's death haunting his dreams, even though they hadn't plagued him for years. That damn letter. At six, he gave up on sleep and took a long hot shower. Two cups of tea later—the only thing he had in the house—he felt little better than he had the night before.

He'd dawdled as long as he could. Seven fifteen. Still too early. But fuck it. He punched in Trucco's number and waited for someone to pick up. Just as he thought the call would go to voice mail, a man answered in Italian. *Bollocks.* He should have anticipated that. His Italian was still only rudimentary.

"*Ciao.* This is Nick Clarkston, calling from London, England. By any chance, do you or someone there speak English?"

"*Sì,* Signor Clarkston. How may I be of assistance?" The man's English was good, if stiff, his accent as British as Nick's own, though tinged with the exotic.

"I received a letter from a man named Franco Trucco."

"You are speaking to him."

Surprise hit him like a bullet. How stupid did this man think he was? "Ah, I am? I mean, great. It's good to speak to you. I've been away and saw your letter only last night. It was troubling."

"I meant it to be. Your father has caused me enormous grief."

I can relate to that. "I understand. And I'm sorry."

"Why would you be sorry? You were not the cause."

"Why did you write to me?"

"I thought I explained myself. I want justice. You are the only one who can give it to me." Oddly, the man seemed to believe his own words, even if he wasn't the real Franco Trucco. Whoever he was, Nick's father was definitely in the man's black books.

"Perhaps. But first tell me who my father is. His real name."

The man's voice grew sly. "You do not know it?"

Nick's mouth filled with a bitter taste. "No."

"Well then, you must come to Italy, meet your father, and learn who he is. And then together we will crush him."

Time to gamble. "No."

"No?"

"Franco Trucco is dead. And you are a liar. Who are you? Did one of my friends pay you to do this?"

The man chuckled. "I assure you, this is no joke."

"Stop fucking with me, mate."

"Very well. My name is Dario Andretti. When you research me, you will find that I have certain ties. You will think you cannot trust me. But I tell you, Signor Clarkston, I am the only person you *can* trust."

Nick laughed. The guy had bollocks. "And why is that?"

"Because your father will never be honest with you. But I will."

"Tell me then. What is his name?"

"Enrico Lucchesi. Not that it will help you much. He has constructed a rather clever front for himself. Trust me, the law has tried many times to pin him down, but he always manages to slither away, rather like a snake."

"So how is this time any different?"

"Because I can give you everything you need to put him in prison."

Blood thundered in his ears. "Who is he? What has he done?"

Andretti laughed. "All in good time. Come to Milan. I will explain everything."

"Wait a minute. I'm not going to hop on a plane just because you say so."

"Call me when you arrive."

"I'm not—" *Click.* The line went dead. Nick stared at the phone. *What now?*

———— ◆ ————

Blevio, Lake Como, Italy

Despite herself, Delfina Andretti admired the A-line cut of the new dress her father had bought her for her upcoming twenty-second birthday party. She twisted back and forth in front of the floor-length mirror in her bedroom, watching the cobalt-blue dress flare out around her legs, then settle back with a gentle flounce.

"You like it?" her mother asked. Her furrowed brow and darting eyes gave her away. She was worried. And ever determined to keep the peace. No matter what the cost.

"Of course, Mamma. It's beautiful. Papà has good taste."

Her mother smiled. "He'll be glad to hear you've finally forgiven him."

Delfina met her mother's gaze in the mirror before turning to face her. She crossed her arms. "I didn't say anything about forgiving him."

Her mother tried to smooth her hands up and down Delfina's upper arms, but Delfina pulled away from her touch. "You know he's sorry about that."

He's never sorry. "He's only sorry he agreed to marry me off to Enrico Lucchesi in the first place."

"He knows he should have consulted you."

She turned away from her mother. "You mean Nonno Carlo should have consulted me. And of course *that* was never going to happen."

"Delfina, stop acting like a child. I thought you learned your lesson with that boy."

7

His name is Teo. A ball of fire filled her chest. She glared at her mother over her shoulder. "When's the last time Papà asked your opinion on anything of consequence? That's right. *Never.*" Her mother flushed, and Delfina regretted her nasty words. It wasn't Mamma's fault. Mamma was just as powerless as she was. "I'm sorry." She touched her mother's arm.

"You are full of foolish notions. I should never have let you watch all those American movies." Mamma looked as weary as Delfina felt. How many times had they had this same fight?

"It isn't foolish to want to be an equal partner in my marriage. It isn't foolish to want independence and freedom. Do you really think I want to live this life?" Delfina gestured at her well-appointed bedroom. Other than the mannequin in the corner and her half-finished sewing projects, the room was like something out of a five-star hotel, all showy fabrics and dark woods.

"Why not? You have everything you could possibly want."

"Except a *choice*. I won't even get to choose my husband." Delfina's hands twitched. She wanted to shake her mother, hard. "Maybe *you* didn't mind when it happened to you, but I don't want to marry someone just to strengthen Papà's business. I especially don't want to marry someone who's almost twice my age!"

"Well you don't have to. Not since that whole business with your grandfather."

Delfina practically rolled her eyes at the way her mother described what had happened. Less than two weeks ago, Enrico Lucchesi had shot and killed her grandfather Carlo right in front of her father Dario. And then he'd married another woman—her late cousin's wife, no less. What a tangle.

She should be happy things had ended that way. At least she could be thankful that her engagement was over almost before it started. She had nothing against her uncle Enrico—he was a fine man, and the world was certainly better off without her grandfather. But she hadn't wanted to marry Enrico. Aside from him being old enough to be her father, she'd have been stepping into the shoes of her late Aunt Toni, and those would have been difficult to fill.

Her chest and throat ached. Aunt Toni had encouraged her to follow her dreams, to become a fashion designer and get far away from the family. But she'd also told Delfina it was important to find someone to love. To marry the right man.

Aunt Toni had been content with Enrico Lucchesi, even though their marriage had been arranged. Shortly before her death, she'd told Delfina the secret to a happy marriage: "Make sure he cares about your happiness more than his own. And if you feel the same way, you'll always be glad you're together. No matter what happens."

She hoped to find that kind of love someday. But it wasn't going to happen unless she could escape this life, somehow, and that was close to impossible. She looked at her mother. "Haven't you ever wanted anything different?"

"This is all I know. It's not a bad life."

"But it's not a good one either. Doesn't it bother you how Papà makes money? Doesn't it bother you to think that people have died for what we have?"

"Of course, Delfi. But most of them made the same choice your father did."

"Not all the dead were criminals."

"Your father isn't some thug. He's a man of honor."

"Dress it up how you like. That doesn't make it any less ugly."

Her mother sighed. "Fine. Pout all you want. Just remember that your father loves us and he puts the pasta on our plates."

"I'm aware of that." She watched her mother leave the room. How could she ever forget? She was a Mafia princess, after all. Delfina smiled, but it was wry. The label fit perfectly, like the dress. She smoothed her hand down the layers of chiffon and ruffles. So pretty. But it had been bought with ugly money. Dirty money.

Reaching behind her, she yanked the zipper down and shrugged off the dress. She left it in a heap on the floor, then reconsidered and picked it up, smoothing the fabric and laying it on the bed. It wasn't the dress's fault. It was too pretty to mistreat. In her head, she deconstructed the pattern, admiring how the designer had put the dress together to flatter and conceal. The cut would work for a great many body types, not just hers. It was the kind of style she'd like to be known for. Something that would work for the average woman. A touch of beauty that was within reach of everyone. Not just the stick thin or the super-rich.

She sat down on her bed and fingered the chiffon. But how would she ever get to follow her dream to leave Italy, to seek her fortune in Paris or London, far from her family's influence? Her father had barely agreed to send her to university. If Aunt Toni hadn't interceded, she'd have been stuck at home. Her father had flat out told her it was a waste of time, that he intended to marry her off soon, and what would she need a career for? Fortunately, he'd never been able to resist his sister when she wanted something. But Aunt Toni was dead now, and there was no one to persuade her father to change course. No one but Delfina, and her arguments fell on ears deafened to her reasoning and even to her pleading. So now it was all-out war between the two of them.

Delfina went to her desk, pushed aside a pile of *Vogue* back issues, and picked up the thick notebook that contained her sketches. She flipped through the pages idly. How would she ever get to make her designs real? If only her father would let her alone, if only she were free. A thought teased her. What if he were in prison? What then?

Don't be stupid. She couldn't betray him. She couldn't do that to him, to her family.

Or could she? He'd betrayed her, hadn't he? He'd known what she wanted, and he'd tried to strip her of it anyway. Just like with Teo. Her father had never let her choose a single thing for herself, certainly not a boyfriend, much less a husband. That whole business with her uncle proved it. Her father didn't care about her. What had he done to earn her love, other than providing a few genes? He treated her like a game piece. Not like a daughter.

The heat of tears burned her eyes, and she took a deep breath. No. She was not going to cry over this. Crying never solved anything. Her tears hadn't spared her, or Teo. With a sigh, she thought about the boy she hadn't seen in six years. What was Teo doing now? Had he ever forgiven her?

With a soft whine, her Rottweiler, Zeta, approached and bumped her broad head under Delfina's hand, making her smile. "Silly beast, you always know when I need a distraction," she murmured while stroking Zeta's black fur, her fingers working around the dog's ears. Her grandfather had given her and her brother Cristoforo two pups when Delfina was fourteen. Zeta had been by her side ever since, had offered Delfina comfort whenever she needed it, had licked away Delfina's tears after Teo had been taken from her.

From her earliest days, Delfina had been told—*reminded*—that she had everything. She was an Andretti, and that name carried with it power, privilege, prestige.

But as with all gifts, there was a price to pay: her freedom.

When she was sixteen, she'd shared an infatuation with Teo Mancuso, the seventeen-year-old son of one of the family's guards. She and Teo had snuck off together several times, stealing kisses in the olive grove, in the guest cottage, deep inside the hedge maze. Stolen kisses and hasty, fumbling caresses. Until they'd been caught by her grandfather Carlo.

Because Teo hadn't taken her virginity, his life had been spared. But Carlo had branded Teo's right hand with an "L" for *ladro*, forever marking Teo a thief. And she'd been forced to watch. Delfina had appealed to her father, begging him to spare Teo, and her. But Papà had been unyielding. She'd had to witness every minute of Teo's ordeal.

After the branding, Carlo had told her, in gruesome detail, the story of his brother Remo, of how Remo had paid for his defiance of the rules. For putting his own needs above those of the family. At the end, Nonno had taken her by the chin and forced her to look into his cold dark eyes. "You are an Andretti. You are not some alley cat, lifting her tail for anyone who struts by. Do you understand?"

The scent of burnt flesh lingered on his fingers. All she wanted was to vomit. But she wouldn't let him see her weakness. Delfina sniffed back her tears and nodded. She understood. Clearly.

That evening, after Teo had been driven away in a black car—at least she could be glad it hadn't been a hearse—Mamma and Papà had taken her aside. "You must never defy your grandfather," Mamma said.

Delfina looked to her father, but he averted his gaze.

"He has plans for you, and you cannot ruin them," her mother continued. "You *cannot*." Her voice took on a shrill tone.

She's afraid. But all Delfina could listen to was Teo's screaming in her head, how his voice had gone hoarse from begging her grandfather to stop, to have mercy on him. The scent of charred flesh seemed to fill her nose again.

"Delfi, are you listening?" Papà said.

"You're a coward!" Delfina spat at her father.

His face turned stony, and he held up his maimed right hand. "*This* is how my father shows his love. He let Rinaldo Lucchesi do this to me. He gave my sister to Rinaldo Lucchesi's son."

She repeated the slur. "Coward."

Mamma slapped her, the blow swift and stinging. "Stop it! Stop it *now*," Mamma hissed, her lips quivering.

"It's true. I can at least tell the truth, can't I?"

"Not if you want to live." Her father said the words slowly, his tone dry, defeated.

"Then kill him," Delfina said. She was shaking inside, whether from anger or terror, she wasn't sure.

Her mother sucked in a breath, then clamped a hand over Delfina's mouth, mashing her lips against her teeth. "*Basta*! You stupid, stupid, child. Must you misunderstand?"

Delfina tore her mother's hand away. "Oh, I understand. When it comes to your children's happiness, the only thing that matters is what's best for the family."

Her father stepped closer, towering over her. "Don't ever forget it." His hands curled into fists before he jammed them into his pockets. "Or the next time, it won't be the boy who pays."

With a sharp whine and an insistent bump of her head, Zeta called Delfina back to the present. She scrubbed her fingers through the dog's short fur and dried the tears that had crept down her cheeks. She needed to forget the past. Forget Teo. Forget everything that never was and never would be.

If her father had started bribing her with dresses, that meant he still cared what she thought. He still cared, at least a little. Now that her grandfather was in his grave, perhaps things would change for the better. Perhaps the dress was her father's way of telling her that?

When Zeta tired of the renewed attention, Delfina sat down at her desk and pulled out a pencil, going to work on a new sketch. Who was she kidding? She needed to stop fantasizing about her father changing. That was never going to happen. And she needed to stop thinking about him going to prison. That kind of thinking was traitorous. And she knew what happened to traitors.

Everyone did.

And yet, as her pencil outlined a new design, her thoughts kept returning to the same idea, worrying it like a loose tooth. What if she were free of her father? What might she become then? What kind of life might be within her reach?

———— ♦ ————

After the phone call with Andretti, Nick spent the next couple of hours researching the man. Andretti hadn't lied—he did have certain ties that made Nick think he couldn't trust him. Mafia ties. Specifically, ties to the Calabrian Mafia, also known as the 'Ndrangheta, the Honored Society. A prickle of unease made him shift in his seat.

The 'Ndrangheta weren't as well-known as the Sicilian Cosa Nostra, but they should have been. Due to the low profile they'd kept, few outside law enforcement had heard of them, even though they were arguably the most powerful organized crime element in Italy and Europe. Maybe even the world. Their reach had spread from southern Italy to the north, then on to strongholds throughout Europe, before branching off to Canada, South America, Mexico, even Australia. The recent recession had only furthered their influence, as desperate business owners, unable to get cash from legitimate banks, turned to the 'Ndrangheta for loans and investments, thus giving the Honored Society more outlets for laundering their profits.

The main reason for their vast success was twofold: the 'Ndrangheta recruited almost exclusively along blood ties, which ensured that the members of each criminal clan were also blood relatives. On top of that, they maintained a low profile: few public killings, especially of civilians, and few *pentiti*, or witnesses for the state. Almost no men who were captured were willing to turn on family members. Thus, law-enforcement efforts against them had little information to go on, little leverage over the members who had been apprehended, and little hope of ever infiltrating the organization.

If Andretti were telling the truth, Nick's father was one of these men. Maybe even a don of one of the families.

His fingers trembled as they hovered over the keys. He'd delayed the search into his father long enough. Now that he was on the brink of knowing, an unending drop yawned before him. If his father were in the 'Ndrangheta, Nick was in trouble. Big trouble. Interpol would consider him compromised, and his career would be over.

Nick typed in his father's name, then snatched his hand back from the keyboard before pressing ENTER. Once he knew, he could never unlearn his father's identity. Why had he never thought of this before? Was it because he'd hoped he was wrong?

"Bugger," he muttered aloud. "Bugger, bugger, bugger." He swallowed against the gastric acid burning his esophagus. The pain was piercing, immediate, and overwhelming. Why did stress always go straight to his belly?

"Fuck it." He had to know. He had to. Curiosity would eat at him until he did. He pressed the key and waited for the search results, his stomach in knots.

What he got back on Enrico Lucchesi was a puzzle. Nothing definitive. He'd expected a long record of offenses compiled by the Italian Direzione Investigativa Antimafia. Instead, the DIA record on Lucchesi consisted of four entries, only one an arrest.

He reviewed the entries in chronological order. Several years ago, his father had come up on possible tax-evasion charges in front of an anti-Mafia judge, Federico Dinelli, who had later been murdered, allegedly by Sergio Grantini, a man who was rumored to have worked for Enrico Lucchesi. But Grantini was missing, the murder weapon had been lost, and the case was in limbo due to a lack of new leads. The tax-evasion case had dissolved in the wake of Dinelli's death.

The second entry regarded a suspected drunk-driving incident from April that was later dismissed due to missing blood-alcohol results. His father had been driving and lost control of the car. The young woman who'd been with him, Fiammetta Trucco, had been killed in the crash. A fresh rush of acid flooded his throat, and pain spread through his jaw and chest. The incident mentioned in Trucco's letter was true. And once again, important evidence that might have implicated his father had disappeared.

He almost moved on to the next entry, but stopped. The incident was true, but he didn't know if Andretti was telling the truth about his father's identity. There was one way to know for sure. He pulled up the mug shot and exhaled hard.

There was no doubt: Enrico Lucchesi was his father. Nick would have recognized him anywhere. He hadn't changed much in the nineteen years since Nick had last seen him. There were faint lines around his eyes and on his forehead, but his hair was still black and thick, and the face that stared back at him was nearly a mirror of his own.

Andretti hadn't been lying.

Taking a deep breath, Nick read the third entry, which concerned a murder committed in self-defense at Lucchesi's home on 15 September—just shy of one month ago. Apparently, he'd gotten involved with an American woman who'd been married to Vincenzo Andretti, one of Dario Andretti's cousins. Vincenzo had broken into Lucchesi's home and attacked them. The woman, Kate Andretti, had shot her husband. The physical evidence supported self-defense, and the case was closed without arrests.

The fourth entry detailed the murder of Rinaldo Lucchesi, Enrico's father. Nick's grandfather. The man's severed head and hands had been delivered to Enrico on 4 October—just twelve days ago. There were abundant signs of torture, with extensive damage to all ten fingers, all of which had also been severed ante-mortem. The investigation was open, but the rest of the body hadn't been found, and there were no leads. Nick started to open the file with the crime-scene photos then stopped. He hadn't known his grandfather, but he didn't want those images in his head. Reading about the case was bad enough. Even if the man had been a mobster, that was no way to die.

Nick moved from the legal details to the business ones. His father was listed as CEO of a major Italian bank, Banca di Falcone, and apparently owned a number of other businesses throughout Milan and around Lake Como, where he lived. Aside from the notation regarding tax evasion, and the missing evidence in the two cases that might have resulted in arrest, he appeared to be clean.

Except there was another curious tie to the Andretti family. Lucchesi had been married to Dario Andretti's sister, Antonella, now deceased a little over a year ago from ovarian cancer.

Why would Andretti hate his former brother-in-law? Could it have something to do with the recent death of his father, Carlo Andretti, who'd been killed in a possible Mafia hit? Andretti had been found shot dead along with several associates in a burnt-out house in the hills above Lake Como. There were no leads in the case and little physical evidence. The bodies had been identified through dental records.

A detail gnawed at him. The letter had been postmarked 29 September. Trucco's body was found on 1 October and Carlo Andretti's on 4 October, the same day Enrico Lucchesi found out his father was dead. That could not be a coincidence.

Trucco didn't write the letter. Dario Andretti did. Had Trucco supplied him the details?

Something dark and twisted was going on between the two families, the Andrettis and the Lucchesis. A silent war of sorts.

And now Andretti was trying to draw Nick right into the middle of the conflict.

CHAPTER 2

They should talk face to face, if Nick wanted to catch Delacourt in a lie. But the trip to Lyon would take too long. And Nick had to be careful not to get caught in a lie himself. How was he going to convince his boss to let him meet with Andretti, without revealing his father's identity?

He dug out his secure mobile, the one he used to discuss Interpol business only, and hit Delacourt's speed-dial number. The man answered straight away, as if his wrinkled hand had been resting on the sleek black phone on his desk. "Nicolas, it is good to hear from you."

A grin crossed Nick's face in response to the smile in Delacourt's voice. "You as well."

"I am sorry you had such a rough time in Sicily, and nothing to show for it." Delacourt's English flowed smoothly, his native French seasoning the words.

Nick swallowed, the grin fading. "I wanted to talk to you about that."

Delacourt paused a beat too long. "What about?"

"Émile, be straight with me. You sent me down there for a reason, but it wasn't to follow leads, and it wasn't to collect information."

Delacourt laughed. "Your imagination is quite fertile. Perhaps you should write for the cinema?"

"I'm not imagining things. First off, I was too junior for an assignment on my own. Second, I haven't trained as a field operative. Third, everything our so-called informant gave me was rubbish, the whole lot."

"I do not know what to say."

"How about the truth?" There was a long pause, during which Nick pictured Delacourt running his free hand through his snow-white hair, pulling it into tufts, as if he took his styling tips from Albert Einstein.

"Nicolas, if we are to continue this discussion, it must be in person. Certain things cannot be discussed on the telephone, even on a secure line."

Nick needed something to counter the sudden dryness in his mouth, the uptick in his heart rate. What couldn't Delacourt discuss on the phone? He took a sip from the steaming mug of tea sitting on his kitchen table. "Shall I come to you?"

"No need. I have business in London tomorrow."

"What time shall I see you at SOCA then?" The Serious Organised Crime Agency was the National Central Bureau for Interpol in the United Kingdom and Nick's home office in London.

"I do not wish to meet at the agency."

Nick's pulse accelerated again. They'd often met before at Nick's office. Why was Delacourt avoiding SOCA? "Then where?"

"Trafalgar Square, next to Nelson's Column. Thirteen hundred hours. We will talk more then." Delacourt ended the call without a goodbye. Odd. The old man was typically the picture of decorum and politeness. Something had him rattled. Something he didn't want his colleagues to know.

Something that affected Nick as well. That case had definitely been a ruse.

Since he couldn't make further progress with Delacourt, it was time to talk to Edmund Tyrell again. Now that Nick knew his father's real name, Tyrell could no longer deny the Mafia connection. Maybe he could trick Tyrell into giving him something useful. The man had a silver tongue, but even the devil made mistakes.

———————◆———————

If she hadn't already had lunch planned with her best friend, Delfina might have been tempted to continue driving north into Switzerland, to go somewhere her father couldn't find her. If such a place existed.

Brushing off her gloomy thoughts, Delfina ascended the stone steps that led to her favorite trattoria in Bellagio. She was nearly to the top when she heard Giovanna's excited voice. "Delfi!" She waved at Delfina from one of the outdoor tables and jumped up and gave her a quick hug and kiss on the cheek.

Like Delfina, Giovanna d'Imperio loved fashion, and she always had all the latest styles; however, that didn't mean she had the best taste. Today Gio was in a crisp black miniskirt and black platform heels; the riveted straps of leather crisscrossing her feet gave her the air of a dominatrix. She'd topped off the outfit with a conservative silk fuchsia blouse that was tucked in but only half buttoned, so that the sheer lace of the black cami she wore underneath peeked out through the deep V. Her black bra was clearly visible.

Delfina surveyed her up and down and put her hands on her hips. "Gio, really. What did your father say when he saw you in that?"

Giovanna wrinkled her nose in distaste. "You too? Next you'll be commenting on my scandalous lack of underwear."

"Tell me you're making that up."

"I have a date."

Delfina couldn't help smiling. "And what did your father say about that?"

Gio grinned and waggled her eyebrows. "Papà doesn't know."

"You can't be serious."

Gio plopped down in her chair, crossed her legs, and swung her foot. "Well, I *think* I have a date."

"You *think*?" Delfina took her seat. "What's gotten into you?"

"It's more like what *hasn't* gotten into me. You know him better than I do."

"Who are you talking about?"

"Antonio Legato. Your 'good friend' Antonio."

When would Gio learn? They were both off-limits to Antonio. Delfina laughed. "Okay, now I *know* you're teasing me."

Gio studied her manicure. "I am not. He asked me out." She picked at one of her cuticles. "At least I think he did."

The waiter brought their standard orders along with steaming cups of espresso. Delfina picked hers up and took a sip. Perfect, as always. "Gio, if he asked you out, you'd know. Antonio is a big flirt. With everyone, including me."

"He said I should meet him tonight at Barfly."

Delfina laughed. "That means he just wants to make sure he has someone to dance with. Not that he ever lacks in that department."

Gio pushed her lips into a pout. "*Davvero?*"

"I hate to disappoint you, sweetie, but yes. Really."

Sinking back against her chair, Gio twirled a few strands of her blond-streaked dark brown hair around one finger. "You really know how to wreck a party, Delfi."

"I'm just trying to save you some heartbreak."

Her friend leaned over the table, tapping the wood with her manicured nails, each one painted fuchsia to match her blouse. "You invited Antonio to your birthday party, yes?"

Delfina nodded as she chewed a forkful of lake trout. "That's the whole reason I'm having it at your place, remember? My father would never let Antonio set foot in our house."

Giovanna's face suddenly lit up. "Oh my God, I completely forgot! There's something I have to tell you. You'll never believe it."

"Out with it."

Gio scanned the other diners as if suddenly worried that they'd be overheard. "My dad says your uncle Enrico has a grown son. An *illegitimate* son."

The news struck Delfina like a bullet to the chest, the wound sharp and deep. Her uncle had cheated on Aunt Toni? "That can't be true."

"It is. Your dad and your grandfather knew about it. I guess it happened while he was engaged to your aunt."

Delfina swallowed hard, trying to mask her hurt, but it must have showed, because Gio raised a hand to her mouth. "Oh Delfi, I'm sorry. I didn't think. It was just good gossip to me. But it's about your family. I'm *such* an idiot."

Delfina set down her fork and pushed her plate away. "It's all right. It's just a shock." *How could he?*

Gio pursed her lips. "Good thing you didn't end up married to him, yes?"

She nodded without thinking. Her father knew? How? And why hadn't he told her? "Do you know anything more?"

"I wasn't supposed to know even that much. I overheard him discussing it with Leandro."

"And you didn't ask Leandro for details?"

Gio rolled her eyes. "Of course I did. But he told me it was 'business' and that

16

I should stay out of it. He thinks he's so far above me now that Papà's made him *capo di società*."

"Yeah, Cristoforo's acting the same way. Just two weeks ago he was my little brother. Now he thinks he's king of the mountain."

Gio pushed her salad around her plate, as usual not really eating it. She hated her tendency to be curvy, but Delfina envied her the generous breasts that captured every man's attention. "Leandro acts like he's joined some exclusive club. A boys-only club. It galls me."

"I second that." Delfina flashed back to the traitorous thoughts that had engulfed her that morning. "I wish I'd never heard of the 'Ndrangheta."

Gio wriggled her wrists, her many bracelets jingling and her rings flashing. "Well, it does have its benefits."

"I hate it. I loathe it."

"You're still upset with your dad."

"Of course. He's going to do it again. Just wait—I bet he springs someone else on me in a week or two. Once he thinks I've forgotten about it."

"Well, I want to get married. The sooner the better. I have *needs*." Gio took a sip of her pinot grigio. "It's too bad Cris is only nineteen. Do you think he'd like a slightly older bride? One with experience?"

Delfina laughed. "Your 'experience' is not much more than mine. Unless there's something you haven't told me?"

"Not yet." Gio tugged her blouse open a little more. "But maybe after tonight, if I can get your blond Adonis to do me right…"

Delfina broke into a fit of giggling. "You think Antonio would mess around with Gianluca d'Imperio's daughter? He's no fool, Gio. No man in the business will ever touch you until he's married to you."

"A girl can dream."

She can. I can. "But nothing's going to come of it."

"Speaking of Adonis," Gio said with a sigh, "how about we go to Greece this summer? We haven't got much more freedom left, you know. I'd rather not be a virgin on my wedding night."

For the right man, I would. "If I'm not married off by then, yes, definitely."

Giovanna patted Delfina's hand. "You look like you're attending your own funeral. He said he'd let you pick, right?"

"I'll have as much choice as a cow going to the slaughter."

"Sweetie, chin up. He won't force you to marry some horrid old man."

"Don't be so sure." She finished off her espresso. "If I could, I'd run off to Paris or London. I could design clothes and live my own life, make my own choices."

"There are worse lives than ours. Think about all those poor starving kids in Africa."

"At least they're free."

"I'm sure they feel very sorry for you, Delfina Andretti, in your fancy clothes. Those Ferragamos I'm sure cost as much as most of those people make in a year. Maybe two."

Delfina reddened and studied her gorgeous black patent heels. Gio was right.

"Okay. It could be a lot worse."

"I hate to point this out, but your whole *life* revolves around money. Which one of us wants to be a designer? You're not exactly signing up to be Mother Teresa."

"True." She laughed. "You love giving me a good kick."

Gio grinned. "Sweetie, you're young, gorgeous, thin, and have more money than you deserve. Embrace it. Love it. Someday you'll be old, fat, and wrinkled." She winked. "If there's any justice."

If there was any justice, someday she'd be *free*. That was the only thing that mattered.

———————◆———————

Nick wished he'd never heard of Edmund Tyrell. The rubbish that had come out of that man's mouth… All of it was untrue. It *had* to be. Well, what had he expected? The truth from a bloody lawyer?

He slammed out of Tyrell's office and stalked to the Tube station, taking the first train that arrived. Nick got off at Trafalgar Square, the mid-October wind whipping his open jacket about his body as he left the station. At least it wasn't raining.

Wandering the square, Nick angrily kicked at bits of trash in his path. He heard giggles and whispers to his left. The source of the noise was a couple of young girls, who were watching him and laughing. "Oughtn't you be in school?" he said to them. One of the girls imitated his scowl, then stuck her tongue out. The two girls laughed harder. He turned away, his face growing hot.

Yeah, he was acting like a child, down to the petulant expression that was no doubt on his face. He stopped walking and took a deep breath, staring up at Nelson's Column. Lord Nelson had probably never acted this way. At least not as an adult. What was wrong with him? Why couldn't he get a hold of himself when his father was involved? Why did he always lose all control?

It wasn't rational. It wasn't logical. And it wasn't who he wanted to be. He prided himself on his analytical powers, on his ability to spot patterns where others saw random behavior. That ability, that very essence of reason and rationality, had served him well on the job. It had led to this posting with Interpol. But he was anything but rational now.

He'd been working in the new cyber-crime unit at Scotland Yard when he heard about the Criminal Intelligence Officer opportunity within the UK National Central Bureau at SOCA. Working at the NCB meant working for Interpol, and Interpol was the big-time, where Nick would have a chance to make a worldwide difference. And a chance perhaps to investigate his father, to find out who he really was. And if he could, to make him pay for his crimes.

He checked his watch. Twelve forty-five. Fifteen more minutes to fret before Delacourt arrived.

That bloody arsehole Tyrell… He wished he hadn't gone to see him. He'd thought he'd catch Tyrell out, surprise the man with what he knew, yet Tyrell had hardly blinked at Nick's revelations. He shouldn't have been surprised, but the man's unflappability could drive a nun to drink.

Though the topper was one particularly infuriating thing Tyrell had said, about the only thing of substance. After Tyrell had refused to answer Nick's questions, Nick had muttered to himself, "Why do I care anyway?" Tyrell had perked up then, after ignoring everything else.

"You care, young man, because he is your father. I assure you that he cares about you very much. Much more than you appreciate."

"He has another family. That's how much he cares about me."

"True. But you are his only son. In fact, his only child at the moment."

The news had struck him with wonder, a wonder he still couldn't shake. Prior to seeing the file on Enrico Lucchesi, he'd never really considered that his father could have another family, other children. A wife. For some reason, he'd always pictured his father alone. Much like himself. And yet, what did he really expect? That his father had missed him all this time? That he thought of his son with the same intensity, the same longing, that Nick had felt for him?

It was foolish to think that way. Not a single thing about his father's actions suggested that he'd loved Nick, not really. He may not have forgotten him financially, but that could be nothing more than the nagging of a guilty conscience.

And yet... Nick remembered, still remembered, the tears in his father's eyes that last time he'd seen him, the pain on his face, the way he'd held Nick's chin and told him that he had to go. "I can't keep doing this to any of us," he'd said to Nick. "I know you don't understand now, but someday you'll see that this is the best thing for all of us." His father had wiped the tears off Nick's face, had crushed him close in a tight hug, had planted a soft kiss on his forehead. And then he'd said, "Someday you'll forget me, someday you'll have another father. But I will never forget you, Nico. Never." And then he was gone.

Nick swallowed hard, hot tears stinging his eyes at the memory. He breathed in deep through his nose, fighting for calm, for control. His father had been wrong on every count. His leaving had been horrible, the worst thing to ever happen. Nick had never had another father. And he'd never forgotten the one he'd been supposed to have.

If his father had truly loved him, he would have come back for him. Tyrell had spouted nothing but a complete and utter load of bollocks.

He swung away from Nelson's Column, gazing unseeing across the square when a movement caught his attention. Delacourt at last. Now he'd get some answers about his mysterious assignment—and hopefully permission to meet with Andretti.

Delacourt approached with his customary loping stride, his white hair lofting up in the breeze. Nick smiled and waved in greeting, but his hand dropped to his side when he saw how his boss's gray trench coat hung off him; he'd lost a lot of weight. As the man drew near, Nick took in the dark circles and the sunken cast to Delacourt's eyes. He appeared not to have slept in weeks. Nick dashed forward. "Émile, what's wrong?"

Delacourt's bushy white brows popped up, his watery blue eyes troubled. "Is it so obvious, Nicolas?"

"You don't look good."

The old man swiped a hand across his forehead. "Let's walk."

"Why are we meeting here instead of the office?" Nick asked as they set off across the square.

"I wanted fresh air."

Nick let out a groan. "Quit toying with me. You're avoiding having this discussion where SOCA or Interpol might hear us. What do you need to say that you don't want them to know?"

Delacourt stopped walking and pinched the bridge of his prominent nose. "Tell me first why you were reading the files on Enrico Lucchesi and the Andretti family."

A punch of surprise hit Nick in the chest. "You've been tracking my searches?"

Delacourt pressed his lips together. "I had to know what you know."

"What the fuck is going on?" Nick planted his fists on his hips and rocked back on his heels.

"I might ask you the same thing. But with less swearing." Delacourt's lips curved up. He was forever chastising Nick over his foul mouth.

"I've bloody had it, Émile. Tell me."

Delacourt studied his shoes. "Do you know who Enrico Lucchesi is?"

"Besides a mobster?"

Delacourt turned back to him. "He's your father."

Nick's gut lurched and rolled. Delacourt was going to fire him. "How did you know?"

Jamming his hands in his coat pockets, Delacourt strode away and Nick followed. "You must swear to never tell anyone." He gave Nick a pointed look. "*No one.* Or both of us are out. *Tu comprends?*"

Adrenaline danced down Nick's spine. "Not a word."

"About three weeks ago, a man named Tyrell telephoned me. He said he worked for your father, a very powerful man. A man who could help me with a problem of mine, if I helped him with a problem of his."

"What problem of yours?"

Delacourt stopped and scuffed a shoe over the blocks of stone beneath their feet. "My wife has late-stage pancreatic cancer."

"Jesus." Nick touched Delacourt's arm. "I'm so sorry, Émile. Why didn't you say?"

He met Nick's gaze. "And suffer the excess of kindness I see on your face?"

"What's wrong with other people caring about you?"

Delacourt turned away. "My wife's only treatment options were in the United States, but of course, we have no health coverage there, and we could not afford the cost. Time was running out. And this man, Tyrell, said his employer would pay for her treatment indefinitely. If I did one thing for him."

"Which was?"

"Keep his son out of harm's way for several weeks. Send him on an assignment put together by Tyrell."

Nick laughed. "So it *was* all rubbish." Jaw tight, Delacourt dipped his head. "Why did you trust him?"

"He told me I could verify it myself. He sent me surveillance video of a man watching your flat and the SOCA building. Face recognition confirmed the story.

The man worked for the Andretti family."

"How did you know Tyrell wasn't working for the Andrettis?"

"He told me the whole story, who Enrico Franchetti was. He knew every detail about you, including items that aren't public record, things you'd told me. I verified that he'd paid for your tuition at Cambridge. I also double-checked with your grandfather, to make sure he knew who Tyrell was. It all checked out."

"Why didn't you fire me? I'm compromised."

Delacourt shook his head. "You don't know your father. There's been no contact, no taint from the association. As far as I'm concerned, he's not your father." He paused. "And in case you haven't noticed, I can't very well point a finger at you without pointing one at myself."

"True." It was a bitter pill to swallow. "I never thought, in a million years, that anyone could get to you."

Delacourt's eyes watered. "Neither did I. But I love her." He swallowed. "And if I had a son, I'd want him to be like you."

A lump rose in Nick's throat. "I wish you hadn't done it."

"I'd do it again," Delacourt said with a defiant jut of his chin. "She's getting better. And you're still alive."

"If you think I'm going to thank you—"

"I don't."

"So what happens now?"

Delacourt ignored Nick's question and asked one of his own. "Why were you accessing those files?"

Nick recounted the letter he'd received and his discussion with Dario Andretti. "I want to go to Italy and meet with him. I'm thinking of posing as a dirty agent. One who can be bought."

Delacourt let out a whistle. "That's a dangerous game. Too dangerous. No one's ever got inside the 'Ndrangheta."

"Because no one has an 'in' like I do. Think about it."

"There's a reason for that. Family ties have a way of twisting one's priorities."

"No worries there. I want my father in prison."

"I cannot let you do it, Nicolas. It's far too dangerous."

Nick smiled. "You can't very well stop me, can you? Now that I know what I know."

Delacourt frowned. "You'll get yourself killed."

"I think I'm smart enough to manage."

"You haven't trained for undercover work."

"I'm not exactly going undercover, am I? All I have to do is pretend to be dirty. It can't be that hard. And if I need tips, I know who to ask."

Delacourt's face took on a red tinge. "Enough of your tongue. I have revealed nothing to your father, nor have I compromised the agency or any investigations."

Nick crossed his arms. "You no longer get to tell me what to do."

"I am sad to hear you speak that way."

When would he ever get a handle on his temper? "I'm sorry. I'm just... upset."

"Will you at least take some advice, then?" When Nick didn't object, Delacourt continued. "I want you to check in with me once a week. And I want you to work with the local anti-Mafia contact. The man's name is Fuente; he works for the *carabinieri*. I'll get his details to you."

"Agreed."

"Remember, you are not to mention a word of this to anyone. I don't care who it is or how much you trust them. *I* don't trust anyone."

"Because everyone has a price." Damn, he'd done it again.

The old man's lips compressed into a hard line, but he didn't respond to the jab. "When do you leave?"

"Tonight. I've already bought the ticket."

Delacourt started to reach out, as if to touch Nick's shoulder, but he pulled his hand back. "I wish you luck."

"I'll need it."

After a sharp nod, Delacourt left without another word. Nick watched him walk away, regret eating at him. Why had he been such a bastard to the man? He'd probably saved his life, after all. So Delacourt had been bought. At least his price was saving the lives of two people he loved.

What was Nick's? What would cause him to abandon his principles, to make a deal with the enemy? The answer was instantaneous: his grandparents. He'd sacrifice anything for them. He sighed. Love was a merciless bitch, always had you by the short hairs.

When Nick could no longer see Delacourt, he headed to the nearest Tube station. He had a lot to do before the plane left.

He was probably going to regret this, wasn't he? He might very well end up in the same position as Delacourt—or worse. But how else was he to get answers? To get justice?

No risk, no reward. No doubt the famous last words of many a fool.

CHAPTER 3

As the plane touched down at Milan's Malpensa airport, Nick balled his hands into fists and bumped them down on the armrests. *Show time.*

Hefting his carry-on case, he hailed a taxi and directed it to his hotel in Milan. He flipped his mobile over and over in his hands, itching to call Dario Andretti and berating himself at the same time. *You're walking into a trap, you idiot.*

Delacourt had warned him, and Nick wasn't such an idiot that he couldn't see the danger himself. And yet, how else was he ever going to get answers? How else was he ever going to get justice for his mother or for his father's other victims? Fiammetta Trucco hadn't deserved to die any more than his mother had. Enrico Lucchesi had used both women and discarded them like so much used tissue. And who knew what else he'd done. Maybe he'd killed that judge too.

Never again.

If he was smart, the first thing he'd do would be to talk to Silvio Fuente, the local *carabinieri* contact. The question was: could he trust the man? Delacourt seemed to think Fuente was reliable, but more than one officer of the *carabinieri* had been caught taking bribes from the Mafia.

Nick did need backup though. And some sense of who Andretti was. If he consulted Fuente, it had to be off the record. And without letting Fuente know his true purpose.

——— ◆ ———

Even amid the mid-morning bustle of the Piazza del Duomo in the heart of Milan, Silvio Fuente was hard to miss. He was in full *carabinieri* dress uniform, the long black cloak over his shoulders making him look like a cross between a Nazi SS officer and an eighteenth-century soldier. Fuente was fit, dark-haired, and somewhere in his forties. A pair of tourists snapped Fuente's picture as he stood beneath the weathered bronze statue of Vittorio Emanuele II astride his horse.

When the tourists moved on, Fuente tipped his black officer's hat at Nick.

"Signor Clarkston?"

Nick held out his hand to shake. "Signor Fuente."

The man smiled, revealing a flash of white teeth beneath a dark mustache, as he took Nick's hand in his gloved one. With his other hand, Fuente pointed to the rank insignia at his neck. "*Sottotenente*. Lieutenant second class."

"I apologize." *Firm shake, strong, direct eye contact. All good.*

Fuente waved off Nick's words. "No need. My promotion was hard won, and perhaps I am too proud of it." He laughed at himself. "What brings you to Milan? You told me precious little on the phone."

"We've run across some data that indicates a major drug shipment is coming to Milan."

The lieutenant raised a brow. "Who are the involved parties?"

Deep breath. You can do this. "We believe half of the transaction involves the Andretti and Lucchesi families. The drugs are coming out of Spain."

With a chuckle, Fuente stroked his mustache. "You are at least part wrong. Enrico Lucchesi may be many things, but he is staunchly anti-drug. His family is not involved."

Sure. "Sometimes people say one thing and do another."

Fuente's mouth twisted. "I am sure this will sound strange, but Lucchesi is a man of his word. I would trust him above many others."

"You know him personally?"

"I have met him in the course of my duties, yes."

"I find it odd that a man in your profession would defend a mobster."

The lieutenant's dark eyes locked on to Nick's. "Are you implying something about my character?"

"Not at all. Just remarking on a curiosity." Nick paused. "But sometimes we can get too close to the men we chase."

"Silvio Fuente is *not* for sale."

I wonder. "So, if Lucchesi isn't involved, what about Andretti?"

Tilting his head, Fuente shrugged. "It is certainly possible. Though we have not heard anything to corroborate your intelligence."

"Do you know everything these men are up to?"

"You would be surprised."

"How?"

A half-shrug this time. "I have my ways."

"I thought we would be working together, not playing games."

Fuente pulled out a pack of cigarettes. He offered them to Nick, and when he declined, Fuente lit one and took a drag before answering. "I have a network of paid informants."

He needed that long to say so? What was the man up to? "And they're reliable?"

"For the most part."

"So this Andretti family. What do you know about them?"

"Regarding the Milan branch, the old don, Carlo Andretti, was recently murdered. We have not found the killer yet. His son, Dario, has taken over."

"You think he killed the old man?"

Fuente blew out a stream of smoke, politely directing it away from Nick.

"Possibly, but Carlo had many enemies."

"His primary one?"

The man smiled. "Enrico Lucchesi."

"That name again."

"The very same." Fuente scanned him up and down. "Tell me. What is your interest in Lucchesi?"

"He's a suspect."

The lieutenant seemed to be holding back amusement. "May I give you a word of advice?" Nick nodded. "You seem awfully young. Fresh to the job, yes?" Nick's jaw tightened. Fuente had seen right through him. "Go home, Signor Clarkston. Before you are killed. These men, they have little patience."

"I'm not afraid."

"Then you are a fool. Dario Andretti would have you for breakfast. Before breakfast."

"You know Andretti?"

Another draw on the cigarette, another pause before answering. "We have met. He is a real dark horse, as you English say. A rather cunning one, I believe. Stay away from him."

"And Lucchesi?"

Fuente smiled. "Go home, *signore,* while you still can." He tipped his cap at Nick and set off across the park.

Nick flushed, his cheeks heating. *Idiot. Fucking prat. You thought you could fool him?* The man had probably seen every liar and con man there was. And Fuente had very nicely told him he was out of his league, though he had barely held back laughing. Nick couldn't have been a bigger fool if he'd charged out onto the football pitch during the World Cup and tried to play striker for England.

He ought to turn back, if he knew what was good for him. But there was no other way. If even the local police were on his father's side, the man would never see justice. Unless Nick kept pushing.

What was it about his father that seemed to charm every person he encountered?

Nick laughed. He was probably the only person immune to that charm. Well, except for Dario Andretti. Which was why the way forward pointed to Andretti.

Nick had no choice—it was into the lion's den or back to a life of toothless outrage.

———◆———

Dario Andretti hung up with Fuente and smiled. Interpol was so predictable, and so was the boy; the first thing he'd done was reach out to Fuente for information, though he hadn't received anything of substance—just enough of a tease to keep him intrigued. Fuente had even thrown in a warning for good measure, like some grizzled police veteran warning off a "rookie" in an old American film noir. He really didn't pay Fuente enough.

Dario let out a chuckle. That wasn't true, but Fuente had a way of pleading poverty that was highly amusing. The man was forever wheedling raises from him, first to fund his children's education, now to refurbish his ramshackle home. Dario had never been there, but it must have been an utter shambles considering how many euros it had cost so far to renovate. Someday he'd have to look in on it. For all he knew, the man was building a palazzo to rival one out of imperial Rome.

But he was worth every cent.

As Fuente had predicted, Clarkston called Dario anyway, less than fifteen minutes after his meeting with the *carabiniere*. Gutsy little *stronzo*. Dario had to admire him a bit. The boy didn't give a damn about his own safety. That would probably make him easier to control, easier to manipulate. Easier to manage, in whatever way he wished.

Dario sent one of his men in Milan to get Clarkston and bring him to the lake, over his objections. Didn't the boy realize he'd displayed fatal weakness by coming to Milan? This game would be played on Dario's terms, or not at all. The boy seemed not to realize how vulnerable he was. How vulnerable his grandparents were.

The question now was what to do with Clarkston. With Enrico Lucchesi's son. The thought rolled through Dario's mind with great satisfaction. He had Lucchesi by the balls, and Lucchesi didn't yet know it.

Even though Lucchesi had killed Dario's father Carlo, Lucchesi thought Dario had agreed to a détente. Forever the optimist, forever the fool—Lucchesi, like his son, was utterly predictable.

Killing Clarkston would be easy, but not satisfying. No, the revenge Dario wanted was more complicated. Lucchesi would beg and crawl before Dario was done with him. Lucchesi had insulted him too many times over the years. First he'd stolen Toni away from him, all those years ago. Most recently, he'd implied that Dario hadn't earned his place as *capo*. That Enrico had given it to him by killing Carlo, that Carlo would have never willingly let Dario have it.

There was a grain of truth to that, but things had changed by the end. Carlo had saved Dario's life by not revealing his role in Rinaldo Lucchesi's death. Enrico's father had died hard, his death savage and brutal. Not at Dario's hands, but by his order. He looked down at the void on his right hand, at the little finger that was no more.

Rinaldo Lucchesi had taken that finger from Dario when he'd discovered that Carlo had murdered his wife and sons in retaliation for Dario's kidnapping. Dario supposed Rinaldo had been sorely provoked, but he'd never forgiven the man. A true man of honor would never have maimed a fourteen-year-old boy. Never. And then on top of it, it was Enrico who'd stopped his father from doing worse, from taking Dario's whole hand.

The humiliation still burned. No wonder Lucchesi still thought of him as a child who couldn't fend for himself. Who had to be helped.

He was no child. He needed no one's help. Certainly not Lucchesi's.

So what to do with the boy? Kidnapping was an option; the boy was delivering himself, and even if he did resist or escape, there were the grandparents to keep him in line. Once he had the boy, he could lure Lucchesi in and kill him. But that was too easy, too swift. Lucchesi needed to suffer.

He could certainly feed the boy information, point him in the right direction, use Fuente to lead him along to certain conclusions, conclusions that would put

Lucchesi in jail for the rest of his life. That was good; Lucchesi's confinement would be especially bitter if his own son were the one who put him away.

But perhaps he could try another tack, one that would require finesse and time: turning the boy. Making him part of the Andretti *cosca*. The payoff would make the delay worthwhile. Lucchesi would be devastated to lose his son in such a manner. And once Lucchesi was crushed, Dario would swoop in for the kill, and Milan and the lake would be his alone.

It was a brilliant idea, but a tendril of unease wound through his gut. What if somehow this were all a trap? What if the boy were in league with his father, what if Enrico Lucchesi were behind the boy's foolhardy, nonsensical behavior? He must proceed with caution, take his time. Study the boy. And then make the move no one would suspect.

Someone tapped on the door to his study. He glanced at his watch. It couldn't be Clarkston; the trip between Milan and the lake took at least forty-five minutes. He didn't expect the boy for another half hour at the earliest. The door opened a bit. "Papà?" Delfina. She'd cracked at last. He'd known she would. Everyone did in the end.

———◆———

Delfina stepped into her father's study. The smile on his face sent guilt arrowing through her. He stood up and greeted her, placing his hands on her upper arms, holding her still while he planted kisses on her cheeks. "Your mother tells me you've finally forgiven me."

She started to object, then realized it would be better if he thought she had; then maybe he'd take the news that she'd invited Antonio to the birthday party a little better. "Yes, Papà." She tugged on the hem of her blouse, acting contrite. "I know I've been..." She cast about for the right word.

"Ungrateful?" he suggested, his tone light.

"What about we just say I've been angry?" At least it was true.

He smiled, chuckling. "Okay, Delfi." He rubbed her arms, squeezing her biceps lightly. "You know I love you, yes?"

"I know." She looked up, her eyes wet. Why did he have to be so nice to her now? "I love you too."

His smile broadened and he hugged her close. "I've learned my lesson."

"What's that?" she asked, her voice muffled by his shirt.

He let her step back. "Next time I find a suitor for you, you get to meet him first. And if you say no, I won't argue." He raised his brows in a silent plea. "Is that reasonable?"

Why couldn't he have been like this before? "But I don't want to marry just yet. Maybe after I find a job."

"You know you're just wasting your time."

"A career is *not* a waste of time. I'll need something to do before and after I have kids."

"You'll have a household and a husband to take care of. Won't that be enough? It makes your mother happy."

Does it really? "I want more. I have dreams. I have talent. Can't I do both?"

He pursed his lips, letting a breath out through his nose. "*Cara,* that's up to your husband."

She lost her patience then. "Why is it that women have careers in America and women here are stuck in the past?"

"You really think they're any happier? They say half of American marriages end in divorce. That means many people are unhappy. And I think it's *because* the women are trying to do too much."

"Well then, I won't marry." She crossed her arms.

Her father laughed and pulled her close again. "You're not quite twenty-two yet. Listen to your old father for once. You're going to want to marry and have a family. And it's best to do that when you're young. Maybe when your children are older, you can do something else. If you married now, by the time you're thirty-five, you could be making dresses, if your husband doesn't mind."

She twisted out of his embrace. "Why does *he* get to decide?"

Her father's face grew somber. "You know in our business that it pays to keep a low profile. Maybe your husband wouldn't want a famous fashion designer for a wife."

There was so much wrong with what he'd said, but she couldn't help smiling. "You think I could be famous?"

"Of course. With my money behind you, you could be anything."

The air leaked out of her, her chest shrinking like a balloon days after a party. She searched his face. He hadn't a clue.

"*Cara,* what did I say?"

"If you can't figure it out, I can't help you." He loved her, but he didn't believe in her. He just didn't think of her as a person. She turned on her heel and fled.

In her room, she grabbed her sketchbook from her desk and sat down on the bed. Dropping the book onto her lap, she curled herself over it, her cheek pressed to its cover. Tears welled up in her eyes. She would never get what she wanted. She might as well face that now. Hers would be a life of yearning, not fulfillment.

Part of her had always known it would be this way, but the dreamer in her had resisted, had insisted she had rights, choices. But that was all fantasy; no one born into this life escaped it without dying young. Her role was to bear the next generation of the 'Ndrangheta, nothing more. Her father's legacy would haunt her all her days. Oh yes, she'd be rich; she'd never lack for anything. But her heart would be poor.

There was a rap on her door; it opened before she could answer. "*Cara?*" Her father poked his head in.

Delfina raised her head, hastily wiping her wet cheeks and shoving the sketchbook under her pillow. But her father wasn't fooled.

"What is that?" he asked, coming into the room.

"Nothing."

"It's not nothing. You're crying." He sat down next to her. "Show me, please. I can't bear to see you so unhappy."

She pulled out the book and tossed it to him. "Just a bunch of silly dreams I'll never see come true."

He opened the book and flipped through it. Despite herself, she studied his face, searching for clues as to what he thought of her sketches. "I'm no expert," he said after a while, "but these seem to be very good."

She smiled. "Thank you, Papà."

He closed the book and held it for a few moments. Then he said, "Delfi, if you wanted, I could help you with this. If it would make you happy."

A spark of hope lit up her chest, filling it with warmth. "It would, very much. But what do you mean? How can you help me?"

"The recession has hit the fashion industry just like everyone else. There's a designer, Enzo Morelli, that I've bankrolled. I can get you a job in his shop."

"I don't want to get in that way!"

He raised his hands in surrender. "Okay. It will be just an interview. I'll make that plain. No problems if he says no."

She thought about it. She still had another year before she finished her bachelor's degree, then two more to finish a master's in design. Was she even ready for such a challenge? "I don't know, Papà. I haven't finished school."

"All the more reason to do an internship. To be sure you want to devote another three years of study to this."

Maybe he just wanted to save money, but part of her saw the wisdom in what he was saying. What if she hated working in fashion? Then she'd have wasted a lot of time and effort. And even once she did finish her degree, it could be years—if ever—before she'd be able to get such an opportunity on her own. Signor Morelli would probably say no anyway. What could it hurt? An interview would let her know what to expect, and hopefully she could learn something too. "Don't you dare threaten him. If he gives me the job, I want to have earned it."

"I know. I promise." She gave him a hug and he returned it. She started to pull back, but he kept her close. "I would like you to do me a favor."

Uh-oh. "What?" she asked, focusing on the fine weave of his shirt.

"At your birthday party, I want you to spend time with Leandro d'Imperio. Be nice to him. Get to know him."

"I already know him."

"You know what I mean."

Unease snaked through her belly. "No, I don't."

He sighed, his breath ruffling her hair. "Must you make this difficult? I'm doing something for you. Can't you do something for me?"

She planted a hand on his chest and shoved, breaking their contact. "You're asking me to consider marrying a drug addict!"

"I'm aware of that. I thought perhaps you'd appreciate being a young widow. Then you'd be free to marry who you like. Or pursue a career. I don't much care. All I want is Gianluca d'Imperio on my side. Give him a grandchild quick, that's all I ask."

Her face blazed with heat and her ears buzzed. "I see how much my happiness means to you. All this *merda* about a happy marriage."

"Delfina! You will not use such language with me."

"Stop me." She folded her arms and glared at him. If he thought she'd been difficult before, he didn't know a thing about her. "You told me minutes ago that I could say no to any prospective suitors. And I'm saying no to Leandro. Or did you not mean what you said?"

His eyes narrowed. "Do you want the interview with Morelli?"

She did, but she wasn't going to say so. When she didn't answer, he said, his voice soft, "You know I can make it impossible for you. I can have Morelli spread whispers about you, make you unhireable."

"You wouldn't."

"Would you care to find out?"

He held her in his fist. He always had; he always would. "Fine. I'll 'be nice' to Leandro. But I interview with Signor Morelli, and if he gives me an internship, I keep it. Even if I do eventually decide to marry Leandro—or anybody else. Agreed?"

He shrugged. "That last part is up to Leandro."

Maybe that was for the best. Leandro had a horrible crush on her. And he was a mess. And that made him easy to manipulate. Far easier than her father. She'd thought she could play the good girl and get what she wanted. She should have known better. But she'd have her revenge.

"Do we have an agreement, Delfi?"

She stared up at her father, making her face and eyes as cool as she knew how. "We do." She smiled, picturing his expression when he found out she'd invited Antonio to the birthday party. It would be her little surprise.

CHAPTER 4

The doorbell chimed, and Delfina stormed downstairs to answer it, her father right on her heels. Gio was early, but her timing was impeccable. Wait until she heard about her father's latest trick. Leandro, of all people!

"Delfina!" he called behind her. "You're still upset?"

"Leave me alone," she tossed over her shoulder, turning her head to give him one last glare. She sailed off the last step into the foyer and plowed into a hard body. A hard body that smelled delicious, sexy. Two strong hands gripped her arms to keep her from falling.

She gawked at a face that was eerily familiar. The young man standing in front of her wasn't Enrico Lucchesi—his wavy, tousled hair was a rich reddish brown, not onyx, and his eyes were mossy green, not chocolate. But the strong blade of his nose, the high prominent cheekbones, and the full, generous mouth were all Lucchesi. "Who are you?" she blurted.

"Nick Clarkston," he answered, his accent British, upper crust. "Who are you?"

"My daughter, Delfina," her father said from behind her. His hands came to rest on her shoulders, and the young man abruptly released her and stepped away, almost bumping into Orsino, one of her father's men. He must have brought Signor Clarkston here.

Signor Clarkston glanced from her to her father. "Is everything all right?" he asked.

"Not really," she said. *Could he be…? But if he was, what was he doing here, in her father's house?*

"Delfi, please leave us. We have business to conduct."

"What business could you possibly have with…" She hesitated, then forced the words out. "Enrico Lucchesi's son?"

The young man raised a dark eyebrow. He truly was handsome. "How did you know?"

She raked him with her gaze. "You must not spend much time looking in the mirror, Signor Clarkston."

His forehead wrinkled in confusion. Ignoring his silent question, she scowled at her father. "We're not done, but I'll leave you to your guest." The clatter of her heels echoed on the marble as she stomped off down the hall.

No, they weren't done. Not at all. What could her father be up to now? Nothing good, that's for sure. Did Signor Clarkston—Nick—did he know who her father was? Was he aware of how much her father hated his? She ducked into the library and waited for them to pass by. Her father's study was two doors down. She wished there was some way she could listen in. Why was Enrico Lucchesi's son here?

———— ◆ ————

Nick watched Delfina Andretti strut away, her black hair swinging behind her, the long strands brushing the small of her back. Good God, he wanted every fiery inch of her. She was gorgeous—large dark eyes, full red lips, an exquisitely shaped nose, high cheekbones, her face a near perfect oval. She could be a model, or whatever the hell she wanted. Her low voice purred in his skull. *You must not spend much time looking in the mirror.* The resemblance to Enrico Lucchesi must be as obvious to others as it was to him. Damn, he hoped word didn't get back to the man that he'd come to Italy. That could ruin all his plans.

"Shall we?" Dario Andretti started down the hall in his daughter's wake. When they passed the room she'd disappeared into, Nick couldn't help peeking in. Delfina was paging through a book and glanced up. He smiled, but she didn't return it. Instead she mouthed something—maybe "Go"?—and shook her head, her eyes a warning.

Okay, he got the message. She didn't like him. He didn't usually have that effect on women, but maybe it had something to do with his father. Maybe she wasn't a fan.

He snapped his gaze away and followed Andretti into a nicely furnished study. A wall of windows faced Lake Como, a strong wind whipping waves across it. The other walls were taken up mostly with books. A large globe occupied one corner, and a massive cherry wood desk sat in front of the far wall, its legs carved to suggest the paws and claws of a large savage animal. Symbolic? His pulse rate kicked up; he hadn't liked the whole idea of coming to Andretti's home, and now he downright hated it. But he was trapped, for the time being. And by his own arrogance.

Dario stepped behind the desk and gestured for Nick to take a seat before it. "So *signore*, what brings you here?"

"You said you had information about my father."

"I did." The man said nothing further. Seconds ticked by while he contemplated Nick, a curious expression on his face.

"Well, do you?"

The door behind them opened, and a huge man, a big meaty Tony Soprano-type, with a smashed nose, stepped inside. At the nod that passed between the men, adrenaline licked down Nick's spine. The giant's eyes were flat, dead. And so was Nick, to judge from the man's impassive face and the bulge under his arm.

Fuente was right—he shouldn't have come. Dario was going to eat him, even though it was well past breakfast.

The reassuring weight of his Glock was no longer with him. Andretti's driver had insisted on taking the gun and his knife when he'd picked Nick up in Milan. He'd resisted giving up the weapons, but the man had made plain he was getting nowhere near Andretti with either one. He'd finally caved, against all his better judgment, judgment that was screaming at him now. *Fool. Idiot. Fucking moron. Cretin. Imbecile.*

Before his brain exhausted its thesaurus of intelligence-related insults, the large man pushed his suit jacket back, revealing the butt of a gun, large caliber from the looks of it. Nick's heart thrashed in his chest. Jesus Christ, he'd done it now. There was only one shot, and he took it. With every ounce of self-possession he could muster, Nick turned his back on the large man and gave his attention to Dario Andretti. "You surprise me, *signore.*"

"How is that?"

"I hadn't thought you'd be so crude as to kill me. At least not straight away."

"Why not?"

"You're a smart man. If I'm dead, you won't get to take advantage of what I have to offer."

His brows lifting, Andretti held up a finger to the brute behind him. "And what is that?"

Nick sprawled back in the chair, opening his hands wide. "Why, the resources of Interpol, of course. I knew this was *quid pro quo* going into it. You scratch my back, I scratch yours."

"And just how were you prepared to 'scratch' me?"

Nick sat forward. "I take my father out for one. Him in jail and out of the way—that would help you, yeah?"

"I need more than that, *signore.*"

"How about advance intel on every move the *carabinieri* is planning? How about your men never being in the wrong place at the wrong time? How about knowing when your enemies are about to fall? I'm sure it would be advantageous to know when the Russians are about to lose a cocaine shipment or when Cosa Nostra is about to be plunged into chaos by a major raid."

Dario nodded, looking speculative. "Such information would be useful. But how do I know you are a man of your word? You seem quite willing to turn your back on those you have taken an oath to."

"What would reassure you, *signore?*" Blood pounded in Nick's veins as he stared at Dario Andretti, his mouth full of sand. Would Andretti take the offer, or was he about to find out how cold and deep the lake was?

"I am not sure I can ever trust a Lucchesi."

Fuck, fuck, fuck. "My father's blood may flow in my veins, but I assure you, I am no more a Lucchesi than you are."

"And why is that?"

"He killed my mother."

Andretti scratched his chin. "I find that hard to believe."

"Well, not directly. She killed herself because he left us."

"And when was this?"

"When I was eight."

Andretti flushed dark red, his fingers forming into fists. "Do you know why he left you?"

Though he knew, Nick shook his head, curious as to what Andretti would say.

"He was married to my sister. My twin, Toni."

His twin *sister? No wonder he hated Lucchesi.* "I'm sorry. But I'm not surprised. The man's a bastard."

Andretti smiled. "On that, we agree."

Nick uncurled his fingers from the armrests. Maybe he wouldn't end up in that lake after all. "We have a deal, then?"

Andretti sat back and studied him. "Perhaps." He made a flicking motion with his hand. "Flavio, you may go."

Nick watched the mountain that was Flavio lumber out the door. He swallowed. So far, so good.

"You will stay here, in the guest house, while I decide what to do with you."

"What to do with me?" When had he turned into a bloody parrot?

"I am not sure you are trustworthy. Until I know, I want you where I can watch you."

"My things are in Milan."

"No, they are not. They are on their way here." Andretti smiled. "And before you ask, your bags have been thoroughly searched and anything of interest has been confiscated. And now"—Andretti held out his hand, a hand that was missing a bloody *finger*—"your mobile, please."

Fuck. Fuente's number was on it.

"Do not worry. I know you met with the *carabinieri* today."

"How?"

Andretti's smile widened. "You think I do not have people watching Sottotenente Fuente? Where he goes, who he meets? One must keep an eye on the enemy."

Well, at least now he knew Fuente was clean. If he could ever get to the man again, that is. He dug the phone out of his pocket and handed it to Andretti, his stomach leaden. His last link to the outside world, gone. His eyes flicked to Andretti's desk phone. Perhaps...

Andretti chuckled. "If you try to leave or contact anyone, I will know it. And Neil and Sharon Clarkston of Belsize Road, St. John's Wood, will be dead in minutes."

A cold sweat broke out over his body. His grandparents. He kept his shoulders rigid as the room began to swim. "I understand."

"I hope you do, *signore*. Their lives depend on your actions."

Nick nodded, swallowing hard. *Idiot, idiot, idiot.* It was one thing to play with his own life, but theirs? Never. He could almost feel Dario Andretti's fine Italian loafer pressed firmly into the back of his neck, waiting to crush vertebrae and sever his spine.

————— ✦ —————

Delfina waited until it was full dark before she put a leash on Zeta and took her for a 'walk' around the grounds. But her true goal was to sneak out to the guest cottage and see Nick Clarkston. The cottage was a miniature copy of the great house; it had been built years ago to house her great-uncle Benedetto when he came up north to visit. He'd wanted more privacy than the villa could afford, all so he could see his Milanese mistress on the sly. Her grandfather had fixed the privacy problem though—he'd had bugs planted in the guest cottage so he could keep abreast of his brother's doings. They were that kind of family.

Those bugs made her task tonight more difficult to keep secret, but not impossible. She tapped on the door and had the piece of paper she'd prepared ready. She held it in front of her face so it would be the first thing Nick saw. It read: "Silence. The guest house is bugged. We must talk. Follow me."

Nick opened the door, parting his lips as if to speak, but said nothing as he read the paper. She lowered it after a moment. His eyebrows shot up when he saw her face. She held a finger to her mouth, then made a "hurry up" motion with her hand. He went back inside and returned in a well-cut tan suede coat. He stepped out, shutting the door behind him.

Delfina led Nick along the side of the guest house, keeping to the shadows afforded by the line of cylindrical cypresses that separated the cottage from the adjacent garden. They'd have some privacy in the hedge maze.

It was hard going in the dark—the night was cloudy and the moon was new. She tripped over a tree root, and Nick caught her about the waist and pulled her back against his hard chest. She gasped at the jolt of adrenaline his touch roused in her. When he spoke, his voice, low and velvety, was so close to her ear that she shivered. "All right?"

"*Sì, grazie.*" Her heart slammed against her ribcage as he held her, his large warm hands on her hips. She had a sudden, entirely insane, desire for him to kiss her. She turned her head toward his and felt his breath, warm against her cheek. Every millimeter of her skin danced with electricity. She waited, the only sound the rush of blood in her ears. Was he feeling the same way? He seemed to be breathing a little fast. She angled her mouth toward his. Would he...? His hands fell from her waist and he released her.

"Where are we going?" he asked. His voice sounded even. Heat flooded her face. Her imagination had gotten away from her. *Cristo.*

"The maze. We're almost there." She inhaled deeply and motioned to her left with her chin as she led him past another cypress and then along a high hedge. When they came to a break in the greenery, she stepped inside the maze and Nick followed. Zeta trotted obediently by her side, the chain clipped to her crystal collar jingling. Delfina tightened up the leash to minimize the sound.

She took several turns she knew by heart, Nick close behind, every molecule of her body aware of him. When they came to an alcove with a stone bench, she stopped. "Here," she said, taking a seat and patting the stone beside her. "We need to keep our voices low. The guards don't patrol the maze itself, but they pass by at intervals." She took a mini flashlight out of her pocket and checked her watch, then laid the flashlight on the bench between them to shed a little light. "We've got fifteen minutes before the next guard comes by." Zeta circled a couple times, then curled up at their feet and let out a soft exhale. She snuffled at Nick's shoe, and he offered her his hand to inspect.

After the dog had accepted his touch, he turned to Delfina. "Why did you want to talk to me?"

She blurted out her purpose, too rattled by her body's reaction to him to play games. "Why are you here?"

"I'm a business associate of your father's."

She laughed, and the tension leaked out of her. This game—this thrust and parry—*this* she could handle. "You must think me a fool. What business could he possibly have with you?"

"He needs someone to run an operation in London for him."

"And so he turns to Enrico Lucchesi's son—the son none of us knew about until recently—for help? How did he even *find* you?" She held up a finger. "And don't tell me it was a coincidence."

He sighed. "I don't know what to tell you."

What could she say to make him trust her? "Listen. I'm here because I'm concerned. Do you have any idea how much my father hates yours?"

"About as much as I do, I suppose."

That was about the last thing she expected. "You hate your father? Why?"

"I'd rather not say." Silence fell between them. After a while, he said, "I thought you disliked me for some reason. Earlier, when you were in the library, you were telling me to go."

"I was telling you it isn't safe for you here. My father is up to something."

"I can handle myself."

She gave him a smirk. "What do you know about my father and yours? You weren't raised here, you don't know these men. How they think, what they're capable of. The way they can stretch grievances into vendettas and then into wars."

"I know more than you think."

Oh he was the devil's own. "Prove it."

"Jesus, you're bloody persistent."

"Like a mosquito?" A little humor never hurt.

He chuckled, shaking his head. "Yeah. Like a bloody mosquito."

"I can always ask my father if you won't tell me."

"Do that."

"He might not tell me the truth."

"And I would?"

She stared at him for a few seconds. Time to gamble, to bet on his good nature. "Yes."

It was his turn to laugh. "You're awfully confident too."

"My brother would say I was just awful."

He smiled. "I wish I had a brother or sister."

"You will soon."

———— ◆ ————

Nick's eyes snapped to Delfina's. What was this about a sibling? "Pardon?"

"Your father, my uncle, recently remarried. His wife is pregnant."

So that's *what Tyrell had meant.* "Let me guess—he got her that way, *then* he married her."

"It happens."

How could she be so bloody casual? "That's what he did to my mother. Only he never married her."

"That's because he was already promised to my Aunt Toni."

"Fucking bastard," Nick muttered. His gut twisted, his pulse revving up.

"I was upset about it too when I heard. But I've had time to think it over. How would you feel if some girl you barely knew was forced on you—as your future wife—when you were only sixteen? He was being a normal teenage boy having a fling before marrying a girl he didn't choose. Trust me, I've been in his shoes, and it's horrid not having a choice." She paused, her gaze roaming his face. "Besides, God knows, all of us make stupid decisions when we're that young."

How dare she make excuses for him? "His 'stupid decision' ruined two lives."

She put a hand on his forearm. "I'm not making light of what he did. Just giving context."

"He was old enough to know better."

"And so was your mother." Her voice was cool, matter-of-fact.

Heat flared over his skin at the insult. "*She* wasn't the one who had a fiancé."

She held up her hands in a gesture of surrender. "True." She said nothing for a moment, then continued. "So you've never, *ever* slept with a girl when you weren't completely honest?"

And now she was accusing him of pulling the same rubbish move his father had? The bloody cheek of this girl! "I've always been upfront—I'm not interested in marriage, or a relationship. Just a good time. Take it or leave it. I've never led a girl on."

She clasped her hands on her lap and studied them. "Well then, Signor Clarkston, you are a better man than most." The softness of her voice pulled him up short.

What did that mean? Had some arsehole played a game with her? He almost asked, but forced himself not to. What did he care anyway? This whole conversation showed how different the Italians were. She was so bloody... *calm* about all this, while he wanted to break something.

They stayed silent for a while, and she checked her watch. She put a finger to her lips to signal him to remain quiet. Soon he heard the guard's footsteps on the grass outside the maze and smelled the smoke from his cigarette.

He held his breath, willing the guard to keep walking, keep moving. *Nothing of interest here, old chap.* His anxiety was a sudden reminder that she'd taken a risk coming to talk to him. Maybe he was reading her wrong. That last thing she'd said... maybe she was no stranger to hurt. And maybe she had a perspective he was sorely lacking.

After the guard had been gone for a few moments, Nick leaned toward her, his hands jammed deep in his jacket pockets. "I know I'm not perfect."

She snorted. "You don't say."

Nick had to smile. Even in the poor lighting, she looked gorgeous. "Yeah. I'm quite the horse's arse, sometimes."

She pressed a hand to her mouth to stifle her laughter. "I know you have no reason to trust me. I might not be as angry at my father as you are at yours, but I would bet I'm very close. He keeps trying to marry me off to better his business. Now he wants me to consider the drug-addicted brother of my best friend, all so he can secure their father as an ally."

Ah, that must be what was bothering her. "Being the wife of a junkie holds *no* appeal at all?" He asked the question as seriously as he could manage, and she let out another unladylike snort.

He liked her, despite himself. And, after the way she'd seen right through his cover story, it was clear he needed someone to help him through this mess. "Can I trust you?" he asked.

She held his eyes. "I won't repeat anything you tell me."

"That's not what I asked."

"It's what I can promise. And I never break my word."

She could have glibly reassured him. That she didn't was a good sign, but he needed to tread carefully. "You asked why I'm here," he said. "I'm here because I want to put my father in jail. And your father can help me do that."

"*What?* Why?"

Let's see her defend him now. "My mother killed herself when I was eight. Care to guess why?"

Averting her gaze, she said, "He wouldn't leave my aunt."

"He turned his back on us. Just walked away." He almost added the most horrible part, but stopped himself. He was tired and upset. The last thing he wanted was to turn into a puddle in front of her.

After a moment, she said, "How are you going to put him in jail?"

Big breath. "I work for Interpol." At the expression on her face, he raised a hand. "Your father knows."

"What?" Her voice was too loud, and he made shushing motion.

"It's a *quid pro quo* thing. I help him, he helps me."

Her eyes grew wide. "You're saying you're a dirty agent?"

Another big breath. "Yes."

———◆———

Delfina stared at Nick, unable to do anything else. He was dirty? *Porca miseria...* just like everyone else she knew. Why had she expected him to be any different? "That's why you think you can handle yourself." He nodded. *Madonna,* he was in over his head. And he had no idea how badly. "Signor Clarkston—"

"Nick."

"—Nick, you are playing a very dangerous game. I don't think you understand how dangerous."

"Your father is a mobster. I get it."

She shook her head. "My father is unpredictable. He hates your father. He would do anything for revenge. *Anything.* And he won't care who suffers. All he cares about is winning."

"He and I have a deal."

She laughed. "You have nothing."

"Not true. I can be useful to him."

"I'm sure he's considering your offer." She pushed off the bench and started circling it, needing to do anything but sit still. "And maybe he'll take it. But only if he decides it's in *his* best interest. You mean nothing—less than nothing—in the equation. I'm his daughter, and *I* mean nothing to him."

"So we have something in common."

"We're not the only ones he doesn't care about."

"I meant, we both hate our fathers," he said.

Hate was such a strong word. She loved her father—she did. But today, when he'd said he was considering marrying her to Leandro d'Imperio—hadn't that washed away the last bit of mortar holding them together? "I'm very angry with him, yes."

Nick grabbed her arm, stilling her. "But you haven't written him off yet."

For some reason, her eyes welled up. She wiped them. "I keep hoping he'll change."

He took her hand and pulled her down beside him. "For your sake, I hope that he does."

"But you don't believe he will."

"I think you're going to have to work within his limitations."

She smiled. What a funny way to put it. But apt. "You may be right."

He squeezed her hand. "I wish I could help."

"I have to manage this on my own. Besides, as my friend Gio pointed out, there are worse things than being a Mafia princess."

"Joe? Who's he?" He gave her a look that was hard to read.

"Giovanna. My best friend in the world."

"Ah."

Maybe there *was* something he could do for her, after all. If Leandro thought she and Nick had something, maybe he'd reject her and squash her father's plans. "Would you come to my birthday party tomorrow?"

"I'm not sure your father would like it."

"I don't care what he likes. He *owes* me."

"If you can arrange it, then yes."

"I will."

He said nothing for a moment. Then he asked, "How old will you be?" His voice was playful.

She *tsk*ed at him and wagged a finger back and forth. "A lady never tells."

He smiled, his white teeth flashing in the dim light. "And would a *lady* be skulking about at all hours in the dark with a man she doesn't know?"

"But I do know you."

"Very little. And you knew almost nothing just a bit ago."

She shrugged. "I suppose I'm no lady then." *I wanted you to kiss me; that's how much of a lady I am.*

———◆———

A mysterious look crossed Delfina's face, intriguing him. What was she thinking about? "So, how old are you?" Nick asked.

"I'll be twenty-two."

And probably still a virgin. Such a shame. She was one fine bird. And damn it, when she'd been in his arms back there, she'd felt so good pressed against him, the soft curves of her bum tucked tight against his groin. A few more moments, and she'd have known just how good she'd felt. She'd been breathing hard, and he didn't think it was just from the near tumble she'd taken. There had been that moment when they'd both been quiet, when all it would have taken was one little twist of his head, and he could have kissed her…. But he didn't need any more trouble with her father. He couldn't risk his grandparents.

"And you are how old?" she asked. She was impossible to deter, this one.

"I'm twenty-seven." He grinned at her, unable to help himself.

"It's a shame you're not married."

What an odd thing for her to say. "Why?"

"If you were, you wouldn't be doing such foolish things. Like putting yourself in my father's hands."

Too true. He wouldn't. And maybe that was the problem, the problem with his entire life. He had no anchor, no stability. Other than his grandparents. Without them, he was just floating, adrift. In search of a home, a direction. A purpose. Something positive. Something other than revenge.

But revenge was all he had right now.

"I don't know what else to do with myself," he said.

She searched his face for a moment. What was she looking for? "I think you know that this"—she gestured around them—"isn't what you should be doing."

Her words struck home with a force that rattled him. "You think you know me?"

"I do. I see myself in you. The bitterness. The anger. The recklessness. And it scares me."

He pressed his lips together and stared at the grass under his feet, even though he couldn't see it. "It scares me too." Where had that come from? Seems he had as much control over his mouth as he did his emotions.

"Then stop."

"I'm not sure I can." He let his voice fade to a whisper. "I'm not sure I want to." What else was there for him? He was too much of a mess to marry and have a normal life like everyone else.

"It's not too late, Nick. I can help you escape."

"I got myself into this. I need to play it out. And I need to see justice done."

She said nothing for a moment. "Did you notice the missing finger on my father's right hand? It was removed when he was fourteen."

Where was *this* going? "I noticed. What did he do to deserve that?"

"He did *nothing* to deserve that." Her voice was razor sharp.

"Isn't cutting off a finger a Mafia punishment?"

Her eyes slid from his. "Not always."

"Which means?"

"You remember what I said about vendettas? Your grandfather Rinaldo cut my father's finger off in retaliation for what my grandfather Carlo had done."

"Which was?"

She paused again, and his heart started beating hard. "He killed Rinaldo's wife and two of his sons. Your grandmother and uncles. Your father's mother and brothers."

What kind of sick bastard had Carlo Andretti been? But then, cutting off the finger of a fourteen-year-old boy…. Jesus, *that's* why Rinaldo Lucchesi had died so hard. Dario must have wanted his revenge. But severing all ten fingers? And his hands? *And* his head? Talk about overkill. The man was a fucking psychopath.

Bloody hell. What would he do to Nick's grandparents if Nick stepped out of line? One thing was clear: no matter what Delfina said, he had to stay put. "I can't run away from this. I'm staying, and I'm getting justice for my mother."

———— ◆ ————

Delfina's stomach squeezed into a hard ball and she found it difficult to draw a breath. She couldn't let Nick put Zio Enrico in jail. He didn't deserve it, not for a mistake he'd made so long ago. But Nick couldn't see that. He was still a confused little boy who couldn't move past his own hatred. She felt for him too, oddly enough. "I beg you, think this over. You do not want to tangle with my father. Can't you see that the Lucchesis have been hurt far worse than the Andrettis? You don't want to be on the losing side of this feud."

He crossed his arms over his chest. "I won't be. I'm partnering with your father."

"He'll never see you as a partner. You're a Lucchesi to him, and always will be."

"I'll win his trust, one way or another."

Frustration and fear boiled up in her. She barely knew him, yet somehow Nick had managed to slip inside her defenses. He was a good man, and so naïve it frightened her. Nick was going to get himself killed, if she couldn't make him see the truth, if she couldn't stop her father and thwart his sick need for revenge on the Lucchesis. Her father's plan was clear to her now: Nick's own hatred, his blind rage, made him the perfect tool to wield against Enrico Lucchesi.

There was only one person who could help, who would help.

Nick's father. The last person Nick would ever take help from. Somehow she had to make him see that his father wasn't a monster. That he was Nick's only chance for survival.

CHAPTER 5

Getting Nick to the party had taken some serious arm-twisting, but in the end, Delfina had prevailed with her father. Now she hoped the rest of her plan came off without turning into a disaster. She headed up the stone steps to the front entrance of the d'Imperio home alone. She'd asked for a moment with Giovanna before her family and Nick followed her in.

The front door flew open just as she reached the top step. "Delfi!" Giovanna called as she swept her inside and into a tight hug. "So how's it feel to be twenty-two?"

"Much the same as twenty-one. Still being oppressed, blah, blah, blah."

Gio laughed at her sourness. "Those poor African children still have it better than you, I see." She smacked Delfina lightly on the arm. "If you don't enjoy this party I worked my butt off for, I'm going to start encouraging Leandro. I'll tell him you really *do* like him, you're just too shy to say so."

Delfina made a face. "Somehow I got forced into 'being nice' to him this evening."

Gio smiled wide, her eyes glittering with mischief. "This, I've got to see. The great Delfina Andretti giving my pain-in-the-ass brother the time of day."

"Don't rub it in." Delfina wanted to wallow in her sulky mood, but Gio made it impossible, as always. It was one of the best things about her friend.

Gio lowered her voice to a whisper. "I don't want to make it worse, but here he comes."

As Leandro strolled into the foyer, even Delfina had to admit he cut a fine figure. She hadn't seen him for most of the last four years while he'd been studying abroad, and he'd grown taller and filled out while he'd been gone. His wavy black hair had been freshly cut, and a few locks of it fell across his high forehead, nearly brushing his dark blue eyes. He'd apparently decided to grow a mustache and goatee, since stubble lingered under his long nose and on his square chin. He probably thought it was sexy that way, and maybe to some women it would have been. With his slick hair and slicker suit, in a navy blue to match his eyes, he could have just walked out of a Gucci photo shoot.

Leandro made straight for them. He took Delfina's hand without saying anything and pressed a kiss to the back of it, his stubble scraping her skin and making her want to snatch her hand back. Oh God, how was she going to get through this? His gaze flickered over her body in a distracted way, and he rubbed the end of his nose; he was high already. Cocaine, from the looks of it. "Delfi, my treasure, I wish you the happiest of birthdays."

His heavy, musky cologne made her queasy and reminded her how angry she was with her father. "I am *not* your treasure."

"Is that any way for my intended to speak to me?"

"What?" She yanked her hand away, and he grabbed it again, holding it too tightly.

"Didn't you know? It's already arranged."

She glanced at Gio, who appeared equally flabbergasted. Delfina wrenched her hand from his grasp again and he frowned, stepping close and putting his arm around her. "Stop acting like this, *cara*. People will talk."

"Let them talk then," she said, trying to shrug him off. His arm slid down the outside of hers, then he clasped her wrist, his fingers squeezing too hard.

"I will not allow you to treat me this way in public," he hissed in her ear.

A by-now familiar voice interrupted them. "Oi, mate, let her go." Nick. Delfina felt relief wash over her, but it was short-lived as Leandro tightened his hold and turned to face Nick.

"Leave us be."

"I said, let her go." Nick shouldered past Cristoforo and stepped up close to Leandro. "I won't ask again."

Leandro's response was to jerk her against his side and let loose a string of insults in Italian, which Nick, mercifully, seemed not to understand. When Nick didn't react, Leandro switched to English. "Only trash would interfere between a man and his fiancée."

Nick's brows winged up and his eyes snapped to hers. "You're engaged?"

She shook her head. "This is the first I've heard of it."

He turned back to Leandro. "Then you're not engaged, mate. Let her go."

Leandro released her arm, but only to take a swing at Nick. Nick easily evaded the blow and lashed out himself, nearly connecting with Leandro's jaw. The only reason he didn't was because Cris managed to grab Nick's arm at the last minute and haul him bodily back and away, quickly inserting himself between Nick and Leandro. Cris placed a restraining hand on Leandro's chest while guards from the d'Imperio and Andretti families surrounded them, guns pointed at Nick.

"Stop this. Now," her brother growled, his voice deep and commanding, using a tone Delfina had never heard from him before. Shocked, she saw him with new respect. He was the same old Cris, with his curly dark hair and heavily muscled build, but his usually laughing eyes and mouth were stern now, grim even, as he scowled at Leandro and Nick.

"No one insults me in my own home," Leandro said, his voice low.

"I wasn't insulting you. I was defending a woman from being manhandled," Nick said.

"I do not know this word, 'manhandled.'"

"Roughed up."

Leandro rolled his eyes. "Are you hurt?" he said to Delfina.

"No." She resisted rubbing her wrist and gave Nick a pleading look.

Nick let out of gush of air. "I must have been mistaken. You two seemed to be struggling."

"Just a lovers' spat." Leandro straightened his jacket. "My fiancée doesn't like public displays of affection."

Delfina ground her teeth together. If he thought she was marrying him, especially after this, he was out of his mind. "Cris, can you take Nick out back? We need a minute alone."

"You're sure?" Nick said.

She nodded and watched Cris escort him out to the party, then she turned to Leandro. "You are not to touch me again without asking."

He put his hands up in the air. "Delfi, you wound me."

"You've been acting like an ass, and you know it." She stared at him hard. "How can you expect me to love you when you treat me like a possession? I'm a *person*, Leandro, not a thing. You can't just grab me, no matter what our fathers think or say. Understand?"

He said nothing. Gio poked him in the arm. "She's right, you idiot. If you weren't so damn high, you'd know better."

Leandro ignored his sister. "I'm sorry." He rubbed his face and gave Delfina a half-smile. "I was so excited and happy, and you weren't. I got angry. Who wouldn't?"

Delfina stepped closer to him. "Don't let it happen again."

"Of course." He reached out, slowly this time, and touched her shoulder, his fingers tracing the outside of her arm until he reached her hand, which he clasped loosely. "I wanted to announce our engagement tonight. May I?"

Dread washed through her. "Let's do that another time."

He leaned down, and when she turned her head, refusing him her lips, he pressed a kiss to her cheek. "Fine. But my patience is nearing an end, *principessa*."

So is mine. "May I have a moment with Gio, please?"

He stepped back from her. "As you wish." He left, heading up the stairs to the bedrooms above. Hopefully he'd stay up there the rest of the night.

Her throat started to ache as Gio put an arm around her shoulders. Papà had lied to her. "What am I going to do?" she whispered, her voice cracking.

Gio patted her back. "He's always been an arrogant ass and maybe that's gotten worse lately, but he still worships you, Delfi, the way he always has."

Pushing up the sleeve of her dress, Delfina revealed the red marks on her wrist. "What about these?"

Gio frowned. "I believe him. He didn't mean to hurt you. You know how he's mooned after you since we were kids. The way you reacted—I'm sure it wounded him. Badly. I've never seen him act like that before."

Delfina smoothed her sleeve back down and rubbed her wrist. "How can I marry him if he's like this? The drugs—he's out of control, Gio. Even if he was sober, it'd be hard. But this—it's impossible."

Gio squeezed her shoulder. "You've only got two choices if you won't marry him."

What was she talking about? There were no other choices. "And what would those be?"

"One: you run away." Before she could interrupt, Gio raised a finger for silence. "But we both know that's stupid. Your father would find you. So really, there's only one choice. Get yourself pregnant by someone else."

Delfina coughed with laughter. "*Davvero*, Gio? *That's* my other choice?"

"You'd have to marry the guy, so pick wisely." Gio's face turned sly. "What about your white knight? The one who came to your rescue?"

She pushed a hand against the foolish flutter in her chest. "Not possible."

"Why? Is there something wrong with him? He looked fine to me. Actually, I take that back. He looked positively *yummy*."

"Nick is Enrico Lucchesi's son, that's why." *Unfortunately.*

"What?" Gio's eyes widened and her mouth opened. "*He's* the love child?"

"Yes."

"*Madonna.* I don't believe it," Gio whispered.

"You can't tell anyone."

"What's he doing with *your* family?"

"It's a long story." She glanced over Gio's shoulder and saw Nick's father walking in. "I'm going to have to tell you later."

Gio followed her gaze and gripped her shoulder hard. "You invited your *uncle*?"

"Yes. Just this morning."

"Delfi, what are you up to? Your father will flip."

"And so will Nick. Which is why I need to talk to my uncle. In private."

"Use my room. Now go," Gio said, giving her a little push. "I'll keep your Nick company." As Gio batted her lashes, Delfina suppressed a laugh. It was impossible to rattle Gio for long.

Turning, Delfina lost her smile. She headed toward her uncle with a rock in her stomach. Nick was going to hate her for what she'd done. He'd probably never speak to her or trust her again.

But someone had to save him. Someone had to intervene. She had to be that someone, or she'd never be able to live with herself.

———— ◆ ————

An invitation to Delfina Andretti's birthday party, issued in person by Delfina herself, was the last thing Enrico Lucchesi had expected. Well, next to lasting peace with the various branches of the Andretti family. He was glad she'd come in person that morning so that they could get past any embarrassment in private. Little more than a month ago, they'd been engaged to be married. And now he was married to the love of his life.

Delfina had been matter-of-fact about meeting Kate, and so gracious and direct about facing the discomfort between them, that there'd hardly been a moment of unease between them all.

But now, as he and Kate and Antonio pulled up before the d'Imperio home, Enrico's nerves jangled. He hoped he wasn't putting Kate and their child at risk. It

45

was one thing to face Delfina. Another to face the rest of her family, so soon after Carlo's death at his hands. The truce between their families had always been fragile, never more so than now. But as Delfina had said, what better way to celebrate and reinforce the new peace he and Dario had recently brokered? Still, he'd brought along Ruggero. Just in case.

They walked up to the house amid a crush of young people and members of other families. The d'Imperios had several maids and a butler, who greeted the guests and took their coats. Enrico helped Kate with her coat, encountering a momentary bit of awkwardness when Antonio, his *capo di società,* reached for it at same time.

"Sorry," Antonio mumbled and blushed, his fair skin mottling to the roots of his blond hair. Not so long ago, Antonio had posed as Kate's husband for a couple weeks, during the horrible time when Enrico had wondered if he'd ever win his beloved back. But here she was, smiling at him, her green eyes and auburn hair shining as he took her coat.

"*Ti amo,*" he murmured in her ear.

Kate's smile broadened and she brushed a hand along his shoulder. "Me too." She took in the grandeur of their settings. "I never thought I'd say this, but your home is virtually spartan compared to this."

He put an arm around her and pulled her close against his side. "*Our* home. And"—he motioned at the soaring, glittering space—"our home is hardly spartan. More restrained, perhaps."

"This verges on Donald Trump levels of gaudiness," she whispered.

He chuckled. "Gianluca wants the best of everything. There is no harm in that."

"Unless it's hurting my eyes." Kate pretended to shield her gaze from the sparkling surfaces around them.

He gave her a tight squeeze. "We should meet our hosts; we can talk about how they live later."

She poked him playfully in the ribs. "Yes, Dad."

"You mean Papà-to-be." He placed a palm over the barely discernible swelling at her belly. If he didn't know she was pregnant, he'd never have guessed. She had been too thin when they'd met, but she'd put on enough weight now to soften the contours of her body. Contours he loved to explore, to touch. He let his hand slide down to the small of her back, his fingers resting just above the luscious swell below. His wife. His, at last.

He surveyed the foyer, seeing several people he recognized, but none of the Andrettis. They must have headed to the garden out back, where from the sounds of it, the party was already in full swing. He started to guide Kate that way when someone tapped his shoulder.

"There you are," Delfina said.

"In the flesh." He leaned forward to kiss her cheek, but the crinkle between her brows stopped him. "What is wrong?"

She started to shake her head, then stopped. "I'm not sure if I've done the right thing now."

"What are you talking about?"

"My father is up to something."

"Color me unsurprised," Kate said, giving voice to Enrico's thoughts. Would Dario forever be at his throat? Enrico had tried to forgive Carlo his sins, but Carlo had pushed and pushed until Enrico had no other choice but to take Carlo's life. Couldn't Dario see that? Or could he only see that Enrico was avenging his family?

"What *specifically* is going on?" Enrico asked Delfina.

"I think rather than try to explain, I'd best show you."

Enrico, Antonio, and Kate exchanged glances, then they followed Delfina up the stairs to a bedroom with a terrace overlooking the pool, Ruggero bringing up the rear. Delfina beckoned them out onto the balcony. Music and chatter from the clumps of guests below drifted up to them. "Do you see that young man by the pool? The one talking to Cristoforo and Giovanna?" She pointed to a tall, dark-haired man Enrico would have recognized anywhere.

An electrical sizzle shot through his body, arcing down his spine and settling into a roiling mass in his belly. *Nico.*

Kate turned to him, an uncertain expression on her face. "He looks just like you. Is that Nick? Your son?"

Antonio let out a grunt of astonishment. "*What?*" he asked, his eyes darting from Kate to Enrico. "What son?"

I should have told him. Too late now. "I fathered a child in England during my betrothal."

"And *that* is him?" The hurt on Antonio's face made Enrico's throat tighten. "So what was I? The stand-in?"

"Tonio, no." Enrico stepped forward, reaching for his shoulder.

Antonio shrugged away from him. "I suppose now you will want to install him as your *capo di società.*"

The roiling in his belly settled into a hard lump of clay. "That will never happen."

Antonio snorted, and Kate put a hand on his arm. "Nothing's going to happen to you, Tonio," she said.

"*Signora,* no offense, but blood is thickest. It is bad enough the rest of the Lucchesis hate me. Now I learn there's a *son.*" Antonio turned to Enrico. "You should have left me in that orphanage in Rome where you found me."

This was all going so wrong. If only Delfina had prepared him. But even if she had, would it have made a difference? He took a deep breath; only the truth would assuage Antonio. "Nico will never replace you. He works for Interpol."

He might as well have set off a bomb. Antonio, Kate, and Ruggero stepped away from him. Delfina was the only one who stayed put. "You knew," he said, turning to her.

She nodded, her face miserable. "He's a 'guest' of my father's. I didn't know what else to do."

Madonna! The air slammed out of his lungs, and he grabbed the railing of the balcony. His eyes darted from Cristoforo Andretti standing beside Nick to Dario, Benedetto, and Lorenzo Andretti standing off in a group across the pool. He'd thought Nico was safe. But here he was, surrounded by Andretti wolves. How had this happened?

And how was he going to save his son?

47

"I need to speak to him. Now." He spun around, heading back into the room, ready to charge downstairs. Delfina stopped him before he reached the hall.

"Wait."

"I have to go to him." He started to push past her, but she dug her fingers into his arm.

"Zio, he might not react the way you'd expect." Delfina hesitated. "He's got very strong feelings about you." She dropped her hand from his arm and stepped back. "They're not good."

The words shredded his skin like shards of glass. "That does not matter. I am still his father, he is still my son."

"I don't think it's that simple."

"It *is* that simple." But perhaps their meeting shouldn't be public. "Figure out a way to bring him in here."

"Do you need help collecting the heir?" Antonio asked her.

Delfina crossed the room to him and placed a hand on his shoulder. "Tonio, don't be like this."

"How should I be?" Antonio's bitter tone cut through Enrico's worry about Nico. His son wasn't the only pressing problem. He should've officially adopted Antonio a long time ago. Now…. He looked at Antonio, who looked away. Now it was too late.

Maybe it was too late with both of his sons.

———— ◆ ————

Delfina's brother guided Nick out to the gardens at the rear of the house. His heart had slowed, but when he thought about that guy's hand squeezing Delfina's wrist, his ears roared with white noise. No wonder she didn't want to marry the bloke. He'd wanted to pound the guy silly, but that sudden display of firepower had snapped him out of it. He wasn't in England anymore; he was surrounded by mobsters, men who settled disputes with guns instead of fists. He had to find some other way to help her. "Fucking bastard," he muttered.

Cristoforo scooped two glasses of champagne off the tray of a passing waiter and led them over to a table by the pool. "I wanted to let you do it, Nick. Hell, I wanted to do it myself. But I can't cross my father, at least not publicly."

He took the champagne flute Cris offered and downed the sparkling wine in one gulp, the bubbles fizzing in his nose and making him cough. *Christ, Clarkston. It's not a bloody pint.* He caught his breath. "You can't let him marry her off to that tosser."

"I know." Cris twirled his champagne flute, watching the bubbles rise up the sides of the glass. "I'll talk to Papà. He's going to be hard to shake—he wants the d'Imperios in his pocket—but Leandro's behavior disrespects my sister and our family name."

"What if you can't persuade him?"

"Then Delfi is going to have to cope." Cris took a swallow of his drink. "But don't worry—if Leandro gets out of control, there are ways to handle it. Even if my father doesn't approve."

He leaned closer to Cris. "What do you mean?"

Delfina's brother stared at him for a long moment. "Drug addicts overdose all the time."

"You'd do that for her?"

His eyes were dark and still. "She's my sister."

At least someone in her family gave a damn. "How can your father treat her like this?"

Cris signaled a waiter for two more glasses. Nick sipped his carefully this time, waiting for Cris to speak. Finally he said, "You didn't grow up here. It's hard to understand, but what we do, it doesn't work without a strong family, without strong connections. Blood connections, ties between the families. All of us—we marry for the right connections. Delfi complains, but I have no more choice than she does. I'll marry the daughter of someone my family needs as an ally, and I'll smile when I do it, even if she has the face of a goat. It's my duty."

"Fuck." Nick sipped the champagne again.

Cris grinned. "That's what a mistress is for."

A hand slid across Nick's back. And then a short curvy girl—Delfina's friend—appeared beside him. "Who's talking about mistresses?" she asked.

"Me, of course." Cris's eyes did a slow pass over the girl's body, and Nick had to admit that what he saw from the side looked very fine.

"You wouldn't need one if you married me," the girl said.

"I wouldn't want one."

Her smile broadened, then she turned to Nick, her fingers twirling a few strands of her hair. "Aren't you going to introduce me, Cris?"

"Forgive me. Giovanna d'Imperio, Niccolò Clarkston."

"Nick," he said. He took the delicate hand she held out to him. She ran the fingers of her other hand through her blond-streaked hair while she inspected him from head to toe. "You're Delfina's friend," he said. "She calls you Gio."

"She told you about me?" Gio asked, her voice lilting up in surprise before falling to a lower tone. "Whatever she said, it was *all* lies."

Nick chuckled. "So you're *not* the most wonderful person in the world?"

Gio rolled her eyes. "That bit *is* true. But the rest most certainly is not."

"How is she?" Nick asked.

"Delfi will be fine. My brother's an ass. But I truly believe he didn't mean to hurt her. He adores her."

"Strange way of showing it."

Gio sighed, tipping her glass of champagne to her lips. "This is *supposed* to be a party. Let's talk about something else." She questioned Nick about where he was from, and he answered automatically, his mind on Delfina. There had to be some way to help her. But he couldn't afford to anger her old man. If only he didn't have to worry about his grandparents, he'd snatch Delfina up and figure out some way to make her disappear. It was the least he owed her for trying to help him.

As if he'd willed her there, Delfina appeared by his side, her face taut. "What is it? Did that bastard try to hurt you again?" Nick asked.

"I need you to come with me." She turned to leave.

"What's this about?"

She ignored the question. When he didn't follow, she grabbed his hand and led him through the crowd. Her small hand practically disappeared as he wrapped his fingers around hers. Along the way, they were stopped several times by friends wanting to wish her happy birthday. He got a lot of questioning glances, but Delfina ignored them all and got moving again as quickly as civility allowed. Why had she taken his hand? Was she one of those birds who liked to stir up trouble? Eventually they reached an obstacle she couldn't rush past. Her father.

Andretti was with two older gentlemen and another who appeared to be his contemporary. Dario looked pointedly at the two of them holding hands and frowned. She let go instantly, her shoulders pulling back and her whole body going rigid.

"Delfina, who have you got there?" the oldest man asked. He was well into his eighties, his wispy hair a mix of white and silver, but something about the man's autocratic bearing and superior, demanding, tone chilled Nick.

"Bisnonno, this is Nick Clarkston. Nick, this is Lorenzo Andretti, my great-grandfather."

Nick took the old man's gnarled hand, surprised by the strength in his grip. "There's something familiar about you," Lorenzo said, peering at Nick closely.

Nick shrugged. "I must have one of those faces."

Delfina then introduced him to her *prozio*, her great-uncle, Benedetto Andretti, a balding, well-dressed man in his sixties who also studied him. He was no warmer than his father, Lorenzo, and said even less. Then she introduced him to the youngest man, a sturdy fellow in his mid-forties, with close-cropped graying hair and a black mustache and beard. "This is Gianluca d'Imperio. Our host."

Bugger. The father of the guy he'd nearly clocked. "Pleased to meet you, *signore*," he said, taking the hand d'Imperio offered. D'Imperio's fingers were surprisingly calloused. The man appeared fit, but something about him said he'd never done a minute's manual labor.

D'Imperio grunted in response and drew on a thick cigar as he studied Nick. "I heard you and my son Leandro… met earlier."

Nick shoved his hands in his pockets. "We did." He wasn't going to apologize.

"My son was asking for it, I'm sure." D'Imperio chuckled. "However, Delfina shouldn't appear to be attached to anyone else, yes?"

He was referring to them holding hands. "She was just getting me through the crowd, *signore*."

D'Imperio took another draw on the cigar. "Be more careful."

Nick nodded, then glanced at Dario. The man was glowering at him. This wasn't good. "No harm meant," Nick said, holding his hands up in surrender.

Next to him, Delfina shifted from one foot to the other. "I wasn't thinking," she blurted.

Dario put a hand on her shoulder. "I thought I made myself clear earlier."

The look she shot her father was pure venom. "Had I known I was engaged *before* the party, everything would have been different."

D'Imperio raised an eyebrow. "You didn't know?"

"That was the cause of the… confusion earlier," she said.

D'Imperio's eyes flicked between her and Nick. "Is the 'confusion' cleared up?"

She glared at her father as she answered. "Yes. Now may we get on?"

"Enjoy the party," Dario said, waving for them to go. Delfina spun away. No handholding this time. Nick rushed to follow her through the press of bodies. He'd never seen so many people at a birthday party. Where the hell was she taking him? And why the hurry?

He caught up with her at the foot of the grand staircase in the foyer. "What's going on, Delfina?"

"You'll know in a minute." She started up the stairs, beckoning him to follow.

Bloody hell. He trotted behind her up the plushly carpeted stairs. Beneath that pretty blue dress, Delfina was wearing sheer black hose with sexy seams that ran up the backs of her legs. He followed the lines of them up to where the hem of the dress hit her, just above the knees. Too bad he'd never be able to follow those seams all the way to heaven. If he did, Dario would make sure Nick joined the missing-finger club. Or worse.

They entered a room partway down the hall. A tall dark-haired man stood with his back to them, an arm around the shoulders of a woman with auburn hair, the two of them facing the double doors leading to the balcony. A few paces off was another man, blond and young. Along the opposite wall stood a dark-haired, powerfully built man, his hands clasped behind his back in the stance common to bodyguards everywhere. Nick checked and saw the bulge under the man's left armpit that indicated a handgun. Who were these people? The tall man turned and Nick froze. *No. No. No.* "Nico," the man said, stepping toward him.

Nick shook his head violently. This wasn't happening. His stomach lurched, his insides going to paste. A red-hot ball grew in his chest until the heat flooded up into his face, making his ears roar and his throat go tight. When his hands started to tremble, he clenched them into fists, at which point the blond on his left and the guard on his right started toward him.

"Antonio, Ruggero, no," Delfina said. The blond stopped, but the other guard didn't. He was on Nick in a heartbeat, cranking Nick's right wrist up between his shoulder blades, his other arm locking around Nick's neck before he was almost aware of it. Nick tried to fight, but the guard's hold on him was solid, unshakeable, the man displaying a massive force that surprised him. The guard was an inch or two shorter than Nick, but clearly he spent far more time in the gym. Hard cords of muscle, apparent even through the man's suit jacket, crushed into Nick's throat, cutting off his air supply.

"Ruggero." His father's voice, controlled, commanding. Seemingly unaffected. How could he be so cool, while Nick was on fire?

The guard, Ruggero, tightened his grip on Nick's neck and gave his right arm a wrench. His shoulder exploded with pain, the arm threatening to burst from its socket, narrowing Nick's world down to a single point of agony, surpassed only by the burning need for oxygen. The guard spoke in his ear, his voice a rough rumble. "Bones break like sticks, yes?" *Yes, yes, they do, you fucking sociopath.*

"Ruggero, let him be." His father spoke again. He was right in front of Nick, so close they could touch.

Nick opened his mouth. *Bastard. Bloody bastard,* he wanted to yell. But nothing came out, and not just because his air was being cut off. Ruggero let him loose, but

Nick could only stumble back a few steps, unable to speak, unable to do anything but stare at the father he hadn't seen in all this time. He shook out his right arm, wincing with pain, but that pain was nothing compared to the storm raging inside him. His father, the mobster. The murderer.

His father stepped forward, closing the gap that had opened between them. "Nico," he said, his voice gentle and choked, that little betrayal of emotion transfixing Nick, as his father reached out and touched his shoulder.

The urge to surrender, to throw his arms around his father, gripped Nick hard, and tears—bloody, traitorous tears—burned his eyes. Seeing them, his father reached out with his other hand to fold him into an embrace.

"No," Nick moaned and backed away. He wanted to run, to get away. He wanted to vomit. He wanted anything but to stand there, panting and shaking. His father tried again, and this time Nick's voice was stronger. "Don't bloody touch me." His father's hands dropped to his sides and Nick saw tears in his eyes. "You're nothing to me. Understand?"

"Nico, I am your father."

"You stopped being my father nineteen years ago."

His father—*scratch that, he's bloody Enrico Lucchesi, he's no father to me*—pinched the bridge of his nose. His voice was hoarse. "You never stopped being my son. Never."

"You're the reason she's dead. You killed her."

"Not true. You know that, Nico."

"Stop calling me that."

"Nick then." Lucchesi reached out again, then stopped himself. "I am sorry for everything that happened."

The roar in Nick's ears intensified. "You didn't even have the decency to come to her funeral."

Lucchesi focused on the floor. "I thought it best to stay away."

Nick smirked at him, triumphant. "You couldn't face me or my grandparents."

"That was not the reason, Nico."

"Nick." He waited, but Lucchesi said nothing more. "You're a coward and a liar."

"He is neither," the blond—Antonio—said.

Nick looked at Antonio, really looked. He was young, around twenty or twenty-one. "You think he's told you everything? Let me guess—you never heard of me, never even knew I existed, until just now." Antonio turned red. "As I thought."

"There's a good reason for that," the red-haired woman said in an American accent.

"Kate, please," Lucchesi said. "He is upset. Justifiably."

Nick let out a snort. '*Justifiably.' What an understatement.* He turned to Delfina. "Why did you arrange this?"

"Because you need help with my father. Your father is the only person who can—who *will*—do anything."

She had so little faith in him? "I have the situation under control."

With a raised eyebrow, she asked, "What about your grandparents?"

"He'll accept the deal."

"Even if he does, you don't understand."

"What don't I understand?"

She threw her hands up in exasperation. "You never should have come here. You keep insisting you're Nick Clarkston. But you're not. In Italy, you're Niccolò Lucchesi, and you will be until the day you die."

Lucchesi spoke up then. "That is why I avoided the funeral. You would have wanted me to take you to Italy, and I could never have said no."

Nick's throat tightened, making it nearly impossible to speak. "I kept thinking you'd come back."

"I missed you so much. But I wanted more for you than this. I wanted you to have all the choices I never had."

"You had choices."

"From the moment I was born, my destiny was written," Lucchesi said, his tone weary. "Those who are born into the *malavita* can never leave it."

"You don't *want* to leave it. You have everything you could possibly want."

"I never wanted any of this, for myself or my sons. I had hoped to keep you free."

"I'm *not* part of it."

"Your name makes you part of it. There is no going back to your old life. You think Interpol will trust you once they know?"

They wouldn't, that was true. "They don't have to know."

"And you accuse my husband of being a liar," Kate said.

"What difference does it make who my bloody father is? He might as well have been a sperm donor for all the influence he's had on me."

"You're acting like a child," Kate said. "You have no idea the sacrifices he's made."

"And you have no idea what it's like to know you didn't matter to either parent." The words slipped out, hot and bitter, and for a moment he was flung back to that horrible moment of discovery, when he'd learned his mother was dead, gone forever beyond the reach of his tears, his pleading. It took everything he had not to sob like the little boy he'd been that horrible day. Delfina tried to touch him, but he flinched away. If she succeeded, he'd crumple, he'd lose what little control he still had.

The whole room was silent, seconds ticking by, Nick's breathing sounding harsh in his own ears. Then Lucchesi spoke. "You matter—you will *always* matter—to me. Let me help you. Let me make it up to you."

"Make it up to me? I don't need your bloody help. What a load of bollocks."

He slammed out of the room and ran smack into Leandro, who started to laugh. "I heard the whole thing. What kind of fool walks away from the Lucchesis?"

"This one. Now get out of my way." Delfina came up behind him and tried to grab his arm, but he shook her off. "Go play with your fiancé," he snarled at her.

He stormed out to the rear gardens. The mass of people outside held no appeal, other than that he could get lost in the crowd. Just find a quiet corner and drink until he didn't care anymore. About his father. His mother. Dario. Delfina. Just forget it all. Just forget he existed.

Nick Clarkston was a sham, a fiction, as Delfina had pointed out. And a bloody liar. His grandparents weren't safe. And he'd been the one to put them in danger.

Who the fuck was he anymore? Did he even care? Why couldn't God take pity and toss him down a deep dark hole, like Alice, so he'd wake up in Wonderland? Instead of where he was: the eighth circle of hell. Where he belonged, with all the rest of the liars.

CHAPTER 6

Dario had barely finished smoothing over Gianluca's concerns about Delfina's behavior when Leandro strolled up to them, a sly smirk on his face. Of all the men in Italy, *this* had to be the one destined to be his son-in-law. *God must hate me.* "You'll never guess who's here, Papà," Leandro said to Gianluca.

"The Pope? We seem to have everyone else."

Leandro licked his lips. "Enrico Lucchesi." An unpleasant prickling peppered Dario's skin. What the bloody hell was Lucchesi doing here?

"You're not serious," Gianluca said.

"He's upstairs, in Gio's room, with his wife. But that's not the best part." When Leandro paused, Gianluca motioned for him to spit it out. His son's smile widened, grew nasty, and Dario's pulse slammed into overdrive. "That idiot who tried to hit me? He's Lucchesi's son. And"—his eyes slid to Dario—"he works for Interpol." Dario's hands clenched into fists. He'd love to knock that grin off Leandro's face. And the good-for-nothing junkie knew it too.

Gianluca coughed mid-draw on his cigar. "What the hell?" He rounded on Dario, and Benedetto and Lorenzo stepped closer. "You've brought fucking *Interpol* into my home?"

Jesus and all the saints… Dario took a breath. "Not exactly."

"What the fuck does *that* mean?" Gianluca's face turned red.

"The boy works for me. He's Interpol, but he's mine."

"But he's Lucchesi's son."

"His bastard, you mean," Leandro said.

"Shut up," Gianluca said, stealing the words Dario wanted to say. "Explain yourself, Andretti."

"Yes, please do," Benedetto said. "You've been holding out on us."

When he found Delfina, he was going to kill her. Inviting Lucchesi here *had* to be her doing. "I'm not holding out on anyone. I'm still finalizing the deal. The boy wants to work for me."

"Sounds like a Lucchesi trap." Lorenzo pursed his lips in disapproval. "Your father was right; you *are* a fool."

Dario's cheeks burned. "It's not a trap. *I* approached the boy, not the other way around."

"So, what, he just threw himself in your lap?"

"I can give him something he wants. Something we all want."

Gianluca's meaty forefinger stabbed him in the chest, connecting right over the sternum. "What game are you playing, Andretti? Are you planning to turn *pentito*?"

"Me roll over and testify? Never." Dario spat on the flagstones.

Benedetto circled around until he was just to Dario's left. He leaned in when he spoke, his voice low. "My brother never saw anything in you. I thought he was missing something, but now I'm not so sure. Either you're an idiot, or you've cooked up a scheme to take over."

The quivering began in Dario's belly, then burrowed deep into his bowels. *Remember Remo.* He was moments from death, unless they believed what he said next. "What I've done is figure out a way to eliminate Enrico Lucchesi."

Benedetto cocked a brow. "Go on."

"The boy hates his father. Says he killed his mother. He wants his revenge, wants to put Lucchesi in prison. I told him I could help, but for a price. The boy offered information. It's that simple."

Leandro, of all people, came to his rescue. "It's true. He hates Lucchesi. You should have heard them."

"It could have been an act," Lorenzo said.

"I know when people are lying," Leandro said. "They weren't."

"You're sure of the boy?" Benedetto asked Dario.

"More or less."

"What kind of answer is that?"

Dario met his uncle's gaze. "An honest one. I want insurance, of course. I just haven't figured out what would be most effective."

"How Carlo resisted strangling you, I'll never know," Benedetto said, continuing to study him.

"I think we're forgetting something," Gianluca said. They all turned to him. "Lucchesi runs the banks we use. Can any of us take his place?" When no one spoke, Gianluca continued. "I don't have anything against Lucchesi. He's never screwed me, and I trust him not to turn on us." He stared at Dario. "He killed your father, but even you have to admit he'd been sorely provoked. You can't kill a man's entire family and kidnap his fiancée and not expect payback."

"He soiled my sister's honor. Our family name. You've seen the proof now; Clarkston is his son, without a doubt."

Gianluca puffed on his cigar. "La Provincia ruled against your father's claims." He turned to Benedetto. "That ruling was final, was it not?"

Benedetto's lips twitched. As head of the commission, he could reopen the matter. "Yes." He focused on Dario. "Be thankful Lucchesi didn't bring a grievance against your father for the unsanctioned murders of his family."

"I could do the same to him. He didn't seek permission to go after my father."

Lorenzo chuckled. "Just like the old days, before we got so civilized." He gestured to Benedetto. "So, my son, what odds do you think your nephew would have if he were to bring such a grievance before the commission?"

"Poor." Benedetto brushed a piece of lint off his sleeve. "Many would take Lucchesi's side."

"Exactly." Lorenzo turned to Dario. "Many would. Many, like Gianluca here, would question your judgment. Lucchesi has brought us a security we'd been lacking. The banks were always the weak link. The DIA will never get Lucchesi to cooperate."

They weren't going to win so easily. *Lucchesi* wasn't going to win. "It's dangerous to rely on him. We've all been lazy. We've been sitting back and letting him handle our money because running the banks is complicated. We could learn. We could set up our own banks."

Benedetto smiled. "And how do you propose we do that?"

"Lucchesi will make me his partner."

Lorenzo laughed. "You will accomplish that how?"

"I have the boy." Triumph surged up in him. It was a change of plan, but a clever one. And it didn't mean he couldn't kill Lucchesi once he knew how to carry on without him. His vengeance would be delayed, but not denied.

Silence fell between them until Gianluca broke it. He smiled and clapped Dario on the back. "Well-played, my friend."

Dario looked at his uncle and his grandfather. They remained silent, then exchanged a glance before turning back to him with smiles. "Yes, well-played," Benedetto said.

But the smiles didn't reach their eyes. The quivers in his gut returned.

———— ◆ ————

Delfina had been searching everywhere, but Nick was nowhere to be found. Could he have left the party?

She circled back to Antonio, Gio, and Cris, who'd all assisted with the search, but who'd now reconvened by the pool. "Anything?" she asked when she joined them.

A chorus of shaking heads greeted her. "Damn it! Where can he be?" She turned to Gio. "Did you talk to the valets and the drivers? Did he leave with anyone?"

"They haven't seen him." Gio stroked Delfina's forearm. "He's got to be here somewhere. Maybe he's wandered off into the hills?"

Delfina cast a despairing glance at the mountains rising up past the front of the house. If he'd gone up there, they'd never find him at night. But it was so damn dark beyond the reach of the party lights, she couldn't imagine him getting that far.

"He snagged a bottle of whiskey from one of the bartenders," Antonio said. "So I bet he's still here."

"You're probably right." She turned to Gio. "If you didn't want anyone to find you, where would you go?"

Gio thought for a moment, then snapped her fingers. "The garden shed. Or the boathouse."

"Okay, Antonio and I will take the shed. You and Cris go to the boathouse."

"We'll find him, sweetie. We will," Gio said, giving her arm a sympathetic squeeze. Then she turned to Cris and laced her arm through his. "I don't want to trip and fall in these heels," she said.

"Happy to oblige," Cris murmured as they walked away, a half-smile on his face.

He'd never taken much notice of Gio before. Delfina wondered at the change, but Nick was foremost in her thoughts. "Come on," she said to Antonio.

They set off through the garden, following the stone paths laid down in a circuitous route through a labyrinth of hedges, topiaries, rosebushes, clumps of flowers, statues, urns, and fountains, all strewn picturesquely throughout the garden. Domed lights on posts lit the flagstone paths.

"This has turned out to be one hell of a birthday party," Antonio said.

She hugged her arms around herself. "I shouldn't have done it. I knew how Nick felt. I just thought… I don't know what I thought."

Antonio slung an arm around her shoulders and kissed her cheek. "It's not your fault. You didn't know how bad it was."

"Nick hates him, he really does. And he just doesn't understand what a mess he's in. How can I make him understand who my father is?"

Antonio let go of her and was silent for so long she momentarily forgot about Nick. "What's wrong?" she asked.

"Nothing."

"Hmm… you've gone all silent over *nothing*."

He sighed. "Do you think Don Enrico meant what he said about not wanting this life for his children?"

"Yes. I think he was sincere."

"Then why did he let me join up?"

Her heart squeezed. She put a hand on Antonio's shoulder. "Oh, Tonio. Don't take what he said the wrong way."

"How *else* should I take it?"

"Well, did he encourage you?"

Antonio hesitated. "No. He tried to talk me out of it. Made me wait until I was twenty to take my vows."

"And he's tried to get you to attend university."

"He's always bugging me about it. But how can I, now that I'm *capo di società*?"

"I'm sure something could be arranged."

"With his godsons breathing down my neck?"

"They're upset?"

He stopped walking. "If your father passed up Cris for some no-name, low-level, completely unqualified *paesano*, he'd be furious."

"I suppose." She rubbed her arms; she should have picked up her jacket before they left the space heaters by the pool. "Why *did* he choose you over them anyway—not that I'm saying you're unqualified."

He hesitated again. "I don't know."

"Yes, you do." Didn't he realize what a miserable liar he was?

"Delfi, I'm sworn to secrecy."

She sighed. "Okay then. But what's really bothering you?"

"Don Enrico plans to take the vow of *comparaggio* toward his godsons."

"He does?" Since their father was dead, it was understandable. But still, it was a big step.

Antonio nodded. "They'll be his sons then, in effect."

She detected a hint of strain in his voice. "He's not taken such a vow toward you."

He turned his face into the shadows. "No."

"Did you ask?"

His eyes flashed back to hers. "One does not *ask* someone to be his *compare*."

"Between that and Nick's appearance, you must be feeling left out."

"Don't psychoanalyze me." He started walking again, faster than she could easily manage. She hurried to catch up, her shoes clattering on the flagstones. The heel of her left shoe caught in a gap between the stones, and she went down with a yelp.

"Delfi!" Antonio hurried back to her. "You okay?"

He helped her up, and she dusted herself off. Her ankle was sore, but it would hold her. She couldn't say the same for the shoe. The heel had snapped off and the ankle strap had torn. "*Porca miseria.*"

Slipping off the other shoe, Delfina proceeded in her sheer hose. Pebbles and twigs bit into the soles of her feet; she was limping by the time they reached the gravel path that veered off to the garden shed. She paused, nerving herself up for the trip across the sharp stones. "Let me carry you," Antonio said. "It's not far. Or you can wait here."

"If he's there, I'd better be with you."

"You think it'll make a difference?" Antonio said. "He wasn't too happy with you either."

"But at least he won't punch me."

"Good point." He swung her up in his arms. She put her hands around the back of his neck, holding herself stiffly away from his chest. She couldn't help smelling him though, and his light, citrusy cologne reminded her of Nick's. Now if *he* was the one holding her.... She pushed that thought away.

Antonio's shoes crunched on the gravel as he headed toward the shed. An owl hooted nearby, and the night sounds of insects filled her ears.

When they reached the shed—it was nearly a small barn—where the gardening equipment was kept, Antonio pushed the door open with his shoulder. "Nick?" she called. No answer. If he wasn't here, and if Gio and Cris didn't find him, what then? Antonio stepped inside the shed, then set her down on the dirt floor.

She heard the slosh of liquid in a bottle, but no other noise. "Nick, I know you're here."

A small electric lantern flicked on in response. Nick was sitting next to a mower, leaning back against a broken garden bench, a bottle of Scotch between his knees. "Haven't done enough damage for one evening?" he asked, his voice slurred.

Her stomach cramped into a ball. "I'm sorry. I should have told you."

He pointed a finger at her. "No. You should have *asked* me."

"You would have said no."

"Exactly."

"You cannot manage Andretti alone," Antonio said.

The finger shifted to Antonio. "Stay out of this. Run back to my fucking father for all I care. You can have him."

Two bright spots of color appeared on Antonio's cheeks. "You do not know him."

"You're right. I don't. And whose fault is that?"

"He is a good man."

"He could be a fucking saint and I'd still want nothing to do with him." Nick took a swig from the mostly empty bottle. "But he's not. He's a goddamn mobster. About as far from a saint as you can get."

"I will not argue with you, but—"

Nick cut him off. "You're right. You're not going to argue with me." He hurled the bottle at Antonio, clipping him on the shoulder. The bottle bounced off and broke on the wall behind his target, littering the doorway with shards of glass. The smell of whiskey permeated the shed.

Antonio rubbed his arm, his mouth compressed into a thin line. "*Basta!*" He started toward Nick.

Delfina intercepted him and put her hand on his chest. "Tonio, go, please."

"I will not leave you here with this pig."

"It'll be fine. I can leave if I need to."

"The glass."

"I'll manage." She surveyed the shed and spotted a heavy canvas tarp thrown over some equipment. "I'll use that," she said, pointing to it.

Antonio blew out in exasperation. "I do not like this."

"Who do you think you are—her boyfriend?" Nick asked. "Is that why you carried her in here? Maybe you were hoping for a snog or two, maybe even a quick shag?"

Antonio's forehead creased. "Snog? Shag? I do not know these words, but I do not like the sound of them."

"How do 'kiss' and 'fuck' sound?" Nick asked, enunciating the words so they felt like punches to the gut. Could he possibly be jealous? Of Antonio?

"You should not speak that way in front of her," Antonio growled.

"So she *is* your girlfriend." Nick gazed at Delfina. "That's why you're not keen on the fiancé, even though he is a rich prick."

Before she could answer, Antonio cut in, his voice cold and hard. "I told you. Do not curse around women. And I am not her *ragazzo*."

"Yeah, the *principessa* wouldn't look at you twice. You're just a *fucking* bodyguard."

The taunting curse lingered in the air. Delfina stared at Antonio, willing him not to take the bait. She hardly dared breathe. For a second, Antonio didn't reply, then he said, "Not anymore."

Nick glared at him while Delfina counted her heartbeats, then a sly grin crossed Nick's face and he shook his head, the movement exaggerated, slow. "You think you're my replacement. The son that never was. Am I close?" Antonio swore. "Hit a nerve, did I?"

Color rose to Antonio's cheeks again and his hands formed into fists. Delfina's pulse spiked. She had to stop this. Nick tried to stand, but lost his balance and fell back against the bench.

"See? He can't hurt me," Delfina said to Antonio, switching to Italian. "I can handle him."

Antonio held her eyes in silent protest, then raised his hands in surrender. "I'll tell Gio and Cris we found him." His face wrinkled with disgust when his focus swung back to Nick. "I don't know why we bothered."

Delfina didn't relax until Antonio left. Now that she and Nick were alone, she sucked in a breath, her nerves flaring. Nick was a mess, and it was her fault. But he needed to see sense. Could she get through to him?

Grabbing the tarp, she spread it out on the floor next to Nick, hoping it was clean enough to save her dress. She eased herself down beside him. Neither of them said anything.

Finally he broke the silence. "Why don't you leave me alone?"

"Because I like you." She said it without thinking. But it was true.

He rubbed a hand across his face. His voice when it came sounded broken, weak. "Why?" Tears gathered at the corners of his eyes.

"Oh Nick," she said and rose up on her knees, putting her arms around him. He didn't respond at first, then his arms closed around her. He was shaking. After a moment she realized he was crying without making a sound. Something in her chest squeezed. What must it have been like for him, growing up without a mother, a father? And she'd been the one to stir up all those bad memories.

She stroked his hair, saying nothing. After a time, his hold slackened, then he pulled away, wiping his cheeks on the sleeve of his suit. She started to sit back on her heels, trying to figure out how to broach the subject of his father, but he took her face in his hands and pressed his lips to hers, stunning her. She started to resist, but he let out a little sound of protest. What could it hurt, really? She relaxed into him. It was just a—what had he called it?—a snog. A silly word for a silly thing. But it did feel good, the brush of his lips on hers, his fingers caressing her cheeks and jaw, the way he tugged her closer until she was sitting on his lap. He kissed her gently for a while, then with a moan, his mouth opened slightly and his tongue sought hers. A thrill ran through her body at the invasion, at his deepening desire for her.

They shouldn't be doing this, she shouldn't be letting him kiss her, but she didn't want to stop. He tasted of Scotch, the liquor dark and smoky. She let him in, parting her lips beneath his, her eyes closing and all her senses concentrating on the touch of his mouth, his tongue. His hands left her face, one of them twining in her hair, the other spreading across her upper back, enclosing her in his warmth.

She'd been kissed before, but only by Teo, and he'd been a boy. Nick was a man—there was nothing tentative about his kiss. Nothing rough about it either, even though he was drunk. He didn't grind his lips against hers, though their touch was firm, insistent. And his tongue was wicked—light and flickering one moment, demanding the next.

She didn't know how long they kissed before he broke it off. She raised a hand to her mouth, caressing her lips where they tingled. Still holding her by the back of the neck, he rested his forehead against hers, both of them breathing hard. "I'm sorry," he whispered.

"For what?"

"For being an arse." He paused. "For kissing you."

"Don't apologize for kissing me."

He let her go and shook his head. "I shouldn't have."

"I wanted you to."

"You're engaged, remember?" He wagged a finger at her, but the movement was slow, almost lazy. "Besides, your father will... skin me and my grandparents alive if he finds out."

And there it was—the solution to both of their problems, a solution Nick would like far more than asking his father for help. Gio was right. There was a way to get rid of Leandro and save Nick, a way to pursue her dream of a career in fashion. And maybe even, a way to save her father from himself.

"Not necessarily."

He squinted at her. "Pardon?"

"Never mind." She'd better handle this on her own. He'd think it too risky, but she knew her father and exactly how to handle him. Nick just had to play a part. And he had to play it well. He had to believe his role in it, or it would never work.

She checked her watch. It was close to midnight. They were supposed to cut the cake then, and everyone would be searching for her. Sooner or later, they'd be found. And it had to appear convincing when they were.

She reached up behind her neck and unzipped her dress. Cool air touched her back, making her shiver.

"What are you doing?" Nick asked. He blinked at her in alarm.

"I'm hot."

"You... can't be." He seemed to be having increasing trouble choosing his words. Good.

"I am."

He averted his gaze as she let the dress slide down her arms. "Stop it," he said as she rose up, stepping out of the dress.

She hugged herself, shaking in the cold. "Look at me," she demanded.

"No."

"Do it, Nick. You want to."

He tried to rise again, but couldn't do it. "Why are you... doing this?"

"It's for your own good." She unhooked her bra, letting it fall to her feet, then couldn't stop herself from cupping her hands over her breasts to shield them from his view. *Silly girl.* Her face reddened, and she dropped her hands. If she was going to do this, she couldn't do it halfway.

She peeled off her hose and panties with haste, then stood before him, her hands at her sides. The cold tightened her nipples, turning them into pebbles. "Look at me," she whispered again, her voice cracking, drying up in her throat. A flock of birds swooped round and round in her belly.

He glanced at her, then quickly away. She waited, shivering, then he turned back, his eyes traveling over her breasts and hips, then up to her face. "You're... beautiful," he murmured, his voice reverent.

She sank to her knees beside him, the tarp icy beneath her bare skin. She leaned toward the heat radiating off him. "Kiss me."

Pulling her onto his lap again, he crushed her to his chest, his lips finding hers with a suddenness that alarmed her. Heart pounding, she responded to his kiss, opening her mouth beneath his, unable to stop a moan from escaping when one of his hands tweaked her hard left nipple. *Dio mio*, this was what Gio was always going on about.

After a while, Nick pulled back, trying to struggle out of his suit jacket. She helped him shed it, then she spread it beside them. With a nervous flip in her belly, she lay down on the warm silky inner lining of his coat and propped herself up on an elbow, her legs tightly closed as she lay on one hip. She had to convince him, but she didn't want to go too far.

He followed her, rolling onto his knees, his head swaying as he crawled up next to her. "We shouldn't... do this," he mumbled. His words were becoming more indistinct. He'd have to pass out any minute, yes?

"I want to. Who's going to know?"

"Good point," Nick slurred. He dropped down beside her, and for a second she thought he was out. But then he raised his arm and placed a hand on her hip, his thumb resting on the front crest of the bone.

She didn't feel cold anymore. In fact, her whole body felt superheated, nowhere more so than between her legs. She was too aware of his hand, of how close it was to her sex. Of how much she wanted him to touch her there.

Placing her fingers over his on her hip, Delfina warred with herself. She had to stay in control of the situation. Even though all she wanted to do was the exact opposite and surrender.

He leaned in to kiss her again. She met his lips eagerly and let go of his hand, which immediately traveled exactly where she wanted it to go. He cupped his fingers over her sex, tickling the hair there with exquisitely soft strokes. She moaned into his mouth and relaxed her legs the slightest bit, which he took as a signal to go further. He rolled her onto her back and his fingers slipped down between the lips of her sex, finding that spot she'd stroked in secret.

"No!" she gasped, grabbing his wrist.

"*Now* you want to stop?" he asked, but he didn't obey, as if daring her to say no again. As if he knew she didn't want to.

She blushed fiercely as his fingers continued to move on her, evoking the most amazing sensations. His fingers felt different than hers. Stronger. Thicker. Insistent. *Madonna*, what was she doing? She'd thought him too drunk to go so far, but apparently he was not drunk enough. She was going to have to go through with it. Here, in a garden shed. On a tarp.

She let go of his wrist. He held her gaze with difficulty, blinking slowly. "You're sure?"

She nodded and lay back. His fingers moved lower, dipping inside her, pulling more moisture up between the lips to her clit, where he made lazy circles around and around, driving her mad whenever his fingers grazed across it. His head dipped down, and he took one of her nipples in his mouth, his tongue swirling around the sensitive tip. She bucked upward against his hand, the excess of sensation startling her. "*Cristo*," she moaned. This felt better than she'd ever imagined.

After a few minutes, just as she was close to her peak, he stopped. "What's wrong?" she asked, surprised at how irritated she sounded.

He rolled off her and onto his back. "We need... to stop."

She couldn't let his conscience take over. "Why? No one will ever know."

"Not... good idea," he mumbled.

What would Gio do in a situation like this? Trembling inside, Delfina unzipped his trousers, then placed her hand on the swelling at his crotch. She moved her fingers lightly over the cloth of his underwear. He wrapped his fingers around her wrist as if to restrain her, but he didn't pull her hand away, only trapped it. She held her breath and waited, afraid that if she said anything he'd stop her. Finally he closed his eyes and pressed her hand more tightly against himself.

She found the opening in his underwear and slipped her fingers inside. He felt so warm, the skin silky beneath her fingertips, his flesh thrillingly hard.

Her stomach flipped over, and she inhaled deeply in response. What would he feel like inside her? He guided her fingers upward, toward the head, which filled her palm. When she cupped her hand around it, he let out a soft, low moan that sent shivers through her. Moving her hand up and down, she squeezed him lightly. No response. His lids were still closed, his mouth slightly open. "Nick?"

Nothing. She shook him. A soft snore came out of his mouth, and a wave of disappointment rolled through her. But this was what she'd wanted. For him to *think* they'd had sex, without her actually losing her virginity.

So why did she feel let down?

Gravel crunched outside. Someone was coming. She rolled over and grabbed her dress, pulling it up in front of her body.

Gio burst through the half-closed door, her shoes snapping shards of glass in the doorway. "Delfi! *Dio mio!* Put your clothes on. Everyone's hunting for you." Delfina scrambled up, turning her back to Gio as she dressed. Nick didn't stir. He must have been out cold. Gio didn't seem to notice. "I can't believe *you* did it before *me*. What was it like?"

"Can you keep a secret? I mean it, Gio."

"Of course. I won't tell anyone." Delfina waited until Gio added, "I *swear* it. On my *nonnina*'s grave."

"He fell asleep."

"After? They all do, from what I've heard."

"No. *Before*."

Gio let out a peal of laughter. "*Davvero?*"

"Help me with this," Delfina said, gesturing to the zipper on the back of the dress. Gio crunched through the glass and zipped her up. "What do we do with him?" Delfina asked. "We can't carry him."

"Throw his coat over him. I'll send Cris back for him."

"*You* will?"

Gio shrugged and smiled coyly. "I think your brother likes me."

Uh-oh. Gio had always ignored Cris before. "How long were you two in the boathouse?"

"Long enough for him to kiss me. Then Antonio barged in. Too bad they didn't want to share."

Delfina rolled her eyes. "You're impossible." She pulled her panties up under her dress, doing her best to appear stern while doing something so undignified. "You do *not* get to break my little brother's heart, Gio. You hear me?"

Gio flashed her a naughty grin. "Come on, we'd better get going. Where are your shoes?"

"Somewhere in the garden. I broke a heel. Can you drag a tarp over to the door so I don't cut my feet?"

They left the shed, Delfina wincing across the gravel back to the main path. Where was Antonio when she needed him?

"Gio, you have to promise me something."

"Anything."

"You have to promise to tell your brother what you saw."

"What I *think* I saw, or what I actually saw?"

"He has to think I've been unfaithful."

"Well, sweetie, you *have*."

"Okay. He has to think I'm no longer a virgin. And you know, possibly pregnant."

"You're going with my plan?" Gio's voice rose excitedly.

"More or less. Papà can't kill Nick if he's got to marry me."

"Are you so sure?"

"I'll make him see the wisdom in keeping Nick around. It'd be better to have my uncle Enrico as an ally instead of an enemy."

"What if you're wrong?"

"I'm not. He'll go for it. I know Papà."

"I'll do whatever you ask. If you're sure."

"I am."

Gio twisted a hank of hair around her fingers. "When do I tell Leandro?"

"I've got that job interview tomorrow, and I don't want this to erupt before then. Give me a week. Then tell."

"But why would I wait?"

"Pretend you've been struggling with your conscience, that it's been waging a war of loyalty between him and me. And he won."

Gio coughed. "You must think I'm a hell of an actress."

"You could charm the paint off a Botticelli. How hard can it be to snow your junkie brother?"

"Point taken." Gio took Delfina's arm, her tone filling with excitement when she spoke. "Tell me, how was it, whatever you *did* do."

Delfina couldn't help smiling wide. "Amazing."

"Details!"

Delfina opened her mouth, then clamped it shut. She didn't want to spoil the moment, didn't want to share it with anyone else, not even Gio. "It's private."

Gio's shoulders slumped. "Delfi!"

"No."

They were silent for a minute, then Gio said, "You care about him."

"I do."

Gio put a hand on her arm and stopped them both. "You can't have him, you know that. Even if your father doesn't kill him, he works for Interpol."

A gasp flew out of her mouth. "How do you know that?"

"Leandro overheard."

The blood drained to her feet. "*Porca miseria*! He's probably told everyone."

Gio nodded. "He went right to Papà and your father, who explained."

"What did he say?"

"I don't know all the details. Leandro was vague about that. Said it wasn't my business. But he said something about Nick being useful—for now."

Delfina felt sick. Could her plan tip the balance against Nick?

"You still want to go through with it?"

Her heart fluttered wildly in her chest. What should she do? She took a deep breath. She knew Papà, she did. He hadn't been the one to hurt Teo. She had to gamble that he wouldn't hurt Nick either. "Yes."

CHAPTER 7

Delfina had managed to elude him last night, and he'd had enough drama at the party already. But Dario wasn't going to wait a minute longer for answers.

"How did Enrico Lucchesi end up at your birthday party?" He frowned at his daughter across the expanse of his desk, drumming his fingers on the dark wood.

"I invited him, Papà. He is my uncle, after all." Delfina flipped her hair back over her shoulder and met his gaze straight on. But she was chewing at her lower lip.

"You do realize you landed me in a lot of trouble."

Her eyes widened. "What do you mean?"

"That wretch Leandro heard our guest arguing with his father. Were you there?" When she nodded, he continued. "So then you know what Signor Clarkston does for a living."

"Did you think you'd keep that secret forever?"

"I'd rather control that kind of information and release it in my own time, if I choose."

"You can't control the world."

How obtuse was she? He leaned forward. "I can't even control my own daughter!"

"What made you think you could?"

He wanted to strangle her. And yet, her fire was so much like Toni's.... An arrow of grief pierced him. Would he never get over the loss? He cleared his throat. "Delfi, you ought to know by now that we can't always do what we want." He gestured around them. "Everything we have comes with a price—obedience, and secrecy."

She looked away from him. "I didn't choose this life, and I don't want any part of it."

Must she always resist? "Are you still planning to interview with Morelli?"

Her eyes turned back to his, wariness in them. "Yes. I've set it up for this afternoon."

He hated to threaten her, but she'd forced his hand. "I promised I'd stay out of that, Delfi. But if you persist in dragging Lucchesi into my affairs, I will do what I must." Her mouth dropped open, but she said nothing. He pressed forward. She needed another reminder that she wasn't in control. "Did you discuss the job with Leandro?"

Her face hardened, and she pushed back her left sleeve and extended her wrist. Light bruises circled it. "*This* is how he discusses things."

Heat flashed through him and his fingers tightened on the edge of the desk, though for once she wasn't the cause. But given all that Gianluca had learned last night, the engagement had to stand. If Benedetto and Lorenzo were turning on him, he'd need d'Imperio's backing to survive the coming battle. He couldn't fight both Lucchesi and his own family alone. "I will speak to Leandro."

She pushed the sleeve back down. "A lot of good that will do." She wiped at her glistening eyes.

Her tears made his chest go tight. "Delfi, I'm sorry. But what's done is done."

"You didn't have the guts to tell me yourself. You let Leandro do it. Do you know how *humiliating* that was?"

About as humiliating as finding out that his uncle and his grandfather thought he was expendable. "Gianluca d'Imperio is key to my future plans. I need him unequivocally on my side."

"You have only one daughter. Are you sure you're 'spending' her wisely?" she asked, her voice sharp enough to cut stone.

Dario rose, coming around to her side. He sat on the edge of the desk, placing a hand on her shoulder. "*Cara*, if there was another way, I would take it."

"You're just like Nonno Carlo. Selling the daughter you claim to love."

Her words were a slap in the face. He was nothing like his father. Besides, his father hadn't done anything Toni hadn't begged him to do. Sorrow lanced through him again. Toni had given herself to the Lucchesis, to free him, her twin, from their clutches. And he'd never thanked her. Not once, his bitterness over her choice rendering him mute.

Delfina was too old to easily placate anymore. He reached down and picked up her bruised wrist. "Leandro won't hurt you again."

"Are you giving me a bodyguard?"

"I promise you. He won't ever again lay a hand on you in anger."

She yanked her arm from his hold and jumped up from her chair. "I see where I rank in this family. Right below the dogs." She marched out of his study and down the hall, her heels echoing on the marble.

Porco Dio! He slammed a fist on his desk. Why could she never see his side? Why could she never trust him? Why must she continually defy him?

Inhaling deeply, he flattened both hands on the polished cherry. Would she prefer it if he acted like his father and tried to grind her to dust? Is that what she wanted? He shook his head. He was losing control, losing sight of who he was as a man. His father was the last role model he wanted to follow.

And yet, his father had had one thing right. Enemies had to be crushed. God help them both if she became one of them.

———— ◆ ————

"I *must* get my son away from Dario." Enrico slapped the desk in his study, startling both Antonio and Ruggero, making them shift in their chairs. Taking a deep breath, Enrico searched for calm. *Damn it.* He mustn't let his emotions get away from him. He hadn't slept since his disastrous meeting with Nico the night before.

"I'm quite sure he doesn't want our help," Antonio said, rubbing his left shoulder. "I've got the bruises to prove it."

"Even drunk, your son has your aim," Ruggero joked, but Enrico couldn't laugh. After a brief silence, Ruggero added, "I could make him leave—if I can get to him."

Enrico shook his head. "You aren't supposed to even be here. I want you to take that vacation we talked about. I've let you delay it for too long. Your family needs you."

The skin around Ruggero's dark eyes tightened. "No. Andretti is up to something. I told you they would come at you through your children."

Antonio's mouth opened and his eyebrows popped to his hairline. "You *knew*? Am I the only one who didn't?"

Ruggero ignored the question, his gaze sliding to Enrico. Yes, it was his problem to deal with. Not Ruggero's. Enrico cleared his throat, a sudden constriction nearly clamping it shut. He'd never thought he'd speak to Nico again. In fact, he'd been thinking of formally adopting Antonio, of making him his heir, of taking the vow of *comparaggio* toward him, no matter the sex of the child Kate was carrying. Tonio deserved to be recognized for who he was to Enrico, for who he'd always been, and who he'd always be. A son. But now…

Now Enrico was lost again. Dom's sons were baying for both his blood and Antonio's, and Nico was in danger. Again Enrico took a deep breath. One thing at a time. Nico first.

"Ruggero, you are going to Calabria. No arguments. Antonio, you will be in charge of retrieving Nico."

"I'm a horrible choice." Antonio's cheeks reddened. "For obvious reasons."

"And I'm not going anywhere," Ruggero said.

Enrico met the challenge in Ruggero's stare. "You're defying a direct order?"

Ruggero bowed his head and spoke to the carpet. "With respect, *capo*. You are in severe danger."

"Perhaps."

The guard's eyes snapped back to Enrico's. "There is no 'perhaps.' You can *never* trust an Andretti." Ruggero let out a soft growl of frustration. "I should have shot the bastard when I had the chance."

"Dario surrendered. He agreed to a truce," Enrico said.

"A truce he does not intend to honor." Ruggero raked a hand through his dark hair. "The Andrettis are snakes, the whole lot of them."

"Cris and Delfina are all right," Antonio said.

"The females perhaps. The males—never," Ruggero said, slamming a closed fist into an open palm.

Enrico sat forward. He had to get Ruggero to see reason. "Dario is playing a game, yes. But if he intended to mortally wound me, my boy would be dead already."

Ruggero's brow wrinkled. "You truly believe so? You told me once that Carlo liked to play with his food before he ate it. What makes you think his son is any different?"

Nothing. Not now. Dario had played him, in the worst possible way. And he'd fallen for it. And now Dario held Enrico's heart in his hands. All he had to do was make a fist and he'd crush it. Who would have thought Dario would prove more devious than Carlo?

That cunning made Dario many times more dangerous. At least Carlo had never hidden his feelings. But somehow, after all these years, Dario remained an enigma. Ruggero was right about the danger. And yet... "I made a promise to you, Ruggero. I intend to keep it."

"I got my Maserati. *Mille grazie.*"

"Not the damn car, and you know it. Your family needs you."

"You need me more."

"I have Tommaso, and Claudio and Santino."

"Claudio and Santino are still boys. And Tommaso is going gray."

"He's still effective."

"*Sì.* But you need more than 'effective' right now."

"There is no budging you," Enrico said, letting a hint of a question into the statement.

"My brother-in-law has a few months left."

Enrico swallowed hard, his throat squeezing shut again. The Velas had had sacrificed too much for the Lucchesis. Ruggero's father had even died in their service. Now Ruggero was putting his family aside again, as he'd done so many years ago when he and his father had followed the Lucchesis north. Enrico's voice rasped when he spoke. "I owe you a debt I can never repay."

"You have repaid it. Many times over. My family would be suffering were it not for yours."

"That may be—"

Ruggero cut him off. "We both know it's true. My whole family has benefited from the connection between our families. The Velas would still be poor farmers, scrabbling in the dirt, with too little in our bellies. My family swore to serve the Lucchesis. *I* swore it. And I will never turn my back on that oath."

So much he owed this man. "When this is over—"

"Yes, I will go. When Dario Andretti is dead."

"Then you are in charge of bringing my son back to me."

Antonio swiftly rose from his chair and paced to the window overlooking the lake. Though he said nothing, he clasped his hands behind his back, his stance stiff and proud. *Madonna.* Enrico needed to deal with Tonio, but not until he knew what to do about Nico. And his godsons. Tonio would have to wait, as painful as it was for them both. It would be worse to make more promises he couldn't keep.

He was the *capo* of the Lucchesi family. A little over two weeks ago, he'd had Dario Andretti at his mercy. And he'd spared Dario then, trying to atone for the wrong that Enrico's father had done to Dario all those years ago. A wrong that Enrico had ultimately condoned. A wrong that he was still paying for.

He was the *capo* of the Lucchesi family. He had everything, and nothing.

Never had he felt more powerless.

———◆———

Delfina fled her father's study and ran smack into Cris. Seeing her face, he took hold of her arms. "Delfi, what's gotten you so upset?"

She threw her hands in the air. "Papà. Leandro." She almost added Nick to that list but caught herself. "Everything."

His soft brown eyes searched hers. "We need to talk." He steered her outside by the elbow and over to the bench under the huge plane tree that shaded much of the grass behind the house. He pulled her down beside him, hugging her close. "I know Leandro's a jerk. But there are worse things that could happen."

She showed him the bruises. "Like this?"

His face darkened as he ran a finger over the marks. "I had no idea. Does Papà know?"

"He didn't care. I'm just currency to him. Something to be bartered and sold."

"It's complicated."

She snorted and shifted away from him. "So I can't count on you either."

"I didn't say that I'd do nothing. I'm just saying it's not going to be easy. And Papà has good reasons."

"He only cares about his business. Not about what's best for me."

"That isn't true. There's a lot at stake. More than you realize. Papà made a mistake. And he can't go back on the engagement without making things worse."

"What mistake?"

"He let you bring Nick to the party. Now that d'Imperio knows about the Interpol connection—no thanks to you—he has lost faith in us."

Tears blurred her vision. "I'm doomed, then."

"Don't worry. I'll fix this." He reached out and wiped away one of her tears with his thumb.

"How?"

He pulled her close and kissed her forehead. "I told you; I'll handle it. Stop fretting." They sat like that for a minute or two, then he asked, "What are you doing with Nick?"

She stiffened, then forced herself to relax. That was the question, wasn't it? "What do you mean?"

"His trousers were unzipped when I went to get him."

Adrenaline spiked through her. *Dio mio!* How could she have been so careless? "I don't know what you're talking about."

"Your dress was dirty."

"I fell in the garden and broke a heel. That's why I didn't have shoes either."

He said nothing for a few seconds. "I found your hose in the shed."

Madonna! "I got a run from walking barefoot."

"I'm sure you did. But why take them off in the shed in front of him?"

71

"He was passed out." She couldn't look at him anymore.

"I'm not an idiot." He squeezed her shoulder. "I know you were upset, but you can't fuck around."

Did everyone think they could tell her what to do? "Isn't that *my* business?"

"Do you want to get him killed?"

A shiver ran through her. "Of course not."

"Then stay away from him and be patient. I *will* fix this."

"How?" She wanted to believe him. But would his plan work better than hers?

He shook his head. "There are some things you're better off not knowing."

Should she call off Gio? "I need to know."

"You just have to trust me."

"What if I can't?"

He turned so he was looking directly into her eyes. "Listen to me. Don't do anything stupid, or Nick will die. Do you hear me? Trust me to handle it."

What if Cris was wrong? Her plan would work; Papà was angry now, but he would get over it. He'd eventually see the wisdom in having Zio Enrico as an ally. The d'Imperios were powerful, but so was Enrico Lucchesi. And her plan would shield Nick too, once her father calmed down. She had to trust her gut. "I'll try."

"Don't try. Trust me."

Delfina swallowed hard. She hated lying to her brother. "I will."

She said a silent prayer. *Please let my plan work. And please don't let Nick be killed.*

———— ◆ ————

Her heart skipping, Delfina reported at one o'clock to an ancient warehouse in the Bovisa district. Beautiful brass lettering spelled out "House of Morelli, established 1890" above the door.

She stepped inside, clutching her portfolio to her chest like a shield. The receptionist led her past a busy workshop and to a small office, where the man himself, Enzo Morelli, was sitting at a desk sketching what looked like a matching ensemble—dress, shoes, and handbag. He continued sketching as she waited, hovering near the open doorway.

Her eyes darted around the room, drinking in every detail of the clutter. Sketches were tacked up haphazardly on the walls in loose clusters by season and year. Swatches of cloth and leather spilled out of a filing cabinet hulking in the corner. A stack of photography and art books sat next to it, threatening to tip over. She wanted to touch everything. And straighten it up too.

With a flourish, Signor Morelli signed and dated the sketch, then set it to one side of his desk. He pushed his glasses down his long elegant nose and peered at her over the rims, his gaze roving up and down her body, but not in a prurient way. "*You're* the Andretti girl?"

"Yes," she said, stepping forward and offering her hand.

He rose and shook her hand loosely, holding it out of the way so that he could scrutinize her outfit. "At least you know how to dress. The cut and color suit you well."

She swallowed hard and squeaked out, "*Mille grazie, signore.*"

72

"Sit," he ordered and put out his hand for her portfolio. "Let's see what you have."

She gave it to him, then didn't know what to do with her hands. She tried to hold them still in her lap, but they kept finding things to do. She settled for clasping them together as he paged through her portfolio, a thoughtful frown on his face. He said nothing for several minutes, instead flipping through the pages, occasionally lingering on one. He folded down the corners on two pages and handed the book back to her. "These show promise. The rest are derivative."

She tried to hold back her dismay, but he must've seen it, for his tone softened. "It's a common mistake for a novice. And how else does one learn, except by imitation? All great artists must study their forebears. And then destroy them."

She nodded, feeling a little better, even though she hadn't gotten the job. She glanced at the two sketches he'd marked; they'd been her favorites too. *"Mille grazie,"* she said. She started to rise when his voice stopped her.

"Be here at nine on Monday."

She settled back into her seat and looked at him sharply. "Listen, just because of who my father is, that doesn't mean you have to give me this job. I don't want it if you don't think I show promise."

Signor Morelli sat back in his chair and took his glasses off, rubbing the bridge of his nose. "I did not get where I am today by letting other people make my decisions. I am no fool, *signorina*. Be here Monday." He put the glasses back on. "And bring some fresh ideas with you."

Had she heard correctly? He made a shooing motion with his hand, then gave her a smile. "I have much to do, *signorina*."

Delfina gawked at him for a moment, warmth spreading through her chest, before returning the smile. The internship was hers! And all her father had done was give her the opportunity. The rest she'd earned.

———— ◆ ————

Nick woke in a sweat, startled by the pounding on his door. Someone had put him to bed the night before; they'd taken off his shoes and his jacket, but he was still in the shirt and trousers he'd worn to Delfina's party. What the hell time was it? He glanced at the clock. Three in the afternoon? *Christ.* He sat up and groaned. His head felt like someone had been using it to mix concrete.

The pounding didn't let up. "I'm coming!" he called as he stumbled to the door. When he opened it, he saw one of the maids, Fulvia. She'd been taking care of him, and today was no exception. She had a plate of mixed cheeses, meats, and olives. Along with a carafe of espresso. *"Mille grazie,* Fulvia," he said, taking the tray from her.

She gave him a sweet smile and a bob of her head. *"Prego, signore."*

His stomach rumbled when he caught a whiff of the coffee. When had he last eaten?

Setting the tray on the kitchen table, he tucked in to the meal and reviewed the night before—what he could remember of it. He had no idea how he'd gotten back to the guest cottage.

All he did have was a dim memory of being in the shed with Delfina, and she'd been naked, and he'd been... touching her? Or maybe his imagination had run away with him. Because the girl he saw in his mind was perfect. High breasts that turned up at the tips, large dark nipples, a narrow waist, skin like satin, black wavy hair that felt like silk.

Exactly how he'd imagined her before. But reality never lived up to one's fantasies. Never, right?

Had he really touched her? He searched his memory some more, remembered her coming into the shed. She'd been in the arms of that blond bloke, Antonio, who he'd thrown a bottle at, though he couldn't remember exactly why. Something about his father.

Jesus. What a cracking mess he'd made of things.

Then again, he had every right. She shouldn't have sprung his father on him like that. It wasn't sporting. At all.

Though he hadn't told her much, it should have been enough for her to have known Nick didn't want to see him.

Ever.

Except behind the bars of a prison cell.

The anger he'd felt during the meeting with his father rose all over again. Though a fair portion of his anger was self-directed, if he were honest.

What had happened to the cool detachment he'd always wanted to show? Why had he admitted he'd missed his father? At least he hadn't done the worst thing. He hadn't flung himself into his father's arms and sobbed like he had the day his father had left them. At least he hadn't done that.

But he hadn't been mature about things either. He could still hear his father's wife saying in her Yank accent that he'd been acting like a child, a charge he couldn't deny.

And Delfina had seen it all. The absolute worst moment of his life, next to finding his mother dead.

Another knock at the door. It must be Fulvia coming back for the tray. He'd be forever grateful to her. The throbbing in his head had receded, and he felt much better with some food in his belly.

He flung open the door, ready to thank her profusely. Instead he saw Delfina, a finger to her lips. The bugs. He'd nearly forgotten about them. She seemed happy to see him, her eyes shining as she beckoned him outside.

"You're in a good mood," he said, following her into the hedge maze, the way much easier in daylight. Maybe he hadn't made a complete cock-up of the night before.

"I just got the job of my dreams."

He'd kissed her, maybe done much more, but how little he knew about her. "What job is that?"

"I'll be working for a designer. Enzo Morelli. I start Monday. It's just an internship. I think Papà wants me to be sure before he invests in three more years of university for me."

Fashion design? She sure looked the part; he'd never seen a girl her age appear so elegant with such ease. "Congratulations. I hope you enjoy the work."

"I'm sure I will. It's all I've ever wanted."

"I didn't realize... women like you worked."

They reached the bench where they'd first spoken at length. Delfina made a sour face. "They don't. Papà doesn't approve. I was supposed to ask Leandro's permission, but I didn't."

He sat beside her. "You need his bloody *permission*? Since when?"

"Since that's how it works for families like ours."

Bloody hell. "And if he objects?"

"I don't intend to marry him." She held his gaze. "I'd sooner shoot myself."

"Don't say things like that."

Twisting her hands together in her lap, she hunched her shoulders. "It's true."

"Listen." He grabbed her forearm, unable to stop himself. "Don't you *ever* think about killing yourself. You hear me? It's bloody unfair to the people you leave behind."

Eyes widening, she covered her open mouth with her hand. "*Dio mio!* Your mother. I wasn't thinking.... I'm sorry."

An awkward silence descended on them. After a while, Nick broke it, a little embarrassed about his outburst. By now, she must think he was a bleeding nutter. "After everything that happened at the party, I wasn't sure you'd ever want to speak to me again."

She laughed, a little too loudly. "I was thinking the same thing." Her smile receded. "I'm sorry about what happened with your father. I truly am. But it had to be done."

"I don't need *his* help."

"You will." He started to interrupt, but she held up a finger to silence him. "I don't mean it to sound like I have no faith in you. It's just that the situation, this world, is utterly foreign to you. You're at a horrible disadvantage. And my father has no scruples. He's not like you, Nick. None of us are. This life requires so many compromises, and if you haven't a strong ruthless streak, you'll never survive it."

He blew out hard. There was no sense arguing. They were never going to agree on this point. Instead, he asked the question that plagued him. "Did we...?" He couldn't quite say the words, so he settled for gesturing helplessly between them.

She tilted her head and smiled. "Yes."

His stomach tightened. "Everything?" She nodded. *Oh dear Lord.* Hopefully he'd done at least one thing right. "Did I wear a condom?" She shook her head. "And you're not on birth control." *Of course not, you berk. She's a virgin. Correct that. Was a virgin.*

"I'm not, but the odds are against a pregnancy. It was early in my cycle."

He so did not want to have this discussion. Ever. And certainly not with the virgin he'd deflowered. And whose father would—literally—kill him if he found out. "Did I hurt you?"

She hesitated, then said, "Not much."

"I'm such a prat." He touched her hand. "Aside from doing it in the first place, I should never have done it while I was drunk. And in a garden shed. Your first time should have been special."

"It wasn't romantic, true, but it was special."

75

She was having him on. "Don't spare my feelings," he said.

"I'm not. When have you ever known me to?"

"True. You don't mince words." He chuckled.

She fiddled with a button on her jacket. "There is a problem though."

"What's that?" he asked, his heart speeding up.

"If I am pregnant, we have to marry."

"Wouldn't your father want to put a bullet in me instead?"

Her eyes flicked to his, then quickly away. "Probably. But he wouldn't. Nobody else would have me."

Nick's stomach twisted into knots at such a future for her. And for the others who might suffer from his stupidity as well. "Even so, do you think he'd harm my grandparents, just to teach me a lesson?"

She bit her lower lip. "I wish I could say no."

He was going to be sick. Not Gran and Grandad. Somehow he had to undo the mistakes he'd made, the mistakes that had gotten him to this point.

Fuente had been right; he was out of his depth, and sinking fast.

CHAPTER 8

"So, my son, what are you going to do about your wayward nephew?" Lorenzo took a sip of his cappuccino and peered at Benedetto over the rim.

Benedetto shrugged. If Dario would not come to heel, he'd have to break him. Eventually. He finished off his own cup and admired the fine view from the rear terrace of Dario's home. Lake Como sparkled in the sunlight, clouds scudding across the blue sky. Still so lovely at this time of year, though a cold bite lingered in the mid-morning air. He burrowed his hands into the pockets of his fine cashmere coat.

"No plan, eh? That's not like you."

Benedetto looked his father over. Like the lake, the old man's eyes glittered, intelligence and cunning in his gaze. Of course, he didn't know everything. Lorenzo didn't know about the debt Benedetto had racked up with the Russians, for example. That debt was the most pressing problem. Dario's compliance—or lack of it—could wait. He had to find someone—someone discreet, someone not tied directly to him, someone who preferably owed him a favor—to meet with the Russians.

He'd considered farming the job out to Lucchesi. The man was trustworthy and could keep a secret, that was for damn sure. Hiding a son all these years!

However, Lucchesi abhorred drugs. And cocaine was how Benedetto was paying off the Russians, with three hundred thousand euros coming back to him in exchange for the extra kilos.

He supposed he could get one of his own to do the deal, but there was always the chance that Lorenzo would catch wind of it. If only Salvatore was out of jail—but that was useless thinking. Sal was stuck behind bars for another two weeks, and the Russians were demanding payment now. As in five days from now.

He could make the delivery himself. But he'd have to go in without backup. He didn't trust his sons to help—they'd as soon shoot him in the back and shake hands with the Russians over his corpse.

Going in alone was risky, possibly suicidal. And certainly bad for business. The

Russians would know something was wrong. *Never let your enemy know when he has the upper hand.* Who'd said that to him? Probably his father.

What about contracting the job out to d'Imperio? There'd certainly been enough friction between Gianluca and Dario at the party to make him think they weren't fast friends, despite the betrothal between Delfina and Leandro. But could he trust Gianluca to keep quiet?

"What's troubling you?" Lorenzo asked. "You've been brooding all morning."

"Nothing."

"Don't try to lie to me."

Adrenaline licked at the base of his spine. He was under no illusions. If his father caught a whiff of the debt and the reason for it, he wouldn't hesitate to get rid of him. Remo, his older brother, had already paid that price, agonizingly so. Lorenzo had plenty of Andrettis to choose a successor from.

Benedetto let out a sigh. "All right. I've been trying to sort out how to get the families in line. La Provincia—that was a stroke of genius. A clever first step."

Lorenzo waved the praise away. "Stop blowing smoke up my ass."

"But the next step will be harder. La Provincia is almost too effective. The families aren't fighting the way they used to, and everyone's making money. So how do we get everyone to see the benefit of consolidated leadership?"

When Lorenzo smiled, the skin on his face creased like fine leather. "You haven't figured it out yet?" He *tsk*ed at Benedetto, wagging a finger at him. "You're off your game."

Taking out his cigarette case, Benedetto lit up. Lorenzo declined to join him. "I do have some ideas, but nothing that will convince everyone. What do you think?"

"Only one thing will work—a strong external enemy. A war."

"Against who? Cosa Nostra has been in disarray ever since the DIA went after them, and the Camorra is too weak."

"But the Russians aren't. And they're eager to come in."

A shiver raced through Benedetto's gut. Inviting them in, when he was in this position—absolutely not. He needed someone else. The answer came in a flash. *Of course.* "Not the Russians. I don't trust them."

"Then who?"

"The DIA." Italo Baldassare, the current prime minister, had long been tied to Cosa Nostra. But he'd recently severed that connection. There was an opportunity, if they were bold.

Lorenzo raised a brow. "You'd trust the fucking DIA over the Russians?"

"Baldassare needs money and votes for his next campaign."

"He threw the Sicilians to the wolves."

"He had to. The journalists were on to him. It was only a matter of time. He'll need a new financial partner. And if he sicced the DIA on us—at least publicly—he'd be a shoe-in for re-election."

"You think you can trust him?"

"Do pigs like to eat?"

Lorenzo shrugged. "Yeah, he's a greedy pig, but he's still a pig. I don't want to put myself in his hands. He's liable to sell us out when he needs to."

"But that's just it. He won't have to. As long as he appears tough on the

'Ndrangheta, as long as we sacrifice a few families—the ones who won't cooperate—he won't need to sacrifice *us*. He won't want to. We keep bankrolling him, he looks tough on crime, and we gain control of the 'Ndrangheta."

Sitting back in his chair, Lorenzo tapped the tips of his steepled fingers against his chin. "There is a certain brilliance to your plan."

Benedetto blew out a long stream of smoke and smiled. "Problem solved." If only he could solve the other one.

Cristoforo stepped out onto the terrace through the rear double doors of the villa. He headed straight for them. "Prozio, may I speak with you alone?"

Interesting. "Certainly." He glanced at his father. "If you'll excuse us, Papà."

Lorenzo picked up his cup and waved them away. The boy headed for the hedge maze. *The stories those hedges could tell.* Who knew how many meetings had been carried out among their twists and turns?

Once they'd walked in some ways, Cristoforo cleared his throat. "Can I speak to you plainly, without fear of our discussion getting back to my father?"

Very interesting indeed. "Of course. You are a man now. You can make your own deals."

His grandnephew let out a breath. "I'd hoped you'd see it that way." The boy's nervousness was almost touching.

"What is on your mind?" Benedetto clasped his hands behind his back, listening to the crunch of gravel beneath their shoes.

"The engagement between Delfina and Leandro cannot stand."

"It is quite an advantageous connection."

"I know. I offered to marry Gio instead, but Papà won't hear of it."

"Gianluca would be insulted."

The boy grumbled something before saying, "Papà can't have that. He screwed things up by not revealing the truth about Clarkston to d'Imperio."

"Or to any of us. He's playing some game."

Cristoforo stopped walking and turned to face him. "Well, I don't like him using Delfi to do it. Leandro got upset and bruised her at the party. We don't need that kind of stain on the Andretti name."

"So what do you want from me?" Benedetto brushed a bit of lint from his sleeve, not wanting to betray his excitement. It would be good to have Dario's *capo di società* in his debt.

"I want you to persuade Papà to see things my way."

"And if I did, what would I get in return?"

"A favor. Anything you want."

Benedetto smiled, his first real one in a long time. *Sometimes one was in the right place at the right time.* He shook the hand Cristoforo extended. *And sometimes one wasn't.*

The boy had so much to learn.

———◆———

When Delfina entered the House of Morelli workshop on Monday at nine sharp, right on time, a hush descended over her fellow apprentices. Was it just her imagination, or were their faces horribly unfriendly? She clutched her portfolio tighter to her chest, unsure what to do next. The receptionist who'd greeted her last time wasn't at her desk. Since no one said anything, she started toward Signor Morelli's office in the back. She'd gotten only a few feet when a tall handsome man in his thirties approached her from that direction. He offered her his hand. "I'm Jacopo Bossi, Enzo's assistant. He asked me to get you settled."

She shook his hand and smiled up at him. With his wavy, sandy brown hair and high cheekbones, Jacopo could be walking runways instead of designing clothes for them. He was casually but elegantly dressed, in a white shirt, unbuttoned at the neck, and a dark navy suit expertly cut to emphasize his broad shoulders and narrow hips. She took her seat at the high desk he led her to.

"This will be your workstation. The lid lifts so you can store supplies in it." He leaned close to her, lowering his voice. "I suggest writing your name in nail varnish on any tools or supplies you want to keep, since things tend to get 'borrowed' otherwise." She stowed her handbag and portfolio inside.

He pointed to a plain wooden table behind her. "That's your work area for anything you can't handle on the desk." Then she followed him into the back, where he showed her the fabric room, crammed with racks of material in a rainbow of weights and colors. She wanted to run her hands over every single sample, but she restrained herself. She'd have time for dreaming later. In the center of the room, a dauntingly huge mound of swatches nearly covered a table.

"Your first job," Jacopo said, "is to sort and hang these new swatches by type, weight, and color family—not by manufacturer. The tulles go with the tulles, starting with white on the left leading to black on the right. Any questions?" When she shook her head, he helped her carry the samples to her work area. "Perhaps some of the others will help," he said.

He then escorted her around the workshop, introducing her to the half dozen other apprentices, all of them in their twenties, an even split between men and women. Or boys and girls, to judge by the less-than-civil interest they showed in her. All of them seemed to hate her on sight. Why?

Just ignore them, Delfi. After Jacopo finished introducing her to the girl whose desk was closest to hers, Delfina returned to her work table and started in on the sorting. The task wasn't difficult, but it was tedious, and she had to be careful not to cut her fingers on the staples that attached the swatches to their cardboard manufacturer tags. After a time, her mind started to wander. Someday she'd have a design house just like this, full of gorgeous fabrics, the bustle of people working, the hum of sewing machines, the rooms perfumed with her own signature scent....

Delfina smiled to herself. That kind of success would be years in the making, if it ever happened. Which reminded her that she wanted to show Signor Morelli the new work she'd done. She retrieved her sketchbook from her desk and set it on the corner of the table so that it would be at hand when Signor Morelli came out of his office. She'd worked feverishly for days, coming up with dozens of new sketches to show him. She'd even included some handbags and shoes.

After a while, she realized that whenever an apprentice walked by her table, he or she muttered something, but Delfina couldn't catch the words. She ignored their behavior, and tried to chalk it up to first-day paranoia.

A few hours into the job, when Delfina had finally made some noticeable headway in her sorting, one of the girls, Ornella, bumped into the table and knocked her portfolio to the floor, scattering her sketches across the thick wooden planks. The girl, a waif with a huge mane of hair, an upturned nose, and a thin mouth, stopped and crossed her arms, staring at Delfina. "I suppose you'll want help with that." A pause, then she added the word they'd been whispering. Only she didn't whisper it. "*Principessa.*"

Delfina's heart sped up. Princess, as in Mafia princess? No, it had to be a coincidence; they couldn't know who she really was. "It's fine. I'll get them myself."

Ornella cocked a skinny hip and crossed her arms, watching Delfina gather up the pile of papers, then she snatched one up just as Delfina's fingers touched it. The drawing was a handbag she'd been playing around with. Ornella's face darkened and she shook the crisp paper at Delfina. "You know, don't you, that most of us have struggled for years to get here. And you just sail in on your father's name."

Blood rushed in Delfina's ears. "Why do you say that?"

"Mario overheard your interview. The old man wouldn't have taken you on otherwise."

"He said I had talent."

"He was blowing sunshine up the rich girl's skirt. Signor Morelli's been having money problems like everyone else. Sooner or later, he'll ask you to talk to your father about a loan." Delfina colored. Ornella had hit too close to the truth.

The girl laughed at Delfina's blush. "My goodness, you are a complete princess, aren't you? You actually thought—"

"Yes, I did. And I *do* have talent."

Ornella raised a brow and raked Delfina's outfit with her eyes. She reached out and fingered the sleeve of Delfina's scarlet jacket, a take-off on the classic Chanel style that Delfina had sewn herself. The jacket suited her beautifully, and she'd always been proud of it. "If ripping off a designer old enough to be my great-great grandmother is your idea of talent, think again."

"The classics are well worth reimagining," Jacopo said as he approached. He stopped and stroked the sleeve of Delfina's jacket. "This is smashing on you, and I think the changes you've made are quite clever. At least you know how to recut a design to suit your figure." He glanced at Ornella, who was wearing a baggy sweater and leggings that made her as drab as a sparrow. "Ornella, Signor Morelli is waiting on those handbag redesigns. You were supposed to have those in first thing this morning."

Handbags? *Cristo.* No wonder Ornella got so upset. Delfina said, "Listen, I didn't know handbags was your area—"

"Like I care about the chicken scratches of the new girl." Ornella crumpled up Delfina's sketch and tossed it at her. Then she glared at Jacopo. "I'm almost done. I'll leave you and your pet alone." She stomped over to her desk and threw herself into her chair, her wild mass of golden brown curls flying around her face.

With a smirk, Jacopo whispered, "Little Miss Drama."

Delfina tried to suppress her smile but couldn't. She blew out the breath she'd been holding. "Thanks for the support."

He smiled and leaned over her table. "Don't let that *strega* get to you. She's just jealous."

"Of what?"

"She can tell by your jacket that you're good."

"She seems to think I was hired because of who my father is."

He gave her a look she couldn't read. Did he know that Signor Morelli had taken money from her father? "Your father owns the largest Fiat dealership in Milan," he said, "along with a slew of other businesses that have the Andretti name plastered all over them. It's no secret that your family is well-off. And it's no secret that Signor Morelli has had money problems."

"All of the apprentices feel the same way she does." She let her shoulders collapse into a hunch and crossed her arms at her waist. It always came back to the way her family lived, didn't it?

He surveyed the room. "Probably, though they're wrong. Signor Morelli recently got a loan from a new silent partner. At least for now, the House of Morelli is solvent. But I won't lie to you. Everything is riding on how well we do at the spring show."

How long would it be until Jacopo learned who the silent partner was? Then even he'd turn his back on her. "They're never going to accept me. Maybe I should leave."

"No, no, no." He wagged a finger in her face. "I did not come over here to join in a pity party. If someone whispering about you bothers you this much, then yes, you don't belong here. Or in the fashion industry, full stop. There are lots of amazing people in fashion, and lots of bitter, no-talent cowards who like to tear everyone else down." He held her gaze. "Decide now whether you want to be in this business. It's not going to get any easier."

He was right. If she were going to be condemned for being an Andretti, she might as well act like one. Aunt Toni had always said the Andrettis were tougher than everyone else. Delfina drew herself up, out of the slouch she'd fallen into. Ornella and the rest of them could go to hell. "I'm staying."

"*Perfetto!*" He rubbed his hands together. "Are you hungry? I know a nice place around the corner."

Crap. The only person who would speak to her was asking her out. "Thanks for the offer, Jacopo, but I'm…" She couldn't force "engaged" out of her mouth. "I'm involved with someone."

He chuckled. "I should hope so. A gorgeous creature like you won't be single for long." He patted her forearm and lowered his voice. "You're not my type, *cara*. Wrong equipment."

She put a hand over her mouth. "Oh, I'm an idiot—"

"And I'm flattered you didn't assume I was gay. I'm sure you have to fend them off constantly. It's become automatic with you, yes?"

He was so kind to give her an out. Her face and neck burned as she nodded. How could she have misread the signs? "If the offer still stands, yes, I'd love to have lunch with you."

"And I'd love to hear all about your man."

She grabbed her handbag and followed him out the door, ignoring the icy looks Ornella and the other apprentices threw her way. If they were going to hate her because of who she was, she'd just have to work hard and prove herself. And if Jacopo was offering his friendship, she'd take it. Even if they hated her for that too.

In time, she'd prove them all wrong. She was a fighter; she was an Andretti. But she was far more than her father's daughter. Somehow, some way, she'd get out from under his long shadow.

———◆———

Nick had just finished wandering the grounds and was returning to the guest cottage when he ran into Cristoforo coming from that direction.

"Nick! There you are!" Cris seemed agitated.

"What's wrong?"

Cris ran a hand through his dark curls, ruffling them up. "Let's take a drive."

"With pleasure." He was feeling a bit housebound. And worried. Dario still hadn't told him whether he'd accept the deal. He was still "thinking." About what? The theory of relativity?

Soon they were speeding off in Cris's red Ferrari 458 Italia. He drove one-handed, using the other to gesture around them when he wasn't changing gears. "Have you seen much of the lake?" he asked. "It's four hundred meters deep. I'm sure there's more than one dead body at the bottom of it."

I'm sure your father's responsible for a few of them too. "No, I didn't have a chance to see any of the lake before your father 'invited' me to stay. But I don't think you asked me along to give me a tour."

Dead silence. Cris chewed on his thumbnail, then said, "You're right. I didn't. But let's enjoy ourselves before we talk business."

At the mention of "business," Nick's pulse revved up. Was Cris the bearer of bad news? Was that little tidbit about the lake a hint? Cris certainly wasn't acting like himself. At all.

The last thing Nick wanted was to find himself at the end of a gun barrel.

Cris took a hand off the steering wheel again and reached across his chest and under his jacket. Exactly where a shoulder rig would be. *Bloody hell.* He'd better scarper, right quick.

The car slowed to take a curve, and Nick yanked on the door handle and threw himself out of the vehicle. He hit the ground hard and rolled on the gravel shoulder. The Ferrari skidded to a stop and Cris jumped out.

Nick scrambled to his feet. Fuck, his shoulder and hip hurt. He should've waited for a stop. Who did he think he was? Jason Bourne?

"What are you doing?" Cris yelled. "You could kill yourself that way!"

Nick turned and ran, searching for somewhere to go. But the road dropped off sharply on his right, and to his left was nothing but craggy rocks. Too exposed. Down the cliff it was. Except… Christ. He'd need climbing gear to get down there without breaking an ankle. Or his neck. He should have thought this through. Story of his life. When the fuck would he learn?

He was starting down the cliff anyway when Cris caught up to him and grabbed him by the collar of his coat. "What's got into you? You can't go down there! You'll get killed!"

Hmm... that was the second time Cris had said that. Why would he be worried about Nick's well-being if he wanted him dead? "You're *not* going to kill me?"

"*Idiota!*" Cris laughed. "Why would you think that?" He let go of Nick's collar and clapped him on the back.

"You seemed upset. Not yourself."

Inhaling deeply, Cris scratched his cheek. "I'm not. But I'm not planning to kill you either." He scrubbed a hand over his head. "Though there's a possibility that I could get you killed if you agree to what I'm about to ask."

"What's that?"

Cris shook his head. "Dust yourself off. Let's talk like gentlemen. Business is best conducted on a full stomach, yes?"

Unless the "business" involves my possible death. "I could use a drink too."

The tiny restaurant Cris took them to in Blevio had a fine bar, and Nick ordered their best whiskey. Just one. After Delfina's party, he'd sworn he wasn't going to touch the stuff ever again, but what the hell. If he were going to die soon, he might as well enjoy himself first.

Throughout their lunch, Cris remained cagey, insisting they eat and drink first, but when they'd finished eating and were both sipping at espressos, he finally got to the subject. "I found a way to get Delfi out of her engagement."

"And you need my help to do it?"

"It will be risky. But I have no one else to ask."

"Are you talking about killing Leandro or something?" Nick surprised himself by not being entirely opposed to the idea. What was happening to him?

"That would be the most direct solution, but it wouldn't be wise."

"Not to mention illegal." Odd. He still didn't really give a rat's arse, despite the words coming out of his mouth.

Cris held his eyes. "Are you ready to marry my sister?"

Nick's stomach contracted. *Fuck.* "I *like* her... a lot. But marry her? Where is this coming from?"

Leaning back in his chair, Cris crossed his arms. "A man honors his obligations."

"How am I obligated to her? I barely know her."

"Yet you slept with her."

Nick froze. Cris's voice had a hard edge to it, an edge he respected but didn't like. "I wish I could take that back. I don't even remember it. How's that for an utter cock-up?"

Cris said nothing, just continued to stare at him.

"Listen, mate, if you want to have a swing at me, go ahead. I won't defend myself. If it turns out I got her pregnant, I'll do the right thing and marry her. I'll take care of her."

Straightening up, Cris jabbed at the white linen tablecloth with a thick forefinger. "If you don't, you'll answer to me. *Capisci?*"

Nick nodded. He got it, loud and clear. "I'm sorry about this whole bloody mess."

"Well, here's your chance to set things right."

Cris explained the plan, while Nick's spaghetti carbonara curdled in his belly. The bloody Russians. He didn't like it. He didn't like it at all. But it did give him a chance to gather intel on the Vilanovich family. And help Delfina. It was the least he owed her.

"I'll do it. When do we go?"

"Tomorrow. Midnight."

So soon. Well, it wouldn't give him long to stew, would it? Nick excused himself to the loo. Just after he stepped inside, someone caught the closing door and followed him in, sending all his senses on high alert. He was turning to face the man when a large hand clapped over his mouth and nose, and a powerful body slammed him against the wall beside the door. What the bloody hell? It was the tough prick who worked for his father. Ruggero. The guard. Or worse, judging from the wicked scar that sliced across his left cheek.

Ruggero's black hair was slicked back, his face naked in its menace. Or was that how the bloke always looked? Yeah, he'd looked downright murderous at the party too. So maybe he wasn't going to kill him, just break a few bones, since he seemed to be into that kind of thing. The guard's voice was low and gruff, his English heavily accented. "You will not make a sound when I release you. Yes?" The hand clamped over Nick's face reeked of tobacco.

Nick nodded, his heart threatening to burst out of his chest, his lungs screaming. When Ruggero's hand left his mouth, he gulped in air. He was developing a real distaste for the hulking bastard. Nick made a show of straightening his clothes while he chose his words. "You don't have to paw me like this every time we meet. If you fancy me, why don't you just say so?"

That ought to have earned him a fist to the jaw, but luckily the man had a sense of humor. He let out an amused grunt. "You have your father's tongue."

Nick's teeth clenched together at the reminder. "Why are you here?"

"Your father sent me for you."

"No."

The guard raised an eyebrow. "You are happy as Andretti's prisoner?"

"No. But he's got my grandparents in his goddamn crosshairs."

"Don Lucchesi can protect them."

"I can't take that chance."

"My orders are to bring you home."

Something in Nick snapped at that word. He stepped up to Ruggero, shoving his face right up to his. "You tell my father to fuck off. I don't need his bloody help."

Ruggero's brows lowered and he moved an inch closer, his chest touching Nick's, as if he were going to embrace him and kiss him on the cheek. When he spoke, his breath, redolent of cigarettes and coffee, was warm on Nick's skin. "I suggest you rethink your options."

Nick blinked as the man stepped out of his personal space. *Rethink my options? What kind of Mafioso is this guy?* "I know what I'm doing."

Ruggero huffed with laughter. "So eager for the coffin?"

That didn't merit an answer. Nick turned his back on the bastard. When he glanced into the mirror above the sink, the room behind him was empty.

He braced his hands on the sink, letting his breath out in a whoosh. His right jacket pocket swung forward and clunked against the porcelain. What the hell? He put his hand in the pocket and closed his fingers over an object that fit easily in his palm and pulled it out. A mobile phone. *Halle-fucking-lujah.*

Flipping it open, he scanned the contact list. Only one listing: "ECL." His father. Making sure the phone was set on silent, he slipped it into an inside pocket. Not that he'd ever take his father's help, but he might need Fuente's or Delacourt's if he continued fucking up.

He splashed some water on his face, Ruggero's question haunting him. *So eager for the coffin?*

Maybe he did have a death wish. But he'd made a promise to Cris; he'd given his word. He couldn't abandon his principles.

Or Delfina.

CHAPTER 9

By the end of her first day working at the House of Morelli, Delfina had one thing to smile about. She had a new friend in Jacopo. And he'd gone over her sketches and approved of several, though he'd suggested a number of changes and had given her ideas for areas she needed to study in-depth. He'd told her to try again, and when she was ready, he'd get her time with Signor Morelli to show him what she could do.

She'd practically skipped out the door, Jacopo locking up behind her and offering to walk her to her car. The streets were dark, and a cold rain was falling. She was about to accept when a harsh voice came from behind her. "*I'll* walk my fiancée to her car." Leandro.

Her blood turned to ice as she whirled around to face him. "What are you doing here?"

He frowned. "Not exactly the reception I was expecting from my bride-to-be."

When Jacopo gave her a questioning look, her face burned. She hadn't mentioned Leandro at lunch. Instead she'd told him about Nick. "Delfi, is everything all right?" Jacopo asked.

Leandro stepped forward and took her arm. "Of course it is." He scanned Jacopo up and down, then turned to her. "We need to talk. Now."

Her heart thumped in her chest. She really didn't want to be alone with him, but she didn't want him to hurt Jacopo. "Yes, we do." She turned to Jacopo. "I'm fine. Thanks for everything."

"If you're sure," he said, raising an umbrella, his tone saying that he didn't think she was.

She forced a smile and nodded, then watched Jacopo walk away, her stomach sinking with his every step. Raindrops pelted her hair and ran down her face and the back of her neck, making her shiver and pull her jacket more tightly about her. When Leandro said her name, none too patiently, she turned to him. "How did you know I was here?" she asked.

"Giovanna isn't exactly quiet when you two are on the phone." He started off in the direction of her car. Judging by how wet his coat and hair were, he'd obviously been stewing out here for a while. Possibly he'd prowled the whole neighborhood, searching for a dealer.

Her mouth was so dry. She tried to inhale, but her lungs wouldn't expand. All she could feel was the bite of his fingers into the soft flesh of her upper arm. He was hurting her, again. And this time Nick wasn't there to stop him.

She glanced behind them, but the streets were empty. She'd stayed too late with Jacopo; they'd been the last ones to leave the shop.

"So who's the *finocchio*?" he asked. There were worse words he could have picked, she supposed.

"A friend. He's Signor Morelli's assistant."

His fingers tightened on her arm. "When were you planning to tell me about this job?"

"When it was your business to know."

"It *is* my business." He let out a little sound of irritation and muttered a curse.

They took a left at the corner, and she spotted her silver Alfa Romeo parked at the end of the next block. The sight made her breathe a little easier. "You don't own me, Leandro. I've already told you that."

He yanked her to a halt. "Delfina, I'm not a boy any longer. You can't boss me around like you used to. I'm a man, and I'm going to be your husband soon. You had better realize that right now. I deserve your respect."

"Respect is earned. You can't demand it."

His eyes narrowed and his lips tightened into a thin line. "And you can't run around like my opinion doesn't matter. You should have asked my permission before you got a job."

A bitter taste filled her mouth and she stamped a foot, her shoe splashing in the river of water running down the sidewalk. "We live in the twenty-first century. Or hadn't you noticed?"

"You know the rules."

"The rules, the rules, the rules! Don't you *ever* get tired of them?"

"Of course." He sighed. "Listen, all I want is some acknowledgment that I matter to you."

"Would you have let me take the job?"

"Maybe." He stroked the black mustache and goatee that had grown in since the party.

One more day, and then this is over. "You're lying."

He squeezed her arm until she winced, then he abruptly let go, as if he'd touched a hot kettle. He inhaled deeply, then blew out while she rubbed her arm. "I'm sorry," he said, his voice cracking, then he raked both hands through his wet hair and paced a few steps away before wheeling back toward her. "I love you, you know that. You drive me mad, Delfi, you always have."

"A strong man doesn't hurt his woman." Why couldn't she stop goading him?

Leandro let out a groan and stepped close, looming over her. "I wouldn't have to, if you'd let *me* be the man in this relationship!" His voice was low and edged by something sharp. "I'm warning you, Delfi. Do not push me too far."

She fought to keep her voice from quavering. "I'm keeping my job."

"We'll see." He went to take her arm again, and she shrugged him off.

"I can walk the rest of the way myself." She turned away from him and started toward the car, her back and shoulders tensed for a blow.

After she'd walked halfway up the block, he called out. "Wait." She stopped, but didn't turn. When he caught up to her, he said, "This job means that much to you?"

"It's everything I've dreamed of." She looked up at him, blinking water out of her eyes.

Leandro cupped her face in both hands. "All right, then. But I want you home every day for supper. No late nights, no weekends."

"I'll try." She offered him a tiny smile, hoping to placate him so he wouldn't see the lie on her face.

He rubbed her cheekbones with his thumbs. "See? I *can* be reasonable, when you don't fight me." He grinned at her, but she wasn't reassured. Not in the slightest. "I want to announce our engagement."

"Can we wait three weeks?" Better to spare him the humiliation of inviting people to a party that was never going to happen.

"What does it matter?"

Delfina brightened her voice and forced another smile. "It'll take me a while to find the right dress for such a special day. You want me to look radiant, yes?"

He returned the smile, then leaned toward her. She started to turn her head to avoid his lips, then thought better of it. Best to humor him a bit more. She accepted his kiss stiffly, and he stepped back with a frown. "What's wrong?"

What *wasn't* wrong? "We shouldn't get carried away."

He nodded and gave her a grin. "You have more sense than my sister." He held out his arm to her and she took it, praying he wouldn't try again. To his credit, when they reached the car, he just kissed her on the cheek, then waited while she opened the door, her hands trembling so violently that she fumbled with the handle.

She got inside and locked the doors, starting the car and waving at him until he turned to leave. He headed up the street away from her, his tall figure receding into the darkness. She tried to slow her breathing, but her mind was racing. What was she going to do? He hadn't seemed high, and yet his self-control had been razor thin. If they ended up married, she'd have to turn into a meek little mouse to survive with him.

Marrying Leandro would be worse than anything else her father had ever done to her. Her plan *had* to work. If it didn't… she'd lose everything she was.

By the time she returned home, Delfina thought she'd sufficiently calmed down. But when her mother greeted her at the front door, something must have shown on her face. "What's wrong, Delfi?"

Delfina waved a hand in the air. "Nothing. I'm fine." But her strained voice betrayed her, and her mother clucked her tongue, as if to say "Don't try to fool me."

"What happened?"

"Leandro was waiting for me. And he wasn't happy."

Her mother patted her cheek. "You should have told him."

"It's *my* decision. It's *my* life."

Her mother sighed. "You knew this day was coming. You need to handle all of this with more grace, more regard for his feelings. I know he's... excitable, but I believe he has a good heart."

"And what about *my* feelings?"

"I know it's not fair, *cara*. But it's how things are. The sooner you accept that—"

"I will *never* accept it."

"Never accept what?" Cris asked as he came in the door.

She turned at the sound and saw Nick beside him. Nick took one glance at her face and stepped toward her. "What happened?"

"Nothing." She gave her mother a meaningful look, swearing her to silence without saying a word. "I'm going for a walk. I need to think."

"I'll go with you," Nick offered.

"I'd rather be alone," she said, heading down the hall to the sitting room, Nick following her anyway. She crossed to the double doors that led to the rear terrace, and he opened them for her. She stopped him with a hand on his chest. "Please let me be."

"You seem like you could use a friend right now."

"Is that what you are?"

"Of course." He reached up and wrapped his fingers around the hand she'd placed on his chest.

A lump formed in her throat. Nick was the kind of man Leandro would never be. She pushed past him, hurrying toward the hedge maze. It hadn't rained in Blevio, but a light wind blew through her damp hair. She was being foolish. What was she going to do? Sit outside and cry all night?

At first she thought he hadn't followed her, but she soon heard footsteps behind her, and he called her name. She kept moving, hoping he couldn't see her that well in the darkness. But the moon provided a lot more light than she wished, and he caught up to her. "There you are," he said as he came up beside her.

"Have you gone deaf? I want to be alone."

"Something's happened. Did something go wrong at work?"

She shook her head. "Work was fine. Parts of it."

"And parts of it weren't." When she didn't say anything, he continued. "But that's not why you're upset."

She ducked around the cypresses that bordered the maze. Why wouldn't he just leave her alone?

He was silent for a while, following her into the maze, then he said, "As far as I know, there are two things you desperately care about: getting that job, and not marrying Leandro. So if it's not the job, I'm guessing something happened with him."

She whirled around to face him and threw her hands in the air. "Yes! Are you happy now?"

"No, I'm not. Not when you're upset like this."

Nick's voice was gentle, his hands in his pockets, his entire stance nonthreatening. Everything that Leandro was not. The lump in her throat came back, and hot tears pricked at her eyes, then they spilled onto her cheeks. She wiped at them and tried to take a deep breath, but she couldn't. All she could do was stand there and try not to sob out loud.

He stepped forward, cupping her cheek and stroking it with his thumb. His hand felt so warm on her chilled skin. The tears came harder, and he pulled her into an embrace, murmuring soft words of comfort. After a while, he said, "Why don't you tell me about it."

She did, and all the while he stroked her hair, his heat soaking into her, his touch soothing her. When she finished, he kissed her temple. "You won't have to marry that bastard."

"You say that like it's a fact."

"It is."

She laughed. "I wish I shared your certainty." What if her plan didn't work? What then?

"Trust me. It won't happen."

Something in her gut tingled. "How do you know?"

He shrugged. "I just do."

She stared at him. He seemed so confident, so sure of himself. Perhaps too sure of himself. Too bad she couldn't believe him. Too bad she couldn't trust him to know the future.

Too bad he wasn't the man she was supposed to marry.

———— ◆ ————

Leandro's visit yesterday plagued Delfina to the point where she couldn't concentrate on any of the tasks Jacopo had assigned her. Any minute now, Gio was supposed to tell Leandro what had happened in the shed. What if Gio told him today, and he confronted Delfina alone after work again? What if he didn't believe the story? What if he wanted proof? Nick didn't remember a thing, and if a doctor examined her, it'd be obvious she was lying.

And then she'd be trapped.

She had to seduce Nick in truth. She had to. It was the only way to ensure her plan would work. But when would she have the opportunity? Since the guest cottage was bugged, getting Nick alone somewhere outdoors was the only option, and though it was sunny today and warm, it would be dark and chilly by the time she got off work.

Ironic. The job she'd wanted so badly was now standing in her way. She couldn't possibly go home sick so early in her employment. Delfina sighed and let her shoulders slump. She'd just have to put off any hope of seducing Nick until the weekend. She'd call Gio, tell her to wait until Sunday. Though that was cutting it awfully close; Leandro would certainly send out the engagement party invitations by Monday at the latest.

Dio mio! She'd forgotten all about her parents. If Leandro sent the invitations and then broke the engagement because of her infidelity, he'd be sure to tell everyone why. She knew him; he was that sort. Mamma and Papà would be humiliated.

She couldn't call Gio; she couldn't put it off any longer. She had to seduce Nick today, and she didn't have a moment to lose. But how was she going to get off work without getting fired?

"What's wrong, *cara?*" Jacopo asked.

She straightened up with a guilty start. She hadn't sorted the dresses in the storeroom, hadn't prepared the fall catalog mailing, hadn't sewn up the half-finished pantsuit prototype yet. "Everything's fine."

His hazel eyes fixed on hers. "Does this have something to do with that handsome but scary fiancé you told me nothing about?"

Heat crawled up her neck and into her cheeks. "I'm sorry I put you in a spot last night."

"Lucky for you, I pay attention. You stiffened like a scared cat when he showed up." He leaned his elbows on her desk. "How about you tell me the gory details while we tackle the storeroom?"

She shook her head. "That's my job. I can't waste your time on that."

He smiled. "*Cara*, a juicy story is never a waste of time." He stepped back and held out his hand. "Come."

She followed him to the storeroom, where they started organizing the mass of dresses they'd received from the vendors who had replicated the designs. Jacopo handed her a dress to place on her rack. "Spill."

"It's way too personal."

He pretended to frown at her, and when that didn't work, he put a hand on her shoulder. "Think of me as a priest. Not a word of this will ever pass my lips." When she dropped her eyes to the floor, he added, "Confession *is* good for the soul, you know."

She chuckled. "And when was the last time you confessed?"

He squeezed her shoulder. "*Cara,* I am a responsible person, and therefore morally obligated to stay away from church. My sins would set the confessional on fire."

Delfina laughed. Jacopo was a man of the world; perhaps he could help her with her dilemma. "All right, I'll tell you." As they sorted the dresses by design and color, she told him everything that had happened at the party, including her pathetic attempt to seduce Nick, the plan she'd hastily hatched with Gio, and her worries about the plan's possible failure. Jacopo took it all in silently, though he did raise a brow a few times and gave her an open jaw when she told him what had happened in the garden shed.

When she finished, he took a gorgeous cream dress with silver accents and held it up to her, as if fitting her for it. "What are you doing?" she asked.

"Picking out your wedding dress. You don't strike me as a conventional bride, so you shouldn't have a conventional dress."

She gave him a withering stare. "Jacopo, this isn't helping."

He hung the dress up behind her and put his hands on her shoulders. "You've dug yourself a huge hole, *cara*. There's only one way out of it that I see."

"Which is?" Maybe he had a better idea than hers.

"You've got to seduce your Nick. For real this time."

She let her shoulders slump. "I know. But when? Gio's going to tell Leandro any minute now, and I won't have a chance until the weekend, which is four days away."

"Call her and tell her to wait."

"I can't." She pointed out the timing problem, which he grasped immediately. "So now what do I do?"

He pressed a hand against her forehead. "You seem feverish."

She smiled. "I can't get away with that." She paused, giving him a hopeful look. "Can I?"

"Signor Morelli is terrified of the flu. He had it last year, and he was sick for weeks. But he also has a terrible fear of needles—ironic, no?—so he won't get vaccinated. I think if I tell him you're not feeling well, there will be no problem." He tapped the end of her nose with a finger. "Wait here, look sick, and I'll be right back."

She finished the sorting, her stomach in knots. If Jacopo couldn't convince Signor Morelli to let her go early today, she'd just have to call Gio and take her chances, but the idea of giving Leandro that much power to rub her family's name in the mud sent acid bubbling up her throat. She wanted to vomit. Papà would never forgive her. Maybe Mamma too.

What was taking Jacopo so long?

She heard a rustle behind her and was relieved to see him. "What'd he say?"

"Go home. He doesn't want you back until you're well." He studied her face. "You really are pale, you know."

She rubbed her stomach. "I can take the mailing home with me and do it from there."

Jacopo smiled. "Enzo will appreciate your dedication." He helped her carry the things she'd need out to her car, then sent her off.

Delfina made the drive in record time. It was around one in the afternoon, the sun high overhead, the sky clear and blue, not a trace of yesterday's clouds.

Parking her car in the large garage behind the house, she headed toward the rear terrace, where Nick was reading the newspaper, his face screwed up in concentration as he poured over the Italian words, occasionally consulting the dictionary beside him.

He looked up as she approached and gave her a smile that warmed her heart and made her stomach flutter. "You're home early. Everything all right?" he asked, setting the paper aside.

"I thought I was getting sick, but I'm feeling better now. In fact, I'm quite hungry. Have you eaten?"

He studied her for a moment, then shook his head. "It's gorgeous today, maybe the last good day we'll get this year. Want to make it a picnic?"

She smiled. He was reading her thoughts, making this easy, so far. "I've got just the spot."

They put together a basket of food and wine and headed up the hill to her favorite place, the olive grove, its neat rows of silver green beckoning to her, as always.

She ducked under branches still laden with fruit, Nick following behind with the basket. Crouched over, she headed down the row nearest to the hedge that outlined the grove, then plopped herself onto the thick grass. She'd chosen the darkest corner of the grove, the one concealed on two sides by thick hedges. It was the place she sought whenever she wanted to be alone, and the place guaranteed to give them the most possible privacy.

Nick spread out the tablecloth they'd brought, then set down the basket and started laying out the food, while her stomach clenched up again. Was she really going to be able to do this? She had to. He opened the bottle of wine and filled their glasses, and she took hers, gulping half of it down while he eyed her oddly. "Why are you staring at me like that?" she asked.

"Something's wrong with you. Did Leandro show up again?"

"No." She looked away, her heart beating fast. "Can't we just forget about him for a bit?"

"I'd like to. But can you?"

His gentle voice undid her. She couldn't use him this way, could she? He didn't deserve it. She started to rise, but he snagged her wrist in an iron grip.

"Don't go, Delfi. Talk to me."

She opened her mouth to say something, but no words would come. Instead a sob came out, and then she was crying. Again. *Cristo,* she was acting like a child.

He stroked her shoulder. "Don't worry about Leandro. We'll figure something out."

She let herself collapse flat on her back. She wanted to confess, to tell Nick everything. To tell him the truth. But she couldn't force the words out. Instead, she let him think the best of her. "Maybe." She wiped her tears away and breathed in deeply to calm herself.

"We will." He eased himself down next to her, propping himself up on one elbow, then placed a hand on her belly and splayed his fingers wide. She was overly aware of that hand, how warm he was, how large, next to her. The silence between them lengthened, eased, and aside from their breathing, all she heard was the trilling of birds and the clicking and whirring and buzzing of insects in the olive grove.

After a while, his fingers moved, making circles and patterns on her belly. Her mind traveled back to the night in the garden shed, how he'd touched her then, and she felt herself loosening up, going wet between the legs.

Rolling forward, he angled his body over hers, his mouth hovering centimeters above her own. His eyes, in this light the color of aged copper, a deep smoky green, searched hers, a question in them. Unable to stop herself, she brushed the dark brown hair off his forehead. He smiled, a grin both sweet and devilish, and she found herself returning it. That damn Lucchesi charm. Nick had it in spades, just like his father. His index finger traced her lips, making them tingle, making her want his kiss. Making her want everything he could do to her.

Without warning, he slid a hand under the base of her skull, drawing her up to him, their lips finally meeting in a kiss so tender, so sweet, Delfina could feel the tears about to start again. They couldn't do this. She shouldn't let it happen, not under false pretenses. She should tell him.

But she didn't want to stop. Not ever.

If she just let it happen, would it really be her fault? He wanted this too, he was the one kissing her. If he started it, it didn't count. Right?

His tongue darted out, flicking along her lips, making her want to open to him.

Soon they were locked in a kiss she could drown in. A thrill shot through her, arrowing straight to her sex.

With a soft moan, she slid her arms around his shoulders, feeling the hard muscles under the fabric of his shirt, her fingers finding the short hairs at the nape of his neck. She pulled him to her, greedy for his kiss, his touch. When his mouth traveled to her neck, she let out a sigh, the sensation of his tongue, his lips against her sensitive skin making her think the most naughty thoughts. She wanted his mouth on her breasts, between her legs. She wanted—

No! She pushed against his chest. "We shouldn't."

"The damage has already been done, yeah?"

Delfina bit the inside of her cheek. *Tell him. Tell him now.* She shrugged. "I suppose."

"Well then." His hand slid under her blouse, his fingers gliding over her breasts, finding and rubbing against her aching nipples. *Dio.* What was she doing? She should stop this, she should tell him the truth, but he wanted this too. What did the truth matter?

"Let's get you out of this," he said, tugging on her blouse. She raised her arms and let him pull it over her head. His eyes widened as he ran his fingers over her bra. "Red lace, my favorite. Do the knickers match?"

She blushed. They did. He unclasped the bra, revealing her breasts. He took the left one in his hand and held it in place for his mouth. When he swirled his tongue over the nipple, she arched up and gasped. So good. So delicious. So wicked.

Delfina didn't protest when his hand left her breast and traveled down to her right inner thigh, moving back and forth, but not up to her sex. *Per favore, Nico.* She parted her legs a little, not wanting to voice her frustration, not wanting to admit it. Not wanting to beg. He chuckled when she shifted beneath him. "Greedy little cat," he whispered.

"As if *you* don't want this," she said, rubbing her leg against the bulge at the crotch of his trousers, a bulge that had grown steadily larger and more insistent.

"Oh I do. But I'm not afraid to show it."

Her cheeks and throat flushed, the heat betraying her. Just then, his fingers hit their mark, tickling over the scrap of nylon between her legs. He slid a finger beneath the damp fabric, tracing her cleft. "You're so wet," he whispered as he rubbed over the entire area, his hand massaging her, the indirect contact with her clit making her squirm. Then he slipped a finger down, between her swollen lips, down into her well of moisture and then back up to circle her clit, not quite touching it, instead teasing her, taunting her, as he watched her face.

She closed her eyes, not able to meet his. "Look at me, Delfi," he said. "Look at me."

His fingers stopped moving until she complied. Then he grazed a finger over her clit, making her shiver and moan. He smiled, holding her gaze. "I'm sorry about our first time. I'm going to make it up to you."

Pushing her skirt up over her hips, he bent his head. He pulled the thong to the side, his mouth finding her sex, his tongue replacing his fingers, and she thought she was going to die from the shame of it, from the sheer wanton pleasure that made her arch up to him and clutch at his hair, holding him to her as he licked and sucked until she cried out and came in a thrilling rush.

He planted a kiss low on her belly, then sat up, peeling off his shirt and revealing a hard, muscled chest that made her mouth go dry. *Dio,* he was beautiful. Sexy. Everything she'd ever wanted. Everything she could never keep.

Her throat tightened. He wasn't hers. Even if her plan worked, he'd never be hers. Because it was a lie. Because he'd be forced to be with her. Sure, he enjoyed her body, he liked her, but he didn't love her. And when he found out what she'd done, he never would.

But this wasn't about love. For either of them. This was about lust, and she'd best not forget. She'd best remember. Between her and Nick, it was lust only; lust, and the fulfillment of her plan to escape Leandro. That's what she had to remember. That's what she had to concentrate on. Anything else between them was a dream she could never have. She swallowed hard and pasted a smile on her face. If all they ever had was this one perfect moment, she'd remember it always. She repeated that to herself, making a silent vow. *Remember this moment. Remember him.*

When he shucked his trousers, she learned that he wore black boxer shorts. *Her* favorite. Her smile widened, became something real. He was hers for now, and she couldn't help her curiosity. Though she'd touched him in the shed, she hadn't seen what she'd held. He shoved the trunks down, and his erection sprang free.

Madonna. Not that she had anything to compare it to, but it seemed too large to fit. Much too large. Her heart skittered in her chest. What was she going to do? She didn't want to tell him, didn't want to see his disappointment, his anger. But maybe—maybe she wouldn't bleed? Maybe he wouldn't notice?

Nick produced a condom from a pocket and held it up with a grin. "In case it's not already too late," he said. She nodded and attempted to swallow, as if this were no big deal, as if she did this every day, at least as if she'd done this once before.

He settled down beside her, his cock pressing against her thigh while she tried to relax beside him. "You *can* touch it, if you want," he whispered.

"Would you like me to?"

He chuckled. "What do you think, *bellissima?*"

She came up on her side and reached for his cock, her trembling fingers passing over the velvety skin, gliding around the head, making him moan low in his throat. The sound made her shiver and flush with heat. She clasped her hand around him loosely, and stroked up and down, enjoying the sounds she elicited from him. "Tighter," he groaned.

Closing her fingers a bit more, she concentrated on rolling her palm over the head. He'd liked that last time. "Lick your fingers," he said. "Get them really wet." She did, tasting a faint hint of him on her skin. The saliva made it easier for her hand to slide up and down, and he moaned again, propping himself up on his elbows to watch what she was doing.

A powerful thrill traveled through her; all his focus was on her hand, on the pleasure she was giving him. She wanted nothing more than to give him the same delicious release that she'd experienced earlier. Did he feel the same way when he was touching her?

When a clear drop wept from the head of his cock, she used the extra lubrication to speed up her strokes. His hips bucked upward, and his right hand snaked out, grabbing her wrist to stop her. "Enough," he said. "Don't want to disappoint you." He picked up the condom packet, ripped it open with his teeth, started rolling it on. *Dio mio.* What now?

She must have tensed up because he stopped. "What's wrong?" he asked. She didn't trust herself to speak. "Ah Christ, I *did* hurt you last time."

She started to shake her head, then froze. "I'm scared."

"Listen, love, it won't hurt this time, I swear. I'll go slow."

He rolled over her, and she put a hand on his abdomen, the hard muscles shifting under her fingers. She kept her legs clamped together, every muscle rigid. He gazed into her eyes. "Trust me."

She tore hers away from him, tears starting. She had to tell him. He took hold of her jaw and forced her to look at him. "Delfi, what's wrong?"

Dio, she couldn't tell him. "We never—" she started to say then faltered.

"We never what?"

Her voice cracking, she whispered, "We never got this far." His face darkened, and he rolled off her in one swift movement.

"Fuck!" He ran a hand through his hair, ruffling it up. "*Fuck,* Delfina. You *lied* to me? I *never* had sex with you?" She shook her head, unable to say it aloud. "Right. That's just fucking lovely." He whipped off the condom and started to dress. "Why did you do it?"

She sat up and grabbed her blouse, using it to cover her body. "I can't marry him. I can't." She let go of the blouse and thrust forward both arms, showing him the bruises from the party, the ones from last night. "Look what he did to me."

He focused on the marks, his face softening as he buttoned his shirt. "You could have told me."

"You had to believe we'd slept together. That was the only way my plan would work."

"*Your* plan?" His eyes snapped to hers.

"Yes."

"What *plan?*"

"Gio's going to tell Leandro what happened. He'll want to break the engagement if he thinks I've been with someone else. Especially if I might be pregnant."

"Did you stop to think about what would happen to me? What would happen to my grandparents?"

"Of course. But I told you, my father—"

"Fuck what you told me. What if you're wrong?"

"I'm sorry, Nick. I shouldn't have done it."

"You're right. You bloody shouldn't have. And now you're going to *un*do it."

Sniffing miserably, Delfina nodded as she unzipped her handbag and pulled out her phone. Just as she pressed the power button to turn on the display, the phone buzzed in her hand, and she yelped. When the caller's name appeared, all the blood drained from her head. "It's Gio."

He motioned for her to hurry up. She didn't even get out a greeting before Gio's words rushed over hers. "I told Leandro, Delfi. He's furious. He and Papà are headed your way."

No! "*Now*? Right now?"

"Yes. I hope you know what you're doing," Gio said.

Nick glowered down at her. She didn't have a clue. Not a one. "I'll figure it out." Delfina ended the call and shoved the phone back in her bag. "It's too late. Leandro knows. He and his father are headed here now."

"Bloody *fucking* hell." He pressed a palm to his forehead and closed his eyes. Without opening them he said, "Will you tell the truth?"

"Of course." She dressed slowly, mechanically. *Porca miseria,* she was in the shit. She'd ruined everything. Nick hated her.

And if she thought Leandro was already mad at her, wait until he found out about the lie.

There was no escaping the truth. There never was. She'd been a fool to think otherwise.

———— ◆ ————

Nick followed Delfina toward the house, then stopped her just outside the olive grove to get the leaves out of her hair and the dust off her clothing and his. "I don't want to give them any reason to believe your lies."

She crossed her arms, hugging herself. "I'm sorry, Nick. I really am. I didn't know what else to do."

"Cris and I—" He shut his mouth. Cris had sworn him to secrecy.

"What?"

"Nothing. We'll figure something out."

"You and I will? Or you and Cris?"

Worst undercover agent ever. That's what they'd put in his file after this. *If* he lived. *If* he were still in Interpol. "We'd better get moving." He put a hand at the small of her back, then jerked it away. He mustn't touch her like that, even though every instinct screamed at him to protect her. Despite her lies, she hadn't meant any harm.

But she'd put his grandparents at risk. Him too. He hoped to God she could fix this.

They entered her father's study to find Dario and Gianluca seated on either side of the massive desk. Cris was sitting on the sofa, and Leandro was standing by the window, arms crossed, the muscles in his jaw jumping, his lids twitching. High again.

When he saw Delfina, Leandro turned dark red and started toward her, covering the distance in a few long steps. "*Puttana!*" he roared, and before Nick could react, he backhanded Delfina in the face.

Nick leapt at him, taking Leandro to the floor. Without thinking, he punched him, an uppercut to the jaw that snapped Leandro's head back so hard it bounced. Cris was on Nick before he could strike again. "You *must* stop this," Cris whispered in his ear as he pulled Nick off Leandro. "*Per favore.*"

Delfina was pressing a hand to her cheek, her mouth open in shock, her eyes moist. "Are you hurt?" Nick asked.

Her expression blank, she turned to face her father and Gianluca as Leandro scrambled off the floor. When Leandro stepped toward her again, Dario jumped

98

out of his seat. "*Basta!*" he shouted. "Stay away from her, or I'll beat you myself."
Leandro's father let out a sigh. "Do you disagree with me, Gianluca?" Dario
asked, his voice filled with challenge.

"No. But remember why we're here."

Dario turned to Delfina. "You have shamed this family."

"I didn't Papà, I swear it. This has all been a mistake."

"A mistake? Why would Giovanna, your closest friend, tell this... story about
you?"

"I asked her to."

"Why?" Gianluca asked.

She pointed to her cheek and showed him the bruises on her arms. "He has no
self-control."

Leandro let out a choked sound. "If you loved me—if you at least respected
me—I would not do such things."

"How can I?" she spat, her voice thick with emotion. It sounded like her own
self-control was about to snap. Shame rolled through Nick at what he was forcing
her to do. He had to stop this. And he had to trust her. He stepped forward.

"Delfina, tell them the truth." Her brows popped up, and she shook her head.
"Tell them about us."

"I *am* telling the truth."

He put an arm around her. "We've been together twice," he said to the room.

"I'm still a virgin," Delfina insisted.

Dario raised a hand for silence. "What is going on here?"

"She's trying to protect me," Nick said.

"No," she said, clutching at his shirt front. "Stop this, Nick. Stop it."

He closed his hand around hers and gave it a light squeeze. "Trust me."

Dario's eyes darted between the two of them, then they settled on Gianluca,
who leaned forward and said, "A doctor can settle this." He focused on his son. "I
suggest you be forgiving."

Leandro slapped his right palm over his left bicep and shoved his middle finger
high in the air. "Forgiving? She's given me the horns!"

The horns? Nick gave Delfina a questioning look. "He means you've made him
a cuckold," she whispered.

"As long as she's not pregnant, there's no real harm done," Gianluca said to
Leandro. "Besides, it's not like the other families are knocking down our door,
eager to give their daughters to you."

"Fine." Leandro glared at Delfina. "You may sleep in my bed and bear my
children, but I will never call you *wife*." He stalked out of the room, and seconds
later the front door slammed.

Dario stepped around the desk. "I expected no less from you, Lucchesi," he
said. "But you, Delfina, *you* disappoint me." He watched her for several seconds,
then his face tightened and his upper body tensed, his hands balling into fists. Was
he going to hit her? Nick lunged forward to shield her, and Dario's face changed.
"You thought I would strike her?" he asked.

When Nick nodded, Dario's right hand shot out, his fist connecting squarely
with Nick's left eye. Pain shot through his face, and it took all he had not to return

the punch. "Do not interfere," Dario spat.

He couldn't hit the man back, but he could say his piece. "If I ever hear that you've hit her, I *will* take you down."

Dario's stare frosted over. "You are alive now only through my grace. Unless you want that to change."

Stepping between them, Delfina put both hands on her father's chest. "Please stop, Papà. I beg your forgiveness. I didn't know how else to break the engagement." Her voice broke, and Nick wanted to pull her close and comfort her.

"I thought Teo was lesson enough," Dario said.

Delfina stiffened and stepped back, her voice turning to steel. "I'm a slow learner when it comes to my captivity."

"Who's Teo?" Nick asked.

"A boy who dared touch me when I was sixteen. He was branded a thief. Literally."

Jesus. Would like to have known that *earlier.* Nick looked at Dario. Time to lighten things up. "Well then, I got off easily. You may knock me about whenever you get the urge."

Dario's face darkened. "If she is not telling the truth, bruises will be the least of your concerns." His gaze dropped to the vicinity of Nick's crotch.

Fuck. The Andrettis took "an eye for an eye" a little too seriously. "So does this mean the engagement is still on?" Nick asked, rubbing his eye socket.

Gianluca answered. "Unless the doctor proves her a liar, then yes."

Cris stepped forward. "If there's a... problem, I could marry Giovanna."

With a weary shake of his head, Gianluca said, "You know the old saying, 'Don't add insult to injury'?"

Cris apologized. If Gianluca's comment infuriated him, it didn't show. Cris glanced at Nick and gave an almost imperceptible nod. The plan was still on. Nick hoped to God that it worked. Something had to.

She may have left some bloody important things out, but he still couldn't bear Delfina's suffering. Even if alleviating it put him and all he held dear in jeopardy.

*

CHAPTER 10

Cris eased the silver BMW between the rows of cars parked outside the marina in the heart of Bellagio. Nick popped his knuckles, his heart revving up, his senses heightening with the first tingles of adrenaline. What the hell was he doing? The Russian *Mafiya* made the Italians look like gentlemen farmers. Tangling with them, especially with the Vilanovich family, was beyond stupid. It was suicidal.

The Vilanoviches were well-known for their ruthlessness, which was legendary, even among the Russian *Mafiya*. One of Nick's first assignments had been updating the dossier on the family. He hoped never to meet their patriarch, Ilya Vilanovich. The man had committed atrocities that made war crimes look like jokes. Hopefully Nick would have some useful intel after this evening. Provided he survived, he might even earn the opportunity to do legitimate field work.

"Everything set?" he asked Cris again.

Cris flashed him a grin as he backed the car up to the dock. "You asked me before. The answer hasn't changed."

Once he had the BMW where he wanted it, Cris shut off the car, pulled a gun out of his jacket pocket, and handed it and a spare magazine over to Nick. "In case. You are familiar with the Beretta Storm?" Nick took it and shook his head. "No? Well, it's easy. Seventeen rounds. No safeties. Just point and shoot."

"Double-action only?" Nick asked.

Cris nodded. "I should have given you a shoulder holster earlier. Too late now."

Nick's heart sped up again. What else had Cris forgotten? "Don't worry," Cris said and clapped him on the arm. "This isn't my first time."

"You've dealt with the Russians before?"

"*Nyet,*" Cris said in a convincing Russian accent. "But how hard can it be? It's an exchange, that's all."

Nick thought about the twenty kilos of uncut cocaine stacked neatly in the boot. This wasn't a trivial deal—that much unadulterated cocaine was worth nine hundred thousand euros, easy. His underarms and back went damp. Christ. "So now what?"

Cris checked his watch and adjusted the mirror on his side of the vehicle. "We wait. They should be here any minute."

As if he'd summoned them up, four men in black leather strode up to the BMW from behind, two of them tall muscular blonds, the other two dark-haired, one stocky, the other small and wiry. All four wore sunglasses, though one of the blonds removed his as they approached the car.

"This is it," Cris murmured and got out of the car. Nick followed suit, but was careful to keep the car between him and the approaching men. Cris, fearless, walked forward, his hand outstretched. The blond without the glasses took the offered hand. "Yuri?" Cris asked.

"*Da*. Cris?" When Cris confirmed, Yuri rubbed his hands together, as if they were cold. Even though he wore leather gloves.

A look passed between Yuri and the other men. Something wasn't right, and it wasn't just that look. But what was it? Nick slid the Beretta from his pocket and palmed it, keeping the gun hidden behind the car. He wished Cris would look at him so he could convey his concern, but Cris kept his eyes on Yuri instead. "We have the product," Cris said. "You have the payment?"

Yuri giggled like a schoolgirl and covered his mouth with a large hand. Odd. What did the man find so funny?

"*Da,*" Yuri finally said, motioning the stocky man forward. The man carried a silver metallic case.

Cris hit a button on his key fob and the BMW's boot unlatched with a pop. Nick was supposed to come forward and open the boot. But he didn't want to turn his back to these men.

When Cris cast him a sharp glance, Nick shook his head the barest bit. Cris probably thought him an utter wanker, but it was safest if only one of them were vulnerable.

Yuri stepped forward, gesturing toward the boot. "We sample first, *da*?"

With a nod, Cris turned away from Yuri to open the boot. Nick tensed, not liking how close all the men were, but Cris seemed cool, in his element. The perfect Mafioso. No fear, no hesitation. As if he did this kind of thing every day. Maybe Nick's father had done him a favor by staying away from him and trying to keep him out of this life. Suddenly Nick's nice quiet desk job, analyzing data amassed by the people on the front lines, seemed a lot more appealing.

When Cris opened the boot, Nick had to step away from the side of the car to keep the other men in sight. He kept the gun flat against his thigh, concealed from their view.

Yuri flicked open a switchblade and stabbed one of the kilos. From his pocket, he produced a glass ampoule that contained a liquid. Yuri snapped the top off the ampoule, used the blade to tip some powder into it, then shook the mixture.

Within seconds, the liquid turned bright blue, and Yuri smiled in approval. He pulled off a glove, dipped a pinky in the powder, and dabbed it on his tongue, running the finger along his teeth and gums. Then he rubbed some powder between his fingers, testing for the silky, soapy, texture of high-grade cocaine. He smiled. "Good quality. Pure."

Yuri put the glove back on and motioned the man with the briefcase forward. The man popped the case open, and Cris riffled one of the thick stacks of euros. He looked at Yuri. "Where's the rest?"

Yuri's gaze narrowed to a squint. "This is all. As agreed."

Cris shook his head. "You think I'm a fool? That can't be more than three hundred thousand euros."

Yuri slammed the case shut, muttering in Russian. In English he said, "Fucking Italians."

"*What* did you say?" Cris asked.

Nick raised his gun simultaneously with the three Russians behind Yuri. "You try to change deal," Yuri said.

"You're trying to cheat us."

Yuri's pale skin reddened. "Cheat? Vilanovich family no cheat no one."

"That is not enough money," Cris said, enunciating carefully.

"Is agreement."

"Cris, why don't you call your uncle to verify?" Nick suggested.

"*Verify?*" Yuri snapped.

"It will only take a minute," Nick said, keeping his tone soothing, placating, while inside, his gut churned.

Cris hissed in frustration and reached for the phone in his inside pocket. Yuri coughed loudly, and that's when Nick saw it. The grin half hidden behind his glove. One of the Russians fired, the sharp report making Nick flinch. For a moment, no one moved, then Cris crumpled to the ground, and Nick's stomach plummeted to the pavement along with his friend.

Without thinking, Nick squeezed off two shots at the tall blond behind Yuri, and then dropped into a crouch beside the BMW, his heart hammering, his lungs gulping down oxygen. He scrambled to the rear bumper, where he could duck down and still see the men.

The blond had fallen. Nick went for the stocky man next. He hit the man square in the chest, scarlet streaming down his white shirt.

Yuri pulled a gun of his own and returned fire, squatting near the bumper on the driver's side. A shot whizzed by Nick's knees and struck a metal rubbish bin behind him with a sharp ping. Fuck. Yuri was too close. The vehicle wasn't effective cover.

He had to get to Cris, who lay far too still on the ground, blood spreading in a pool under his head. *Please God, please God. Don't let him be dead.* Nick thrust a hand under the bumper and blind-fired several times at Yuri, who let out a grunt and dropped to the ground.

Just the wiry little one left. The man shot at Nick, hitting the lid of the open boot, then sprinted away from the car, heading for the dock. Nick rose, blood roaring in his ears, and fired, four quick pulls, but missed. He wanted to chase the little man down, but first he needed to check on Cris. He hurried forward and bent over Cris, who was lying on his side, his eyes closed. Blood ran from a wound above his left temple. Nick patted his cheek. "You all right?"

When Cris didn't respond, Nick shook him a little and shouted his name. What if he was in a coma? Had the bullet punctured his brain? "Cris!" No response.

A powerboat started up and zipped onto the lake. *Bloody fantastic.* There was one alive to finger him.

Nick shook him again. "Cris!" At last, his eyelids fluttered, then he looked up at Nick.

"What happened?" he asked.

"You were shot. The *polizia* will be here any minute," Nick said. "What do I do?"

Cris pulled out his mobile. "Get the money and get me in the car. Call Delfina. *Not* my father."

Nick checked on Yuri, who was lying still, eyes closed, bleeding heavily from a hole high in his belly. When Nick nudged him with his foot, Yuri's eyes flew open and his gun arm snapped up, sending a shiver down Nick's spine. He fired again on reflex, two quick shots, hitting Yuri in the neck and upper chest. The Russian's arm dropped to the pavement, the gun falling from his fingers.

He checked the other blond, and the one with the suitcase. Neither one was breathing, but Nick's own breath came in quick shallow gasps. He was dangerously close to hyperventilating. He'd just killed three men. Three. Without a fucking thought, with hardly a pause.

"Hurry," Cris hissed from his left. Nick forced himself to inhale deeply. He had to hold it together, had to get Cris to safety and medical help. He grabbed the briefcase from the stocky man's hand, tossed it in the boot on top of the drugs, then slammed the lid shut and helped Cris onto the backseat of the car. Getting behind the wheel, he hit Cris's contact entry for Delfina as he drove away, careful to keep his speed reasonable. Nothing would attract more attention than a car screeching off.

The phone rang and rang. "Come on, answer," he growled. Finally she did.

"Cris?"

"It's Nick. Cris has been shot."

Her scream pierced him, but he didn't have time for niceties. "He's alive. But he's hurt. Where do I take him?"

"What were you *doing*?"

"No time to explain. He needs a doctor. And your father can't know about it."

"Okay. Someone will call you back."

He hung up. Nick hit a pothole, and Cris groaned. "Sorry, mate." He should pull over somewhere. He turned down a dark alley, making note of the cross streets nearby. He stopped the car, but kept the engine running.

"Are you pressing on the wound?" Nick asked, mouth parched, chest tight.

"*Sì.*" Cris grunted out the word. He sounded bad.

The phone rang. "Hang on," he said to Cris. The number showed on the display as Private. "Yes?"

"Where are you?" a familiar voice asked.

"Bellagio." He gave the cross streets.

"Go south on Via Valessina, until you reach a roundabout, then go east on Via per Lecco, until you come to a private road. Turn there. You are searching for this address." The caller rattled off a location. "I will meet you there in thirty minutes with a doctor."

Nick hung up and glanced at his watch. After conferring with Cris, he decided to stay where they were for the next fifteen minutes.

"I'm sorry," Cris said. "I don't know what happened."

"I just killed three men, that's what happened." Nick slammed his fist against the steering wheel. Cris said nothing, and Nick finally realized what had been bothering him ever since he'd laid eyes on the Russians. "Those fuckers planned to kill us all along."

"What do you mean?"

"They didn't bring anything to transport the cocaine to their boat. They meant to get rid of us and take the car." He paused to let that sink in before he said, "Do you think your great-uncle was in on it?"

Cris's answer was instantaneous. "Of course not. Damn Russians. They probably thought they could fuck with me because I'm young."

Maybe. Maybe not. Nick kept his doubts to himself. They waited the rest of the time in silence, the air in the car thick with the scent of blood. Nick thought about calling Delfina back, but he'd wait until he was sure Cris was okay. He was talking and he seemed relatively alert, but you never knew with head injuries.

Finally it was time to go. Nick backed out of the alley. He followed the directions, puzzling over where he'd heard the caller's voice before. It wasn't until he turned onto the private drive and saw the flash of blond hair on the man waving him down that he realized. Antonio.

He was with a tall, thin dark-haired man Nick didn't recognize. Nick pulled up and lowered the driver's side window. Antonio opened the back door. "Keep the car running," he said to Nick.

Another man approached, gliding out from the shadows. The bastard from the loo. Ruggero. He motioned Nick out and slid behind the wheel. "There's cocaine and cash in the boot," Nick said to him.

"Who do they belong to?"

"The cocaine belongs to the Russians. The cash to his uncle," Nick said, flicking a thumb at Cris.

A look passed between Antonio and Ruggero. "Which Russians?"

"Vilanovich. Yuri."

"How many down?"

"Three. All dead."

"Any others?"

"One. He got away on a boat."

"So, have you selected your coffin yet?" Ruggero grinned.

Heat flooded Nick's face. "What are you going to do with all this?"

"Put it in storage." Ruggero held out a hand encased in black leather, palm up. "The gun." Nick gave him the Beretta and the spare magazine. "And him?" Ruggero indicated Cris, as Antonio and the other man carried him inside.

"He didn't fire."

Ruggero's grin widened. "You *are* your father's son." Then he put the car in drive and took off.

Nick scrubbed his hands over his face. His legs felt weak. There was no telling what Dario would do once he knew about Cris getting shot.

Nick pulled out the mobile Ruggero had given him the day before and placed a call to France. Hope surged in him. Maybe, just maybe, he could minimize the fallout.

———— ◆ ————

Nick's call had roused Delacourt from bed, but Émile sounded overjoyed to hear from him—at first. After Nick recounted everything that had happened, Delacourt fell silent. Finally he said, "Nicolas, you must come home immediately. Perhaps, if we put you and your grandparents in protective custody, we can save you."

"I can't do that. Not yet. But things would be much easier for me if I knew Gran and Grandad were safe."

"I'll see what I can do." Delacourt paused and said, "Do you believe me now? That this was a fool's errand?"

Nick flushed. He had to prove Émile wrong. He knew he could accomplish something here, knew he could bring down his father and the Andrettis. As long as he didn't have to worry about his grandparents. "Trust me, Émile. I know what I'm doing here."

"Do you? Need I remind you that my wife is alive because of your father's generosity? I hate to think what will become of her if that generosity disappears."

"You're asking me to compromise my investigation."

"*What* investigation?" Delacourt asked. "Everything you're doing is unofficial."

Ice showered over him. "What's my status?"

Silence. Then: "I put you on administrative leave. Family emergency."

"You're hanging me out to dry."

"What did you expect? I couldn't very well reveal what you're doing and why. Difficult questions would come up. Questions you would not want answered."

"My career is over, isn't it?"

Delacourt sighed. "I sincerely hope not. If you give up on this madness and come back, all can be as it was. If you persist, I cannot save you from the inevitable questions that will arise."

"So I'm fucked."

"As far as staying in Interpol is concerned, yes."

He'd forced Delacourt to let him go, and here was the payback. "Need *I* remind *you* that your career is in as much jeopardy as mine?" Nick snapped.

"I had hoped you would not be vindictive."

"That's rich, coming from you." Nick's fingers tightened on the mobile. It was all he could do not to throw it.

"Nicolas, you engineered all this. You brought it all upon yourself with your shortsighted impulsiveness."

How blind he'd been when it came to Delacourt. "The pursuit of justice is never shortsighted."

"What you're pursuing isn't justice. It's retribution. You would like the world to be black and white. Most people would, but it is many, many shades of gray. It's time you learned such a basic fact."

"Said by the corrupt to the righteous."

Delacourt laughed, but it was bitter. "You know what happens to the righteous, yes? They become martyrs."

Nick's stomach sank. Everywhere he turned, people were planning his funeral, even though Dario hadn't yet delivered the killing blow.

He had to make his case with Fuente, or else everything he'd done, he'd done for naught.

———————◆———————

Nick walked inside the clandestine clinic, then wished he hadn't. The doctor and a nurse were working on Cris, a small mound of bloodied gauze in a pan by the bed. Nick swallowed hard, suddenly feeling woozy. He found a chair next to Antonio and sat. "How is he?"

Antonio ran a hand through his hair, leaving it sticking up in tangled clumps. "*Molto fortunato.* The bullet did not enter his skull. He has a... crease in the skin?"

"You mean the bullet grazed his skull?"

Nodding, Antonio continued. "*Sì.* Much bleeding, he needs stitches. The doctor says he has a...." Antonio knocked himself on the skull with his knuckles.

"A concussion?"

"*Sì.* But he will be okay."

"That's a relief."

Nick's stomach was just starting to unclench when Cris's phone buzzed in his pocket, making him jump. Delfina. "How is Cris?" she asked, her voice trembling. Christ, he should have called her.

He filled her in. Then he asked, "What do we do about your father?"

"What were you two doing?"

He sighed, then said, "A job for your great-uncle."

"Why?"

"Delfi, I can't tell you more."

"This is part of Cris's plan to fix things for me, isn't it?"

He looked over at Cris, then quickly away. "Yeah."

She took in a choked breath, then a string of affectionate curses came out of her mouth, a lovely stream of Italian. He caught only a few words. After a moment she stopped herself. "Benedetto is going to want to talk to you—I would be surprised if he's not here by morning."

"So, do I tell Dario?"

"No." Her voice was rushed, urgent. "Prozio must not have wanted Papà involved for some reason. You don't want to cross him. Trust me on this. He is far worse than my father. And far more powerful."

Bloody hell. This just got better and better. "So what do I tell your father?"

"Make something up, but keep it simple."

"Someone tried to steal the car?"

"*Perfetto.*"

If he could carry out the lie. "How will I explain why we didn't go to him in the first place?"

"*Merda.*" She paused for a long time. "Tell him Cris told you who to call. He'll have to handle it when he wakes up."

The whole thing was as shaky as a pub crawler after a weekend binge. But it would have to do.

Antonio drove him back to the Andretti estate, an uncomfortable silence lying thick between them. Finally Nick broke it. "I'm sorry I was such an arse to you at the party."

"It's not me you need to apologize to."

"*He* can rot."

Antonio glanced at him. "Your father is heartbroken."

"You assume I care."

Nick's words hung in the air as they lapsed back into silence. Resting his cheek against the cool glass of the car window, he stared out, though there was not much to see other than the occasional light where someone had stayed up late. He'd killed three men, but the one that counted was Yuri. Nick had murdered him.

He could argue that it was self-defense, but that was a flimsy excuse for how he'd handled things. He hadn't tried to disarm Yuri or somehow disable him before approaching, so that he wouldn't be a danger. So that he'd be alive when the police and medics came. No. If he were entirely honest with himself, he'd *wanted* an excuse to shoot the man. He hadn't wanted to leave any witnesses. All he had needed was an excuse, some justification for what he'd done. But that was all it was. A justification.

Hell, he'd tried to murder the other one too. The wiry little guy that got away in the boat. Who the hell had he become, shooting at someone who was running away?

Antonio broke into his thoughts, his words laden with heavy emotion. "I would give anything to have my parents back. *Anything.* But your father, he has been good to me. He helped me when no one else would. Or could."

"So what are you? His assistant, or something?"

"His second."

"I thought you were a guard."

"I was. Until recently."

"So I'm kind of the fly in the ointment, yeah?"

Antonio's brow wrinkled. "I do not understand."

"You think he'll replace you with me."

"*Sì.* He says he will not, but he would if you asked."

"Don't worry. I won't be asking."

Antonio's hands clamped down on the wheel, his knuckles going white. "I almost wish you would."

Nick felt a tightening behind his eyes. "You would want that?"

"If it would make him happy, yes."

"I don't get it. Why do you all kowtow to him?" At Antonio's puzzled look, Nick added, "You treat him like a king." Then he shook his head. "No, it's more than that. Like he's... I don't know." His throat constricted. He *did* know. "Like he means something to you." *Like a father would.*

Antonio didn't answer. Instead, he stopped the car at the gate and called Delfina, who buzzed them through.

When they reached the front door, Antonio turned to him. "You want to know why? Your father is a good man. A true don. You would see that if your eyes were open."

Nick started to get out of the car, but Antonio stopped him. "It's not safe for you here. Come with me. Your father can protect you."

Shaking his head, Nick stepped out, then leaned back in the open door. "*Grazie.* For everything."

"*Prego.* Think about what I am saying, yes?" Nick shut the door without answering. Antonio shifted the Mercedes into first gear and left in a spray of gravel.

Oh he'd think about it. But it wouldn't change his mind.

Nick turned toward the house. Delfina stood in the open doorway, silhouetted in the light streaming from behind her. She closed the door and ran down the steps and into his arms.

When he caught her against him, her body shook with sobs. Tears pricked his own eyes, though he wasn't sure of their origin. Everything had gone wrong. Everything. The only thing that felt right was the woman in his arms. The woman he couldn't have, the woman he'd never forget, supposing he lived long enough for regrets.

Delfina tilted her face up to his, and without thinking, he kissed her, long and passionately, all the blood in him raging.

With a sigh she pulled back, then nestled her damp face against his chest. He stroked her back, murmuring that Cris would be okay, that everything would be all right.

After a time, she looked up at him. "Let's go to the guest house before someone spots us."

"But we can't talk there."

"Who said we were going to talk?" The lilt in her voice and the smile behind her words called to him, even though he knew they weren't entirely real. But if she wanted to put on a brave front, he'd let her.

She slipped her hand in his and started toward the guest cottage. He said nothing, just wrapped his fingers around hers and followed. On the doorstep, he stopped her. "Are you sure?"

"I want to."

So did he, but… could she still be trying to stop the engagement? He shook his head. "Cris is hurt, and you're upset."

"Maybe I want some comfort," she whispered.

So do I. How he wanted to forget this night, to bury himself inside her and forget everything else, forget every horrible thing he'd done. How he wanted to wipe away her tremulous smile and the bruised look in her eyes.

And lingering beneath all that, his whole body screamed to finish what they'd started in the olive grove. But for the first time in his life, Nick didn't give in to such demands. For some reason he didn't understand, he wanted more than a romp. He was starting to feel something for her. Something that frightened him. Something he didn't want to feel.

And right now, he really needed to be alone with what he'd done to those men.

"This should be more than a shag—at least for your sake," he said and gave her a gentle nudge in the direction of the villa. "Go home, Delfi."

She stared at him, gobsmacked, her face flooding with color. "You're serious."

He nodded, hardly believing it himself. But it was the truth. "Go on."

She dried her wet cheeks, her motions jerky, and sniffed loudly. "I've made a dog's breakfast of this, haven't I?"

He cracked a smile. "No more than I have."

The funny thing was, as she walked away, he felt he'd finally done something right. One tiny thing, in a universe of mistakes.

CHAPTER 11

As Delfina had predicted, Benedetto arrived around dawn. Nick hadn't even spoken to Dario yet when the knock came on his door. Benedetto barged in, leaving a guard on Nick's doorstep. "Where is everything?"

Blood thundering in his ears, Nick put a finger to his lips. "Let's take a walk."

Benedetto followed him outside and into the garden, the guard trailing them just out of earshot. "Why are we out here?"

"Dario is keeping tabs on me." Nick inhaled deeply, taking in the piney scent of the cypresses they walked past, trying to calm himself. It wasn't working. He'd had precious little sleep that night, and what he did get had ended each time with him waking in a sweat, heart thrashing against his ribs, his ears full of the roar of gunfire.

"Ah." Benedetto clasped his hands behind his back. "Tell me everything." When Nick finished, Benedetto said, "So again I ask, where is my property?"

Nick swallowed, certain the pounding of his heart was audible. "I want something in exchange."

Benedetto stopped walking and turned to stare at him, his eyes tundra cold and lethal. "*You* demand nothing. *I* make the demands."

Nick's stomach contracted into a ball. Everything hinged on what he said next. What if during all his ruminating overnight he'd come to the wrong conclusions about Benedetto? He chose his words with excessive politeness. "I mean no disrespect. But my position is precarious, and I've done my best to salvage the situation for you. Is it so unreasonable to beg a favor?"

Benedetto didn't relax. "We will see."

Not good enough. Nick went with Plan B, which was much less polite than Plan A. "Something was wrong with the deal, the amount they were paying. I can only conclude that you owe the Russians. And I would guess that you owe them more today. And tomorrow, it might not be only a debt you owe them."

Something flickered in the man's eyes, and the sudden tightening of his neck and shoulders told Nick he'd guessed correctly. He tensed for a bullet from behind, but Benedetto didn't signal the guard. Instead he looked away from Nick, but Nick

111

didn't dare do the same. Finally Benedetto took a deep breath. "What do you want?" He almost sighed the words.

Triumph surged through Nick, but he kept it off his face. "I want my grandparents safe, and Delfina's engagement over. And I want you to finance a design company for her. Make things happen for her, without her knowing it." He paused. "And one last thing: don't let Dario force her to marry someone else."

Benedetto's eyebrows rose. "You don't want her?"

No point in giving the man extra ammunition. "I've had her. And I don't do relationships."

"If you want all this, you'll have to do something more for me."

Nick crossed his arms and nodded, trying to ignore the tightening in his gut. He was going to regret this.

"Dario may be scheming against me. You will work for me—supply *me* information from Interpol. Not him."

"That's going to be hard to do, seeing as he'll kill me if I don't."

Benedetto smiled. "That brings us to my next request. When I ask, you will kill my nephew."

Nick couldn't hide his surprise. "You do mean Dario?"

"Of course."

Cold-blooded son of a bitch. Nick was no fan of Dario's either, but then again, he wasn't a blood relative. "And how am I supposed to do that?"

"You're a clever boy."

Nick shook his head. "What you're asking—I'm not sure I can do it."

"I don't think you have much choice." Benedetto raised a finger and beckoned his guard.

Nick's pulse beat wildly as the guard approached. Benedetto stopped the man with a gesture just two feet away from Nick.

"Have I told you about Eusebio? He's a man of remarkable talent. I believe he knows at least one hundred different ways to kill a man."

"Like everyone else around here. Is there some special Mafioso-ninja school all these guys go to?"

"Would you like a demonstration of these skills?"

No sense of humor, this guy. "No need. I can imagine." *All too well.*

Benedetto held Nick's gaze for a few moments. "So, have we a deal, as the Americans are fond of saying?"

Fuck, fuck, fuck! But what choice did he have? "Yes. When do you want me to do it?"

"I'll contact you. My nephew may prove useful for some weeks yet." Benedetto checked his watch, before focusing on Nick again. "Now, where is everything?"

"With my father."

Benedetto's face fell and he cursed.

"Would you rather it was with Dario?" Nick asked.

"This complicates things."

"I've been told my father is a reasonable man."

Benedetto snorted. "He has no love for cocaine. He will be anything *but* reasonable."

So it must be true. His father didn't deal in drugs. Nick found the idea oddly comforting. "Everyone has a price," he said.

Benedetto jammed his hands in his coat pockets and looked Nick up and down. "You *are* a Lucchesi, through and through."

"I am nothing like my father."

Benedetto laughed. "You have his balls. And his brains. Be grateful," he said, then he walked away.

Nick started to follow him but stopped short when he felt a vibration against his chest. The phone from his father. He turned and hid the mobile as he read the incoming text message. "N and S are safe. Let me know if you wish to talk to them. E."

Stunned, Nick stared at the message. He hadn't asked his father to do anything for him, and yet he had. Did he actually give a damn, or was he just trying to win Nick's favor?

Either way, at least his grandparents were safe. And for that he could be thankful. He texted back. "Thank you. Their number?"

A set of digits with an Italian country code came back to him. He dialed the number, almost dizzy with relief when he heard his grandfather's voice. Tears pricked his eyes. They were safe. *Safe.* He hung up without speaking. At the moment, he didn't have it in him to hide his emotions from them. Anything he said right now would be more worrisome than reassuring.

Now all he had to do was figure out how to save his own hide. And determine what to do when Benedetto issued the order against Dario.

———— ◆ ————

Benedetto must have evaluated and discarded a dozen approaches before he reached Enrico Lucchesi's door. He'd finally settled on one he thought was foolproof, though there was no telling with Lucchesi. The man was bound to make things difficult, if not impossible. But as Lucchesi's son had said, every man had his price.

Besides, as Dario had pointed out, Lucchesi had value. His control of the bank was pivotal to the 'Ndrangheta's continued success. But Benedetto would rather have that business in *his* pocket, not Dario's. His nephew was up to something, and that made him dangerous.

But that was a problem for another day.

A maid ushered him into Lucchesi's study. He left Eusebio outside, trusting that Lucchesi would not be underhanded.

Lucchesi was pouring over something on his laptop, a frown of concentration furrowing his forehead. Perhaps business wasn't that good? Or perhaps Lucchesi was tired of playing *contabile* as well as *capo*. He had yet to replace the traitorous Franco Trucco. Trustworthy accountants were hard to find.

Gesturing for him to take a chair, Lucchesi said, "What can I do for you, Don Andretti?"

Benedetto raised a brow. "So formal, Enrico?"

"Considering that your family seems bent on destroying mine, my formality is understandable, no?" Lucchesi gave him a tight smile.

Benedetto returned the smile, even though he felt like clenching his teeth and leveling Lucchesi with a stare. "*Per favore,* I beg you not to hold me accountable for the actions of my brother and my nephew."

"Are you saying you had no influence over Carlo—or Dario, for that matter?"

The barb hit home. And it was impossible to answer without appearing a fool. So he said nothing.

"The fox has lost his tongue," Lucchesi mused. "For once."

"Shall we speak plainly?"

"Always."

"You have certain items that belong to me. I want them back."

"I believe the money belongs to the Vilanoviches."

"It is none of your affair."

Lucchesi leaned forward and placed his hands flat on the desk. "Oh but it is. Once you involved my son, it became my business."

"*I* didn't involve him."

"Doesn't matter. You found someone to do a risky job for you and you didn't care who got hurt. Even if it was your own flesh and blood. Have you bothered to visit Cris?"

Benedetto's cheeks burned. "You seem bent on provoking me."

"Tell me, Don Andretti, why I should do otherwise."

Here it was. The demand, ever so subtle. Benedetto smiled. "I can help you get what you want most."

"And what do you think I want so badly, that I would consider working with you?"

"Peace. And a return to the old codes. No drugs, no prostitution, no pornography." He could always find some sacrificial lambs to make Lucchesi happy.

"You can give me neither."

Acid scalded Benedetto's throat. "You question my authority?"

"You run La Provincia. Not the whole of the 'Ndrangheta. And by your own admission, you have no control over Dario."

"What I meant was that I did not order—or condone—any actions against you. I would rather have you as a friend, Don Lucchesi."

"Would you?" Lucchesi's gaze sharpened, as did his tone. Time for some reminders of what a good friend Benedetto Andretti could be.

"When my brother Carlo brought you before La Provincia, when he accused you of breaking the truce between our families, did I not treat you fairly?" Benedetto asked, keeping his voice mild.

With a curt dip of his chin, Lucchesi said, "I cannot fault you in that matter."

"Well then. I believe that demonstrates my intentions toward you. I had nothing to gain then, and much to lose."

"As you do now."

He was going to put a bullet in Enrico Lucchesi the minute he was no longer useful. "Ah, but I do have something to gain this time. Your friendship. Your partnership."

Lucchesi snorted. "You think I would take on an Andretti as a partner?"

"Hear me out, *per favore.*" When Lucchesi crossed his arms and nodded, Benedetto continued. "Despite the success of La Provincia at negotiating disputes"—Lucchesi snorted again—"there is still too much strife between the families. It would be in everyone's interest to form a permanent advisory council that would coordinate the efforts of the families and keep and enforce the peace."

"And you would be in charge of this council, of course."

Benedetto shrugged. "That position could be permanent. Or it could rotate, or be elected."

"And I suppose this council would collect a percentage from all the families?"

"Naturally, to fund peacekeeping and military operations and certain administrative expenditures."

"I have noticed, Don Andretti, that expenses for La Provincia keep increasing. Why is that, I wonder?"

That bullet would go right between Lucchesi's dark eyes. "As more families have turned to La Provincia for mediation, my travel expenses have increased."

Lucchesi waved his words away, as if they smelled of pig shit. "What does this partnership you speak of have to do with this council?"

"To be effective, the council would need regional heads. You would be the head of Lombardy."

"Not Dario?" Lucchesi asked, arching a dark brow.

"My nephew has less foresight, less patience, less... restraint, than you."

"And in exchange, I return your property?"

His pulse quickened. He had Lucchesi now. "Yes."

"No."

"What?" His stomach sank, the breakfast he'd eaten on the jet going sour.

"You are right that I want peace with your nephew. But I will not have it unless my son is free."

Benedetto smiled and stretched, reaching for a confidence he didn't feel. "Done. Now return my property."

"You will understand if I remain skeptical."

Lucchesi had gone too far. "No, I won't."

"Then we are at an impasse." With a shrug, Lucchesi sat back in his chair.

"You forget that I could press my nephew to dispose of your son."

"You won't. Or you wouldn't be here right now." He wanted to shove that self-confident grin, those shiny white teeth, down Lucchesi's throat. "Bring me my son. Then we'll talk," Lucchesi said.

"Give me my property, and you will get your son."

Lucchesi held up his watch and tapped its face. "The Russians are waiting. They are not known for their patience."

"Your boy killed Yuri and Gregor Vilanovich. Perhaps I should turn him over to their father?"

His stare unwavering, Lucchesi touched the lid of his open laptop. "I've been going over certain accounts today. Yours and La Provincia's. I found some suspicious activity. Transfers that could be considered irregular. Transfers it might interest the other families to know about."

Fuck. Him. "You can prove nothing."

A self-assured smile spread across Lucchesi's face. "You are certain?"

"The Vilanoviches will burn him with a blowtorch. They'll pour acid on his skin. Maybe cut off a hand or a foot before they tire of his screams."

"At least he won't die alone. You'll be right beside him."

Benedetto searched Lucchesi's face for weakness, but all he saw was a cold, implacable man. His brother Carlo had pushed Lucchesi too far, had changed him. The man who ruled with his heart was dead.

Benedetto had fatally underestimated Lucchesi. He raised his hands in surrender. "Fine. I will free your son."

"Do it, and I will return your property."

"I need the product now."

Lucchesi leaned forward. "What you need is an incentive. Tick tock." He sat back in his chair and studied his nails. "The clock runs backward for no man. Not even you, Benedetto."

Stomach churning, Benedetto rose and headed for the door. As he reached it, Lucchesi's voice stopped him. "I am a man of my word. Demonstrate your friendship, and you will have mine in return."

Fuck Lucchesi and his friendship. That's what he wanted to do.

But the Russians were coming. And Lucchesi was right—they were not known for their patience.

Or their mercy.

What the hell was going on with Dario's family? First Delfina defying him and defiling herself with Clarkston, now Cris getting shot?

Clarkston's story stank like week-old fish. Now that Cris was home and had slept, it was time to get some answers.

At least Lucchesi had sent his personal physician to accompany Cris home. Dottor Beltrami had recommended that Cris stay at the clinic overnight, but Dario didn't like the idea of Cris being in Lucchesi's hands. The man might get ideas.

Odd though how Lucchesi let Cris go without a fight, without a single demand.

Dario didn't like that either. Not one bit. Lucchesi was up to something. Perhaps he somehow thought to broker a true peace between their families.

Over Dario's maggot-ridden bloated corpse.

If Lucchesi wanted to play nice and remain naïve, that was hardly Dario's problem. But Cris and Delfina were.

He left his study and headed upstairs, pausing outside Cris's door when he heard low voices. Cris and his wicked older sister. Dario shook his head. She'd nearly ruined his plans to create an alliance with Gianluca. And if she turned up pregnant at the doctor's appointment tomorrow, she still could ruin everything. The ungrateful little *troia*.

He regretted the insult the moment he thought it. He shouldn't blame her— Delfi was an innocent, still a girl really. It was Clarkston who was to blame for all of this. Clarkston who had no doubt led her astray. Clarkston who would pay if things went wrong. The boy had all the charm of his father, the kind of charm that led young women, like his dear sister Toni, astray.

Dario turned the doorknob without knocking, wanting to catch them unawares. When the door unlatched, Delfi snapped around to face him and color flooded her cheeks. Clarkston's gaze slid away the moment Dario turned to him. But Cris—Cris lay still, his pale face washed out in its nest of dark brown curls, a white bandage above his left temple showing where a bullet had almost ended his life. A few millimeters to the right, and his boy would be dead.

Dario's throat went tight. He'd meant to bark out an accusation, to put Cris off-balance, to get him to confess the truth, but seeing his boy lying there, his boy who'd nearly died, his boy who was on the cusp of being a man, undid him.

He swallowed, his hand still on the knob. "I wanted to see how you were." His voice sounded strained, weak. Not the image he'd wanted to convey at all.

"I'm fine, Papà," Cris said. He tried to push himself up on the pillows and winced. Orfeo, Cris's Rottweiler, stirred beside the bed and rose, placing his large head next to Cris's hand, and let out a gentle *woof.*

Delfina put a restraining hand on Cris's chest. "You heard Dottor Beltrami. You don't want to overexert yourself."

He shook his head. "I wasn't."

"You were."

Dario's eyes grew hot and wet at the sound of them bickering, reminding him of when they'd been children. Reminding him of when he'd feared for them, always worrying that something would happen, a kidnapping or a random, stupid accident. He hadn't worried about Cris and Delfina for some time now. He'd thought those days were gone.

So why did he fear for his children now?

"*Bambini*, hush and listen to your father."

They both turned expectant gazes to him. "What, Papà?" Cris asked.

"Tell me the truth, Cristoforo. Tell me everything."

Delfina jumped in. "Someone tried to steal the car. Nick saved Cris's life."

A fire sparked in his gut. A lie. Fuente had confirmed it when he'd checked on Clarkston's story. Three Russians were dead, two of them Vilanoviches. Of course, Fuente couldn't say for sure that Cris and Clarkston were involved. But the timing was suspicious. And why else had Clarkston involved his father?

"Let your brother speak for himself. Cris?"

Cris averted his eyes and scratched his nose. Preparing to tell a lie to match his sister's—the gesture reminded Dario of when six-year-old Cris had tried to blame Delfina for a bit of writing on the dining room wall. "I took Nick to Bellagio. For fun."

"Do you think me an idiot?"

Cris's mouth dropped open. "Of course not."

"Then don't treat me like one." He glanced at Clarkston, who was studiously examining Cris's football trophies.

His son shifted on the bed, twisting the edge of the sheet in his fingers. "I made a deal with the Russians to sell them some cocaine. And they tried to cheat me." Cris held his eyes without wavering. Perhaps that part was true. But that wasn't all of it. *Dio,* he wanted to scream at his son. The Russians!

Clarkston jumped in. "They were acting strangely. I wish I'd been able to get Cris's attention before the shooting started."

Dario exploded, at last having a target for his wrath. "What the *hell* were you thinking? How could you let him do such a stupid thing?"

"I asked Nick to help me—"

"I'm asking him, not you!" he barked at Cris. Turning, Dario stared down Clarkston. "You're a *man*, he's just a boy. Don't you have a *shred* of common sense?"

Clarkston's gaze fell to the carpet. "You're right. I should have stopped him."

"Enough, Papà." Delfina lurched to her feet. "Cris is *capo di società*—would you expect any of his men to defy him?"

She had a point. However... "Clarkston isn't one of his men." And they still hadn't told him the entire truth. He turned back to Clarkston. "Why did you go to the Lucchesis for help?"

"That was my fault," Delfina said. "Nick called me, and I called Antonio. I knew you'd be angry."

"So angry I'd let my son die?"

"No. But..." She paused and licked her lips. "I thought you might do something stupid. Like try to go after the Russians."

"You *do* think I'm an idiot."

"No." She patted the air in a placatory gesture. "I just worried that you'd overreact. I didn't want you to start a war over this."

"And you think I won't now?"

She shook her head. "You've had time to think about it."

"And you know stirring up the Russians isn't a good idea," Cris said.

"A clear case of a rag speaking ill of a cloth."

Cris reddened and sighed. "I thought I could handle them."

Dario stepped to his son's bedside and took his hand. "Leave the deals to me for now, *capisci?*" He leaned down and kissed his son on the forehead. When was the last time he'd done so? Not for a decade perhaps. His heart squeezed painfully, and he rubbed a thumb over the ache in his chest.

"I understand, Papà. And I'm sorry."

Someone knocked on the open door. Dario turned. Benedetto. His uncle's eyes lit on Cris, then Clarkston, the look in them troubled.

And suddenly things started to make sense.

CHAPTER 12

After a quick visit with Cris, Benedetto asked Dario for a private word. They headed down to the study, Dario's gut burning again. This time, his uncle was the cause. How dare he endanger his son?

Dario inhaled deeply, trying to tamp down his emotions. He had to play this carefully. He didn't actually know anything.

But why else would Benedetto have flown all the way from Calabria? It certainly wasn't to check on Cris. And how else could he have known? Dario hadn't called him. The only person he'd spoken to was Fuente. Unless…

Unless Lucchesi had involved him. That could explain Lucchesi's willingness to let Cris go.

So what deal had Lucchesi made with his uncle? If Lucchesi thought he was getting his boy back, he could rot.

They took seats in the study, Dario choosing two chairs across from each other rather than putting his desk between them. The maid brought in steaming cups of espresso and they each took one from the tray.

Dario watched Benedetto carefully, studying his uncle. He'd never trusted the man, blood or no. He'd always had the sense that people had dollar signs on them in Benedetto's eyes. Blood or no.

And lately, he felt his worth to Benedetto had gone down to zero. And it was all because of Clarkston.

If Dario hadn't been the one who'd lured Clarkston in, he'd have sworn Lucchesi had engineered some clever plan against him.

His gut tingled. He'd had such thoughts before and dismissed them. But perhaps he'd been too hasty.

Taking a sip of his espresso, Dario studied Benedetto over the rim. Whatever the man wanted, Dario damn well wasn't going to make it easy for him. He knew how this worked—the one who made the first request was the one in trouble. Always. It was one of the few useful things his father had taught him.

Benedetto drank from his cup, then set it down. "I'm happy to see that your son will be all right, *grazie a Dio*."

"Perhaps we should thank Enrico Lucchesi instead."

"Certainly." Benedetto idly ran a finger around the rim of his cup. "I'm glad to hear that your hatred of Lucchesi has abated."

"I assure you, it hasn't."

Benedetto's mouth pursed. "That is a shame."

"Why? Are you saying you bear him no ill will? He did kill your brother. *My* father. Unless you've forgotten."

"I haven't." Benedetto sighed. "But let's be honest. Your father was a thorn in my side—yours as well. I was relieved when he died."

His uncle was ever the politician. "*Died?* Lucchesi executed him."

"A mercy killing. Sooner or later it would have happened. And considering the torture your father inflicted on his, I'd say Carlo got off easy."

Dario glanced at the floor. He'd played his part in that. He'd wanted revenge on Rinaldo for taking his little finger. He absently stroked the stump on his right hand. But his father had taken it too far. Much too far.

As always.

With a shrug, Dario said, "Perhaps. Still, had you seen my father die, I do not think you'd be so sanguine."

"Feeling guilty? After all, you were the only one who walked away that night. What did you do to save your soul, I wonder?"

Made a deal with the devil. "You didn't fly all this way to rehash the past."

His uncle smiled. "I have an opportunity to make us both very rich."

Interesting. "How so?"

"Your grandfather and I have always felt the Andrettis should have a strong role in guiding and shaping the 'Ndrangheta. La Provincia in its current form was a good first step. Now we are poised to implement the next phase in our plan."

Very interesting. "Which is?"

"We form a permanent advisory council. A council that will set direction and guide the families. A council that will keep the peace between us. A peace we all enjoy." He paused. "A peace you endanger if you persist in your dislike of Lucchesi."

Dario snorted. "Dislike. You always were master of the understatement."

Benedetto's voice sharpened. "Sometimes I wonder if my brother was right about you. I always thought you had brains hidden away somewhere. Right now, you're as clever as a bull charging a red flag."

Dario took a deep breath and let it out slowly. "What do you want of me?"

"Your cooperation. I need to bring Lucchesi in line with this plan. He does run the banks, as Gianluca pointed out."

"I told you at Delfina's party. I'm already working on a partnership with Lucchesi."

"Are you?" Benedetto took a gulp of his coffee. "Considering your attitude, I don't see how you'd ever be successful without my help."

Adrenaline shot through Dario's system. "Your *help?*" Benedetto's tone raised his hackles. Condescending. Dismissive. Patronizing. Only one person had ever dared speak to him that way: his late father. He didn't need a new one.

His uncle nodded. "I've spoken to Lucchesi. He'll agree not to oppose us, in exchange for his son back."

Dario's ears flooded with the pounding of his heart. Benedetto had been making deals behind his back. Benedetto was trying to cut him out. "And what do I get out of this?"

"My eternal gratitude. And a seat on the council. As head of Lombardy."

"The pot isn't sweet enough."

"Tell me. What is it you want? Did you intend to kill Lucchesi's boy, or just let him waste away in your guest cottage?"

"I want Lucchesi to suffer."

"If you're not going to kill his boy, then how?"

It was time to commit to a particular course. He'd dawdled long enough, trying to determine if Clarkston and Lucchesi were playing some elaborate game with him. In the end, it didn't matter. He'd play the game his way. "I want the boy to be mine. Not his."

Benedetto's brow furrowed. "Yours?"

"Part of my *cosca*. Mine."

"You would have him take the vows?"

"*Sì.*"

Benedetto gaped at him. "I take back what I said earlier. You're no charging bull. You're *insane*."

Dario smiled. "Having the one thing Lucchesi wants most—next to his firecracker of a wife—and forever denying him it will bring me immense pleasure." Stealing away Lucchesi's son was the perfect payback for his father's death. And for losing his sister to Lucchesi, a man who'd never deserved her love. A man who hadn't cherished her love, her friendship, the way Dario had. The way only a twin could.

"Lucchesi will never stand for this."

"His boy won't be dead. He'll have to settle for that."

Benedetto tapped his fingers against his lips. "Lucchesi will go to war against you without some guarantee of a truce. What about a marriage?"

He wasn't serious. "Delfina is marrying Leandro d'Imperio. It's already been decided."

"But it hasn't been publicly announced. You can still back out."

"No."

"Neither Lucchesi nor I will trust you without some other bond to keep the peace."

"I will not marry my daughter to an illegitimate son. She will have no standing."

"What if his last name was Lucchesi instead of Clarkston?"

He looked away from Benedetto. As much as he hated to admit it, there were good reasons to agree. They didn't align with Benedetto's plans—not entirely—but if he could bottle his anger and bide his time, he could have it all in the end.

The banks. The Lucchesi fortune. An inside man at Interpol.

And power, real power, that his uncle couldn't take away.

He met his uncle's eyes. "If Lucchesi makes me a partner in the bank, we have an agreement."

———◆———

Had Dario bought their story? And what had Benedetto said to Dario? Nick almost didn't want to know. He reviewed his early morning discussion with Benedetto. Should he tell Delfina and Cris about Benedetto's plans for their father? But would they believe him over their own flesh and blood? Delfina, maybe. Cris… it was hard to say. He seemed to trust Benedetto far more than she did. Nick had best keep Benedetto's betrayal to himself until he had specifics to offer about the attempt on Dario's life. Maybe then—if they believed him—they could catch Benedetto.

Dario had been gone a little more than an hour before he returned to Cris's room. His stony gaze met Nick's first, then shifted to Delfina. "You two come with me." He turned and left without checking if they were following.

His pulse racing, Nick glanced at Delfina, then followed Dario out the door. Her father led them to the library and gestured for them to take the sofa. He sat on a chair directly across from them. "What is this about, Papà?" Delfina asked.

"Your future. Both of yours." He rubbed a hand over his face. "I have made a decision."

"About what?" Nick asked.

Ignoring Nick, Dario focused on his daughter instead. "You will not be marrying Leandro."

Relief washed over Nick. "Why not?" Delfina asked.

"Because you will be marrying someone else."

Nick's heartbeat ratcheted up. He tried to catch Delfina's eye, but she wouldn't look at him. "Who?" she asked.

Dario nodded in Nick's direction. "What?" Nick asked, his voice sharp. "What game is this?"

"You would refuse my generous gesture? My mercy?" Dario leaned forward, picking up a heavy crystal tumbler half-full of liquor, weighing it in his hands as if he were going to throw it. The glass looked like it could leave a sizable dent in the wall—or in Nick's head.

"Of course not. But—"

"But what, Signor Clarkston? You told the d'Imperios that you'd bedded her twice. Surely you have no objection?"

"I thought forced marriages went out with the Middle Ages."

"I am giving you an incredible opportunity. An opportunity that no one of your station has ever been offered."

"My *station*?"

"You are illegitimate. But you won't be for long."

Nick's gut twisted. "Stop talking in riddles."

With a smile, Dario sat back in the chair. "Your father will legally recognize you. You will take the Lucchesi name. But you will join my *cosca*. You will be an Andretti, part of this family. And you will work for me, be my eyes and ears in Interpol."

Fuck that. "I will never take his name." Nick wanted to punch something. "I came here to ruin him. You promised to help."

Dario spread his hands and shrugged. "My plans have changed."

"I refuse."

"You'd prefer to take a ride with Flavio to the countryside?" Dario stared at him, his eyes going dead.

Delfina gripped Nick's knee. "Don't fight," she whispered.

He brushed her hand aside and stood up. She was right, but he just couldn't do it. He paced over to the far wall, sucking in air. Then he realized he had a reason for refusing that Dario couldn't ignore. He turned to face Dario. "If I am legally recognized, I can no longer be in Interpol. That's not what you want."

Dario pursed his lips. "I can give that up if I need to."

"But *I* can't. I won't. I will do the rest."

"For someone disloyal to Interpol, you seem awfully interested in staying part of it," Dario said.

Uh-oh. He'd almost given himself away. "I'm much more valuable to you if I'm in Interpol. Call me suspicious, but I think that improves my position with you."

Dario's brows rose. "What makes you think we are negotiating?"

"You want this for a reason. And you need my cooperation. I've given you my terms."

"And I've given you mine. You have an hour to decide." Dario rose. "I will leave you to talk." He stepped out, closing the door behind him.

As soon as her father was gone, Delfina was by his side. She placed a hand on his forearm. "You need to pick your battles carefully, Nick," she said, her voice low and firm.

Of course she'd say that. He jerked his arm out of her hold and stepped over to the window. Breathing in deep, he tried to slow his racing thoughts and quell the anger that threatened to swamp him. Dario was right about one thing. Part of this was an incredible opportunity. If he took Dario's offer, he'd be inside the 'Ndrangheta. He'd have access to information that would be impossible to get any other way. He could blow the lid off the organization, expose the rats to the light.

But the price Dario was asking.... The name change and legitimation aside—and *those* he was never going to agree to—there was the marriage to Delfina to consider. If her heart were pure, he could fall for her—*would* fall for her. Maybe he already had. But she seemed just as self-interested as everyone else in this twisted, tangled life. How could he be happy if he was constantly questioning her motives?

She touched his shoulder, shaking him out of his thoughts. He turned to snap at her, but stopped when he saw the tears streaming down her face. Damn him, but he couldn't yell at her when she looked so miserable. "What?"

"Just listen to me. For five minutes. Please." Her voice sounded broken. She should be happy. So why wasn't she? He gestured for her to go on.

She wiped her cheeks and sniffed. "I know you hate this whole idea. And with good reason. But I don't want to see you dead. I promise I'll give you a divorce or let you live separately with a mistress—whatever you want—as soon as I have a child."

Her words confirmed his thoughts. She just wanted what was most expedient. Whatever would get her to her ultimate goal. Freedom. "There won't be a child."

She twisted her hands together. "But we must have one to bind the families. After that, we can divorce."

"No. And that is final." She blanched, but he didn't care. "What kind of heartless bastard do you think I am? Children aren't bargaining chips. And no child of mine will ever be fatherless."

Delfina smoothed her hands over her belly. "I understand. But you cannot tell my father."

"Do I look stupid to you?" he snapped. When she turned away from him, he softened his tone. "Was there anything else?"

"You *cannot* take the vows, Nick. That's the thing you need to fight."

What was she talking about? "How can I marry you if I don't take the vows?"

"I mean the vows to join the 'Ndrangheta. The vows to follow my father, to be part of the Andretti *cosca*. That you cannot do."

"Why not?"

With a wild shake of her head, she muttered "*Madonna.*" Then her hands flew up from her sides and she hissed, "Those vows are forever, Nick. To the grave. Anyone who violates them dies. *Anyone.*"

"You think they're invincible."

She stared at him, her eyes like black pools, every muscle of her beautiful face set like stone. "Listen to me. Traitors are never forgotten, never forgiven. They will hunt you to the ends of the earth. There is nowhere you can hide from them."

"I'll take my chances."

"*Idiota,*" she spat, her eyes flashing fire, then she crossed her arms and blew out. "Let me tell you a story."

He checked his watch. "Is it long? Because you've already used up two of your minutes."

She hissed in frustration, but continued. "My great-uncle Remo betrayed this family once, long ago. My great-grandfather, Lorenzo, his father, saw to it that Remo, his oldest son, his own flesh and blood—"

"Nice buildup, Delfina, but this is boring me," Nick said, feigning a yawn.

"Damn you, listen!" she snapped, her gaze burning into him like a laser.

"Well, what did he do?"

"When he was twenty-five, Remo felt he was ready to head the family, but Lorenzo thought him too hotheaded. He told Remo to wait. Remo went to the Russians and made a plan with them to start dealing in arms. He was going to carve out a whole new territory for himself, establish his own branch of the family."

"That doesn't sound so bad."

"He disobeyed his *capo*, Nick."

"Sounds like a son getting out from under his father's thumb to me."

She shook her head. "To seal their arrangement, Remo gave the Russians some inside information. That information cost my great-grandfather a lot of money and compromised our operations in Eastern Europe."

"So what happened?"

"Remo thought his father would forgive him, write the loss off, if he ever found out. But to my great-grandfather, to my great-uncle Benedetto, to my father—money is all that matters. Money and pride. Remo had hurt his father on both counts." She swallowed. "Lorenzo ordered Remo's death. But first he was to be tortured. What they did to him—it was horrible. He had to be buried in a closed casket. And Lorenzo witnessed it all. He made Benedetto and my grandfather Carlo watch too. To this day, that story is passed down to everyone who joins the *cosca*. It is not just a warning. My great-grandfather is *proud* of it."

Nick's stomach curled in on itself. If a father could kill a son like that—but Remo hadn't had the benefit of Interpol's vast resources. They could hide him. And if they couldn't... maybe he'd have to take out his own insurance before he left Italy. Maybe he'd have to make sure Lorenzo and Benedetto and Dario were dead.

Christ! What had gotten into him? Was he seriously considering murdering them? He was an officer of the law. Not a judge. Not a court-appointed executioner.

But in the big scheme of things—really, did it matter? If he stopped the Andrettis, if he got rid of Benedetto and Lorenzo—Dario too—if he did that, wouldn't he be doing a good thing? They might never see justice any other way.

"You haven't heard a word I've said." Delfina glared up at him.

"No, I haven't. Because it doesn't matter."

She tore at her hair, the black locks sliding through her fingers when she released them. "You are impossible."

"I've been told that before." He consulted his watch. "You've gone past your five minutes."

She started speaking again, her voice low and intense, drilling into him. "They kept Remo alive for hours and hours. Burning him bit by bit. Breaking his bones. Pulling out his teeth. His fingernails. They cut him open, carefully, so he wouldn't die straight away. Imagine seeing your intestines in a pool at your feet."

She was a damn good storyteller, he'd give her that. "Has it occurred to you that this story is exaggerated? That it's just Lorenzo's brand of PR?"

"I heard it from my grandfather Carlo. He was there."

"Maybe he was just trying to scare you."

She laughed. "He hated his father. He told me that story after Teo because he wanted me to behave."

"I don't think Remo's death made much impression on Benedetto. And he was supposedly there."

"Why do you say that?"

"He's in league with the Russians. I can feel it."

"He wouldn't do such a thing."

"I think he already has."

Delfina crossed her arms. "He'd never take such a risk."

"He didn't. Not exactly. He tried to get Cris to do it for him."

"That was just about money."

"I don't think so. He acted rather strange about it." He raked the hair back off his forehead. "I would bet that Lorenzo knows nothing about Benedetto's deal with the Russians."

"You had better hope he does," Delfina said. "Or Benedetto will find a way to tie up all the loose ends." She swallowed hard and her eyes widened. "You and Cris—"

She clapped a hand over her mouth, her lower lip trembling.

"You think he wants us dead."

She nodded, the fear in her expression arrowing through him.

Maybe he ought to be afraid.

But if he was already damned, how much worse could it get?

———————— ◆ ————————

Delfina's father returned all too soon, before she could convince Nick to refuse the offer to join the *cosca*. At least he'd agreed to the marriage. And marrying him had to be far better than marrying Leandro.

Nick had to have some feelings for her, or he'd have slept with her the night before when she'd offered. He'd tried to help her, several times now; he'd almost gotten himself killed last night trying to do just that. He even seemed to have forgiven her lies, and if that wasn't love, at least it was affection, compassion.

He was a good man, if a flawed one, and the time she'd spent with him—especially those quiet, intimate moments when it was just the two of them—haunted her thoughts. Was this the great passion the poets talked about? Was she falling in love with Nick Clarkston? An odd thrill traveled through her chest. Maybe she was.

But even if she was falling for him, how did he feel about her? He cared for her; that was clear. Perhaps in time his feelings could deepen into love, and they could have a marriage in truth, and a child or two to go with it. A child who would bring lasting peace between their families.

However, if Nick took the vows to join the *cosca*, neither of them would ever escape this life. And even if he came to love her, she could never truly be happy. Because they'd never be free.

What was she going to do?

Papà closed the door behind him and remained standing. "Well?"

Nick rose. "I will not take the Lucchesi name, and I will not be recognized as his son. The rest I will do."

Her father's mouth tightened and he shook his head. "You are a fool."

"I've been accused of that, once or twice."

Papà pulled out his mobile phone. "Then this will be the last time you hear it."

Delfina's heart lodged in her throat. She couldn't let that happen. "Papà, is this how you treat the man who saved Cris's life? We owe him a huge debt."

Her father stilled and after a moment heaved out a breath. "*Madonna*," he grumbled, but he put the phone away. "No name change. But your father must amend his will and recognize you in it. The will can be amended privately, and it will remain private until his death."

"I don't like it, but... I'll agree."

"However, since you have defied me, you must first pass a test of loyalty, a test of worthiness, for entry into this *cosca*."

A shiver ran down her back. This couldn't be good. "Papà, surely that isn't necessary. He's already killed for the family."

"Yes, but can he follow orders?"

Nick stroked a hand over his face. "What would I have to do?" He looked a bit uneasy. Good. Perhaps the danger was finally sinking in.

"A small task."

"How illegal is it?"

"A bit of insurance fraud. Burn down a warehouse for me."

"That's all?"

Her father smiled, his eyes glittering like obsidian. She knew that smile. He had something up his sleeve. "That's all."

Nick shrugged. "No problem."

"Nick—"

Her father cut her off. "Enough, Delfina. Haven't you interfered plenty?" His voice was low, commanding. The one he used when he was stretched to breaking.

A lump formed in her throat, a lump with sharp, jagged edges. She'd failed to stop any of this from happening. Nick was walking into a trap.

CHAPTER 13

Ornella had been at it all morning, one dig after another. Delfina was close to shoving a wad of tulle down the girl's throat. But Delfina was taking Jacopo's advice to ignore her. And there was one good thing about Ornella's jabs; they gave her less time to worry about Nick. And those same jabs made her want to prove herself more than ever.

Since that first day when Jacopo had gone over her sketches and advised her on how to improve them, Delfina had been working on revising them. And today, finally, she'd created a design that sent him over the moon.

The dress was daring while still being conservatively cut. It was a riff on the typical "little black dress." Except that the long-sleeved top was cut entirely from a semi-sheer black gauze, and the skirt had peek-a-boo panels in the same gauze interspersed with panels of black velvet. The woman who wore the dress would be showing the world her undergarments—or lack of them. Jacopo urged her to clean up the sketch, then show it to Signor Morelli.

She'd just finished the new version when she heard a voice beside her. "Delfina," Cris said, and she raised her head, startled. "That's the second time I've said your name."

She smiled. "I guess I got caught up."

"You love this. It really shows," Nick said on her other side, startling her again.

Her cheeks heated. She could barely look at him. If only he knew how much time she'd spent worrying about him. And wondering too. Had he really meant what he'd said the night Cris had been shot? "Why are the two of you here?" she asked.

"Gio invited us out," Cris said. "Didn't you get her call?"

"No. I turn the phone off when I'm working." She started digging for it in her handbag, but Cris stopped her. "I told her we'd collect you."

Nick took the sketch from her hands, then let out a low whistle after scanning the drawing. "What I wouldn't give to see someone in this," he said, his eyes catching hers.

Does he mean "someone" as in me? She blushed furiously, imagining herself in the diaphanous gown, her body boldly on display. Her father would kill her, but the idea made her flush with heat.

"Let me see," Cris said.

Dio mio, no! She tried to intercept the sketch, but Nick and Cris held it up too high for her to reach. *Bloody children.* "Give it back," she demanded of Cris.

He chuckled. "Not on your life." He glanced at the sketch and his eyebrows popped up. "Now I see why Nick likes it." He scanned it again. "Papà would kill you if he saw this."

"I know. But he's not going to see it."

Jacopo approached. "Who are your visitors, Delfi?"

Cristo. She never should have told him about Nick, but then she'd never thought they'd meet. Would Jacopo give her away? She made the introductions, her heart jittering in her chest when she said Nick's name.

To his eternal credit, Jacopo said nothing obvious as he shook Nick's hand, though he mouthed *"molto bello"* at her when Nick and Cris were looking elsewhere. She couldn't help grinning at her friend. Nick certainly was *"molto bello"* worthy. *Very* worthy.

He was wearing the same suit he'd had on at her birthday party. It had been properly cleaned and pressed since then, and the cocoa brown shade brought out his coloring in a way that made her flash back to that night in the garden shed, to that afternoon in the olive grove.

And most of all to how he'd rejected her advances, how he'd said no to them having children after they married. Had she traded a horrible marriage for a hollow sham? Couldn't he see that she cared about him?

Nick Clarkston had gotten into her blood like a virus. The question was whether she'd ever recover.

"So let's see it," Jacopo said, putting out his hand for the sketch. Cris gave it to him and Jacopo beamed at her once he finished studying it. *"Cara,* I've got to show this to Enzo. He'll love it."

Her heart rate spiked. "Are you sure?"

Jacopo nodded. Signor Morelli came out of his office, his hat and coat on, clearly on his way home. "Enzo, you must see this," Jacopo trilled.

Does he have to be so loud? And so obviously in love with what I've done? Delfina felt the stab of every apprentice's gaze. She looked over at Ornella. The girl straightened up and pushed back her mass of golden brown curls, her face taut with anger as she tracked Signor Morelli's progress toward Delfina's desk.

Jacopo practically forced the sketch into Signor Morelli's hands. "What do you think of Delfi's design?" Jacopo was all nervous energy and smiles, like a boy who'd been told he was getting a puppy. What a good friend he was. Even if he was embarrassing her to death.

Signor Morelli pulled his glasses out of his pocket as Nick and Cris crowded around, dwarfing Signor Morelli and Jacopo. Every second of the wait was torture. She wanted to crawl under her desk and hide.

At last Signor Morelli perched his glasses on the end of his nose and peered at the sketch, a frown on his face. Her stomach sank. *Madonna. He hates it. He just doesn't want to say so.*

Cris butted in. "It's amazing, isn't it?"

She wanted to cuff him on the arm, but restrained herself. It wouldn't be professional. "Ignore him," she said.

"I know what I like, Delfi," Cris said. He turned to Signor Morelli and tapped the paper. "This should be on the runway, don't you think?"

Signor Morelli looked up at Cris. "You're Delfina's brother."

Cris stuck out his hand. "Cristoforo Andretti."

Signor Morelli took Cris's hand. "I see the resemblance now."

"So, what do you think?" Cris asked. "It's damn good, yes?"

Signor Morelli cleared his throat and nodded, then he smiled at Delfina. Her heart cartwheeled in her chest. "It *is* good. Stunning, in fact."

"So when will we see it on actual women?" Cris asked.

"Soon." He focused on Delfina. "I'd like to feature it in the spring show."

She blinked. Had she heard correctly? "You want it for the show?" Her voice came out in a barely audible squeak. She hardly noticed though. All she heard was the slam of a ruler on Ornella's desk and her muttered curse.

"Yes. Start working with Jacopo on the patterns."

Jacopo turned to her and said, "I told you so. You owe me lunch, *cara.*"

"Monday."

"It's a date."

Signor Morelli put his glasses away and said to Delfina, "I'd like to see it in black, burgundy, and white. And two other colors of your choice."

"How soon?"

"Two weeks. That will give us plenty of time to adjust it before the show."

"*Mille grazie, signore,*" she said as he walked to the door. Delfina felt light-headed, as if she might faint. She was going to have a design in the show!

The only sour spot was the glare on Ornella's face. If the girl could kill with a glance, Delfina would have been bleeding out.

Jacopo followed her gaze. "Ignore that one. She's always bitter. That's why Signor Morelli hasn't promoted her to second assistant."

She patted him on the arm. "You always know just what to say."

Which was when Nick cut in. "Time to go." He offered her his arm. Could he be jealous? He flashed an insincere grin at Jacopo. "Pardon me, mate."

Jacopo eyed Nick up and down, then raised his hands in surrender. "I see my Delfi has attracted a real he-man."

Nick shrugged as she took his arm. "No hard feelings."

Jacopo looked at Delfina, amusement written all over his features. She could imagine what kind of "hard feelings" he might harbor toward Nick, and the thought made her snicker.

"What?" Nick asked, his gaze darting from one of them to the other, Jacopo dissolving into laughter and pressing a fist to his mouth.

Cris rolled his eyes. "No idea. Come on, let's go."

"Just a minute," Jacopo said. "Delfi, come to the back with me. There's something I need to show you."

What was he talking about? Mystified, she grabbed her bag and followed him into the storeroom. "What's going on?" she asked.

"You're going out dancing, Delfi. We need to sex you up a bit." Jacopo removed the scarf from around her neck and undid her top three buttons. He stepped back to survey his work, then grabbed a seam ripper off the table. Before she realized what he was doing, he'd lengthened the slit in her skirt, raising it to mid-thigh.

"Hey! This skirt cost a fortune."

"No harm done. A few stitches, and it'll be good as new. I'll fix it myself."

"I feel like a slut."

"You look like a goddess. You want your he-man worshipping at your feet, yes?"

She did. Looking down at her exposed cleavage, she suppressed the urge to button back up. How would she have the courage to model that dress for Nick if she couldn't stand to show a little skin? Taking a big breath, she gave Jacopo a smile. "I hope this works."

"*Cara*, it'll work. Trust me. If there's anything I know, it's men."

She swiftly kissed him on the cheek. "See you Monday."

He shook his head. "We've got a ton to do, so I'll see you tomorrow at ten. Don't let those two run you ragged."

She couldn't wait. Getting a dress in the show was only the first of many small steps, but she was on her way to the top already. She could feel it in her bones.

Now if only she could sort things out with Nick. When it came to him, she felt anything but certain.

——————◆——————

Nick looked around Barfly and sighed. The flashing lights and the psychedelic décor—a whirl of purple, magenta, acid yellow, and lime green that looked like something Willy Wonka had chucked up—grated on his nerves, but anything was better than another night cooped up in the guest cottage.

And what was up with that Jacopo guy and Delfina? He was calling her "dear" and taking her to lunch? And she was kissing him on the fucking cheek? And then when she'd come back from the storeroom, her blouse was unbuttoned, her skirt had a slit he hadn't noticed—had Jacopo done that? Had he touched her?

Not that he had any right to object, but—*Don't go there, Clarkston. Don't.*

This just showed that he'd made the right choice when he'd turned her down. If she could move on from him so easily—

Stuff it. Right now.

He jammed his hands in his trouser pockets and scanned the club for Giovanna d'Imperio. He didn't see her anywhere, but then he heard her voice from above. Turning, he saw her hanging over the second-level railing, her generous breasts threatening to spill out of her skin-tight red dress. She waved at them. "Delfi, Cris, Nico! Come up!" She beckoned them upward with rapid flicks of her hand, as if a fire were licking at their heels.

Nick followed Cris and Delfina up the stairs, unable to stop admiring her bum and legs. Damn her. Why did she have to be so bloody captivating? She'd be the woman of his dreams—if there were such a creature—if she wasn't a mobster's daughter. And if she had a sincere bone in her body.

Clarkston, you pillock. She's a good girl trapped in bad circumstances.

Who would he have been with that upbringing? A spoiled rotten tosser, no doubt. And he'd probably think he was the next best thing to God. He might have even put Leandro d'Imperio to shame.

They reached the top of the stairs and headed toward Giovanna's table. When they got close, the girls gave each other a hug, and that's when Nick saw who Giovanna was sitting with. Antonio.

Fuck me. Antonio gave him a nod and Nick returned it. That would be the extent of their communication if he could help it. He didn't need any more of Antonio banging on about his father.

He took a seat between Cris and Delfina, which put Antonio and Gio on the far side of the table. Cris turned to say something to him, and that apparently was when Gio noticed the bandage on the left side of Cris's head. "Cris! *Dio mio!*" She popped out of her seat and hurried around the table, practically sitting in Cris's lap to inspect his injury. "Delfi told me you were hurt, but not like this." She stroked a hand over his curls, and Cris blushed and smiled, looking like a puppy about to roll over and show her its belly.

"It's nothing, really. Just a scratch."

"It certainly bled a lot," Antonio said. Then he grinned. "Don't forget to tell her about your concussion."

"A concussion! What happened?" This time she did settle onto Cris's left knee and leaned forward, giving both Nick and Cris an eyeful of her bountiful cleavage.

Cris didn't answer straight away; instead his gaze seemed locked on the view in front of him. Nick elbowed him and spoke. "He hit his head hard when he fell. Got knocked out. Gave me quite the scare."

Cris clapped Nick on the shoulder. "But my friend saved me."

"You did?" Giovanna gave Nick a slow bat of her false lashes. "Tell me all about it."

Nick smothered a chuckle with a cough. The girl was an incorrigible flirt. "Nothing to tell. I'm sure Cris would have done the same for me."

Gio slipped a hand around the back of Cris's neck and turned her attention to him. "Of course you would have."

Cris held her gaze and said, "You know me so well." Nick wanted to pat him on the back and say *Well done, mate. Didn't think you had it in you.*

She tucked her chin down and smiled. Nick suppressed another laugh. He really did like the girl. He hoped there was something genuine in the attention she was showering on Cris, because he recognized that look on his friend's face: Cris fancied her. Badly.

Nick glanced away from the show beside him and caught Delfina staring at him, but she seemed far away. "Still on top of the world?" he asked her, trying not to let his eyes stray to her breasts. But it was impossible. Fortunately, she wasn't looking at him that closely. God, she was amazing.

She shook her head. "Just thinking."

"About what?" He leaned in close, trying not to shout in her ear, but also wanting her to hear him. It was a tricky balance. He inhaled her fragrance, so sexy, so enticing.

"The night Cris was shot." She threaded her fingers together and he couldn't resist putting a hand over them.

"Let it go, Delfi. He's fine."

"But he might not have been."

He squeezed her hands, her bones feeling delicate, easily crushed. "Your brother is one lucky bloke."

She flashed her large dark eyes on him. Eyes he could get lost in. "He's lucky to have you."

He opened his mouth to say something self-deprecating and witty, when three dark-haired young men stopped beside the table. "Well, it *is* true," the tallest and oldest one said, glowering at Nick.

"Who are you?" Nick asked, putting an edge in his voice. Delfina clutched his forearm.

The guy smiled, but it wasn't the least bit affable. "Your cousin. Fedele Lucchesi." He motioned to the other two blokes with him. "And these are my brothers, Sandro and Matteo."

Matteo appeared to be around Cris's age, but Sandro appeared to be in his early to mid-twenties like Fedele, both of them broad in the shoulders and heavy with muscle.

The looks the Lucchesis gave him, Antonio, and Cris were anything but kind. In fact, they were downright murderous.

"Nick Clarkston," he found himself saying. "Should I be pleased to meet you?"

Fedele smirked, then let out a chuckle. "You remind me of your grandfather. Big balls." He cupped his crotch to illustrate. "But you don't want the Lucchesi name?"

"It's not mine, mate. Never was, never will be."

"You are certain of that?" Fedele motioned to Antonio with his thumb. "This one is all too eager to be a Lucchesi. But he never will be."

Antonio was on his feet in an instant, his chair hitting the floor with a crash, his hands balled into fists.

"*Basta!*" Delfina yelled, rising herself and leaning across the table.

Fedele's eyes flicked to her. "I don't take orders from Andretti trash."

Nick's blood pressure surged, rocketing him to his feet. "You heard her. That's enough."

"*I* decide when it's enough," Fedele said. "I also don't take orders from bastards"—his gaze darted to Antonio—"or motherless orphans with no names."

"I am your *capo di società*," Antonio hissed. "You will not disrespect me."

Fedele laughed and took a step toward him. "Aside from the bastard, *I'm* the closest thing Enrico Lucchesi has to a son. Remember your place."

Antonio's face flooded red and a vein pulsed at his temple. "Get out of my sight. Now."

"Gladly," Fedele said. "I don't want any of the Andretti stench to rub off on me."

Cris set Gio on her feet and rose. "Would you care to repeat that?"

Fedele's face hardened. "Your grandfather killed my father. You're lucky I'm in a good mood, *figlio di puttana*."

Before Nick could stop him, Cris threw a punch, his fist smashing into Fedele's jaw, knocking him back a few steps. The youngest, Matteo, had the common sense to grab hold of Fedele's arms as Nick did the same to Cris.

It was like trying to restrain a bull. Nick had eight years and a few inches on Cris, but Cris was built like a wrestler, solid muscle with a low center of gravity. "Come on, mate. He's not worth it," Nick said in Cris's ear.

Abruptly Cris stopped struggling. "You're right. He's not."

Fedele rubbed his jaw and shook his head, murderous eyes locked on Cris. "Next time we meet, I won't be so nice, Andretti." He spat at Cris's feet and turned, his brothers following him.

"Christ," Nick muttered. "What a fucked-up mess."

Cris clapped him on the back. "Imagine what it was like having your father married to our aunt. Would you care to guess what Natale—Christmas—was like every year while we were growing up?"

"Insufferable?"

They took their seats and the waitress came by and asked if they were okay and wanted drinks. They each ordered, then Cris said, "Usually my Aunt Toni came by herself, and no one would mention Zio Enrico in her presence. The times he did come, he and my grandfather circled each other like lions." He played with a napkin the waitress had left in front of him, then he leaned forward, catching Delfina's attention. "Remember how many stomachaches I had?"

She stared at the table. "I miss her."

After the waitress brought their drinks, Cris raised his glass in a toast. "To Aunt Toni. *Salute.*"

Nick felt strange toasting the woman his father had married instead of his mother, but it was obvious from the looks on Cris's, Delfina's, and Antonio's faces that she was well-loved. He raised his glass, though when he took a drink, it was hard to swallow past the lump in his throat. His mum would never have fit in here. She would have hated Italy, would have cried for her parents, would have refused to learn Italian. If his father had married her, she never would have been happy.

But at least she would have been alive.

He took a deep breath to tamp down his emotions. Their fun night out had certainly been anything but.

Giovanna let out a theatrical sigh and searched their faces. Then she threw up her hands. "Seriously, *ragazzi*. Are we going to let the entire evening be ruined?" She batted her eyelashes at the lot of them, then gestured to her clothes. "I did not put two hours into hair, makeup, and clothes to just *sit* here." She looked at Antonio, then Cris. "Which one of you is man enough to dance with my fabulousness?"

Nick couldn't help it. He cracked up at the stricken expression on Antonio's face, which Antonio tried to hide by taking another sip of his drink. Cris stood and extended a hand to her. "I'm your man."

She took his hand and sashayed around the table, ruffling Antonio's blond hair as she passed him. "You disappoint me, Adonis," she tossed over her shoulder.

Antonio slumped back in his seat. "*Grazie a Dio*," he muttered.

Delfina laughed. "She loves to take the starch out of you."

Antonio straightened and leaned forward. "I'd love to give her what she's asking for, but her father would have my head on a platter."

"She knows. You're just fun to tease."

Antonio turned to watch the dancers below and Nick followed his gaze to Gio and Cris. Cris surprised Nick again. His mate had moves.

"Well, I wish him luck," Antonio said. "He's going to need it." He addressed himself to Nick. "And so are you."

Nick pretended he hadn't heard, but when Delfina left the table to go to the loo, Antonio leaned forward and raised his voice, and Nick had to stop pretending. "I don't understand you. Let your father help. You don't know how worried he's been."

"I'm fine. I've worked things out with Dario."

Antonio raised a brow. "What do you mean?"

"It's none of your affair. Not now, not ever. You understand me, mate?"

Antonio shook his head, but said nothing further. Nick took another sip of his drink, his guts churning. If he had it all under control, why he did still feel sick?

———— ✦ ————

Delfina surprised Nick when she came back to the table. She didn't sit; instead she whispered in his ear, her voice a low purr. "Dance with me."

Tingles raced down his spine at the sound. "I'm not much of a dancer."

"I don't care." She tugged on his hand, urging him out of the chair.

Cor, she was determined. He rose and followed her down to the floor. Some crazy house number was playing, the beat too frenetic to follow. But Delfina seemed oblivious to both the song and the other couples; she wrapped her arms around his neck and nestled in close to him, as if they were about to slow dance. "What are you doing?" he said in her ear.

"Dancing." She pressed her breasts and thighs into him as she moved in a slow, languid flow, tugging and pushing at him so that he moved with her.

He slid his hands around her waist, resting them on her hips, enjoying the feel of her so close. God she was gorgeous, smiling up at him, her lips red as rubies, her eyes dark as night, her jasmine scent teasing his nose. Her high breasts rubbed against his chest, and he remembered how good they felt, how sweet they tasted. How many times had he wanted to have them in his hands again, in his mouth? He understood now why so many poets had waxed on and on about the women they'd adored. She was intoxicating.

If only she weren't the daughter of a mobster. If only...

But those were silly thoughts. Useless thoughts.

Except that his cock disagreed. His mind disagreed. He'd been thinking about her too much lately, almost obsessing, when he wasn't worried about getting shot. Did she think about him the same way? He almost laughed. They were going to be married, and he knew so little about her. They were going to be married, and he couldn't even ask her such a simple question. Because the possibilities were too frightening. How was he ever going to keep his distance from her?

Closing her eyes, she drew his head down to hers. At first he thought she was going to kiss him, but she didn't. Instead she said in his ear, "It's a shame you're not interested in me."

"Not interested?" He slid his hands down to her bum and crushed her against his aching cock. "Does that feel 'not interested' to you?"

"Then why did you turn me away the night Cris was shot?"

"Delfi, it's complicated."

"Did I do something wrong?"

He shook his head. "It's me."

She opened her eyes; they glistened with tears. "I don't understand."

How could she? He'd been lying to her about so many things. How he really felt about Interpol. His deal with Benedetto. How he felt about her. He had to try to be at least a little honest. "I can't let myself get carried away. It would be very easy to forget everything but you."

"Maybe you should." She held his eyes, the promise in them magnetic.

Maybe he should, just once. He bent down, bringing his lips to hers in a kiss that sent fire racing along his limbs. When she let out a moan, he deepened the kiss, invading her with his tongue. Damn it, he wanted her. He wanted her to be his. Always.

But they were not meant to be, not in any lasting sense. As long as he remained true to Interpol, he could never be true to her.

———— ◆ ————

It had been murder to leave Delfina's arms, but Nick had been forced to do it; he'd had to put some distance between them before he did something foolish. Breaking off their kiss, he'd insisted they return to the table, ostensibly to keep Antonio company.

Delfina had been hurt, and now she'd spent nearly an hour dancing with Antonio. Probably trying to make Nick jealous. Well it worked, but he couldn't let her know that. He had to keep his cool. He'd come dangerously close to telling her too much.

Just after one in the morning, they finally stumbled out of Barfly, Cris and Gio hand in hand, the rest of them following. *Thank God that was over.* How was he going to survive being married to Delfina when he could barely resist her for one lousy evening?

Gio beckoned Antonio to her. "I'm going back with them. It was sweet of you to bring me." She kissed his cheek. "*Ciao ciao!*" She waved at Antonio as he turned away.

The screech of tires attracted Nick's attention to the street, where a black SUV hurtled up the road toward them, gun barrels sticking out the driver's side windows. Adrenaline hit his system like a body blow, his heart slamming against his ribs, his breathing turning frantic. "Get down!" Nick yelled, just before the men in the SUV opened fire.

Fortunately the club had a smoking area outside with tables, chairs, and a low hedge that marked off the space. Nick grabbed Delfina and shoved her under a table.

Bullets slammed into the windows behind them, adding the crash of broken glass and the blare of the music inside to the roar of the guns and the SUV's engine.

Nick wasn't armed, of course, but Cris and Antonio had both pulled handguns and fired at the SUV's back end as it sped away. Poking his head out from under the table, Nick tried to get the license number, but he could make out only the first two numbers before it rounded the corner. He wasn't even sure of the vehicle's make. Some cop he was. He turned to Delfina, who was lying on her side under the table, arms over her head, eyes squeezed shut. She wasn't moving. Oh God. Had she been hit? He shook her hard. "Delfi!"

She opened her eyes and lowered her arms. "I'm all right," she said, an edge to her voice.

Nick almost asked her why she was angry, then he saw it: her hands were shaking. He pulled her out from under the table and put his arms around her. "They're gone," he murmured into her hair.

She clutched the lapels of his coat and buried her face in the crook of his neck. She trembled in his arms, but didn't cry. He stroked down her back to the ends of her thick dark hair, but didn't say anything.

Antonio, Cris, and Gio crowded around them. "Is she hurt?" Gio asked.

"No," Nick said. "Just rattled."

Delfina pulled out of his arms and accepted a hand up from Cris. One of her knees was skinned, but she seemed all right otherwise. Nick stood up, realizing he was going to be sore tomorrow from throwing himself so violently to the ground. "Anyone hurt?" he asked as Antonio and Cris holstered their guns.

People started pouring out of the club and sirens wailed in the distance. Cris nudged Antonio. "We should go."

"Who was shooting?" Nick asked Cris, his voice low. "The Russians or my cousins?"

Cris shrugged. "I don't know. Hell, I wouldn't rule out Leandro, except that I don't think he'd endanger his sister." He addressed Antonio. "Do the Lucchesis have a black Fiat Sedici?"

"Not that I know. But it could have been stolen."

Delfina poked Cris in the shoulder. "You shouldn't have punched Fedele."

"He shouldn't have insulted us." Focusing on Antonio, Cris said, "If you don't exercise your authority, you'll never gain their respect."

"All I'll get is their hate if I do."

"They don't have to love you. Just respect you. And if they can't respect you, they have to fear you." When Antonio nodded, Cris took Gio's arm. "Let's go."

A man in the crowd tried to stop them, saying they should wait for the police, but Antonio and Cris just stared at the man until he gave way, apparently recognizing belatedly what kind of men they were.

They hurried to their cars and drove off. Nick sat up front with Cris while the girls huddled in the back, Gio stroking Delfina's shoulder, none of them saying anything.

Nick let his head loll back on the head rest as Cris drove them home. On top of everyone else who wanted his head, did he have to add his cousins to the roll call of his enemies?

CHAPTER 14

Delfina and Jacopo worked feverishly on the dresses Saturday, developing the pattern for the first, then cutting it out by hand and pinning it to a mannequin, making adjustments as they went. Her knee was stiff from where she'd landed on it last night. She'd covered the bandage with black opaque tights so she wouldn't have to endure Jacopo's questions.

She was glad they had so much to do and that Jacopo was such a chatterbox. He'd saved her from having to say much. All she could think about was Nick, that toe-curling kiss he'd given her, the sadness in his eyes, in his voice. He did have feelings for her, and they ran deep. And that seemed to scare him. Maybe it should scare her as well, but it didn't. It thrilled her.

And made her miserable. She was marrying this man, and unless something drastic happened, it was going to be one big unhappy disaster.

By one o'clock, they'd cut out and assembled the black dress. It still needed to be stitched together, but a shiver of excitement went through Delfina as she looked at it. "Take a picture, *cara,*" Jacopo said. "Show your family."

"Brilliant idea!" Delfina snapped a photo with her phone. Her first official design.

Jacopo put an arm around her and kissed her on the cheek. "You're the brilliant one." He let out a sigh. "Someday your name will be in lights."

She smiled. "Someday."

"Well," he said, "I think that's enough for today. Go home and celebrate. We'll pick this up Monday. Have you decided on the other two colors?"

"I'm thinking silver and cobalt."

He nodded. "I like them both. Let's go through fabrics on Monday and see what we need to order."

She was flying high, singing along to the radio as she drove home. The future she'd always dreamed of was really happening. She'd been terrified last night, but today, with the sun out and the trees just starting to turn, she felt like nothing could hurt her. Not when she was so close to seeing her hopes realized. Anything was possible now. Somehow things would work out with Nick; she could feel it. They'd figure out a solution to their problems.

As she drove through the gates to the house, her stomach tightened, and her good mood vanished. If she didn't manage to change Nick's mind, he'd take the vows, and nothing good would come of that.

When she stepped inside the villa, she heard her father and Cris arguing in his study. "Why did you have to be so bloody stupid?" her father shouted.

What had Cris done now? She poked her head in the door and stopped dead when she saw a wooden crate covered with Cyrillic writing. The lid had been removed; it was a case of Russian vodka.

The crate was a message—the shooters hadn't been Nick's cousins.

Her father and Cris turned to her, both of them red in the face. Her first instinct was to defend Cris—after all, he'd only gotten involved with the Russians to try to help her. But telling her father the truth was Cris's decision to make, not hers. Instead she crossed the room to Cris and put a hand on his shoulder. "I'm sorry," she whispered. "Maybe you should...?"

He shook his head and addressed their father. "I think I know how stupid I've been."

Their father crossed his arms and stared at them. "What aren't the two of you telling me?"

Delfina tried to make her face as blank as possible. "About what?"

"The night Cris was shot."

"There's nothing more to tell," Cris said.

Papà's eyes moved back and forth as he studied them, searching for weakness. Finally he threw up his hands. "You both think you're adults, that you know everything now. But you don't." His voice was tight, hoarse. "Everything I've done, I've done to keep you safe. To keep this family safe. To make our lives better, more secure. And unless you both trust me to do my job, all of us will pay a terrible price."

The last time she'd seen her father upset like this was the morning after Cris had been shot. Whatever faults he had, he did love them, even if sometimes that love was hard to see. Even if sometimes his love threatened to drive them away.

She cleared her throat. "We understand, Papà."

"Make sure that you do. If we don't stand together, we will fall, and the vultures of this world will be only too happy to feast upon our corpses."

Delfina looked at Cris, suppressing a shudder. No doubt one of those vultures was Benedetto.

———◆———

Enrico's heart thumped against his ribs as he waited in Dario Andretti's front room for his son. He'd insisted on speaking to Nico before he signed the new will, and Dario couldn't very well refuse him.

They hadn't spoken since that horrible fight at Delfina's birthday party. He had no reason to think this discussion would go any more smoothly, but still a part of him hoped.

He glanced at the guards he'd brought—Ruggero, positioned by the door, and

Tommaso by the window. Both men were standing ramrod straight, their shoulders stiff with tension. Ruggero hadn't liked the idea of coming here. He'd wanted to bring Claudio and Santino as well. But Enrico had insisted they show good faith. Two guards were enough. Especially when they bristled with weapons. Dario hadn't insisted on frisking them; in fact, he'd acted as if this were an ordinary social call.

When they all knew it was anything but.

The doorknob turned, and the pounding in Enrico's chest turned painful. He looked up, expectant, his heart slowing slightly when Delfina stepped in. Was Nico refusing to see him?

Delfina smiled and came forward, lightly kissing him on the cheek. "Zio, it's good to see you."

He returned the smile, trying to be easy, but she saw through him. Patting his hand, she lowered her voice to a conspiratorial whisper. "Nick will be along in a minute. He's nervous too."

Nervous would be fine. Angry would not. But he had to make sure Nico knew he hadn't insisted on legally recognizing him; it wasn't even his idea. He'd spent his whole life denying himself the pleasure of raising Nico, of calling him son. All to keep him safe.

And now he had to acknowledge him for the same reason.

Dio mio, he wished now that he'd brought Kate with him. But he hadn't wanted to endanger her and their child too.

The door opened again, and this time, his son was there. His left eye had been blackened, a ring of greenish yellow bruising encircling it. Enrico rose involuntarily. "Who hit you?" he blurted.

"I'm all right," Nico said.

"What happened?"

Nico stepped inside and shut the door, putting his back against it as if he were thinking about the need to escape. "Dario found out that Delfina and I..." He trailed off and glanced at her.

"Oh," Enrico said, retaking his seat. *Dio,* could his son get into any more trouble?

Silence descended on them. Enrico had no idea what to say. He'd prepared a speech on the way over, but the words flew out of his head.

"What did you want to talk about?" Nico asked, his voice creaking like an old hinge.

"The change in my will, the recognition. I wanted you to know that it was not my idea—"

"So you *don't* want me after all."

"It is not that. I just wanted—"

"That's fine. Because I don't want it either."

Enrico's heart cracked in two. "You do not understand. I *do* want this—"

"No. You don't. You've never wanted me. And you don't want me now."

"Listen to me, I just did not want you to think—"

Nico stepped forward, thunder in his eyes, his hands clenched into fists. "Actions speak louder than words, especially with you. You're only doing this because Dario is forcing you to."

"That is not true." Enrico rose, stepping toward Nico. "I *always* wanted you. I wanted you to be my son. I was there, all the time, watching from a distance. I knew what football team you rooted for, I knew what subjects you excelled at, I knew what girls you chased. I was at your graduation from secondary school and at your graduation from Cambridge. I was there."

His son's eyes narrowed. "But you *weren't* there when I needed you most."

The pit in Enrico's stomach grew. It was time to admit what he never could before. "I was there, Nico. At her graveside. I did not know what I was going to do. And then you saw me—I saw the hope on your face—and I knew if I went to you that I would *have* to take you with me. So I left." His voice wavered on the words, his vision blurring. He hated what he'd done.

"It *was* you? I thought I'd imagined it." Nico rubbed his face, then shoved his hands in his pockets. "How could you leave me like that?"

"Carlo would have killed us both if he had known about you."

"You were a coward." The words sliced him like knives.

Delfina sprang to her feet. "He's telling the truth, Nick. Would you rather be dead?"

Nico stared at her, his chest heaving. "Sometimes I think so."

"Oh Nick." She stepped toward him and he retreated to the door. Nico studied the carpet for a moment, no one making a sound.

Enrico rose to leave. He'd ruined everything by coming here. "Nico, I am sorry. I failed you." He needed fresh air, needed to get out of this damn house. He needed anything other than more of his son's hatred and hurt.

Nico's raised hand and his low voice stopped him. "Wait." His son took a breath, then continued. "I was wrong. You didn't fail me when I needed you most. When I truly did."

"What do you mean?" A spark of hope flared in Enrico's chest.

Nico met his eyes. "You saved my grandparents. And you tried to rescue me." His gaze flickered to Ruggero, then returned to Enrico. "Had I taken your help, Cris wouldn't have been shot, and I wouldn't be in this mess today."

"I still failed you back then." Nico nodded, but didn't say anything. His heart pounding, Enrico asked, "Will you ever forgive me?"

Nico shrugged. "I don't know if I can. But I am grateful for what you've tried to do for me now."

So he hadn't entirely failed his son. "Even if it means you will have to take my name?"

Nico's jaw tightened. "I agreed to be recognized in your will, but I keep my mother's name."

Enrico turned from Nico to Delfina. "Certainly Dario will insist."

Nico, rather than Delfina, answered. "He tried. But he gave in. As long as I do everything else he wants."

A frisson ran down Enrico's back. He didn't like the sound of that. "What other things?"

"It's none of your business. I made the deal, I agreed to it, and it's done."

"Tell me."

Nico stepped away from the door, crossing his arms. "You've said your piece. Now go." His face settled into the stubborn cast worn by every Lucchesi male who'd ever refused a request. He looked just like Dom, just like Primo, just like Mario. Just like Rinaldo, his grandfather. All of them gone now.

Dio, *I beg you, don't let my boy end up among the dead.* Enrico glanced at Delfina as he rose, and she seemed just as worried as he felt. Perhaps she knew what his son had agreed to. He'd press her about it later. And then he'd do his best to intervene, even though Nico wouldn't thank him for that either.

Nico was not going to become the latest victim in the Andretti family's pursuit of vengeance. If anyone was going to pay that price, it would be Enrico himself.

Those sins were his alone to bear.

———— ♦ ————

Dario certainly didn't waste time. Barely four days had passed since they'd made their agreement, and despite Delfina's and his father's attempts to dissuade him, here Nick was, sitting in a nondescript Fiat outside an old warehouse in Milan's Rogoredo district with the ever-menacing Flavio and a driver Nick didn't know. Three cans of petrol were sitting in the boot, waiting for the spark from the box of matches Nick clutched in his jacket pocket.

"We go now," Flavio said, startling Nick. He'd never heard the man utter a word before. Flavio's voice was a low rumble seasoned with gravel. The man sounded like he ate boulders for breakfast.

Nick fumbled for the door latch, his fingers slick with sweat. He stepped out into the cold air and inhaled deep, trying to slow his racing pulse. At least Dario hadn't ordered him to kill someone.

What he was doing—arson—was still a major felony, though considering he'd already shot and killed three men, he shouldn't even be blinking at the thought of what he was about to do.

There had to be some catch. Maybe the warehouse wasn't Dario's? Nick chewed the inside of his lower lip as he and Flavio grabbed the cans and headed toward the warehouse. Yeah, that had to be it. A warning to someone who'd royally pissed off Dario.

They rounded a corner and stopped at a side door. The padlock had been cut through and lay on the ground. Someone else had already broken in. Setting down his cans, Nick grabbed Flavio's arm as the big man was about to open the door. He pointed out the broken lock. "Someone's in there."

Flavio glanced at the lock, then pushed the door open. "No worry."

If Flavio was surprised, he hid it well. Nick swallowed hard, his heart tapping his ribs. Something was definitely up. He gripped his two cans of petrol and followed Flavio inside. The driver was waiting in the car behind the wheel, ready to take off as soon as they'd completed the deed.

The interior was dark. Street lights dimly filtered through grimy glass windows, giving enough illumination for Nick to see orderly rows of pallets stacked twenty feet high all about them. This was definitely a well-used space, and between that and the broken lock, Nick felt certain that someone was going to be furious tomorrow. And most likely the owner wouldn't be able to file an insurance claim.

Flavio flicked on a torch, letting Nick see the labels on the pallets. Looked like a lot of clothing, shoes, and assorted designer leather goods. If the high-end labels were real, the merchandise in the warehouse would be worth millions. And if not, imitations would still be worth a small fortune. Someone had definitely gotten on Dario's bad side.

Using the light from the torch, Flavio gestured to the left. "There," he said. "Spread along wall, then we light from door."

Nick nodded and forced his feet to move. He hurried along the row of pallets, heading for the far wall. When he reached it, he unscrewed the cap on the first can, the pungent odor of petrol burning his sinuses. He splashed it along the wall, moving fast, being careful to avoid dripping any on his clothes or shoes. When the can was empty, he retraced his steps and opened the other one, coating the walls and the pallets back to the door where they'd entered.

He met Flavio at the entrance. The big man jerked his head at the partly open door and they stepped outside. Nick pulled the box of long wooden stove matches from his pocket. With trembling fingers, he dragged the match along the sandpaper strike zone. Too slow. The match failed to light. Flavio glared at him, disapproval on his face. Once again, Nick was proving to be a miserable Mafioso. He tapped another match from the box, then heard a muffled crash from within the warehouse. "What was that?"

Flavio shrugged and motioned for him to go on.

"Someone's in there."

"Rats."

Nick raised a brow. "Who is it?"

"No one. You hurry."

Fuck, fuck, fuck. This was a murder. It had to be. He threw the matches on the ground. "I'm not doing it."

Flavio raised his right hand, a Glock suddenly in it. For a big man, he moved damn fast. "Five seconds. *Capisci?*"

Nick went cold inside, his eyes fixed on the gun. *This is it, Clarkston. Save yourself, or sacrifice yourself for God knows who. Probably another gangster.*

For a moment, all Nick felt was the stuttering of his heart, then a pounding reached his ears. The flood of adrenaline was urging him to run, to move, to do something, anything, but stare at the barrel of that Glock. But his legs remained frozen, locked in place. *Run and die. Stay and fight—and die. Or do what he wants— what Dario wants—and live.*

Shaking inside, Nick retrieved the box of matches, surprised to see his hand so steady. He struck a match easily this time and tossed it in the doorway. With a soft *whoomp*, the interior lit up, and Flavio motioned him toward the car, pocketing the gun.

Nick's feet carried him to the little green Fiat, his arms tossed the cans in the boot, his hands closed the door behind him. *Coward, coward, coward...* The insult he'd hurled at his father came back to haunt him. Maybe Nick *was* a Lucchesi, in the worst possible way.

As they drove away from the scene, the driver keeping a controlled yet quick pace, Nick could think of only one thing: his father had been right to abandon him all those years ago.

Even among the Mafiosi, the world they lived in was known as the *malavita*. The bad life.

Nick's stomach curdled and he thrust his head out the open window, vomiting down the side of the car.

CHAPTER 15

Nick burst through the door of the guest cottage. He had to get away from Flavio, the Fiat, every reminder of what he'd done. The smell of petrol lingered in his nostrils. Damn, he must have dripped some on his shoes. He kicked them off and set them outside the door, then he tore off his coat and pulled his wool jumper over his head, dropping it on the tiled floor as he headed for the bath.

In the middle of unbuttoning his jeans, he heard a discreet cough. He turned and saw Delfina sitting on the sofa. Oh why hadn't he listened to her?

His throat clamped shut and he could say nothing. But his feelings must have shown on his face. She jumped up and rushed to him, pressing her slender length against his bare chest as she wrapped her arms about him. "What happened?" she whispered.

He shook his head, afraid to speak, and buried his face in her hair, taking in the scent of jasmine that clung to the strands. He clutched her to him, breathing hard, trying to choke back the tears that wanted to fall. He'd done something horrible, terrible, and he couldn't take it back. He'd made a selfish choice, and now he had to live with it.

Inhaling deeply of her perfume, he took several breaths, willing himself to settle down. He hated to admit it, but she felt so damn good in his arms. So right. Even though everything else was so wrong.

With a groan, he separated himself from her. He couldn't continue down that line of thinking. She didn't care for him the way he did—no, *could*—for her. He had to own up to that and move on. He'd marry her, and then he'd find a way to put enough distance between them that he wouldn't be tempted to believe differently.

She stepped back into his personal space, less than an inch separating them. He could feel the heat of her body radiating outward. She pressed her small, delicate hands flat against his chest and looked up at him. "You're shaking," she said. "What did he make you do?"

Nick wrapped his fingers around hers. "Someone was in the warehouse.

Someone who's now dead because of me."

Her eyes widened in distress. "Tell me everything. Exactly what happened."

He didn't want to, and his mouth tasted rancid. He let go of her hands and headed into the kitchen, drinking glass after glass of water at the sink. He was leaning against the counter when she came up behind him, pressing herself against his back, her slender arms wrapping around his waist. "Tell me, Nick."

He sighed and turned in her arms. He opened the tap again, then started to talk, keeping his voice a whisper. When he finished, she laid her head on his chest. "It's not your fault."

He snorted. "Weren't you listening? *I* lit the match. *I* threw it."

"With a gun to your head. What else were you supposed to do?"

"I'm an officer of the *law*, Delfina. That may not mean much to you, but it's been *everything* to me." His voice sounded raw, choked, and he wished he had more control. Jesus, he was a big girl's blouse, wasn't he? He wasn't cut out for this—not for field work, and certainly not for the *malavita*. At nineteen, Delfina's brother, Cris, had more balls for this than he did at twenty-seven. Had his father known, all those years ago, that he was too soft for this life?

"You still work for Interpol," she whispered, surprise in her voice. "You're not dirty at all."

He hadn't meant to let that slip, but part of him was relieved she knew. "And you're still a Mafia princess."

Her mouth twisted. "And you hate me for it."

He pulled a hand from her grasp and ran it through his hair. "I don't hate you, Delfina. I feel sorry for you."

She pulled back from him this time. "You do?"

"This life has corrupted you, warped you. And it's a damn shame."

She crossed her arms beneath her breasts. "I happen to think I'm a good person. Not corrupt or warped."

He might as well say it. "You're only interested in getting free of your father and pursuing your career. That's the whole reason you got mixed up with me—I was your ticket out of here. You don't care about me—not deeply anyway."

Her mouth dropped open for a second, then she tore into him. "That's not true. Didn't I try to warn you away from the start? And who introduced you to your father? Even you admitted he'd helped you and could've got you out of this mess. If it wasn't for me, you'd be alone in all this, and your grandparents might be dead." She whirled about and started for the front door, her heels clacking on the tiles.

"Damn it." He caught her before she reached the door and turned her around to face him. Holding her by the biceps, he stared into her eyes, not sure what he hoped to see. "What about that trick you pulled?"

She looked down. "That was a mistake. But you said you weren't the type to stick around, that you didn't have serious relationships, so I figured you wouldn't mind that much."

"I wouldn't *mind* you putting me and my grandparents in danger?"

She tore one of her arms free and struck him on the shoulder, tears filling her eyes. "Yes, it was selfish, but what else could I do? I had to get away from Leandro.

You at least have a father who cares what happens to you. Mine doesn't."

The bitterness in her voice struck him hard. He'd always felt the same way about his father. Perhaps he'd been wrong. Perhaps he'd been wrong about everything.

He pulled her tightly to him, wrapping his arms around her. Comforting her this time. "I'm sorry," he whispered.

"Is that an actual apology, or do you just pity me?"

"A little of both."

He felt her cheeks round into a smile. She punched him lightly on the back. "You are impossible."

"I try." A laugh bubbled up in his chest. He stepped back a little to see her. "So to be sure I've got this through my thick head: You genuinely feel something for me—and it's not *just* friendship?"

She held his gaze. "I think I've been trying to tell you that for a while."

He traced a finger along the arch of her brows, then down over a high cheekbone and along the line of her jaw until he reached her full lips. He held her eyes for a moment before leaning down and capturing those lips with his. She melted against him, her hands wrapping around the base of his skull, her fingers playing with the hair at the top of his neck.

A sigh of pleasure left her and slammed straight into his cock, hardening it instantly. He cupped her buttocks, grinding her against the ache between his legs. So good, so damn good, she felt. Just where he wanted her. When she tilted her pelvis, trying to put them in better contact, he lifted her up, and she wrapped her legs around his waist. *Christ.* The heat from her pussy radiated through his jeans. He wanted inside her, now.

But maybe she would want to wait?

He broke their kiss and nuzzled her ear. "This time, I want *everything*, Delfina. If now is not the time, say it. Because I'm not stopping again."

She shivered in his arms. "I want everything too."

"Right answer," he growled and headed for the bedroom, kicking the door shut behind them with his foot.

He carried her over to the king bed and laid her upon it, liking how she didn't take her eyes off his as he finally finished unbuttoning his jeans. He slipped them and his boxers off. Her gaze dropped to his waist and she gave him a wicked smile.

God he wanted that mouth on his cock. Maybe not tonight, but sometime soon. He took a deep breath, forcing himself to slow down, to remember this was all new for her. Her first time.

A curious feeling of pride filled him. She'd chosen him. Him out of all the blokes who'd doubtless approached her. He'd be her first.

Maybe even her only?

His heart beat faster. What had happened to the Nick Clarkston who didn't give a shit? The guy who always kept it casual?

He stepped toward her and she suddenly held a finger to her lips. The bugs. He'd forgotten in the rush of everything that had happened.

But he wanted to hear her, wanted to talk to her. An idea came to him. He crossed over to the dresser and flipped on the iPod he'd brought with him. It was his inseparable companion, and he'd bought some excellent travel speakers for it. He scrolled through his collection, settling on a mix of Roxy Music and Bryan Ferry he'd put together. Lush, atmospheric, romantic stuff no guy in his right mind would ever admit to liking, but Nick had always had a soft spot for it.

Yeah, he was a big girl's blouse all right.

He turned the music up and caught her eye. Was it just his imagination, or had she been admiring his arse? "Watching me, were you?" he asked, keeping his voice pitched low.

She blushed, roses staining her cheeks. His chest felt lighter than it had in weeks. "I'm not answering that."

He strode over to her and leaned in, forcing her to sprawl back on the bed, caged within his arms. He placed his lips near her ear. "Your blush told me everything. Every single naughty thought you were having."

"*Madonna,*" she muttered and braced her hands against his chest. "You're getting a swollen head."

He darted his tongue out and ran it along the edge of her ear. "Most certainly." He put a knee up on the bed and rubbed his cock along her thigh.

She laughed and pushed against him, but he didn't budge. "Time to get undressed," he whispered. Her hands went to the buttons that ran down the front of the silk blouse tucked into her skirt. She played with the top one.

"Now?" she asked, her voice lilting and playful.

"Now." He rumbled the word in her ear and she shivered. "Take it off. I want to see you. All of you."

——————— • • ———————

Delfina held Nick's eyes as she undid the first button of her blouse. Her heart pounded against her ribcage and her stomach did somersaults. He looked so feral, so intent. So... big, looming above her on the bed. The muscles in his arms and abdomen rippled and bunched as he shifted above her, studying her every move.

Dio, he was gorgeous. Those smoky green eyes, that wavy brown-red hair falling over his brow, those lush lashes that hid his gaze as his eyes flicked downward to watch her open her blouse. And that body. He was paler than the men she was familiar with—not as pale as most Englishmen, but lighter than the olive tones that she saw every day. He probably burned when he went to the beach.

Making quick work of the buttons, she pulled the blouse out of her skirt, then reached for the front clasp of her bra. She'd worn red, his favorite color, even though she'd had no intention, no hope, of having sex with him—at least not before the wedding.

That they were going to do so now seemed like nothing less than a minor miracle.

Then again, he probably wasn't thinking that far ahead. His hard cock grazed her thigh. He probably wasn't thinking at all.

He stopped her from undoing the bra. "Skirt first." He watched her slide the zipper down and then helped her wriggle out of it, the crepe fabric feathering over her skin, the sudden coolness reminding her how exposed she was. "Another pair of red knickers. How many do you own?"

Seven, ever since he'd said he liked them. "A few."

He ran a finger along the top edge of the silky panties, where they rode below her navel. Her breath caught at the touch. "How many is a few?"

She smiled. He'd have to find out later. She reached for the bra's clasp again, and again he stopped her. "I'll unwrap the rest of the package," he said, and a rush of liquid dampened the fabric between her legs. It was ridiculous how he could do that to her so easily. How he could make her feel so wicked.

He fanned a large hand over her left breast, his tapered fingers finding the peak of her nipple beneath the lace and expertly tweaking it. The sensation arced to her sex, making her even wetter. She let out a little moan that made him smile. Then he unhooked the clasp and bared her breasts to his gaze.

She knew he'd seen them before, but somehow this felt different. Maybe because he wasn't acting as if he did this every day. As if she were just another notch on his bedpost. No, he was making this special. For her.

Her throat went tight. He really did care.

Lowering his head, he took her right nipple in his mouth, his tongue soft as velvet. She cradled his face in her hands, closing her eyes, savoring the exquisite sensations he was evoking in her. He drew hard on the peak, then took it between his teeth, biting down just enough to send an overwhelming mix of pleasure and pain streaking through her. She gasped and arched, digging her fingers into his hair. "*Cristo*," she murmured.

He backed off and moved to the other one, repeating the process until she begged him to stop. Her nipples were throbbing, two points of heat and fire that seemed connected to her sex.

He lifted his head and grinned, then accepted the kiss she offered. This time she darted her tongue into his mouth, showing him how excited she was. How she was ready for him. For everything.

When he parted from her, he held her still for a moment, his eyes locked on hers, the look in them full of promise. And something she didn't dare put a name to.

Bending, he kissed and licked her neck, then worked his way to her navel, nuzzling and tasting every square centimeter on the way. She squirmed beneath him, eager for what came next, remembering the pleasure he'd given her in the olive grove.

He paused at her panties, blowing on the fabric, making her shiver. "You want this, don't you?" he asked, then planted a kiss on her inner thigh.

She blushed. Why did he insist on making her say it? "*Sì*."

He grinned, a flash of strong white teeth. "Don't be shy. Tell me what you want."

She rolled her eyes. Impossible. He was impossible, this man she—not yet. She couldn't think that way, not until he said it. Not until she knew he wouldn't be taking a bullet from her great-uncle's gun.

When she said nothing, he traced small circles along her inner thighs from her knees to her sex, but went no further. "Come on, Delfi, tell me."

"Why?" Her voice came out in a croak.

"Because I want to know."

"Because you want me to beg."

"That too."

She swatted at his head and he ducked. "I guess that means you're not in the mood." He started to rise, and she grabbed his wrist.

"Tease." He stared at her, unmoving, waiting for her to acquiesce. "Stay where you are," she said, her voice gone breathy. "Don't you dare leave me like this."

A self-satisfied smile curved his lips and his eyes half closed. "Not quite begging, but I like demanding too."

A thrill rolled through her. He was daring her to order him about. "Satisfy me," she whispered, her voice husky and raw.

Nick's cock thumped at the throaty undercurrent in her voice. The princess was coming down off her throne, joining him in the gutter.

"You had only to ask," he said lightly. He settled between her beautiful legs and blew on the scrap of red satin between them. He could smell her arousal, a heady, musky spice that somehow made him harder. His cock could punch through a door.

He peeled her panties down over her black curls, which had been neatly trimmed. Had she done that thinking of him? His pulse accelerated. Had he ever wanted a woman this much?

Hooking his fingers around the edges of the thong, he tore it off her. She shifted and let out a whimper, spiking his pulse even higher. Parting the glistening lips of her pussy, he flicked her clit with the tip of his tongue, just the barest touch, and she thrashed and shuddered beneath him. Cor, she was close. He'd barely touched her.

Backing off, wanting this to last, he circled that tender nub, then slipped first one, then another finger inside her, testing her, as he swept his thumb over her clit. She was so damn tight. He tried to add a third finger, but she flinched and tensed. He wanted her to be ready for him, but this didn't seem to be helping.

What could he do to get her to relax? He crawled back up her body and found her breasts again. Lightly squeezing them with his hands, he asked, "What do you call these?"

She gave him a puzzled look. "*Le tette.*"

Moving back down her body, he cupped her pussy with his hand. "And this?"

This time she smiled. "*La figa.*"

"Like the fig, the fruit?" When she nodded, he slipped a finger between the lips of her pussy and stroked her clit, eliciting a shudder from her. "And what's this?"

She blushed. "*Il grilletto.*"

"What does that mean?"

"The cricket."

He chuckled. "Because when it's touched, you make noise?"

She sat up, bracing herself with her hands behind her. The wry look on her face was exactly what he'd hoped for. "*Cazzo.*"

He smiled up at her. "I know what *that* means."

This time she snorted. "Of course you would. Every man wants to know what to call the thing between his legs."

"It *was* one of the first words I looked up."

Shaking her head, she laughed hard, and lay back on her elbows. "You *are* impossible."

"I aim to please." He settled back between her legs. "I'm going to make your little *grilletto* play some music."

She let out a groan. "You are awful, yes?"

"Yes," he murmured, then parted her lips and latched on to her clit, sucking it into his mouth and making her moan. Swirling his tongue, he concentrated on her pleasure. He wanted her first time to be amazing, perfect. Fun.

Her thighs quivered with each draw on that tender spot, and when he slipped two fingers inside her, she was wetter than before, a little less tight. Maybe if she came, she'd relax completely.

Moving his fingers in and out, he focused on her little *grilletto*, lavishing it with attention, making her thrash and moan until she shuddered and clamped her hands on his head, crying out loudly. No doubt *that* could be heard above the music. Hopefully her father wasn't listening in real time, or he'd come barreling through that door.

Delfina lay back panting. *Dio mio,* she'd never had an orgasm like that. Not even the last time with Nick. She'd felt like she was coming out of her skin.

He climbed up beside her, his hard cock pressing into her thigh. *Dio*, what if he wanted her to reciprocate? She hadn't the faintest idea what to do. Her pulse beating fast, she reached down and touched him. "Would you like me to...?" Her mouth dried up and she couldn't say the words.

Wrapping his fingers around hers, he said, "I'd love it."

Biting her lower lip, she looked into his eyes. "I'm not sure how."

"Almost anything you do will feel good. Just don't bite."

That made her laugh, and she took a deep breath. She eased down to his waist, getting her first close-up view of him. She'd pleased him before with her hands, so she'd start there.

Wrapping a hand around his shaft, she stroked up and down, then tentatively swiped her tongue across the head of his *cazzo*. When he let out a moan, she repeated the action, this time running her tongue all around him, as if she were licking an ice cream cone. Since he seemed to enjoy that too, she took the tip of him in her mouth, rolling her tongue around and around, enjoying the way he sucked in air and shivered. "Good?" she asked.

"You're bloody brilliant. Keep doing what you're doing."

Emboldened, she sucked the tip of him into her mouth, remembering what he'd done to her *grilletto*, and he grabbed hold of her wrist. "Harder," he grunted. "Deeper."

Widening her mouth, she took him in as far as she could stand, then swirled her tongue around him in a crisscrossing motion as she moved back up to the head. His grip on her wrist tightened. "Christ," he groaned. "Stop."

She released him and looked up. "Did I hurt you?"

He blew out a breath and shook his head, giving her a lazy grin. "Not at all. But I can't take too much right now. I've been thinking about this for too long, and having it actually happen... It's shot my control all to hell."

He rose off the bed and dug around in his dresser, then came back with a foil packet in his hand. She watched him roll the condom on, her heart dancing in her chest. It was finally going to happen. After this, she'd be a woman in every sense of the word. No longer a girl. No longer an innocent.

And perhaps, no longer alone.

He lay down beside her, running his fingers over the hills and valleys of her body until his hand came to rest between her legs, his palm pressing on her still swollen flesh. He flexed his hand, sending aftershocks through her. She sat up and grabbed his wrist. "*Per favore,*" she whispered.

"Stop or continue?"

Despite everything they'd done, an emptiness, an ache, remained between her legs. "More."

"Ah Delfina, you are the woman of my heart," he murmured as he rolled over her.

What did that mean? Was he saying he loved her? Or just that he loved that she wanted him? Damn him for being so damn confusing!

He drew her legs up, wrapping them around his waist. "This is going to hurt a bit, love. Can't be helped. Stop me if it's too much."

She tensed. The blunt head of his *cazzo* nudged her entrance, then he surged into her in one stroke. The pain was sharp and she inhaled harshly.

"Okay?" He lay still over her. All she could feel was the length of his cock, the pain giving the illusion that he was throbbing inside her like a second heartbeat.

She nodded. "Go on," she whispered and relaxed her hold on his shoulders.

"*So* demanding," he teased as he shifted his weight.

She cuffed him on the shoulder, wincing a little as he moved, but the pain was starting to fade. He reached down between them, found her clit, and rubbed it with his thumb. Oh yes, the pain was fading fast.

When she widened her legs and slid her hands down to his firm buttocks, pulling him closer, he responded with a growl and sped up his strokes, occasionally slowing to add a swivel of his hips that made her moan. Before she knew it, he was pounding into her, each stroke exquisite torture, his thumb on her *grilletto* taking her higher and higher until she came again. He stiffened moments later, his body going rigid as he joined her.

Panting, he rolled to the side, but came up on his elbow and slung an arm over her breasts. He kissed her cheek, her lips, her neck. "I adore you," he whispered. Then he lay back.

"I love you," she blurted. *Madonna!* Had she said that aloud?

He said nothing for a moment, then he chuckled. "Delfi, don't be silly. Let's stick to the plan."

Let's stick to the plan? Her stomach rolled. She was an idiot. "Shouldn't I at least pretend to love you?"

He laughed this time and rolled over her again. Stroking the hair off her face, he studied the blush that colored her cheeks and neck and that deepened with every second of his scrutiny. Finally she could take the embarrassment no longer and tried to push him off. "You don't have to laugh at me," she huffed, hating how close to tears she sounded.

He held her still. "I'm not. I'm happy."

She froze. "Happy?"

"Yeah." He kissed her, the softest, tenderest, kiss he'd ever given her.

A lump filled her throat. He loved her, but he couldn't say it. And she knew why. Her voice came out strangled. "Even after how selfish I've been?"

"You were desperate. I've been there myself. Made a few bad decisions too."

Tears pricked her eyes, and she took a deep breath to hold them back. He might not be able to say he loved her aloud—not yet—but at least he'd forgiven her. That was something. "Those decisions led you here."

He smiled again, though it was wistful. "Yeah. I just hope I don't eat a bullet because of them."

Maybe *now* he'd understand. She pitched her voice even lower. "It's not just Benedetto you have to worry about. You *can't* take the vows, Nick. If you do, who knows what else my father will make you do? And if you refuse to do what he says, he'll put a bullet in you before my great-uncle does." Besides, she didn't want to marry an 'Ndranghetista. That wasn't in her plans. Not that she'd planned to marry an Interpol agent either. But perhaps he'd see reason and give up his quest. Just pretend he knew nothing about the Lucchesis and the Andrettis.

"I have to. If I'm going to do my job, I have to."

"What do mean 'if I'm going to do my job?'"

"I came here with a mission. I'm going to complete it."

What was wrong with him? She'd never met anyone so willfully, pigheadedly stubborn. "Has it occurred to you that 'doing your job' means arresting members of my family? *Your* family? Could you really put your father in jail?"

"Delfi, I admit he's got his good points, but he's still a gangster."

"What about my father? What about Cris? Would you put him in jail too?" He looked away and didn't answer, chilling her. Maybe he wasn't after only his father. "Nick, tell me what you'd be willing to do."

He looked at her then, his voice a furious whisper. "Delfi, this is who I *am*. I've never lied to you about it. How many more murders am I supposed to let them commit?"

"You *did* lie to me. You told me you were a dirty agent. And you're not."

He rubbed his chin, not looking at her. "Yeah. I lied about that."

Part of her was secretly happy he wasn't dirty like everyone else in her life. But if he wasn't dirty, he had a job to do. A job that endangered everyone she knew, everyone she loved. "Let's just walk away. Run off and get married. Your father would help us. He'd set us up somewhere. And my father would eventually get over it."

"Would he? What about Benedetto?"

"If we're gone, he might not consider you a threat."

"Running away like that—it feels like cowardice to me."

"It feels like practicality to me."

"I can't do it."

"If you take those vows, Nick, if you arrest my family, I'll never forgive you."

"And I'll never forgive myself if I don't." He slapped his hand against the mattress, and when he spoke his voice sounded rough, shredded. "I killed someone tonight. I have to make up for that somehow."

"If you put my father in jail, you'd be putting Cris there too."

"He's young; he'd probably get a suspended sentence if he turned witness for the state."

"So you'd have him hiding and on the run for the rest of his life? And what about us?"

"We'd go into protection too. It's not ideal, but—"

"But what? You think I want to trade one prison for another? At least in this one I have a little freedom. And I get to keep my own name." Pushing up on her elbows, she forced him to roll over. She scrambled out from under him, her skin burning with anger. Bloody idiots, the both of them. He was impossible, and she was foolish for thinking he'd ever see reason. "You made a decision, Nick. That's not murder. You chose to save your life. And now you're going to throw it away. Don't expect me to stand by and do nothing."

Her chest aching, Delfina dressed hurriedly while he watched her, saying nothing. The soaring sounds of "Slave to Love" came on, one of her favorite songs, and her throat jammed up. But the storm wasn't breaking like in the song. It was building. She loved Nick, but she wasn't going to end up his helpless slave.

She was going to save herself and her family. And hopefully Nick as well, even though he wouldn't thank her for it.

No, he'd probably hate her to death.

CHAPTER 16

Nick hadn't been able to sleep since Delfina left. He loved her. He knew it now. And yet he hadn't been able to say it. Even after she had. He'd laughed at her instead. Laughed! And acted oh so cool, so casual. Oh, he'd edged around how he felt, he'd given her a hint or two, but the plain truth was this: the idea of pouring his heart into words scared him shitless in a way that nothing else did. The question was why. Why couldn't he bloody *say* it?

He'd never let himself fall in love before. Never let himself spend more than a night, maybe a weekend, with a girl. Never let himself feel any more than lust, any more than a glimmer of affection. Like what you might feel for someone you'd just met and got on with, but weren't sure yet that you'd be mates, because that kind of trust, that kind of connection, took time. Time that he'd never spent with a girl for fear of those feelings deepening, taking on weight. And here he'd gone and gotten tangled up in Delfina's life. And she'd gotten tangled up in his. The thought of losing her, of going back to his old life, appealed less than having his fingernails ripped off with pliers. Which was probably what Benedetto had planned for him. At the least.

But Nick wouldn't care. Because if he couldn't have Delfina, nothing else would matter.

Oh he was fucked now. Bloody, royally, *fucked*.

He'd spent the rest of the night pacing around the cottage, her final words echoing in his head. What was she planning to do? It wasn't like he'd given her any good options.

No, he was forcing her to choose—him, and his pathetic inability to say three lousy words, not to mention the very real possibility he could get her killed—or her family. It was one hell of an awful choice.

He was an utter prick. He'd do his best for Cris, recommend leniency given his age. That was the least he could do.

And what about his own father? Clearly he wasn't all bad. Then again, maybe he was just trying to get on Nick's good side. To make him think he wasn't a horrible person.

Did a few kindnesses wipe away everything else his father had done?

And yet—what other choice had the man had? He'd tried to spare Nick from this life, from these decisions, from the wretched snarl Nick had embroiled himself in.

His father had tried. The failure was all on Nick.

And now he was making a real dog's breakfast of things. The only way to recoup anything, the only way to redeem anything he'd done, was to plow forward. Stick to the plan and take them down. Strike a blow for justice.

But what was he going to do about Delfina?

She'd made it clear she didn't want the life he could offer her. And who could blame her? It wasn't much of one.

The only solution was to divorce her when he had enough evidence to make arrests. Set her free. That was the only reasonable thing to do.

Never mind that letting her go was going to kill him. He'd have plenty of time in protective custody to lick his wounds. He probably wouldn't even have the job to distract him. Delfina was right; Interpol would most likely kick him out, and he'd end up with some dull position teaching computer skills under an assumed name in some tiny village in the back of beyond.

But if he lost his post with Interpol, so be it. He couldn't let his father and Dario and Benedetto get away with what they'd done. No matter the cost to him. He'd known going into this that the sacrifice could be high, that he might not survive. What the hell kind of man would he be if he backed down now?

He'd just stepped out of the shower and was only half dressed when he heard a series of rapid knocks on the front door. He threw on an oxford shirt and opened the door, the shirt still unbuttoned. Delfina. Her face was white, and her hands, clutching a copy of *La Repubblica*, trembled. "What is it?" he asked.

She brushed past him and flattened the newspaper on the kitchen table, stabbing a finger at an article on the front page. His Italian was good enough to translate the headline: "Warehouse Fire; One Dead."

He started reading, but kept stumbling over the words. No point, when he had a perfectly fine translator right in front of him. "Tell me what it says." He pushed the paper at her.

"The warehouse belonged to your father."

An icy shockwave flooded Nick's body. Had his father been inside? "It wasn't—"

She cut him off, anticipating his question. "The man who died—he was Fedele Lucchesi."

Nick's gut spasmed, as if he were about to vomit again. *Ah Jesus.* Sure his cousin was a prick, but he was—he'd *been*—part of Nick's dwindling family. "What the hell is your father playing at?"

"I don't know. I don't think he means to go through with the wedding."

A nasty thought shot into his brain. "Do you think he's turning me over to Benedetto?"

She shrugged. "I have no idea. But I don't like this." She touched his arm. "You have to tell your father what happened. He has to know."

"And then what? What's he going to do?"

"He'll think of something."

Something that would wreck his plans. "No. We have to pretend we don't know anything about this."

"We won't be the only ones pretending."

"What do you mean?"

"Papà told me this morning that he's hosting our engagement party in three days."

"Then why antagonize my father?"

She rubbed a hand down his arm. "Nothing makes sense, I agree."

"I've got to confront Dario about this."

"What you need to do is talk to your father."

His head hurt. Maybe she was right. Something bad was brewing, and he wanted her far away from it. Maybe it was time to use that mobile phone Ruggero had given him. He turned to her. "Can you talk to Cris, see what he knows?"

She bit her lip and nodded. "But I'm not going to tell him our suspicions. In case." Her eyes welled, and Nick pulled her into his arms.

"I know you love him."

"I hate hiding things from him. He's my brother. He's always been there for me."

"He loves you, Delfi."

"I know. But he loves Papà too. And he's taken the vows. He's not going to turn his back on that."

"He might surprise you."

She wiped her cheeks and looked at him. "He might. But maybe not the way I'd like."

———◆———

Her heart tripping in her chest, Delfina pulled herself together and headed to Cris's room. What if he'd condoned Fedele's murder? How would she ever look him in the eye again, knowing he could be so cruel to Nick?

When she stepped inside Cris's room, he was sitting in a chair by the window, reading a book on... economics? "Since when do you read anything but car magazines?"

"Antonio recommended it. Apparently our uncle is pushing an education on him, wants him to attend university."

"Are you thinking of going?"

Cris wrinkled his nose. "You know me. I'm not much of a scholar." He tapped the cover of the book. "Though I have to admit this book has opened my eyes to some things I'd never given thought to."

"Such as?"

"You know how Papà and Nonno Carlo always used to talk down anything Zio Enrico did? How he's not a real Mafioso?" He continued before she could nod. "Well, they're right. Zio Enrico is a businessman in a way they're not." He set the book on the windowsill. "I think he *sees* more than they do. He's not a true 'Ndranghetista."

"You think he's clever."

Cris smiled. "In some ways. Not in others. He's too reluctant to fight."

"And some are too ready." She sat on the edge of the bed and tried to draw a full breath, but her chest was so tight. Cris wasn't going to like this turn in the conversation. "Do you know what Papà made Nick do?"

"Warehouse job."

"Fedele Lucchesi died in that fire."

Cris's eyes widened, then narrowed. "He didn't tell me that."

Delfina let out a breath. *Grazie a Dio.* He hadn't known. But that meant he didn't know Papà's plans either. And that wasn't good.

Shaking his head, Cris murmured, as if to himself, "What's he up to?"

"I have no idea. The engagement party is in three days."

"Does Nick know who he killed?" Cris asked, focusing on her again.

"He does now."

"I don't like this."

The tightness on her brother's face was a kick in the gut. *I don't like it either.* "Imagine how Nick feels."

Cris glanced away, his gaze settling on the book. He'd probably rather be reading it than hearing that Papà had kept the full truth from him. She waited, balling her hands into fists in her lap as the muscles in Cris's jaw jumped. Finally he said, "I shouldn't tell you this, but the initiation ceremony is today."

Delfina's stomach flipped over. "When?"

Cris checked his watch. "One hour. Flavio should be getting Nick right now."

"Where is it happening?"

"I can't tell you that." Then why had he told her anything? *Because he's angry.*

"Are you going?"

"Of course. I'm going to be his sponsor. I have to coach him. I'll be doing that during the drive." Someone knocked on the door. "That'll be Flavio." He started to rise from the chair.

"Cris." His eyes snapped to hers, the look in them as sharp as her voice. "Nick can't do this."

"He has to. You know Papà won't trust him without it."

"He'll never trust Nick, regardless. If he did, he would have told him what he was going to do last night."

Cris shrugged. "Papà doesn't have to explain his every move to subordinates."

"And what about you? You're his second. Shouldn't *you* know what he's thinking?"

The knock on the door was louder this time. Flavio's voice rumbled through the door. "Don Cristoforo, we have to leave."

"Coming!" Cris called, his irritation plain. He rose from the chair without answering her and headed toward the door.

Delfina caught his sleeve as he passed her. "Well?"

"I'm sure he'll tell me when he's ready."

"That wouldn't be good enough for me if I was in your position."

He roughly disengaged her hand from his arm. "It's not your problem." He bit off the words, as if each one pained him.

"This is my family too."

"Delfi, this is a *cosca* matter."

He turned away again, and she grabbed his wrist, digging her fingers in this time. Could she still get through to him? "Don't let the 'Ndrangheta strip away everything I love about you."

He stayed rigid for a second, the muscles of his arm tight beneath her hand, then he sighed, his shoulders relaxing. "I'm still me. Nothing's changed." He leaned down and kissed her cheek.

She stared up into his soft brown eyes as he straightened, hating what she had to say. "The brother I love isn't heartless. Or a blind follower."

Cris's face darkened, and for a second, she glimpsed the man behind the boy. "I am neither of those things. There is blindness and there is obedience. I know the difference." He turned and left the room, not stopping even when she apologized.

She'd been right; Cris planned to walk with their father. No matter what path they took. No matter how cruel the means of their passage.

Cris wouldn't help Nick, but that didn't mean she could do nothing. She jumped up and hurried down the hall, grabbing her handbag and keys. Nick was not going through with the ceremony. She'd make certain of it.

———— ◆ ————

Nick's stomach splatted on the tiles when someone pounded on the door as he was turning on the mobile Ruggero had given him. He stuffed the phone back in its hiding place, then answered the door, his insides not feeling any better when he saw Flavio. It took him a moment to recognize that Flavio's lopsided grimace was an attempt at a smile, and that his heavily accented words meant that Nick was going to be inducted into the 'Ndrangheta instead of introduced to a six-foot-deep hole in the ground.

Unless Flavio was a master prankster. But having a laugh didn't seem to be part of Flavio's repertoire of personality traits.

Nick grabbed a suit jacket and followed Flavio to the main house and waited in a Mercedes limousine while the big man retrieved "Don Cristoforo." He still couldn't imagine Cris as *capo di società*. Cris, with his easy smile, his wavy brown curls, and the traces of baby fat lingering on his cheeks.

Had Cris known that Nick was being sent to that warehouse to kill his cousin?

Nick's hands formed into fists when Cris climbed in the back of the car and sat next to Nick. Flavio took the seat beside the driver.

With a meaningful glare at the two up front, Nick said, "Can we talk privately?"

As the car pulled away from the house, Cris gave him a questioning look and pressed a button to raise the partition between the front and the back. "What is it?"

"Did you know what was going to happen last night?" A frown creased Cris's face, then he shook his head. "That surprises me."

One corner of Cris's mouth turned up. "It surprises me too."

"When did you find out?"

"Just now. My sister is a fount of information. As well as a nuisance." Cris said the words affectionately, but with a hint of genuine frustration.

Nick knew exactly how he felt. "So you don't know what your father is up to?"

"I'm sure he'll tell me." Cris patted Nick's shoulder. "I'm sorry about your cousin."

"What the hell do I say to my father the next time I see him?"

Cris's eyes narrowed, turned to lasers. "Not a damn thing. You know that."

Nick sighed. "This is fucking impossible, you know."

"I know no such thing. This is how things *are*. So far you've been sheltered from some of the less pleasant realities of life, but you're getting an education now. Bottom line—this is a business, and we are always ready to protect it. By all means necessary."

"But this doesn't make sense! Why kill the nephew of the man you're trying to ally with?"

"There must be a good reason. Papà never orders a death without one. Deaths attract attention."

"My father isn't stupid. He'll know who did this."

Cris raised a brow. "Will he?" His tone was crisp.

For a second, Nick didn't catch Cris's implication. "Don't worry. I'm not going to tell him." That much was true, for now. Most likely, Delfina would beat him to it.

Cris relaxed, the challenge ebbing from his face. He pulled a paracetamol bottle from his pocket and tapped a pill into his palm. Then he took it along with a swig from a bottle of water in the bar fridge. He tipped his head back against the leather seat and closed his eyes.

"You sure you're okay?"

"I'm fine. It's just a headache. The doctor said I might have them for a bit."

"Why didn't you stay home? Surely you don't need to be at the ceremony."

Cris turned his head on the seat and looked at Nick. "I'm your sponsor. And I wanted to make you an offer. Something special to acknowledge the debt I owe you."

"An offer I can't refuse?" Nick joked.

"You can refuse it. But I hope you won't."

A herd of elephants stampeded through Nick's stomach. Thank God he hadn't eaten. "What is it?"

"I'd like us to become *fratelli di sangue*. Blood brothers."

"You mean like when kids cut their thumbs and swear to be best mates forever?"

A smile flitted across Cris's face. "It is much more than that. The blood bond is the most sacred vow two men of honor can make to each other. A man cannot betray a blood brother. Such a thing is unthinkable. It is worse than betraying your kin."

"Why?" Nick's voice was hoarse.

"Because you have chosen this brother. A man who would betray a blood brother has no honor and cannot be trusted."

Fuck, fuck, and hell-fucking-no. Nick searched Cris's face for any trace of guile or ulterior motives. All he saw there was earnest friendship.

It was one thing to betray the 'Ndrangheta. Another to betray Cris so completely.

He'd never understand or forgive it. But what other choice did Nick have?

He could refuse. But what reason could he give that wouldn't point to his intention to deceive? He pasted a smile on his face. "I'm utterly gobsmacked that you'd do this for me."

"So that's a yes?"

He was going to hell for sure. "Of course." In a flaming fucking handbasket. Why the bloody hell had he ever thought he could do this?

Sometimes having a conscience was a damned liability. A handicap. What he wouldn't give right now to not give a shit about anyone.

Except Delfina. God help him. Why, of all the women on the planet, did he have to fall in love with her? Why, why, *why* did she have to be part of a family he had to destroy?

Cris grinned and gave Nick's hand a hard squeeze. "You are a true friend."

Nick forced himself to return the squeeze, the open grin. A true friend he was not. But he swore to God he'd do what he could for Cris, though it would never be enough.

Next to killing his cousin, betraying Cris would be the worst sin he'd ever committed.

CHAPTER 17

Delfina followed the Mercedes at a discreet distance, careful to keep a car or two between them. So far, so good as they wound around the lake and headed into Cernobbio. The only problem would be if the Mercedes entered the hills above Lake Como, where traffic was much sparser. In that case, she'd have to stay back and pray she didn't lose them.

She reached into her bag, her fingers easily finding her phone. She flicked through her list of contacts, looking for Antonio. She was under no illusions; her father was probably tapping her phone, especially after the whole incident with Cris getting shot. No other choice.

Antonio answered after a couple rings as she clicked her fingernails on the steering wheel. "Delfi, my goddess."

She almost laughed from nerves. "I don't have a lot of time to explain. Nick is being inducted into the *cosca*. I need Zio Enrico to stop it."

Antonio swore. "Tell me you're joking."

"I wish I was."

"Where?"

"I don't know. I'm following the car he's in, but they've just turned up into the hills above Cernobbio. It's going to get harder to follow them without being spotted."

"Which direction?"

"They're headed northeast on Via Bisbino."

"Does your family own any property around there?"

"Not that I know of."

Antonio swore again. "Let me get Don Enrico."

She looked for the Mercedes. *Porca miseria,* she'd lost sight of them! She pressed the accelerator, her pulse racing along with the car. She hated driving so fast on these twisting mountain roads, but she didn't have much choice. How long could she follow them before they caught on? *Grazie a Dio* that she'd asked Papà for a silver Alfa Romeo instead of a red one.

She rounded a curve and caught a glimpse of the black Mercedes as it started into the bend ahead. Her breathing eased, but she didn't know how much longer she could pull this off.

Antonio came back. "I'm putting him on the line."

"You're still headed northeast?" Her uncle's deep voice made her feel better.

"No. We've curved around southwest."

"There's an old Roman ruin off Via Bisbino. You'll come to two forks; take the southern one each time. The turnoff is a dirt road that doesn't have a name. That may be where they're going."

She brightened. "I remember Cris said his ceremony was done outdoors."

"Then that's probably it. I'm on my way. Be careful."

"You too." She hesitated, then said, "I heard about the fire. I'm sorry."

"*Grazie.*"

"Zio?" Blood rushed in her ears.

"*Sì?*"

"Nick did it."

"What are you saying?"

"My father forced him to set the fire."

Silence filled the line. Finally he spoke again. "I'm going to strangle him."

"Nick?"

"Your father."

Her heart seized up. "I shouldn't have told you."

"Don't worry about it. I'm sure your father would have told me sooner or later."

"He still means to go through with the wedding. I think."

"I find that hard to believe."

"He told me about the engagement party this morning."

Her uncle sighed. "All theater, I'm sure."

She'd already said it, but it bore repeating. Her throat tightened on the words. "Be careful, Zio."

"I always am." The line went dead.

She dropped the phone in her bag, concentrating on the road. The Mercedes was still ahead of her, carrying the two people she loved most in the world.

Had she done the right thing? Or had she just killed them all?

---◆---

The limousine turned onto a dirt road nearly hidden by trees. Nick's heart sped up as they bounced along the pothole-filled road. Everything he'd been told, right down to Cris's offer, might be all an elaborate misdirection, a way of keeping him calm and cooperative until the trap was sprung.

After a quarter mile or so, they rounded a bend and slowed, picking their way between cars parked along both sides of the road. He counted at least a couple dozen vehicles. His heartbeat slowed. This was going to be a gathering, not an execution.

Unless it was going to be like that scene in the "The Untouchables" where Al

Capone uses a baseball bat to kill a guy during the meeting of the bosses.

But that was just fiction. Wasn't it?

Eventually they reached a point where the trees thinned out and the road ended at a small clearing. As they exited the car, Nick gulped down a lungful of crisp air scented by the cypress and umbrella pines in the surrounding forest. If this were going to be his last day, it was a damn nice one. Not a cloud in the blue sky above, though there was a slight chill in the air and fallen leaves crunched underfoot as they headed toward the clearing and the remnants of an old stone temple. A base, a few crumbling stairs, and some chipped columns were all that remained.

At the top of those stairs stood Dario. A table in front of him held a large white ceramic bowl surrounded by lit candles, a stack of thick pasteboard cards beside it. When they drew closer, Nick saw the picture on the top card; it was a reproduction of an old painting. He didn't recognize the woman depicted, but the halo made clear she was a holy figure.

Dario was dressed in a black suit with a white shirt. Perhaps it was the setting, but he reminded Nick of a preacher from a traveling outdoor church. He followed Nick with his eyes, and Nick again felt a stir of unease. The man's stare was relentless. "Are you ready?" Dario asked, but directed his gaze and the question to Cris.

Cris leaned over and whispered in Nick's ear. "You remember everything we went over in the car?"

"I think so."

"I'll prompt you if you forget. But don't forget." At Nick's raised brows, Cris elbowed him in the ribs. "Calm down."

Cris ascended the steps until he stood by Dario. He turned and motioned for Nick to follow, but gestured for him to stop when he was on the second stair from the top. The men of the *cosca* encircled them.

Dario began to speak, raising his voice to be heard. "I have called you here today to witness the baptism of a new member. My son, Cristoforo, has chosen to be his sponsor. I present to you Niccolò Rinaldo Lucchesi." A ripple of comment swept through the assembled men. Adrenaline spiked Nick's blood, making him dizzy and sending his heart into a gallop. He swallowed hard and tried not to meet anyone's eyes. Damn Dario for using that name, the name Nick had never agreed to. He was Nicholas Reginald Clarkston. Not Lucchesi. *Never* Lucchesi. But he should have known his wishes didn't matter to Dario Andretti.

A man in the group below stepped forward. "What is the meaning of this? A Lucchesi? In the Andretti *cosca*?"

"Our families are blending again," Dario said. "Soon Niccolò will wed my daughter."

The man crossed his arms. "So this is what, extra insurance?"

"Something like that."

The man raised his brows, glanced at his comrades, then stepped back with a shrug. "My apologies for the interruption, Don Andretti."

Dario smiled. "Perhaps I should have been less theatrical and informed you all beforehand." The men chuckled and relaxed.

The boss man was a real funny guy, all right. Nick itched to tear into Dario as soon as they were alone.

"My son will conduct the initiation. Cris?"

Nick turned at Dario's words and met his eyes briefly, trying to bore a hole in the man, before turning his attention to Cris.

"Before all assembled here," Cris's voice rang out, "I shall help prove your worth to this society." Cris motioned Nick to join him, and the two of them stood face to face, less than two feet separating them. Cris put his left hand on Nick's right shoulder. "Niccolò Rinaldo Lucchesi, you have come before this society on this day, seeking entry into our ranks. Tell me, what are you looking for?"

"Blood and honor," Nick answered, remembering the ritual responses Cris had taught him.

"Why? Don't you have it?"

"I have it to give and to take." So far, so good.

"As you know, one goes in and comes out of the 'Ndrangheta with blood. It is time to test your courage."

Nick's heartbeat revved up again. Cris hadn't mentioned any test.

Cris produced a switchblade from his pocket and held it so that the point was sticking straight up in the air. "Place your hand above this knife."

Nick extended his hand, feeling the prick of the blade's tip in the center of his palm. Dario stepped forward, the ceramic bowl in his left hand. He held it below the knife. Christ, that bowl was to catch blood. A lot of blood. *His* blood. Dario's right hand hovered over Nick's.

"Ready?" Cris asked.

Tensing for what came next, Nick nodded. Why hadn't he stuck out his left hand instead of his right? Dario raised his hand in the air. Soon that hand would slap Nick's onto that knife. His stomach lurched and he struggled to hold his hand steady. He had to do this. All these other men had survived this ritual. So would he.

Dario's hand swept down toward Nick's, and Nick fought to keep his eyes open. At the last moment, Dario's hand veered away, and it took Nick a second to realize the move was deliberate.

The men of the *cosca* clapped and whistled. Nick had passed.

Relief shuddered through him, even as he pictured that knifepoint protruding from the top of his hand.

Cris beamed at him as he set the knife on the table, before turning back to face the men. "With the permission of all assembled here, I present this man to you for approval. From now on, I recognize him as my faithful companion. I will eat with him, divide right and wrong with him. I will defend his flesh, skin, blood, and bones to the last drop of blood. If he fails and fails again, swindles and stains honor, these crimes are his own charge and to the discredit of the society. And he then shall be punished with death."

Cris motioned Nick toward the table and the bowl. He picked up the knife again. Taking Nick's right hand, Cris pricked the tip of Nick's index finger. The knife was sharp as a scalpel; Nick didn't feel the cut until Cris squeezed his finger to draw the blood out. Dario brought the bowl and one of the cards forward, and

Cris squeezed harder, causing several drops of Nick's blood to fall on the female saint.

It was time to take the oath. Nick took the card from Cris and a burning candle offered by Dario. He lit a corner of the card. "As this paper burns, so must my flesh burn if I betray this society."

The card blackened and curled at the corner, the flame steadily eating toward the drops of blood in the center. "I swear on my honor to be faithful to the 'Ndrangheta, as the 'Ndrangheta is faithful to me. As this saint and these few drops of my blood burn, in the same way I will pour all of my blood for the 'Ndrangheta, and as this ash and this blood cannot go back to their former states, in the same way I cannot leave the 'Ndrangheta."

The solemnity of the oath struck Nick in the chest. In the car, the oath had been just words. Now it was a vow. A vow that couldn't be undone. Not without his death.

Nick dropped the burning card in the bowl as the heat began to bite at his fingers. Cris placed a hand on Nick's shoulder and addressed the men. "Are there any objections to this candidate's membership?"

When no one spoke, Cris continued. "With your approval, he has been made into a man."

A low buzz started up, and Dario addressed the crowd. "Before we proceed to the formal welcoming, there is one more thing we must do today. My son has conferred a great honor upon this man, who has saved his life. He wishes them to be joined by the blood bond, the *vincolo di sangue*."

Another murmur of comment sprang out as Nick and Cris turned to Dario, who picked up the knife from the table. Cris and Nick each held out their right hands, and Dario made swift cuts on the tips of their index fingers, then he pressed their fingers together for a moment, before smearing their combined blood on another holy image.

He handed the card to Cris and Nick. They each held one end of it, while Dario touched a candle to the center.

As the flame burned outward, Dario said, his voice solemn and full: "From now on you are brothers. The blood of one is in the other. Only more blood or an infamous action may untie this bond."

His heart in his throat, Nick looked up at Cris as they let go of the card, then Cris embraced him, kissing him on both cheeks. Nick returned the embrace, his hands trembling with the import of what he'd done. How could he ever betray his new brother?

They descended the stairs, where Nick, Cris, and Dario formed a sort of receiving line. The first member came forward and embraced Nick by clasping his shoulders and kissing his cheeks, then concluded by sucking the bloody tip of Nick's finger. *What the hell? We aren't vampires, for Christ's sake.* "Your blood is my blood," the man murmured. Then the man moved on to embrace Cris and Dario. The next man, and then the next, stepped forward, each repeating the same ritual.

Nick accepted it all in a daze. These hardened killers, these men with scars on their faces, one of them missing an eye, several missing fingers—these men had welcomed him into his ranks, virtually without question. Because Cris and Dario had recommended him. Because he'd saved Cris's life. Because Cris had joined with him as a blood brother.

A humbling sense of duty fell upon him. As of this moment, these men and he had sworn to lay down their lives for each other. To trust each other. If necessary, to kill for each other.

Delfina had been right; he hadn't understood a damn thing. Not until this very moment.

And now it was too late.

As if he'd conjured her up, Delfina flew into the clearing, out of breath, anguish on her face. "Is it finished?" she cried.

Nick nodded, and when she covered her face with her hands, heat flushed his cheeks. He should've listened to her. Why was he always ignoring her good advice?

Right behind Delfina, his father and at least ten men poured into the clearing, all of them packing Uzis. "What is the meaning of this?" Enrico demanded.

Dario answered, and the smug look of triumph on his face deepened Nick's shame. "Your son has joined my *cosca*."

"That is not possible. I forbid it."

"He is of age. He does not need your consent."

Enrico raked a hand through his hair. "He is ineligible."

Dario raised a brow. "Please explain."

"He is illegitimate, as you well know."

"I have consulted with my uncle Benedetto on this matter. Because you have legally and formally acknowledged the boy as your own, and because you and my sister had no children, he feels an exception can be made for you, Don Lucchesi. Are you not happy to have your son as part of our society?"

All eyes shifted to Enrico. He looked down at the ground, then back at Dario. "He is *my* son. He should be part of *my* cosca." His eyes sought Nick's, and in a raw, broken voice, he said, "Nico, why did you do this?"

Nick couldn't tell the truth. So he gave the answer Dario would believe. The one his father would believe. "You never wanted me to be part of your *cosca*. So I have chosen another family."

"Nico—"

Dario interrupted Enrico. "Come now, Don Lucchesi. We are joining the families. Do you begrudge me this extra gesture? Your son has rendered great service to my family. I thought it only fitting to reciprocate."

Enrico's eyes narrowed. "We should talk about that 'service' for a moment. I assume this includes the fire last night."

"You will have to be more specific."

"The one where my godson was killed." *Christ. Fedele was his father's godson?*

"A tragedy."

"You ordered it. Do you deny that?"

"Not at all."

Enrico crossed his arms. "You puzzle me, Don Andretti. You pledge your daughter to my son, you offer an alliance between my family and yours, and yet you kill my godson?"

"Yes."

Surprised noises swept through the assembly.

"Tell me why I should not gun you down this instant."

"Fedele was plotting against you. He didn't like the promotion of your orphan boy to *capo di società* over family members. He approached me and asked for my cooperation... in eliminating you." Dario paused again as the murmur of voices swelled. "I will accept your apology at any time."

Enrico's gaze flicked to Nick before returning to Dario. He bowed his head. "I am most grateful for the assistance, Don Andretti. Please accept my apologies." With one final glance at Nick, a glance that pierced him, Enrico turned and left.

Ruggero stepped forward, his eyes blazing, and hawked a gob of spit at the ground before following his boss. *Was that meant for me, or Dario, or both of us?*

As he watched his father go, Nick rubbed at the ache that had formed in his chest. For the first time in many years, Nick longed to run after him, to throw his arms around his father and never let go.

But now that was impossible. He'd just made sure of it.

CHAPTER 18

Nick and Cris returned to the house, where a great feast had been laid out under the trees on the back garden terrace. The men of the *cosca* streamed through the house and out back to the groaning tables. Dario offered everyone a humidor full of cigars, and the maids brought out grappa, sambuca, limoncello, and whiskey, along with steaming carafes of espresso. Then they withdrew, leaving the men to their celebration.

Except Nick didn't want cigars, alcohol, or a feast. Dario's head was the only thing he wanted brought to him on a platter.

Cris picked up on his dark mood and pulled him aside. "Listen, I know your father was upset, and maybe Papà could have handled it better, but aren't you happy that you helped rid your father of a snake in his midst?"

"*Did* I? How do we know your father is telling the truth?"

"What other explanation makes sense? If I had been in Fedele's shoes, I'd have been upset. Antonio is my friend, but he isn't family, and what Zio Enrico did—well, it's a huge slap in the face."

"I'm sure he had his reasons." Like keeping his godsons out of the family business. The way he'd tried to protect Nick.

"In the absence of his own son, Enrico should have made Fedele *capo di società*," Cris said.

"Perhaps my father felt he wasn't qualified, or that he could have been of more use elsewhere."

Cris shrugged. "You have two more cousins with a claim. Your father will need to handle them as well." He cleared his throat. "Of course, the fact that you were the one who dealt with Fedele complicates matters."

It took Nick a second. "Christ. Now they'll want *my* head." Then Dario's deeper purpose hit him, like a lightning bolt hurled by a vengeful god. "Don't you see? Your father is starting a civil war in the Lucchesi family."

Shaking his head, Cris said, "Your father started it when he chose Antonio. Perhaps Fedele's death adds a bit of wood to the fire, but this problem isn't my father's creation."

Heat flooded Nick's face. "Your loyalty to your father is stunning." He stalked away from Cris before he said something worse.

Nick wound through the crowd, feeling slaps on the back but not acknowledging them as he headed toward Dario, who had a cigar in one hand and a glass of whiskey in the other. "May I have a word?" Nick asked.

"Of course, my son." The endearment took him aback, but it shouldn't have. He was to be Dario's son-in-law, and in the world of the 'Ndrangheta, a *capo* was like a father to his men. But the slight deepening in Dario's tone indicated that he'd chosen that word to underline his victory.

He followed Dario to a spot some distance from the others. "What is on your mind?" Dario asked.

"Where do I start? With the cousin you made me kill? With giving me a surname I never wanted? Perhaps with all the trouble you've caused my father?"

Dario took a long draw on the cigar, holding Nick's eyes all the while. He let the smoke puff out his nose and mouth as he answered. "When you came to me—and do remember, *you* called me, *you* came to me—you wanted to hurt your father. Has something changed?"

The question caught him off-guard, and everything Delacourt, Delfina—even Fuente—had tried to drum into him, hit him in a barrage. He wasn't immune to the bonds of family. Not at all. He was *consumed* by them. Everything he'd done had been driven by his love for his father—a love that had twisted into hate, but that at its core was the plaintive cry of a young boy: don't leave me. *Christ.* Could he be any more pathetic?

"Well?" Dario asked.

Nick focused on the man before him, so smug in his self-satisfaction. Dario had buried an axe in Enrico Lucchesi's heart. And Nick had been that axe. He bit the inside of his bottom lip to keep his face emotionless. "Of course nothing's changed. But you could have let me in on the plan. I feel like a pawn, not a player."

Dario chuckled. "Does a chess master explain his moves to the pieces?"

A white-hot bolt ripped through Nick. "Is that all we are to you? Delfina, Cris, me? Your supposed family?"

"When I die, all of you will reap the rewards of what I've done. And then you can make the decisions." He took another draw on the cigar. "Provided you don't get yourself killed before then."

Nick stepped closer to Dario. "How far are you willing to go? Are you willing to sacrifice your own son?"

Something reptilian flitted through Dario's eyes. "What are you talking about?"

"If you sell me out to Benedetto, Cris goes down with me. Remember that."

Dario looked puzzled. "I am at a loss."

Fuck. Dario didn't know, and Nick had promised Cris he'd keep quiet. Now what? He needed something plausible, but not the truth. "Benedetto threatened me. He thought I was a spy sent by my father. I thought he'd told you."

"What does this have to do with Cris?"

"Benedetto knows the two of us are close, and now that we're blood brothers, it wouldn't take much to convince him we were conspiring against you and the rest of the family."

His eyes unfocused as he mulled over Nick's words, Dario stroked his lower lip with the rim of his whiskey glass. "He hasn't mentioned this to me."

"Your uncle seems to be someone who keeps his own counsel. Am I wrong?" *Please let this work.*

"What you say is true. But you have nothing to fear." Dario took a gulp of the whiskey. "I don't think Benedetto is serious. Rather, I think he does not like the idea of me having a man in Interpol. Someone *he* doesn't control."

Nick's gut uncoiled. "That makes sense."

Transferring his whiskey to his cigar hand, Dario gripped Nick by the base of his neck and squeezed. "So, we are friends, are we not?"

Hardly. Nick forced a smile and a nod. If his plan was going to work, he'd need Dario's trust.

And he'd need an ally in law enforcement. Someone Delacourt didn't have influence over.

It was time to contact Silvio Fuente again. But before that, he needed to talk to Delfina. He owed her one hell of an apology.

———— ✦ ————

Delfina had failed to save Nick. Zio Enrico had practically drawn her a map, yet somehow she'd gotten lost. Worried that they'd spot her, she'd let the Mercedes leave her behind, but once she'd lost sight of it, she'd panicked and had sped past the first turnoff, not realizing her error until many minutes later. On most stretches of Via Bisbino, branching roads and turnabouts were infrequent, and that portion had been no exception. By the time she'd been able double back and find the right road, she'd been too late, arriving at the ceremony just ahead of her uncle.

All her frantic effort had been for nothing. After seeing the devastation on her uncle's face as he'd walked away, she'd regretted called him. He'd have found out eventually, but it might have stung less if Nick hadn't disowned him in front of everyone.

And Nick's betrayal wasn't even true—she was sure of it. He'd say anything to make her father happy and complacent, to get him to drop his guard and let Nick into the inner circle.

But she couldn't let Nick do it. Couldn't let him put Cris in jail. Maybe Papà deserved it, but not Cris.

Somehow, she had to stop Nick. Her mind spun with possibilities. Spun until she was dizzy with options, worries, and second-guesses.

Clearly, Nick wouldn't rest until he'd found some way to wash his conscience clean from Fedele's murder. And for Nick, that meant bringing someone to justice—no matter what a farce that justice might be. If her father went to jail, he'd just run things from there, through Cris. Provided that Cris didn't end up in jail himself. But she couldn't let that happen.

She needed to give Nick some other way to atone. She needed to give him a bigger fish than her father, the biggest fish she knew: Benedetto.

But how?

Taking Benedetto down would require solid evidence. Evidence no one could refute or argue away or hire fancy lawyers to dance around.

The answer hit her like a bullet. The bugs. Of course! Nonno Carlo had taped Benedetto's visits to the guest cottage for years. There had to be something on those recordings.

But where did Papà keep them?

Or did he even have them? So far, he hadn't said anything to her about her visit to Nick last night. Perhaps he was late in reviewing them. But that didn't seem like Papà.

Was it possible her grandfather had taken their location with him to the grave?

Cris would probably know. There should be no reason for Papà to keep such a strategic advantage secret.

Heading through the double doors that led outside to the party, she almost collided with Nick coming back into the house. Delfina had nothing to say to him. She tried to brush past him, a painful lump in her throat almost strangling her.

Nick grabbed her arm, stopping her. "I need to talk to you," he said.

She yanked her arm out of his grasp. "We have nothing to discuss." Her voice came out distorted, laden with emotion, and he looked at her sharply.

"We don't?"

Madonna. She scanned the yard. They were in far too public a place. "If you're going to insist, we'd better find someplace private."

"Agreed." She followed him in the direction of the cottage, but they couldn't talk there because of the bugs. She stopped him and pointed that out. "Where, then?" he asked.

"Follow me." She turned and headed up the hill past the hedge maze, which would be too prone to intrusion right now. The replica temple to Ares that her grandfather had constructed should be relatively safe, if they kept their voices low. The path around it was gravel, so they should hear if anyone approached the arched doorway.

She led Nick up to the marble structure. It wasn't huge, but it was large enough to fit a half dozen people at once.

They stepped inside and she took a seat on one of the benches under the cupola. Leaves and pine needles were scattered about the stone floor; they'd either blown in through the open doorway or dropped through the oculus in the domed ceiling. She'd have to get on the gardeners about maintenance.

Nick sat beside her, his wavy hair showing glints of chestnut in the light streaming from the opening above. Damn her for wanting to touch it. "What is so important?" she asked, an edge to her voice.

"I owe you an apology. A huge one."

"For what?" She could think of several things he needed to apologize for.

He took in a breath and leaned forward, bracing his hands on his knees. "You were right. I should have listened to you about taking the vows." He paused. "On top of that, Cris and I were joined as blood brothers."

A knife pierced her heart. "*Dio.* You didn't."

"How could I refuse without it looking suspicious? But now I don't know if I can go through with my plan. He'll never forgive me."

Hope sparked in her. He raked a hand through his hair, reminding her of his father, who'd done the exact same thing the exact same way at the initiation ceremony.

"What if we found something on Benedetto? Would that be enough to assuage your conscience?"

"Maybe." He scrubbed a fingernail up and down over the stone lip of the bench they sat on, the soft clicking echoing in the silence.

She needed to be sure. "Could you leave my father and brother out of it?"

"If they're not directly involved. But Delfi, I have to be honest—I want your father's hide for what he's done to me. How he's used me."

Her father had used her too. But what hurt Papà, hurt Cris. She stared at her hands, clasped together in her lap. Maybe there was some way. She raised her head, meeting Nick's eyes. She had to trust him. "Please, spare Cris. And..." She hardly dared say the rest.

"And?"

"Your father. He doesn't deserve what's happened."

Rubbing his eyes, Nick averted his gaze. "I've really fucked things up with him, haven't I?" His voice was hoarse, and something tightly wound in her chest let go.

"Oh Nick, why did you have to be so damn stubborn?"

His cheeks curved up into a grin, but still he didn't look at her. "Nature of the beast."

She wanted to laugh, but couldn't quite. He'd joined the 'Ndrangheta. He was an 'Ndranghetista now. How could she marry him? Not only that, but how could she marry a man in Interpol? "Nick, explain something to me."

"What?"

"If you put any of them in jail, that means we'd have to go into protective custody, and you'd have to leave Interpol."

He mulled that over. "Maybe not. My work could be done remotely."

"Nick," she said, careful to keep her voice gentle. "They'll want you out, no matter what you do. You're a mobster's son. You're compromised."

He smacked a closed fist onto the stone bench. "If that's the way they look at it, so be it."

"You keep saying you're an officer of the law. But you can't have both. Either you give up going after them, or you give up Interpol. Which is more important to you?"

"When all this started, I could have given you a clear answer. Now I don't know."

She let out a hiss of exasperation. "You have to decide, Nick. And whatever you decide affects me. It's not just you anymore. If you turn them in, I'll be the wife of a traitor. Do you know what that means?"

"I think I can guess."

"Let me spell it out for you. It means my family would be within their rights to kill me."

"Your father wouldn't—"

"But Lorenzo might."

His shoulders slumped and he let out a sigh. "I'm sorry. I'll think of something. There has to be a way where we can both get what we want." Reaching over, Nick took her hand, pulling it onto his lap and cradling it in both of his. "I know you didn't want to marry someone mixed up in all this. I know you want to get away from this life. So, I want you to know that I'll give you a divorce any time you like." He spoke to her hand, his voice soft, rasping. "But I won't want to."

He was killing her, he really was. "You were easier to handle when I could be angry with you."

Nick caressed her hand, petting it as if it were a fragile bird. "So you forgive me?" He had yet to meet her gaze.

"I might, if you could look me in the eye."

"I'm afraid to."

A fist closed around her heart and squeezed. "Why?"

"After everything I've done, how foolish I've been, how cruel—I don't deserve your forgiveness. I know that. I can't bear to see how unhappy I've made you."

Tugging her hand out of his grasp, she placed her fingertips under his chin, using the barest pressure to turn his face to hers. His eyes were swimming, two shimmering pools of sea green. Her own blurred and tears rolled down her cheeks as she leaned in to kiss him. She brushed their lips together, then pressed her forehead against his, their lips almost touching when she spoke. "Don't ever break my heart again."

He smoothed the backs of his fingers down the side of her face. "I'm an idiot, Delfi. I'm bound to screw up again. But it won't be intentional. I *can* promise you that."

"Set the bar low, why don't you?" A smile filled her voice.

"That way I can wriggle over it on my belly."

She sat back so she could see the amusement on his face. "You're not much of an achiever."

"Not in my personal life, no. That's been one cock-up after another. Best not get your hopes up."

He was hopeless, this man. And now so was she. She loved him, hopelessly, helplessly. Somehow, she'd become his slave after all.

She offered him her best smile. "You really know how to sell a girl."

Laughter huffed out of him. "I truly don't. I've spent my whole life trying not to do that. Doing the opposite, in fact. You're the only one who's made me want to change."

She gave him another smile, this one utterly unforced. "That's better. *Much* better."

"How about this?" He leaned in and kissed her, his tongue sweeping between her lips, invading her, claiming her, making her moan.

Oh, how she loved his touch. She wrapped her arms around his neck and he pulled her sideways onto his lap, then started kissing and nuzzling her neck. Delfina offered her throat up to him, each caress of his lips on that sensitive skin sending a ripple of pleasure straight to her sex. He pushed her skirt up her thighs, his fingers making circles on the soft flesh he found there. She grabbed his wrist. "Not here."

Ignoring her, he pulled his hand out of her grasp and slipped it under the fabric of her panties, stroking her sex. She clamped her legs closed on his hand. "I'm serious."

His eyes met hers, but he continued caressing her, his thumb finding her clit. "Delfi, you didn't care in the garden shed. You didn't care in the olive grove. And you didn't care that your father might have overheard us last night."

"But the party... someone's going to come searching for you."

His lips trailed along her neck again, his thumb doing sinful, wonderful things below. "So? We're engaged."

"I'd rather not get caught."

His response was to slip two fingers inside her, making her breath hitch. "The whole idea of getting caught adds a certain... spice, doesn't it? Someone watching us, maybe getting turned on?"

She moaned. The idea did excite her. "Damn you," she whispered, her voice husky.

"I told you before. You are the woman of my heart."

Was that as close as he'd ever get to telling her he loved her? Some other time she'd ask him, but not now. Now she wanted something else from Nick, something else entirely. She spread her legs wider for him, and his fingers worked faster at her slick, swollen flesh. His erection bumped against her hip. To tease him, she wriggled on his lap, making him growl. "Keep that up and this will all be over in a few minutes," he said. She did it again, and he hoisted her up and carried her to the wall, pressing her against the cold marble. To her right was the alcove that housed the statue of Ares holding his sword.

They were directly across from the doorway. Anyone who looked in could see them. And with how heavily they were both gasping, she doubted they'd hear anyone approach, despite the gravel. This was ridiculous... mad... insane. And so deliciously wicked.

Nick held her in place, his large hands under her buttocks. "Unzip me," he grunted. Wrapping her legs around his waist, she leaned back to see what she was doing. She quickly freed him, his hard cock springing up between them. Unable to resist, she gave him an experimental stroke, grinning like she'd just won the lottery when he shuddered at the contact. "Condom's in my right pocket," he said.

So he's been thinking about this. The idea excited her. She fished around until her fingers closed over a ring wrapped in foil. She held it up for him. "Put it on me," he said.

"I'm not sure how." She hated to admit it, but it was true.

"Well, that tells me something," a voice said from the doorway. Delfina's breath caught and her heart pounded until she processed the voice. Cris. She peeked over Nick's shoulder to be sure.

"Get out of here," she snapped.

"No."

No? "You don't get to tell me what to do, Cristoforo Andretti."

Nick released her legs, easing her back onto her feet, careful to keep his body in front of hers, shielding her from Cris's view. He glanced over his shoulder as he zipped himself up. "Really, mate?"

Cris leaned against the doorway. "I know you're engaged, but could you not treat my sister like a dog in heat?"

Delfina's face flushed and a thrill rippled through her. What they must have looked like. How could she be ashamed and angry and turned on at the same time?

"It's not like that," Nick said as he straightened his clothes.

She could have continued to let Nick handle Cris, but something inside her rebelled. She nudged Nick aside and stepped forward. "What I do and who I do it with is none of your concern."

Cris reddened with irritation. "I am *capo di società* of this family."

Someone had a swollen head, and it wasn't Nick this time. "I'm not part of the *cosca*, and I don't want any part of it," she said. "*I* didn't take any vows. As far as I'm concerned, you're just my little brother. Now leave us be."

"Well, dear sister, anyone could have seen you." Cris jammed his hands in his jacket pockets. "You're damned lucky it wasn't Papà who went hunting for Nick. Engaged or not, he'd take this out of his hide." Cris kicked at the marble flooring. "Use some fucking discretion."

Nick chuckled. "Unintentional pun?"

Cris's mouth quirked up, and Delfina had to suppress a smile. Leave it to Nick to find something funny about the situation. "I suppose." Cris motioned with his head back toward the house and started down the stairs. "They want to toast you."

"You'd think it was my birthday," Nick grumbled. He offered Delfina a hand as they descended the steps and met Cris at the bottom.

"In a way it is," Cris said. "You're a new man now." They headed toward the house, Nick's fingers still wrapped around hers. Cris gestured around them. "You have a new life now, new rules. And one of them is not to disrespect the women in other men's families. Mothers, wives, daughters, sisters. *Capisci?*"

As if she were a child who couldn't defend herself. Or a possession. Delfina rolled her eyes. Her anger flared again, but Nick leaned over and gave her a swift kiss on the cheek. "Message received, mate. It's just that I adore her." Warmth spread through her chest at his words. Even though it wasn't "I love you," it reminded her of the first time he'd said it, of the way Nick had looked when he'd told her he was happy.

"Adore her chastely then. Save the rest until the wedding."

Delfina let out a groan of frustration. Hadn't Cris heard a word she'd said? "I told you, Cris, it's none of your business."

"It *is* my business. *You* may not have taken the vows, but Nick did. I'm his *capo di società* now. And I have to watch out for the well-being of my men and my family, which, by the way, includes you."

She wanted to strangle him. It must have shown on her face, because Cris held up his hands in a placating gesture. "Listen, I know I'm being a pain, but I'm trying to do you both a favor. You don't want your husband to look like a punching bag on your wedding day, now do you?"

Nick squeezed her hand. "He's right."

Was he just saying that to mollify Cris, or did he mean it? She glanced at Nick, and he waggled a brow at her. Incorrigible. Her man did love to live dangerously.

176

But didn't they all? That's what the men in her world did. Risk their lives to earn the euros that brought home the pancetta, prosciutto, and provolone.

Why did she think she'd ever love a man who didn't? What was done was done. The man she loved was an 'Ndranghetista.

She just hoped her man's love of danger didn't get him killed.

Madonna. She must find those recordings. Benedetto had to be stopped before he killed Nick, before he killed Cris, before he destroyed her father. And bringing Benedetto down might be just the thing to assuage Nick's conscience and bring him some measure of peace.

The only problem was preserving her dreams in all the chaos to come. Following Nick's form of justice would mean giving up everything she'd worked for. Protective custody and the fashion limelight didn't mix.

But perhaps there was some backdoor way to get what they both wanted? If she had inarguable proof that Benedetto was a traitor, that he'd lied to his father and acted against the family, perhaps Bisnonno Lorenzo could be persuaded to let Nick send Benedetto to prison as punishment. Jailing an Andretti would be a major coup for Nick, and it would help bolster his standing in Interpol. They'd never suspect that he was an 'Ndranghetista. Especially not one working for the Andrettis.

But there was grave danger in that plan: Lorenzo would own Nick then, body and soul. And of all the vipers in the Andretti family, Lorenzo was the king.

CHAPTER 19

After the shooting at the nightclub, Delfina's father had insisted she bring Orsino, one of the guards, with her to work. Although she was grateful for the protection—there was no reason to think the Russians had given up, and they very well might go after her to get to Cris—Delfina wanted Orsino to wait in a café nearby and pick her up at the end of the day. However, he'd insisted on coming inside and sitting in a chair near the front door.

Orsino was an unfortunate choice. He wasn't as intimidating as Flavio, but as his name implied, he had all the social graces of a bear; he scowled at everyone who came near her, even Jacopo. Maybe especially Jacopo. She tried to ignore her bodyguard, but it was hard when Ornella and Mario kept asking about her entourage, saying things like, "Does it speak?" or "Perhaps it's hungry. How many bananas does it eat a day?"

After this last comment, Delfina's gut burned. How much more of this *merda* was she going to have to put up with?

Despite spending hours searching the house, she'd made no progress on finding the recordings, and it was driving her mad. Much the same way that unfinished business with Nick yesterday was driving her mad. Her damn brother just had to interrupt them at the worst possible moment. Somehow she had to figure out how to steal some private time with Nick. She'd love to model the burgundy dress for him. She could picture her bra showing through the gauzy top, the peek-a-boo panels in the flowing skirt allowing her legs to tease him as she strutted back and forth. Maybe she should forget the bra? A flush of heat warmed her cheeks. The gauze would feel so soft as it rubbed against her nipples...

Focus on the dresses. She and Jacopo were showing the first one to Signor Morelli that afternoon. They had only to put the finishing touches on the black dress and then they'd be ready. Quickly fanning her face and trying to banish all thoughts of Nick, she went back to the rack where she and Jacopo were storing the mockups they'd made so far. Her heart skipped in her chest when she found the rack empty. Where were they? Had Jacopo moved them elsewhere? She searched the surrounding racks, but didn't find them.

Maybe he'd put them in another storeroom. With a fluttering under her ribcage, she searched the room where they kept finished work. Nothing.

Turning, she noticed a heap of fabric in the corner. Black, burgundy, white, silver, and cobalt fabric. Her pulse sped up as she walked over to it. She lifted up the black fabric, a combination of gauze and velvet panels. It was her dress, sliced to ribbons. A bolt of heat flashed through her. She picked up the partials they'd started putting together, all of them slashed and torn. Ruined, every one.

Gathering the damaged dresses in her arms, she strode out, searching for Jacopo. Angry voices streamed from Signor Morelli's office, one of them Jacopo's. She'd almost reached the door when she heard something that made her pause. Ornella's voice. "You've never put a first year's dress on the runway. You're just doing it because you think she can help you. It's not fair to the rest of us who've slaved here for years and never got anything in the show."

Unable to breathe, Delfina clutched the dresses to her chest and waited for Signor Morelli's reply. Jacopo broke the silence. "The design is daring. It deserves to be in the show."

"Do you think this is Jean-Paul Gaultier?" Mario's voice.

"None of this matters," Signor Morelli said. "The dress is in the show."

"Why?" Ornella demanded. "Tell me why."

Signor Morelli sighed, his chair creaking as he shifted. "The dress is good. I'm not embarrassed by it. If putting it in the show makes her father inclined to help us, all the better."

"Perhaps you're worried he'll send one of his apes here if you don't?" Ornella said. "Oh wait. There's one out in the shop *right now* guarding *la principessa*. Make that the *Mafia* princess."

"Get back to work, Ornella. You too, Mario. This matter is closed," Signor Morelli said.

Delfina turned and tried to hurry away, but Ornella saw her as she left Signor Morelli's office. She stepped toward Delfina. "Eavesdropping? I hope you heard everything, you little bitch." The triumph on the girl's face was too much to bear.

Behind Ornella, Mario snickered, but he stopped when Jacopo came out of the office, his handsome face shifting from anger to dismay when he saw Delfina standing there, blinking fiercely to hold back tears.

Ornella crossed her arms and turned to Jacopo. "She knows. You can stop licking her ass now."

Delfina's stomach tightened. Had Jacopo been honest with her at all? "*Cara*," he said. "Don't listen to her."

She hurled the ruined dresses at him. "It doesn't matter. I quit."

Whirling around, she rushed to her desk, grabbing her bag and a few personal items she'd brought. When Jacopo tried to stop her, Orsino lumbered up from his chair. She pointed at the guard. "Stop." Turning to Jacopo, she said, "You can't change my mind. None of them want me here. I'm only here because of who my father is. You know it, and I know it. And I can't stand to be humored."

"I'm not humoring you. I love your work. We make a great team."

A hard lump rose in her throat. They made a terrific team. She swallowed it down and patted his arm. "I know. I'll miss you."

"You haven't seen the last of me, Delfina Andretti," Jacopo said. "We're friends."

She nodded, unable to speak. Then she fled from the workshop, Orsino at her side. She'd been an idiot to think her father could help her without the Andretti name ruining everything.

Clutching her handbag, Delfina raced down the street outside Morelli's, her heels clacking on the pavement. Orsino matched her pace and tried to pat her on the shoulder, but she shrugged him off and stopped. "Get the car," she snapped, then softened her voice and added, *"Per favore."* It wasn't his fault. He was just doing his job, following her father's orders.

While she waited for Orsino, tears slid down her cheeks. At least she'd been able to keep them in until she got outside. She wiped at them angrily, her face on fire. What was she going to tell her family? She'd been so proud of herself, so happy.

But it had all been a sham. Signor Morelli hadn't wanted to hire her, hadn't thought she had talent, hadn't seen anything special in her. She was just an inconvenient but necessary pest. A condition of continued funding.

Her throat aching, Delfina closed her eyes. She was never going to see her dress on the runway. She was never going to see Jacopo again.

Inhaling deeply, she expelled the air out slowly and leaned back against the wall of a warehouse. Maybe this was for the best. Someday she was going to have to leave Italy, and this way, it would be less painful.

For a moment, Delfina indulged herself in a fantasy of her and Nick, free of the 'Ndrangheta, living together in London, her with a design shop of her own. She heard a light tap of a car horn and opened her eyes. Orsino got out and held the door for her, closing it after she got in back. Time to stop fantasizing and face reality. The 'Ndrangheta had always been her life, and that wasn't going to change. She was marrying Nick. And he was an 'Ndranghetista.

All her planning, all her hard work, everything she'd done to escape this life— once again, she'd been outmaneuvered by the master. Her father.

But the battle wasn't over. She'd find those recordings or she'd find some other way to get free—or relatively close to it. If she and Nick were away from the family, they might have a shot at something next to happiness.

———◆———

Now that he was an 'Ndranghetista, several things changed. Nick was moved into the main house and issued a key and the passcode to the front gate. He also received the keys to a red Alfa Romeo Spider and a mobile phone. Lastly, Cris gave him a Beretta and a switchblade, the latter engraved *"Fratelli di Sangue,* C.A. and N.L." Blood brothers.

Nick accepted the knife with a rock in his throat. Even though he'd told Delfi he'd keep Cris out of it, there was bound to be blowback and collateral damage. He might not be able to shield Cris from any of it.

And at any rate, if he did manage to take out Dario, Cris would be thrust into the limelight as head of the *cosca,* a position that would change his life drastically and put Cris square in the sights of law enforcement.

There was just no way that everyone he cared about was going to win. And there was every chance that he would end up the loser. Cris would never forgive him, no matter what he did. Anything Nick did would be a betrayal.

Yet how could he turn his back on everything he believed? How could he let Dario Andretti go free? And letting Cris persist in this life—that wasn't right either. Not for Cris, and not for the people Cris would eventually hurt in some way.

He was going to have to break his promise to Delfina. Maybe she'd hate him for a while, but eventually she'd see reason. Wouldn't she? He had to hope so. He had to hope her core of goodness would win against the corruption she'd been raised to tolerate. He had to hope, or else they had no future together.

Since Delacourt was dead to him, Nick had no other choice but to contact Sottotenente Silvio Fuente again. At least the man was clean. Well, as far as he knew. He'd have to risk it.

They agreed to meet in downtown Como at a café Fuente knew. Nick drove halfway there, then stopped at a church. Getting out of the car, he searched the undercarriage, finally spotting what he'd suspected: a GPS tracking device had been attached to the rear passenger wheel well. He removed it from the car and took it and his new mobile and hid them under a shrub outside the church. He'd retrieve them on the way back.

So Dario and Cris trusted him only so far. He shouldn't be surprised. He'd have thought them naïve if they had granted him their full trust so easily. Still, it stung.

He tried to ignore the worm of unease that tunneled through his belly as he drove to the café where he was meeting Fuente. If they didn't fully trust him, how *else* were they keeping tabs on him?

He checked the rearview mirror several times, but was certain he hadn't been followed. No need really if they thought him too stupid to check for the GPS. Or to carry his mobile with him. Instead, he carried the one his father had given him.

When he stepped inside the café, it took him a minute to spot Fuente. The man was seated in a corner, back to the wall, in an elegant navy suit instead of his *carabinieri* uniform. His dark hair was carefully slicked back, his full mustache neatly trimmed, every inch of him scrubbed and polished. Military neat. Force of habit, Nick supposed.

Fuente was drinking an espresso. He shook Nick's hand when he offered it and motioned for him to sit down. "Thank you for meeting me, Sottotenente."

"Of course. But tonight let's stick to Silvio and Niccolò, yes?"

Smart. Nick leaned forward on the heavily scarred wood of the thick table as Fuente signaled a waiter and held up two fingers, motioning to the cup he held and then Nick and himself.

Nick waited for the coffee, watching Fuente pull out a cigarette case and light up, even though he was seated beneath a sign warning that smoking indoors was prohibited by law. Nick glanced up at the sign, then down at Fuente's lit cigarette. Fuente laughed. "Who's going to stop me?"

Good point. The waiter brought their espressos and Nick inhaled the rich, heady aroma before taking a sip. He'd rather have tea, a nice Darjeeling or an Earl Grey, but the coffee here was growing on him. None of the wretched instant stuff he encountered so often in England. No, here coffee was taken seriously, brewed fresh and presented with care, as if it were a pint of the finest stout back home.

A wave of homesickness struck him. Were Gran and Grandad all right? Could he visit them now, wherever they were? They probably missed their flat. What had they done with their Yorkie, Biscuit?

So many questions he hadn't bothered to get answers to. He'd been so consumed with his own problems that he'd barely had time to think beyond the present moment. Somehow his world had collapsed in on itself, shrinking down to his immediate circumstances and his next move.

And it wasn't over yet.

"So what brings you to me, Nico? I doubt it's the sparkle of my conversation, though I have been told I have a way with words."

Nick chuckled. The man was a handful. In different circumstances, he'd like to get to know him better. No doubt Fuente could be endlessly entertaining. When he wished. "I need help with a delicate matter."

"And you thought of me. I'm flattered." Fuente took a sip of his espresso. "What can I do for you?"

"My superior at Interpol has been compromised. If I try to launch an investigation through him, I'm afraid he will... stymie my efforts."

Fuente smiled, flashing even white teeth. They sparkled too, as if he didn't drink coffee and smoke all day. The dentists in Italy must be amazing. "Tell me they haven't disowned you."

"No. But it's been made clear to me that certain actions won't be supported."

"So who owns him?"

"My father."

"The redoubtable Enrico Lucchesi. My, my, he is a man of many talents. Two men in Interpol, imagine that." Despite his words, Fuente's mocking tone made clear that he wasn't surprised.

"You knew?"

Fuente took a long drag on the cigarette, then blew a stream of smoke away from Nick. "I guessed about Delacourt. But I've known about you for some time."

"You have? How?"

"As I said, your father and I have met."

Fuck no. "So he owns you too."

The man shook his head. "No one owns me. I'm a free agent."

"For sale to the highest bidder?"

Fuente pursed his lips. "Let's not be crass, yes?"

"How about being honest? How about doing your damn job?" Nick kept his voice low, but he practically spat the words at Fuente. Was everyone in this country on the take?

Leaning forward, Fuente stabbed out the cigarette on his saucer. "I do my job. I do *all* my jobs. And I do them well. Or at least according to how well they pay." He tapped a fingernail against the rim of his cup and stared at Nick. "Let me explain something to you. I maintain the balance of power here. I play all sides, but mostly I play for me. Right now, it's in the best interest of this community, these people, and myself, to keep the Lucchesis and the Andrettis in place."

"What the fuck are you saying? Are you even *listening* to yourself?"

The officer's face went dark and he leaned closer. Nick could smell the cigarettes and espresso on the man's breath. "There are worse things that could happen to these people than the Lucchesis and Andrettis. Far worse threats. For the most part, they keep the killings to a minimum and the feuding out of sight. And they bring in a lot of wealth and jobs to Milan and the lake. They invest heavily here, and it's in everyone's best interests to keep things as they are. Eliminate them, and you create a vacuum that will be filled."

"What are you afraid of?"

Fuente ran a finger over his mustache. "The Russians, the Albanians. Even the fucking Camorra. They all want a piece of the north, and they have no scruples about what they'd do to it. The North Africans would love to come in and deal drugs and leave *Dio* knows how many overdoses in their wake. The 'Ndrangheta keeps them all at bay."

"Isn't that supposed to be your job?"

Fuente chuckled. "My boy, you work at Interpol. How are you still so naïve? You've seen the figures, you've seen the changes. The global economy has gone to shit, and the 'civilized' world is losing to the criminal one. Let's not pretend otherwise."

Well, didn't that just put him in his place. "I see we have a fundamental difference of opinion."

Apparently Nick had become quite the comedian. Fuente barked with laughter, and held his hands out like a scale, palms up. "What we have is experience on the one hand and idealism on the other." He dropped his hands and finished his espresso, then leaned back in his chair. "Look, if there is someone who needs to be stopped, I will stop them. I took care of Carlo Andretti."

"From what I've heard, my father took care of him."

"But not without my assistance." Fuente tapped the table for emphasis. "In fact, had it not been for me, you'd have been face down in a gutter with a bullet in the back of your head."

The wild goose chase through Sicily—of course. Delacourt had said he'd done it because Nick's life was in danger from the Andrettis. "Well then, I suppose I'm in your debt."

"Normally I'd ask for euros, but you can repay me by taking my advice."

"Which is?"

"Enjoy the favors life has bestowed upon you. If you must fight battles, fight only those that threaten hearth and home." Fuente's index finger stabbed the tabletop, rocking the cups in their saucers. "And *those* battles I will fight alongside you."

Delfina's concerns about Benedetto and Lorenzo, and her hint that maybe she could find evidence against them, came back to him. Perhaps Fuente knew something useful. "Okay then. There's something you may be able to help me with. What do you know about Benedetto and Lorenzo Andretti?"

Fuente sat back in his chair and picked up his espresso again, his face going perfectly still. "I know they're trouble. Trouble neither of us wants."

"Benedetto already has me in his sights, I think."

The officer sighed and drank from his cup, then set it down. "How you've managed to survive thus far is a miracle. If Benedetto wants you dead, there's nothing I can do for you."

"A man as clever as you must know something."

With a chuckle, Fuente wagged a finger at Nick. "Your flattery is transparent. But it's true. I do know something."

When the man didn't say more, Nick prompted him. "Which is?"

"I know Carlo had something on Benedetto. He wouldn't say what exactly, but I can guess. I heard that a *casinò* owner near Lake Lugano was foolishly complaining about a customer who hadn't paid his markers. That customer was Benedetto Andretti."

"What happened?"

"Can't you guess? The owner with the big mouth was later found floating in the lake. He'd tried to swallow a whole cod. Of course, we had little doubt how an ocean fish found its way into the lake and into the man's mouth."

"But of course, no proof."

Fuente lit another cigarette and shook his head. "There never is."

———— ◆ ————

Delfina had had plenty of time to think while Orsino drove her back from Milan. Her father had certainly played his part in ruining her chances. But so had her brother. She'd been blind to it at the time, how cleverly Cris had manipulated both her and Signor Morelli, that day he'd said her dress deserved to be on the runway.

She should have realized what Signor Morelli had meant when he'd met Cris and said he'd seen the resemblance. Not the resemblance to her—to her father. Cris's praise hadn't been just praise—it had been a demand. Signor Morelli had understood that, even if she hadn't. She'd stupidly continued to think of Cris as merely her little brother. He wasn't, not anymore. Under the skin, he was just like her father, and that incident at the temple yesterday just reinforced it. Well, he wasn't getting away with it unscathed. She might not have been able to stop him, but she could damn well let him know that she knew.

Orsino stopped to let her off at the front door, his gaze troubled as he helped her out of the back. He continued to hold her hand once she was standing beside the car. "*Signorina,* I caused you difficulty today, and I am sorry for it. I hate dealing with outsiders—"

"What happened today is not your fault. It had nothing to do with you."

"They were rude. I wanted to teach them a lesson."

Her chest tightened. "They deserved one, but they'll never learn. It's not our problem anymore."

"Should I go back there? I could—"

"*No.* Do nothing. You hear me?" She pinned him with her eyes. "Not one thing."

He bowed his head. "You're the boss."

If only she was, but that was not how the world worked. Squaring her shoulders, she headed into the house and made a rapid circuit of the first floor. When she found her mother in the kitchen conferring with their cook, Delfina asked for Cris. Her mother ignored the question. "You're home early," she said. "What's wrong?"

"I quit. They know who I am, and they don't want me there."

"Oh Delfi, I'm so sorry." Her mother tried to embrace her, but Delfina stepped away. "Delfi?" her mother asked, sounding wounded.

"I know you didn't approve. You should be happy. Papà got his way."

Her mother shook her head. "How could seeing you hurt make me happy?"

She was being unfair to her mother. "I'm sorry, Mamma. I'm just upset. I need to talk to Cris, right this minute. Where is he?"

"Out back." Her mother touched Delfina's cheek. "Come see me when you're done."

Delfina nodded, but she wasn't sure she could bear her mother's sympathy. Not when her mother believed that women in their world shouldn't have jobs outside the home. Any sympathy she offered would only be accompanied by assurances that Delfina leaving her job was for the best.

When she walked out onto the back terrace, Cris looked up from a book. It was the same one on economics that he'd been reading the day of Nick's initiation. A cup of espresso steamed by his side. Her feelings must have shown because like their mother, he immediately asked her what was wrong.

"I *trusted* you. I trusted you to be my brother, not to act like the Andretti *capo*. But you couldn't resist, could you?"

"What are you talking about?"

"That day where you told Signor Morelli to put my dress in the show."

"I didn't make him do anything."

She snorted. "You practically forced him. 'This should be on the runway.'"

Setting down the book, Cris raised his hands in surrender. "Seriously, Delfi, I don't know what you're talking about."

The more he protested his innocence, the more heat flamed up in her. Her face was hot, her voice thick. "Stop pretending. You knew what you were doing. I couldn't see it at the time, but I certainly see it now." Her blood thundered in her ears, and her hands trembled. "I hate what you've become."

He rose, the metal chair scraping along the stones as he moved. "Are you saying you *hate* me?"

He sounded so wounded, she wanted to take it back. But she said nothing. A gulf had opened up between them. A gulf she didn't know how to close.

"Delfi, I'm your *brother*."

"You are Papà's son. And that means you can't be loyal to anyone else."

Cris let out a small pained sound, and he stepped toward her. "That's not true."

"If I asked you to step down as *capo di società*, would you?" It wasn't fair of her to ask, but she couldn't stop herself.

He reached out, putting his hands on her arms. "Papà would never forgive me."

She twisted out of his reach. "I knew it."

He took her by the arms again. "Let me finish," he said, his voice low and urgent. "It's always been you and me, Delfi. The two of us together in this mess. If that's what you want, I'll do it." His voice was hoarse when he finished, his eyes filled with a vulnerability she hadn't seen since he was a little boy. Maybe he was telling the truth.

"You honestly weren't trying to intimidate Signor Morelli?"

"I wasn't. Look, I forget sometimes. I still think I'm just this kid, you know? I sometimes can't believe anyone listens to me. Or takes me seriously."

She touched his temple, smoothing back the curls that had fallen over his bandage. "I'm sorry, Cris."

"And I'm sorry about the misunderstanding with Morelli. I'll fix it tomorrow." When her vision blurred with tears, he said, "What happened at work? Why are you home early?"

She started to tell him the story. When she faltered, he pulled her close, and that was when she couldn't hold back the tears any longer. She sobbed against his shoulder, not listening to the comforting words he murmured until he said again that he could fix things with Signor Morelli.

"I quit, Cris. I'm not going back there."

"But you were so happy. And Nick seems fine with you working."

Taking a deep breath, she stepped away from him. "It's tainted. Don't you see? I thought I got that job on my own terms, I thought my dress got in the show on its own merits. But it was the Andretti name, the Andretti money, the Andretti *threat* that got me in the door. They don't want me there. They're afraid of us."

Cris slowly shook his head. "I'm sorry." He turned from her, looking out across the lake. "There's no escaping who we are, is there?"

Her throat and chest ached. If she thought she had it bad, Cris had it worse. He truly had no choice, no hope of ever escaping. And the odds were he'd end up dead well before his time. If he didn't end up in prison first.

She embraced him from behind, no longer able to comfortably rest her chin on his shoulder. Her little brother was still growing. "All I do is whine about myself and my problems. I haven't been much help to you lately, have I?"

He shrugged, but put his hands over hers where they circled his chest. "Things could be worse. We could be digging through the trash for our next meal."

She chuckled. "You sound like Gio. She gave me a lecture about how I'll never be Mother Teresa."

He laughed, his chest rumbling under her hands. "She's right."

"I know." Delfina squeezed him hard, then let go. She walked over to the table, taking a sip of his cooling espresso. He followed her, and they both took seats.

After they'd gazed at the lake for a while, passing the espresso back and forth, Cris said, "I know this might sound like a stupid question, but are you going to be happy with Nick?"

"What do you mean?"

"Well, he is an 'Ndranghetista now. I know you didn't want that."

"Beggars can't be choosers."

"Delfi."

She looked at him. "He's a better choice for me than Leandro. Much better."

"I thought you loved him."

"I do." She smiled. "But he's horribly stubborn and he doesn't listen."

Cris chuckled. "Sounds like someone else I know."

That made her laugh. "Okay, we're probably well-matched that way."

"I want you to be happy. One of us should be."

"Are you thinking about Gio?"

He shrugged, his answer for everything. "Maybe."

"Now that Leandro and I—"

"Maybe."

"Cris, you can't give up on what you want."

Eyes hard, he held her gaze. "I will do what's necessary." Then he added, "But I am going to try."

And she needed to try for happiness too. She'd promised Nick she'd help him atone for what he'd done. Now was the perfect time to ask Cris about the recordings. "I need to ask you something."

He ran a hand over his hair. "Ask away."

"I need to know where Papà keeps the recordings from the bugs in the guest house."

"Why?"

"Nick and I..." Though it was the perfect excuse, she still blushed. "The other night—"

Holding up a hand, Cris pretended to shudder. "Say no more. I can fill in the blanks."

"No doubt you heard us well before you saw us at the temple. That was all on you."

"I was curious. I didn't think it was going to be my *sister*."

"Well you certainly didn't walk away."

He pursed his lips. "I was angry. So were you. I think we're even."

"True." After a moment, she said, "I could use your help. I want to get that recording before Papà does."

"I can't help you."

"Can't or won't?"

"Can't. I don't know where they are."

Damn it. Resting her elbows on her knees, she asked, "He hasn't told you?"

"It's not that."

Raising a brow, she said, "What is it then?"

Cris leaned forward. "You can't tell anyone this. *Capisci*?"

"Of course. Now spill."

"Nonno had bugs all over Benedetto's and Lorenzo's homes. Aunt Toni was a genius at planting them. No one suspected her."

Excitement sizzled through her. This could be what she and Nick needed. "But?"

"Nonno never told Papà where the recordings were."

Now that was a surprise. "What if you help me search for them?"

Cris frowned. "You can't let Papà know that I told you. He was furious over the initiation."

"He knows I didn't want Nick to join. That's no secret. And Papà seemed pretty happy in the end."

"No thanks to you."

"Nick didn't know what he was getting into."

Cris's voice sharpened. "What has he said to you?"

"Nothing. He's happy about it. It's what he wanted."

"Then what's the problem?"

"He's not like you. He hasn't been raised for this since birth."

"He got a good taste before the initiation."

She traced a finger over the design on the beautifully painted ceramic tabletop. "I don't want to be worrying that my husband will be gunned down."

"Nick's not going to be doing the typical work." Cris downed the rest of his coffee. "He'll have it quite easy in fact."

"Except that he runs the risk of prison. Or perhaps Benedetto will put a bullet in him."

"Why do you say that?"

She stared at him, openmouthed. "Now who's being naïve? Benedetto doesn't like anyone to have an advantage over him, certainly not Papà. And having a spy in Interpol is a big advantage. And then there's the business with the Russians."

"What about it?" His voice was sharp, defensive.

"Cris, are you being deliberately obtuse?"

"You mean the money. Or the lack of it."

"Exactly. Why were they underpaying?" she asked.

"Maybe they'd paid some other way."

"Or maybe Benedetto owed them a favor or a large chunk of money." Did she have to spell it out for him? *Dio mio,* her brother would be loyal to the family right until Benedetto put him in his grave.

Cris rubbed his chin. "What I don't understand is why he didn't tell me to expect the underpayment."

"Maybe he wanted to weaken Papà."

Cris looked at her, his eyes troubled at last. When he spoke, his voice was little above a whisper. "He suggested I take Nick. And that I keep it absolutely quiet."

Bile rose up in her throat. She didn't want to be right, but... "I'm afraid he's going to try to finish what he started." Chris said nothing, but the expression on his face spoke volumes. He was starting to believe. She took his hand. "There may be a way to save you both. Do you think Benedetto could have been working with the Russians?"

"Possibly."

"Then you've got to tell Bisnonno Lorenzo."

"What if I'm wrong?"

Fire burned in her chest. "Who cares? He tried to get you and Nick killed."

"I don't know that for sure."

"Do the math, Cris."

He focused on the lake for a long time before he spoke. "He's my blood. How could he?"

"Not everyone has honor. We both know that."

"He's the head of La Provincia!"

"I'm sorry, Cris."

He turned to her, eyes blazing, hands balled into fists. "If he set us up, I will hunt him down and shoot him like the dog he is."

Maybe she shouldn't have told him. But if she hadn't, he'd never have seen the danger Benedetto posed. "Be careful, *per favore*. I beg you."

"Only one of us is ending up dead. And it won't be me."

More than ever, she had to find those recordings. *Now.* Before Cris did something they'd both regret.

CHAPTER 20

Ilya Vilanovich's latest call had veered from threatening to homicidal. He wanted blood for his sons. And he made clear if he didn't get the shooter, Benedetto's blood would do just as well. "You are hearing me?" Vilanovich growled in his clumsy English.

"Patience, Ilya. You will have your vengeance. The Lucchesi boy will soon marry my nephew's daughter. Send your men to me the usual way, and we'll go over the plan. My only condition is that the boy's father, Enrico Lucchesi, not be harmed. I need him alive—for now. But you can have my grandnephew, the Lucchesi boy, and my nephew as well."

"Why this nephew?"

"Because he will want vengeance upon you."

"And your father? He will want same, no?"

Benedetto chuckled. "He will see the wisdom of my choices." There was no need to mention that having the Russians strike against two 'Ndrangheta families was exactly the unifying provocation that Lorenzo hoped for, an undeniable catalyst for bringing the clans together. Under Andretti "guidance" of course.

"I will send my men. And I will come also."

Porco Dio! The last thing he wanted was the volatile Russian in the mix. "Scorched earth" wasn't a military policy to Ilya Vilanovich. It was a way of life. The old man had risen to prominence through the ruthless and unstinting application of violence. "There is no need to trouble yourself."

Ilya barked with laughter. "Trouble? Trouble is stepping on landmine and hearing click. Trouble is having RPG pointed at your face. Trouble is running out of credit at casino, and when they threaten to break your legs, you ask Russian friend to help. And you hope his memory is no good from vodka."

Benedetto's face heated. He hated that Ilya knew his weakness and felt free to throw it in his face. The day the Russian finished playing his part, he'd force Vilanovich to eat those words, to plead for mercy. But today was not that day. "I did not mean to minimize your pain, Ilya. I meant only to assure you that I have the situation under control."

Vilanovich laughed again, the sound harsh. "You are referring to how well you handled this?"

Oh yes, Ilya would eat a gun barrel before Benedetto was through.

"Nothing's perfect."

Except revenge.

———————◆———————

After his meeting with Fuente, Nick drove aimlessly around Como. Why was he being thwarted at every turn? Was this a sign from heaven, a sign that he should walk away?

Nick returned to the church and retrieved his mobile and the GPS tracker, placing it back on the Spider's undercarriage where he'd found it. As he was about to turn on the car to leave, a flash of sunlight glinting off the stained-glass window caught his attention.

He'd never been a particularly religious person, and he no longer considered himself a Catholic, but something drew him to the church. Exiting the car, he headed up the walkway to the steps, his chest tight, his eyes aching. He hadn't set foot in a church since his mother's funeral. As he climbed the steps, he rubbed at the ache behind his sternum. What the hell was he doing?

The church, though small, boasted an ornately decorated interior, including a stunning depiction of the crucifixion. Nick walked down the center aisle, his feet drawing him forward. He stopped at the front row of pews and knelt, clasping his hands in prayer. But he didn't know what to pray for. This was daft. He didn't belong here. He rose hastily and hurried back down the aisle. A strong clear voice halted him.

The hairs rose at the back of his neck, and for a second he had the sensation that Jesus himself had said the words. But when he turned, of course he saw a priest, all in black, a short, balding, portly man with red cheeks and kind eyes. He asked again in Italian how he could help Nick.

"I don't know why I came here." Realizing he'd answered in English, he started to repeat himself, struggling to put the words into Italian, but the priest held up a hand to stop him. Then he answered Nick in perfect English.

"There was a reason you came. Perhaps you need to unburden your soul?" The priest motioned to the row of confessionals.

Nick hadn't confessed since he was eight. A light sweat broke out on his forehead. So many sins to catalog since then. He shook his head, but didn't turn to leave.

The priest approached and put a gentle hand on his shoulder. "Come, my son, release your burdens, and you shall be healed."

Numbly, Nick let himself be led to a booth. He took a seat and faced the priest through the grill. "I haven't been to confession in almost twenty years," he whispered.

The priest chuckled. "Well then, only the major sins, my son."

"You cannot repeat anything I tell you?"

"Everything you say here is between you, me, and God."

In a rush, Nick described the shooting at the docks and the warehouse arson and murder. "Four men are dead because of me."

"God understands the intent behind your actions."

"But I chose to save myself each time. Those men died because of my selfishness."

"Do you repent your choices?"

Nick's gut clenched. He hated to admit the truth. But if he didn't do so here, when would he? "I want to say yes, but in my heart…"

"It is the rare man who can willingly sacrifice his life for another's. Even Christ had his doubts."

The answer was little comfort. "How do I live with what I've done?"

The priest drew in a breath, then let it out. Nick heard the creak of wood as the man shifted in his seat. "Are you seeking absolution, my son?"

"I cannot ask for that."

"That is because you haven't forgiven yourself."

"How can I? All I want is to bring the men who ordered these crimes to justice, but the avenues I've tried are closed to me now."

"Is that really true?"

No. He did have one more option: pursue the prosecution through Interpol and accept his own dismissal for Mafia ties. Of course, Émile's wife might die because of his choice. He explained his dilemma.

"Is it certain that she will suffer due to your actions?"

"No. But it's possible."

"You must trust in our Holy Father."

Or maybe, he should trust in *his* father. "Can a man be moral and still be part of the Mafia?"

The priest chuckled. "Anything is possible. But such a thing would be a miracle, yes?"

Nick stared at the dark wood paneling of the confessional, searching his heart for answers. For some reason, he remembered the day his father had left them for the last time, remembered his father swinging him up into his arms and whirling him about in a circle until he was dizzy. Then his father had pulled him close and kissed his forehead. "I love you, Nico." There'd been tears on his father's cheeks. Tears that had prompted Nick to beg him to stay or to take him and Mummy back with him to Italy. "I cannot." There had been such sadness in his father's voice, such regret. A fierce grief in his eyes.

And in that moment, the answer came. It was time to forgive his father. Time to ask his help.

Time to hope for a miracle.

———— • ————

After calling Cris to let him know he was going to visit his father, Nick picked up the mobile Ruggero had given him and placed the call, his hands sweating, his heart running a marathon in his chest. The phone rang three times; Nick wasn't sure what to say if it went to voice mail. Then his father answered. "Nick." Not "Nico." The voice flat, emotionless.

"May we speak?" Nick asked. "In person?"

Silence. Finally: "Come to the house." His father gave him directions, then hung up without saying goodbye.

Nick stared at the phone, his stomach churning. Maybe this was a bad idea. He tapped the edge of the phone against the steering wheel. What other choice did he have?

He could just keep his mouth shut, keep his head down, and do Dario's bidding.

But that wasn't a life worth living. Even if Delfina were his wife. He'd slowly kill himself that way, his self-worth an ever diminishing speck until he shoved a gun in his mouth and made a bullet his last meal.

No, he had to take his lumps. He needed his father's help, his forgiveness. Nick turned the key in the ignition, smiling at the irony. How many times had he fantasized about his father coming to him groveling, begging Nick to let him back into his life? Never had Nick imagined their roles reversed.

How things had changed.

He reached the villa quickly, his mouth dropping open at the beauty and enormity of the estate. He'd thought Dario's house grand and Gianluca d'Imperio's impressive. But this was a true *palazzo*, a magnificent home fit for a king. For a moment, his nervousness ebbed. Just how had his father made so much money?

A maid showed Nick inside and directed him to wait in the foyer, a grand soaring space over two stories high. The expensive décor—marbles, fine fabrics, paintings that appeared to date back at least a century or two—reminded Nick of Versailles or the Palacio Real in Madrid. His father's home was a far cry from the ones Nick had grown up in, even farther from his own tiny flat. Did he truly know this man at all?

His heart started skipping again, and the feeling grew worse when Ruggero appeared, his eyes dark and menacing. He frisked Nick, unburdening him of the gun and knife. "Is this really necessary?" Nick asked.

Ruggero stepped close to Nick, giving him a clear view of the nasty scar that cut across the left side of his face. "You are an Andretti now. No matter what Don Lucchesi says, I do not trust Andretti trash." For a moment, Ruggero looked like he might spit in Nick's face, then he turned without another word and led Nick out back to a stunning garden.

His father sat on the rear terrace with his beautiful wife, who glared when she saw him. His father's face was drawn, his gaze trained on the lake shimmering in the distance.

Ruggero withdrew and took a post out of hearing range. His continued presence unsettled Nick. So this wasn't to be a friendly visit. But he had only himself to blame for that. He was the one who'd decided to join forces with Dario, he was the one who'd insulted his father in front of Andretti and his top men. He was the one who'd killed Fedele, his father's godson.

Nick stood awkwardly, not sure whether to take a seat at the table. After a long silence, his father rescued him. "Sit," he said, motioning to an empty chair. "This is my wife, Kate, if you do not remember."

Nick offered his hand, but she didn't take it. Instead she turned to her husband. "Tell me again why he's here."

His father half-smiled. "*Cara*, your love for me is humbling, and I know you mean well. But we should stay civil, yes?"

She leaned over and kissed his cheek. "I'll do my best."

His father's face brightened, and he took Kate's hand and kissed her knuckles. Then he turned to Nick. "You wished to see me."

Nick didn't know where to start. Now that he was here, all he could think about was the horrible, crushed expression on his father's face when Nick had told him he'd chosen to join the Andretti *cosca*. To be, more or less, an Andretti. His vision blurred with unshed tears and his throat jammed up.

"Well?" Kate asked, her voice softer than it had been, but still with an edge that threatened to slice him.

"I didn't mean it," Nick finally said, his voice choked. "I didn't mean what I said at the ceremony." He risked a glance at his father and saw his eyes swimming as well.

"Then why, Nico?" His father's voice vibrated with anguish.

"I had this stupid idea that I could put Andretti in jail if I got on the inside. But it's all a mess, and I should've listened to Delfina, but I didn't, and now—"

"Slow down. You are trying to put Dario in jail?"

"I want to, yes. He used me to kill Fedele. He needs to pay."

His father's mouth clamped into a grim line. "You cannot do that."

"Why not?"

"They will kill you. The men of his *cosca*." He ran a hand over his face and took a deep breath. "And if they fail, all of us—all of the 'Ndrangheta—will be given the task of hunting you down."

"You mean—?"

His father nodded. "Yes. Even me."

"And if you refused?"

"I would be next."

"But you're my father—"

His father leaned forward, placing his hands flat on the table. "*You* took the vows. *You* said the words. Betrayal means death. Refusal to carry out orders means death. There are no loopholes, no exceptions."

Something with sharp teeth tore at Nick's belly. "So I'm stuck taking orders from Dario Andretti for the rest of my life?"

"You should have given that a little more thought, shouldn't you?" Kate said.

He deserved her scorn. He'd been such a goddamn fool from the moment he'd received that letter purportedly from Franco Trucco. He'd charged into a situation he didn't understand, he'd ignored every single person who'd tried to help him. And now he was reaping the fruits of his foolhardiness.

"Kate, he did not know. And now he does. Maybe I should have been more direct with him."

"No," Nick cut in. "This is my fault. Not yours."

His father raised a brow, but didn't look at Nick. Instead he studied the mosaic on the tabletop. "So, you have stopped blaming me?"

Nick knew what he was really asking. He was asking if Nick still blamed him for *her*. The image of his mother lying in that tub of crimson flashed through his mind. Knowing what he knew now—could he still hold his father responsible? An internal shuddering started in his chest, and despite the breaths he took to quell it, the tremors grew until he felt sick, as if he needed to vomit up the hard truth he'd held back all these years—*she* was the one who had abandoned him. His father had tried to set him free.

Nick lurched away from the table, unable to speak, and started toward a rose garden a few dozen yards away. He'd avoided roses for years after her death, their scent always reminding him of that awful time. But now he had to face the truth, face what she'd done. He stumbled along the rows of fading rosebushes; most had given up all their blooms. Only a few blowsy stragglers braved the cooler days of November. Why had his mum done it? Why hadn't she loved him enough to want to see him grow up?

He'd reached the far end of the rose beds and now stood looking out at the lake gleaming in the sunlight, framed by the high peaks of the Alps. He heard the tread of footsteps behind him, but he didn't turn. A hand cupped his shoulder. "Nico."

Nick leaned into that touch. "Papà." He could barely choke the word out before he released a sob, and then his father's arm slid around his shoulders. "I'm so sorry," Nick finally managed.

His father hugged him from behind, pulling Nick against his broad chest. A rush of warmth filled him and dried up his tears. "I am sorry too. I should have taken you with me after the funeral. We missed so many years together."

"No. You made the right decision."

His father said nothing for a while, just rested his chin on Nick's shoulder. When he spoke again, his voice was a whisper. "So many times I wondered if I had been a coward. If I had made the right choice for you."

"You tried to give me something else, another life."

"But I failed."

"This is all my creation. Let me take the responsibility." Nick stepped out of his father's embrace and took a deep breath, turning around. "I'm not a schoolboy anymore."

"I know." Then his father smiled. "You have turned out well. I owe your grandparents so much."

"So do I." *Christ.* He still hadn't called them. "Where are they anyway?"

Another smile. "Enjoying my godfather's hospitality in Capri."

"You're sure they're safe?"

"As houses. No one crosses Vittorio Battista."

"Fancy that. They had their honeymoon in Capri. Always said they wanted to go back."

"I am sure it is as lovely as they remember."

Nick stuck his hands in the back pockets of his jeans, not sure how to say it, but knowing he had to. "I'm so sorry about Fedele. I had no idea—"

A shadow crossed his father's face. "That was Dario's doing. Not yours."

When Nick tried to say more, his father held up a hand. "I will not hear another word on the subject."

His face flamed. He'd been such an idiot, thinking he could outmaneuver Andretti. An awkward silence stretched between them. Finally Nick said, "So now what do I do?"

"You marry Delfina and hope Dario does not ask you for more than information."

"That's it? *That's* my option?"

"For now." His father shrugged. "Perhaps another possibility will emerge."

That shrug and that tone were far too casual. "You have something in mind."

"Benedetto approached me with an offer. I have not quite accepted it, but if I do, Dario will not be pleased. The mere fact that Benedetto made me this offer tells me that Dario is in trouble."

"As in he might not be alive much longer?"

Another shrug. "Perhaps."

It was time to tell him. "I think Benedetto tried to have Cris and me killed."

"The Russians?"

"Yes. We were supposed to die that night. Delfina thinks Benedetto isn't finished with us."

"He is afraid you will tell Lorenzo, or let something slip that gets back to Lorenzo."

"So what do I do? Let him shoot me in the back?"

"No. Benedetto wants something from me. He will not get it until he swears to leave you alone."

"Cris too."

His father raised his brows. "You are certain you want to vouch for Cris?"

"We took an oath to each other. We're blood brothers now."

"*Madonna.*" His father looked heavenward. "There are no half measures with you."

Nick chuckled. "Especially when I've done the wrong thing."

"I will ensure my agreement with Benedetto covers both of you."

"Thank you." Nick tried to swallow down what else he was feeling, but the words spilled out. "I hate being so fucking powerless."

His father was silent for a moment, then he said, "Nothing in life—especially in our world—is certain. One minute you are on top, the next you are scrambling for your life." He clapped Nick on the shoulder. "Patience is the most important tool in any war chest. *Capisci?*"

Nick nodded. He understood, better than he ever had before. It wasn't the answer he wanted to hear—his store of patience had always run thin. But he'd better learn to cultivate some.

His father turned them back toward the house in an easy meander. "How are things between you and Delfina?"

"Good."

"But?"

It was Nick's turn to shrug. "She didn't want to marry an 'Ndranghetista. She wanted out."

"And?"

Nick chuckled at how well his father read him. "She said she forgave me, but I can't help thinking that she's settling. Like I'm the least obnoxious choice in front of her."

His father stopped. "I know the feeling. I went through that with Kate."

"She certainly got over it. She's like a tiger when it comes to you."

His father smiled, his eyes glowing. "I proved myself to her."

"How?"

"I killed the man holding her prisoner."

Nick clucked his tongue, impressed. "I can see how that would work. Don't know what *I'm* going to do."

"I do not think you need something so dramatic."

"You don't know her."

His father stopped walking. "I do know her, actually."

"Yeah, I guess you do. She was your niece."

"And briefly my fiancée."

"What?" A blast of heat ripped through him.

His father raised his hands in surrender. "It was not like that. I never even held her hand."

How could he have forgotten? Nick calmed down. "Don't know why that took me off-guard."

"Because you love her."

Nick kicked at a rock in his path. "I don't. This marriage is strictly business. I *can't* have feelings for her." He jammed his hands in his pockets. "I wish I could just walk away. She deserves better than this."

His father studied him for a moment, then he said, "I told myself the same thing when I married Antonella Andretti." He smiled. "It was impossible for my heart to resist her." After a pause, he said, "Perhaps you are in a similar situation?"

"Perhaps." He was such a liar. But what kind of future could they have?

"I have an idea. Have you bought her a ring yet?"

Christ. He was some romantic. He didn't have a ring. Hell, he hadn't even proposed. She was going to walk into that party tomorrow with nothing. "No, but I'd better fix that."

"I think I can help. Follow me."

A dozen yards from the house, Nick stopped. "May I ask a favor?"

"Anything."

"If something happens to me, promise you'll help Delfina get free. I want her to have all the things she's ever wanted."

A slight smile creased his father's face. "You do love her."

"I just want more for her." Nick shook his head. "More than this."

"I will do my best, Nico." He took Nick back to the terrace and left him with Kate while he headed into the house alone.

"You two patched things up?" she asked.

"Yeah. He's forgiven me."

"Good." She twisted her hands together, the large diamonds on her left hand sparkling in the sunlight. Delfina should have stones like those. "Listen, I know I was hard on you—"

Nick put up a hand. "No need."

She smiled. "Good. Because I suck at apologies."

"I'm getting some much-needed practice myself."

His father came back outside, and handed a small velvet box to Nick. "Open it."

When he did, an impressive antique ring poked out of the enclosure, sparkling as if it had just been cleaned. He could easily picture it on Delfina's hand; its classic beauty would suit her, and the diamond solitaire was more than big enough. "It's perfect. Where did you get this?"

"It belonged to my mother. I had been saving it for my eldest son." His father touched Kate's belly lightly and Nick remembered. She was pregnant.

"You should keep it. I'll find something else." He held the ring out to his father.

His father refused with a wave of his hand. "This one might be a girl. Besides, *you* are my eldest son. I want you to have it."

Throat tight, Nick put the ring box in his pocket. This was how it should be, right? This was how it should have always been.

And even though he'd made one horrible blunder after another, at least he'd done one thing right today.

Tomorrow at the party—maybe even tonight—he hoped to do another. He was going to propose to Delfina Andretti. He'd never said "I love you" to a woman; he hadn't been able to say those words for almost twenty years to anyone. Not even his grandparents. Not since Mum.

But even if he couldn't say how he felt out loud, he'd make sure there was no doubt in Delfina's heart that he loved her.

———◆———

Nick had just exited his father's house, the ring in his pocket, and was opening the door to the car when he heard someone calling his name. He glanced back and saw Antonio descending the steps. The expression on his face was stormy, and Nick's shoulders drew up in response.

Trying to appear casual, Nick rested one arm on the top of the open car door, which stood between them like a shield. "What do you want?" he asked, when Antonio drew near.

"I just heard the news. About you and Delfina."

Nick noticed that Antonio didn't offer his congratulations. "And?"

A scowl darkened Antonio's features. "I do not know what you have planned, but you had better be good to her, or I will gut you and enjoy every minute."

"You sound like a scorned lover. Not a friend."

"She is special to me. Like a sister." The sincerity in Antonio's tone surprised him.

"I'll do right by her."

"She deserves a husband who loves her."

"You think I don't?"

"I think people are useful to you."

Nick's face grew hot. The accusation was partly true—he had lied plenty to get to where he was. But he hadn't done it for personal gain. And he hadn't used Delfina. He stepped around the car door. Only a couple feet separated them now. "You don't know me."

"I know enough not to trust you."

Nick shrugged. "Your problem, not mine."

Antonio stepped forward and pushed Nick hard. "You joined the damn Andrettis and broke Don Enrico's heart. You will break hers too."

Nick's hands clenched into fists. "I've apologized for that. I made a mistake I can't undo, and I'm sorry for it. What else do you want me to say?"

"Why did you come here?"

"To apologize to my father."

"No. I mean, why did you come to Italia?"

"I was curious about him."

"Then why did you put yourself into Dario Andretti's hands? Why did you react so violently the night we all met?" He didn't wait for Nick's response. "I will tell you why. You hated him. You hated him and you wanted to hurt him. All the rest is a charade."

"That's not entirely true." The words sounded feeble even to his own ears.

"Pack your things and leave. Spare us the rest of the misery you want to inflict on us."

And there it was—Antonio's true fear. "You're afraid of anything good happening between me and my father. Because where does that leave you? With a new baby on the way and my cousins crying for your blood, you must be feeling awfully insecure." He took a step closer to Antonio, staring him in the eyes. The red spots mottling Antonio's cheeks told him he'd hit the truth. He lowered his voice. "I'm only going to say this once—I'm no threat to you."

"Says the Interpol spy who works for the Andrettis." Antonio spat on the ground before walking away.

Nick took a deep breath, then got in the car. Antonio was right to be suspicious. From the outside, it did look bad. Didn't look much better from the inside either.

But he'd prove himself in time. Somehow he'd manage to do what Silvio Fuente did. Play both sides. Maintain the balance of power. Fight like hell when the situation warranted such.

And bide his time until he could get out from under Dario's thumb.

CHAPTER 21

Delfina needed those recordings. If there was any gift she wanted to give Nick after their engagement party, it was the means for him to clear his conscience and save his life and Cris's. And hopefully give her and Nick the relative autonomy of living in England.

But if Cris and her father didn't know where the recordings were, how could she ever lay hands on them? She couldn't believe her grandfather would have died without entrusting anyone with his secret. The only person he'd definitely trusted was Aunt Toni, and she'd been dead more than a year. So who else?

Had he told Nonna Romola? If he had, surely she'd have told Papà, and no doubt Papà had already thought to ask her. Delfina could think of no excuse to ask Nonna herself.

There had to be someone else. Or perhaps her grandfather had written it down?

She paced around her bedroom. She'd searched as much of the house as she'd dared, and so far, she'd found nothing. Her father's study was the place she most wanted to comb through, but doing so was risky. Besides, Papà had certainly done the same search already.

If only she had access to her grandfather's private papers, or to Aunt Toni's… *Think, Delfina.* Her grandfather would have locked up that kind of information, so he must have hidden a key somewhere. But where?

The answer struck her like a thunderbolt. The necklace!

She rushed to her jewelry box and rummaged through it, pulling out the pendant her aunt had given her before she died. Aunt Toni had said something at the time that took on new significance now. "When your grandfather gave this to me, he said I'd always owned the key to his heart."

Delfina held the pendant up to the light. It was made of sterling silver, an oval with a tree in the middle. She inspected it carefully. The trunk of the tree bisected the pendant at the bottom. Perhaps the trunk was a separate piece? She picked at it with her fingernail. It didn't budge.

Setting the pendant on her desk, she rubbed her fingers over its surface. There

200

was something odd about that trunk. It felt a little more raised than the rest of the design.

She scanned the corkboard above her desk. There it was—the needle she'd used to stick up the picture she'd taken of her first official design. The peek-a-boo dress that would probably never see the spotlight. She took the photo down, her stomach doing a funny flip. If she found the recordings, if she and Nick were allowed to go to London—maybe her dress would end up on the runway someday. A smile teased her lips and she pressed the picture to her chest, almost not daring to hope.

With a shake of her head, she reminded herself of her task. If she didn't find those recordings, she wouldn't be going anywhere, and her fiancé very well might end up with a bullet in his back. Setting the photo on the desk, she grabbed the pin and ran it around the edge of the trunk. Just where it met the branches, the pin's tip slipped into a small depression. She tried to pry the trunk up. No luck. Then she pressed down and the trunk gave with a click, flipping down on a cleverly designed hinge at the bottom of the pendant.

She held the "tree trunk" up to the light to see its silhouette. It was definitely a key; small scalloped teeth lined the upper quarter of its length.

Her heart pounded wildly. She had the key. Now where was the lock?

She peered at the underside of the trunk. A symbol appeared to be engraved on it. It resembled a sword. What the hell did that mean?

A sword. Where was there a sword in the house?

She practically slapped herself when the answer came to her. Not in the house—in the temple to Ares. The god's statue held a sword in one hand and a shield in the other.

Excitement fluttering in her belly, Delfina raced out to the temple. Embedded in the marble beneath the statue in the alcove was a brass fitting with a keyhole in the middle. She stuck the key in the opening and turned. The lock clicked and the marble square that housed it popped forward. When she pulled on the piece of marble, it slid toward her, revealing a tiny drawer. Inside she found a ring with two keys and an address in Como followed by one word: Luperca. The name of the wolf goddess who'd suckled the legendary founders of Rome, the twins Romulus and Remus. Fitting, considering how much her grandfather had loved dogs.

She took the address and the keys, then carefully relocked the marble slab.

When Delfina pulled her Alfa Romeo up to the address on the paper, she was surprised to see a small office building. Was this a front of some sort? She scanned the names on the directory, but there was no "Luperca" among them. Taking a breath, she forced herself to slow down and reread the names. Finally she found it: Canis Enterprises. Dogs again.

One of the keys fit in the locked outer door. She hurried up to the second floor and followed the signs to the suite number. Her pulse racing, she tried the other key. It worked. She opened the door and stepped inside, immediately disappointed. It looked like an ordinary office. Dusty, sure, but ordinary.

She walked past a bank of desks, all of them sporting computers, books, and other knickknacks. Had anyone ever worked here, or were these desks just clever window dressing?

Dead plants languished in the corners and the water cooler was full of some awful greenish slime. No one had been in here for at least a month.

There were two rooms at the end of the suite, both with closed doors. She tried the first one. It wasn't locked. There was no name on the door, but the pictures on the desk inside suggested it was her grandfather's—a recent one of her and Cris and several of her father and Aunt Toni as children. The computer was switched off. After she explored the next room, she'd come back to investigate further.

That room was locked. She fit the key in the lock, her heart skipping. This had to be it.

She opened the door to the low hum of computers. The room was dark, except for the blinking of various lights on the machines in front of her. When she flicked on the overhead light, she saw four machines sitting side by side, each with a handwritten label taped along the top of its monitor: Guest Cottage, Home Office, Plane, Watch.

Delfina smiled when she saw the last one. Oh, her grandfather had been sly. He'd given his brother a Patek Philippe for Christmas two years ago, and she'd rarely seen Benedetto without it. *Dio mio,* the things that must be on those recordings!

She sat down in front of the computer that said "Guest Cottage." First order of business—erasing the recording of her night with Nick. Letting out the breath she'd been holding, she moved the mouse and was greeted with the password prompt. She typed in "Luperca" and found herself at the Windows desktop.

What now? Her grandfather hadn't been fond of computers, so the setup had to be relatively simple. She'd try the most likely arrangement. After opening Windows Media Player, she scanned for a playlist—and there it was. A list of recordings with dates and times. She found the first one for the day she and Nick had been together and clicked it out of curiosity. Lots of random noises of Nick moving about and occasionally mumbling to himself. At various points he put on music, making her smile when he sang along to it off-key. She flipped forward to the next recording from that day. Pay dirt—she could hear the two of them whispering, but most of what they said was indistinct. Then the music came on again and a thrill ran through her as an image filled her mind: Nick placing her on the bed, the intent, almost predatory fire in his eyes as he'd watched her undress. If she hadn't been in a hurry, she'd have replayed their entire evening together, but she didn't have that luxury.

She listened for a few more seconds before stopping the recording and deleting it, then emptying the Recycle Bin. At least she didn't have that to worry about anymore. Where to start next? She logged in to each machine and checked the playlists. There were so many recordings to choose from—too many.

Her mobile phone buzzed, making her jump. Nick's name was on the display. "*Ciao, bella,*" he said when she answered. It felt so good to hear his voice after the day she'd had.

"Where are you?" she asked.

"I'm about to leave my father's." He paused, then said, "I just spoke to Cris. He told me what happened at Morelli's. I'm so sorry."

The sincerity in his voice made her chest ache. "*Grazie.* You're lucky—I already sobbed my heart out on Cris's shoulder, so you'll be spared that."

"I wish I'd been there for you."

"Actually, it gave us an opportunity to clear the air."

"Fancy that. I did the same with my father." After a moment, he said, "Any chance we can get together tonight? I have a surprise for you."

She grinned. "I like the sound of that. I might have one for you too." And maybe they could sneak off to the temple again and finish what they'd started. Without any interruptions.

After they hung up, she settled on the machine with "Watch" taped to the monitor. That one had by far the most recordings on the most days, and they were the highest quality and easiest to understand. Of course much of what she heard was banal and sometimes embarrassing: Benedetto and his wife in the bedroom, Benedetto in the bathroom, Benedetto ordering espresso somewhere. Boring, boring, boring. How did the *carabinieri* do it? She'd go mad if she had to listen to wiretaps all day.

Finally something interesting from a few days ago. Benedetto had taken a call from someone named Ilya. That name alone caught her interest. But what she heard next chilled her to the marrow.

She couldn't make out Ilya's side of the conversation. But she heard Benedetto's loud and clear. He was planning to sacrifice them all—all except her uncle Enrico. For some reason, Benedetto needed him. But Nick, as well as Papà and Cris—*his* family, *his* blood—they were expendable. She just didn't know where or when the attack would take place, but since he'd mentioned Uncle Enrico, it sounded like he was planning it for the engagement party.

She'd found clear proof that Benedetto was a traitor. But she wanted to know why—and she needed more if Nick was going to put him in jail. There were too many recordings to review them all. She needed a strategy.

Perhaps if she went back to the day after Cris was shot, she'd find something useful. No doubt Benedetto had received a call from Ilya then. The second recording of the day did yield a phone call from Ilya; Benedetto spent his time soothing the man, saying that he'd find out what had happened. Afterward, he muttered and cursed to himself, nothing she could make out well, other than "the little shits." Did that mean Nick and Cris?

She zipped through the next few recordings—all snippets of Benedetto going about his day, boarding his jet, and so on, as he journeyed north to the lake. Then she heard something interesting: Nick's voice. They were bargaining. Nick was asking Benedetto for several things, including saving his grandparents, breaking her engagement to Leandro, setting her up as a designer, and not letting Dario force her to marry someone else. Her throat constricted. Nick had tried to do so much on her behalf, even if some of it was misguided and insulting. She'd have to tell him what she thought later. Then Benedetto said, "You don't want her?"

Delfina leaned forward. *What was Nick going to say?* "I've had her. And I don't do relationships." She couldn't have hurt more if Nick had punched her in the gut.

She meant nothing to him. Nothing at all.

Pressing a hand to her trembling lips, Delfina stopped the recording, breathing deep to quell the tears that wanted to fall, the sobs that wanted to tear out of her throat. She was not going to cry over this. There had to be an explanation for what he'd said. And that had been a week ago. Things had changed.

She started the recording again and heard Benedetto asking Nick to be his mole in Interpol. Okay, Nick hadn't mentioned it, but she wasn't surprised by the request. She rather expected Benedetto to want that. But what she heard next made her breath catch: Benedetto asked Nick to kill her father. Nick tried to refuse, but in the end, he said he'd do it.

Now she knew why Nick had never mentioned this conversation.

Acid crawled up her esophagus and her gut clenched into a ball. What else wasn't Nick telling her? What were his true intentions, his true plans? Had everything between them been a lie?

She needed to confront him. Right now. Opening the desk drawers, she rifled through their contents, hoping to find a blank CD. Instead she found a flash drive. Even better.

With the copy in hand, Delfina started to rise, but then she sat back down in the chair. What if Nick *did* have some other plan in mind? If she confronted him by herself—she hated to think it—could she trust him not to hurt her?

The Nick she'd heard on that recording sounded mercenary, even if his requests of Benedetto were not entirely selfish. Maybe he did have a shred of decency in him. But if that was true, why hadn't he mentioned the conversation? Why hadn't he warned her, at least?

It wasn't safe to be alone with Nick. Her stomach rolled over. *Dio mio,* she was going to be sick.

When she'd admitted that she loved him, he'd just stared at her; he'd even laughed. And then when he'd said he was happy, that he'd forgiven her, he must have been lying.

Her stomach rebelled again, and she grabbed the rubbish bin under the desk and vomited into it. She heaved and heaved, tears squeezing out from under her closed lids.

Nick never loved me.

She set the bin down and swallowed, trying to clear the bitter taste of bile from her tongue.

He never loved me.

Delfina inhaled through her nose and pressed a fist against her mouth. Papà would know what to do. He'd know how to keep the family safe from Benedetto. And he'd know how to handle Nick. Her own emotions were getting the best of her. She wanted to believe in Nick. And yet, how could she?

A hot tear slipped down her cheek and she wiped it away. How had everything gone so wrong?

She'd hoped finding the recordings would help Nick achieve his type of justice and put Benedetto in jail. But now it was time for a different brand of justice altogether. The only justice recognized by the 'Ndrangheta.

Death.

But would Benedetto be the only one paying that price?

———— ✦ ————

When Nick pulled up to the house, Cris was waiting for him outside, arms crossed, a frown etching deep lines in his normally sunny face.

"What's wrong?" Nick asked as he came up the front steps, clutching the bouquet of roses he'd bought for Delfina in one hand, the bag of funny gifts he'd run all over Como for in the other.

"Follow me." Cris turned without another word and headed into the house.

Nick's stomach flipped over as he followed Cris inside and down the hall. Had they somehow discovered his meeting with Fuente? If they had, they probably didn't know what was said. Perhaps he could claim he was seeking information or just keeping in touch to reassure his superiors? He'd remind Cris that he did call him about visiting his father and produce the ring as proof. That would assuage them, right?

They entered Dario's study, and Nick was surprised to see Delfina sitting behind her father's desk. She was showing Dario something on the computer. When her eyes met Nick's, they were filled with nothing but hurt. He took a step toward her. "Delfina, what's wrong?" She looked away from him, toward the door. Flavio was standing beside it. Not a good sign. What was going on?

Dario straightened up and pinned Nick with a hard stare. "Tell me why I shouldn't shoot you where you stand."

Fuck. Nick almost started to make an excuse, then realized he ought to be careful. He set the roses and the bag of gifts on a table by the window before answering. "Would one of you please tell me what this is about?"

"Play them," Dario said to Delfina.

She clicked something on the computer, and voices flowed out of the speakers. It was the discussion he'd had with Benedetto after the Russian deal had gone south. The discussion where Benedetto had asked him to kill Dario. "How did you get that?"

"Never mind. The more important question is: When were you planning to do it?" Dario asked.

"I wasn't. I only said yes because he threatened me with his guard, Eusebio. You did hear that part?"

Dario crossed his arms. "Why didn't you warn me?"

"What proof did I have? I figured he'd just deny it, and you'd kill me. I wasn't exactly in your good graces then."

"And you certainly aren't now."

"Listen. Why would I do it? You have my grandparents in your sights. If I killed you, Cris would certainly kill them. It doesn't make sense for me to take that kind of risk."

"You might do it to save your own skin."

"How would killing you save me?"

"If I'm dead, that solves a lot of problems for you."

"Does it? If I kill you, then I'd be betraying Cris and my vow. Everyone would hunt me down. I'd be dead myself."

Cris rose from where he'd been perched on the windowsill. "He does have a point. Several of them. And then there's the other recording."

"What other recording?"

Delfina clicked the mouse and Nick heard Benedetto's voice and an inaudible one that he didn't recognize. A Russian accent heavily flavored the second speaker's

English. When Benedetto referred to the man as "Ilya" and then mentioned Ilya getting his vengeance, a chill spread through Nick. Ilya as in Ilya Vilanovich. Father to Yuri and Gregor, the men he'd killed. He listened to Benedetto say that Ilya would soon be able to avenge his sons, and he recommended they take Dario too. Then curiously, Benedetto mentioned Nick's father and specified that he be spared. Why? Did this have something to do with the offer his father said Benedetto had made to him?

When the recording ended, Nick latched onto the thing he thought exonerated him. "Benedetto wants me dead—or at least he's willing to let Vilanovich kill me. That proves I'm not conspiring with him. And this isn't the first time Ilya's tried. Maybe Benedetto had a hand in that too."

"All that really proves," Dario said, "is that Ilya is more important to him."

"I took vows to this family. I made a promise to your son. I'm marrying your daughter. I have no reason to cross you."

"What did you do today?"

The back of Nick's shirt went damp. *Stay calm.* "I went to a church. And I visited my father. And I bought a few gifts for Delfi."

"If you're lying, we'll know."

"I'm not."

Dario turned to Cris. "Check the records."

"What records?" Nick asked, even though he knew.

"There's a GPS tracker on your car," Dario said.

"Tracking me through my phone wasn't enough?"

"A phone is easier to shed than a car," Cris said. He nudged Delfina aside and clicked the mouse several times. Nick met her gaze. She still looked hurt. Why? Did she actually believe what he'd said to Benedetto about not wanting her?

Cris glanced up at Nick and Dario. "The GPS confirms his story. And he did call me. Twice."

Dario pursed his lips, then he said, "Find out what he said while in the car."

Fuck! He should've known the car was bugged. Adrenaline dumped into his system, urging him to run, but that was pointless. He'd never get past Flavio.

Cris clicked the mouse a few more times, then Nick's voice flowed out of the speakers. Thank God he hadn't called Fuente in the car. But he should've called his father from the mobile they'd given him. As long as they didn't think to double-check its call log, he'd be okay.

When the recording ended, Cris said, "There's another."

"Play it," Dario said. Nick's voice again and Antonio's, a bit muffled. *Shit.* Delfina shouldn't be hearing this. What he'd said wasn't terrible, but it wasn't a ringing endorsement of his feelings either. He reached for the ring in his pocket to show her, and Dario put up a hand. "Don't move."

"I wasn't going for my gun."

Dario motioned for Flavio. "Search him."

His heart pounded as Flavio patted him down. Maybe he'd miss the second phone.

Flavio removed Nick's Beretta, the switchblade, the mobile from Cris, and the ring box. So far, so good. Then he patted Nick's chest and found the lump of the other phone. He pulled it out and held it up for everyone to see. "This doesn't look like one of ours," he said.

Nick tried to slow his breathing as Flavio handed the phone to Dario. *Fuck, fuck, fuck!* Dario turned the phone on, pressing buttons as Nick's mind raced. The texts. The phone itself was bad enough. But once they saw those, they'd know he'd lied. Why hadn't he erased them?

After a few moments, Dario's face darkened. "I should have known not to trust a Lucchesi."

"What is it?" Cris asked.

"A text from his father. Nick has known his grandparents have been safe for nearly a week. He found out a few hours after Cris was shot." Dario's eyes bored into Nick. "Which makes you a lying snake."

"Listen, I could've walked away at any time once I knew that. But I didn't. I stayed and I made my deal. And I certainly didn't shoot you."

"All true. But you lied. Which means you're hiding something. Benedetto asked you to spy on us, didn't he? Or did your father?"

"Neither. I'm not spying on anyone. You've got to believe me."

"Yes, you are." Delfina spoke for the first time. "You're trying to put them all in jail. *That's* why you're here. *That's* why you stayed. *That's* why you joined the 'Ndrangheta." Her voice was dry, flinty, and cold as frostbite.

The chill in her tone infected him, moving through him with a shudder. Christ, with that little revelation, he was done for. Even Delfina had lost faith in him. Not even the redoubtable Enrico Lucchesi, as Fuente had dubbed him, could save him now.

He tried one more time. "You don't have the full story on any of this. You need to listen to all the recordings—then you'll see that Benedetto is a master of pulling strings and telling lies."

Dario laughed. "You think I don't know that? He makes you a rank amateur."

None of this was going right. None of it. He tried to get Delfina's attention, but she stared right through him. He motioned to the ring box. "May I?" he asked Dario.

Dario shook his head. "Cris."

Cris picked the box up and opened it, barely glancing inside before shutting it. "It's a ring," he said, his voice sounding flat, hollow.

"It's for Delfina. My father gave it to me. I had planned to propose at the party, but after what happened to her today, I was going to do it tonight instead." Nick spoke to her, but she looked away. When she finally turned back, her eyes were swimming. God help him. He loved her. He truly did. And now she'd never believe it. "Delfi, I swear to you—"

Delfina jumped up and ran out of the room. Cris set the ring box on the desk.

She hates me. Nick slumped into a chair and bowed his head, clasping his hands on the back of his neck. He hardly gave a damn if he lived or died at this point. They'd both probably be the same. Hell, either way. "I'm sorry," he whispered to no one in particular.

Cris slammed his fist onto Dario's desk, making everything on it jump and rattle. "Sorry? You're *sorry*? I trusted you. I put my faith in you. I put the faith of our *cosca* in you. And this is how you repay me. I thought you were trying to save my life that night. But all you cared about was saving your own!"

"If all I'd cared about was myself, I'd have run and let them kill you."

"You are no brother of mine."

Nick studied the carpet. "You will always be mine."

Cris picked up Nick's switchblade and clicked it open. "I ought to slit your throat with this and cut out your tongue for all your lies."

Nick looked up at him. "Then do it. If I've lost you and Delfina"—his voice broke on her name—"I haven't much left."

Some of the heat ebbed from Cris's eyes. He closed the knife and tossed it on the desk. No one said anything for several moments. Finally Dario broke the silence. "As far as I can tell, Benedetto and Ilya are going to attack at the engagement party."

"But it could be at the wedding. Or another event. Maybe the rehearsal dinner," Cris said.

"Have you reviewed the rest of the recordings?" Nick asked.

"There are hundreds of them."

"I know some shortcuts. We could use keyword searches—"

Dario brushed his words away with an upraised hand. "Not enough time. Besides, the only event Benedetto knows the date of is the engagement party. Logic says that's the date."

"How familiar is he with your security?" Nick asked.

"Moderately."

"You should change all the entry codes, all your normal routines."

Dario glared at him. "How nice of you to be so helpful now."

"Listen, my interests haven't always aligned with yours, but when it comes to Delfina and Cris, we're on the same side."

"Behave yourself at the party, and perhaps I will still have a use for you."

"I'd rather not give Nick a chance to fuck things up for us tomorrow," Cris said, each word a punch to Nick's gut.

Dario smirked. "Turning on your blood brother so soon? You always were one to abandon your toys."

When Cris said nothing, Dario added, "I don't want Benedetto to know we're onto him. I'm putting you in charge of watching Nick." Cris nodded, his face flushed and unhappy. "And collect your sister's phone. I don't want her having a change of heart and calling Lucchesi."

Cris nodded again. He handed Nick the ring box. "You'll need this. But not the rest." He left the room, beckoning Nick to follow him.

Nick dreaded being alone with Cris. What could he possibly say?

But Cris said nothing as they tromped upstairs to Nick's bedroom. Just as Cris was about to go, Nick stopped him. "I know you don't believe me, but I never meant to betray you."

"I gave you my trust. I'll never be that foolish again." Cris wheeled about and left, slamming the door, then locking it.

Nick's throat clamped shut. When he'd lost his mother, he'd thought he'd lost everything.

How wrong he'd been.

CHAPTER 22

How many tears could one person cry? Delfina blew her nose again and wiped her eyes, but the tears kept coming. Nick Clarkston was a consummate liar. He'd never truly cared for her. Only for himself. She flopped down on her bed and called Gio, who answered on the second ring. *"Ciao, bella!* Ready for the big day tomorrow?" Gio asked.

Delfina burst into tears again. *Dio mio,* she had to go through with that charade too and somehow make it look real.

"Sweetie, what's wrong?" Gio asked, the levity leaving her voice. "Did something happen?"

Delfina gulped down air and tried to steady her voice. "Can you come over? Now?"

"Of course. I'll be there in a flash. Should I plan to stay overnight?"

"Would you?"

"It'll be just like when we were girls."

Delfina tried to smile. *"Mille grazie,* Gio. You're the best friend ever."

"Any time, sweetie. How often have I been the one crying on your shoulder?"

After they hung up, Delfina heard Cris and Nick come upstairs and Cris lock Nick in his room. Of course her father would make Cris Nick's jailer. Always he had to stick the knife in deeper. It was bad enough that she'd had to hear those recordings once, but by the time Nick had arrived, she'd already heard them three times. And her father had insisted she stay to face her fiancé.

How could Nick listen to what he'd said without reacting? Not even a wince at those callous words. "I've had her. I don't do relationships." And then what he'd said to Antonio. It could've been worse, but it was clear he didn't love her. "I'll do right by her." That was all she merited. His pity. Not his love.

But hadn't she already known that? He'd never said he loved her, not even when she had. She'd been a fool of monumental proportions to believe that he felt it, even if he couldn't say it.

Someone knocked at the door. It was too early for Gio, who'd be at least a half hour, provided she didn't try on four different outfits and twice as many pairs of shoes before coming over. "Go away," she yelled.

"Delfi, it's me." Cris.

He had to be nearly as devastated as she was. "Come in."

"Papà says I need to collect your phone." He held out his hand for it.

"He thinks I haven't received the message?"

Cris reddened. "We all know by now you've got a soft spot for Zio Enrico."

"I've had my fill of the Lucchesi family." She picked up her phone and tossed it to him. "Papà has nothing to worry about."

Cris put the phone in his pocket. "I'm sorry, Delfi." The tenderness in his voice called forth her tears again.

She turned her head away and wiped at them. The mattress dipped beneath her and then Cris took her in his arms. Her chest heaved and sobs tore out of her throat as she clung to her brother. He stroked her hair and upper back, murmuring that everything would be okay. But it wouldn't. It wouldn't be okay ever.

Nick had been her one hope to escape this life. And even when he'd joined the 'Ndrangheta, she'd at least thought that he loved her. That he cherished her and would do his best to make a happy life with her. But she'd been dreaming again. When was she ever going to grow up and face reality?

All she'd been to him was another *figa*. A girl he'd "had." A girl who didn't merit more than his pity. Hadn't he been telling her she was beneath him? All that stuff about her being corrupted and warped. But she'd ignored it when she should have known better. She was tainted in his eyes. Always had been, always would be.

Cris kissed her hair. "Delfi, *per favore,* stop crying."

She took a deep breath and tried to stifle her tears. "I'm sorry," she whispered.

"He fooled all of us. I truly thought he cared for you." He smoothed the hair off her forehead. "After all, he didn't have to try to help me get you out of the engagement."

"I know. That's what I don't get."

Cris shrugged. "Maybe he thought it was a good way to earn my trust."

"Maybe." But he'd really seemed to care. He hadn't wanted Leandro to hurt her. His defense of her had seemed utterly sincere. Was he that amazing of an actor? "What if we're wrong about him, Cris?"

He studied her face, his soft brown eyes holding hers. "I wish we were. But you heard it."

"I can't help thinking—" She stopped herself and shook her head. She was being stupid. "I never thought I could be taken in like that."

"Me neither." He ruffled her hair. "Better?"

She smiled. "I will be. Gio's coming over. We'll make pigs of ourselves on gelato and talk about how all men are dogs. Except you, of course."

Cris averted his gaze. "Is that her opinion of me, or yours?"

"So you really are going to try?"

He lifted his hands and shrugged. "It's hopeless. Her father will never agree to it after the fiasco with you and Leandro."

"You never know." She bit the inside of her lip. "I hope I haven't ruined things for you two."

"Well, if you hadn't broken off with Leandro, there'd be *no* chance, so don't feel bad."

Someone knocked at the door. Or rather tapped a handful of nails on it. Gio. "Come in!" Delfina called.

Gio bustled in, two large Fendi suitcases trailing behind her. "What's all that?" Cris asked.

She pointed to one then the other. "Clothing and shoes. I didn't want poor Delfi to suffer all alone any longer than necessary."

Delfina laughed. "Gio, I know what a sacrifice that was. You are the best friend a girl could ever have."

Simpering and batting her fake lashes, Gio said, "I try." She shooed Cris off the bed. "I know you've been trying to help, darling," she said to him, "but some things are best handled by a woman. Heartbreak is one of them."

Cris rose and scrubbed a hand through his brown curls. "I thought I was doing pretty good."

"You were," Delfina said. "But Gio's right."

Cris turned to go, then paused awkwardly. "Gio, I need your phone."

Gio's eyebrows popped up under the brown and blonde tresses that tumbled over her forehead. "Are you kidding me, Cristoforo Andretti? This phone is my lifeline. I'm not giving it up for anyone. Not even you, as adorable as you are."

He blushed. "Gio—"

Delfina came to his rescue. "Cris, Papà said to take mine. I think you can trust Gio to babysit me. Besides, all my numbers are on my phone. Who am I going to call on hers? Leandro?"

"Okay." He pointed at Gio. "Take care of her."

Gio crossed her heart. "Will do. As long as you promise to hang out with me tomorrow."

"If that's what you want."

She batted her lashes again and smiled. "That's not *all* I want."

"And that's my cue to go." He turned and shut the door behind him.

Gio plopped down on the bed beside her and fanned herself. "Is it just me, or is your brother hot?"

Delfina giggled. "It's just you."

"Well, it would be horribly wrong if you thought he was hot too."

Delfina laughed harder. Only Gio could turn her from tears to laughter so quickly.

Leaning back on her elbows, Gio kicked her feet up in the air, showing off her new sandals and her pedicure. "You like?"

"Fuchsia isn't exactly subtle."

"I wasn't going for subtle. Have I ever?"

Delfina nudged Gio with her shoulder. "Don't ever change."

"No fear of that." Gio let out a sigh. "Okay we're going to have a serious moment. What's going on?"

Delfina filled her in, impressed that she teared up only three times while telling the story. "The thing is, I still can hardly believe it."

"Can I hear these recordings?"

"If you want. I've got the flash drive in my bag."

Gio found it and plugged it into Delfina's computer, her eyes going wide as she listened to the conversation between Nick and Benedetto. "Your great-uncle is a cold son of a bitch."

"Nick's not much better."

"I disagree."

"What do you mean? He doesn't give a damn about me."

"Not true. Did you listen to what he asked Benedetto for? *One* thing for him. *Three* things for you."

"Because he felt guilty."

"Because he *cares*. Do you think he'd admit how he feels to a man he doesn't trust? It would be stupid to give Benedetto ammunition like that."

"What about what he said to Antonio?" Delfina asked.

"What was that again?"

"'I'll do right by her.'"

"No, no. The part where he said he loved you."

"He didn't. Antonio said I deserved a husband who loved me. And Nick said 'You think I don't?'"

"Which means he *does*. He said he got the ring from his father, right?"

"Yes. So?"

Gio poked her in the arm with a long fingernail. "I bet it was Nick's grandmother's ring. You know—*the* ring. The famous one."

Oh *Cristo*. If it was... "Zio Enrico swore that no Andretti would ever wear that ring. Not after what my grandfather did."

"Maybe he's changed his mind."

"How could he ever forgive that? His mother and his brothers were gunned down like dogs in the street." Delfina shook her head. "He never gave my aunt that ring. He certainly wouldn't give it to me."

"But he might give it to his son."

And if Nick had it... Her stomach flipped over. "You really think Nick loves me?"

Gio nodded. "It's all over his face. The way he looks at you. Damn it, Delfi, the man could have run away any time after he knew his grandparents were safe. He didn't have to do a damn thing to try to help you. God knows, things have only gotten worse for him since then."

Delfina thought back to the day when Leandro and Gianluca had confronted them. How Nick had gone after Leandro, how he'd lied for her. Even though she'd lied to him and had nearly gotten him killed.

And then how he'd tried to help Cris with his plan to free her. And had nearly gotten killed again in the process. Her throat tightened. What if she'd been wrong?

She owed Nick another chance, and she needed to make sure her uncle didn't walk into a trap tomorrow. "Give me your phone."

"Why?"

"You've got Antonio's number, right?"

"Yeah, but... "

"But what?"

Gio smiled. "He might've put a block on my number."

"What did you do?"

"I called him a few times."

"A few?"

"I was drunk, sweetie. I'm not sure how many it was."

Delfina rolled her eyes. "Let's hope he's forgiving."

"Or desperate."

Antonio's phone rang several times before going to voice mail. Delfina left a quick message, then texted him. Hopefully he wouldn't delete them without first checking them.

Then they both stared at the phone, waiting for it to ring.

———— ✦ ————

After Cris left Delfina and Gio, he went back to his father's office. He had to convince Papà to change the plan for tomorrow.

When he stepped inside, Flavio and Papà were studying a hastily sketched layout of the Andretti estate, both of them pointing to various locations and naming which guards would be posted where.

Cris's gut roiled as he looked at the paper. "Papà, I think we should reconsider."

His father fixed him with a hard stare. "What?"

"This is mad. Why are we putting our whole family at risk?"

"We don't have any choice."

"Of course we do."

His father stabbed the sketch, his finger crinkling the paper. "No. This ends here."

"What do you mean?"

His father ran a hand through his black hair, thoroughly disheveling it. "We have to stop Benedetto. And Lucchesi."

"Can't we just confront Benedetto with the recording? Bisnonno will handle it."

His father let out a gust of breath and walked around the desk, stopping in front of Cris and taking him by the shoulders. "Cris, everything depends on what we do now. Think about it. Benedetto is a clever devil. He will have excuse after excuse for what he said. And once we play that hand, if he eludes us, we can never have that advantage again. He will definitely put targets on our backs then, if he hasn't done so already."

"Of course he has."

"Benedetto could be planning something else entirely. He could be playing a game with the Russians and Lucchesi."

He had to come clean about the Russian deal. "The night I got shot, the night with the cocaine—that deal wasn't my idea."

Papà's fingers tightened on Cris's shoulder. "I knew you were hiding something."

"Benedetto asked me to handle the transaction for him. And he insisted I bring Nick with me." He could hardly meet his father's gaze.

Papà let go of him and took a step back, muttering a curse. "Why didn't you tell me?"

Now Cris truly couldn't meet his eyes. "I asked Benedetto to talk to you about Delfina's engagement."

"You thought he could convince me to break it?"

Cris shrugged. "It was worth a try."

"No, it wasn't." His father's hand came out of nowhere, striking him hard and fast on the side of the head. Then he grabbed Cris by the collar and pulled him close, his words low and menacing as he spoke in his ear: "Don't you ever undermine me again. You are my son. I am your father. The only people we can trust are each other." He let go of Cris's collar and cupped the back of Cris's head in one hand, his voice going hoarse. "Do you understand? I cannot bear to lose you."

Tears pricked Cris's eyes. "Forgive me, Papà."

Papà rubbed the side of Cris's head where he'd cuffed him. "We have enemies everywhere. If they succeed in dividing us, we're both dead."

A lump sealed off Cris's throat. He swallowed hard. "I'm sorry. I just wanted to help Delfi."

His father stepped away. "Your sister helped herself, yes?"

The bitterness in Papà's voice surprised him. "She was right. I know you want an alliance with Gianluca, but putting her in a bad marriage to get it was wrong."

A tight smile crossed his father's lips. "You cannot resist defying me, not for one minute."

"It's not defiance. It's the truth." A shiver ran through Cris as he said those words, and he inhaled deeply through his nose. Delfina had accused him of following blindly. He wouldn't make that mistake again.

"It's your opinion, not fact."

"Am I not supposed to disagree at times? Am I not supposed to give you my counsel?"

Papà's lips pressed together and his chest rose and fell. "Of course."

"Then let me ask Gianluca for Giovanna's hand."

His father sighed and shook his head. "Remember what he said last time? He said it gently, but he was still insulted."

"He may feel differently now. He obviously wanted to ally with us before. This would give us an even tighter tie, since I'm *capo di società*."

"Perhaps. Let me think about it."

"Did you have another bride in mind for me?"

"I have been considering a few options."

Cris's stomach flipped over. He'd do his duty, of course, but... Gio's beautiful smile made his heart jump in his chest, and her touch was pure electricity. He didn't want anyone else. "Please, Papà." The words slipped out unbidden, making him sound like a child. He wished he could stuff them back in his mouth.

"Let's get through tomorrow. Then we'll talk."

Papà's tone said the discussion was final, but at least he had another chance. "Okay. So now that you know everything, will you reconsider this plan?"

His father frowned. "Benedetto's behavior does seem more suspect now." He put his hands on his hips and stared at the carpet. "But that doesn't change anything. He could still make us look wrong."

Thinking back to his conversation with Delfina, Cris blurted, "When he asked me to handle the deal with the Russians, Benedetto said he wanted me to bring Nick along to test his loyalty to you."

Papà grinned. "See? The perfect excuse. He eliminates you and Clarkston, weakens me, and appears innocent at the same time. Our only hope is to catch him in the act with something he can't refute."

Cris let out a breath. There was no escaping the facts. Benedetto had them outmaneuvered at this point. "You're right. At the least, we should keep Nonna Romola out of this, in case things turn ugly. We can send her to the Villa d'Este and say she's ill."

His father nodded. "Agreed. I'll talk to her."

Cris turned to Flavio. "You've changed all the access codes?" When Flavio nodded, Cris said, "Good. Don't give them to anyone but Papà and me. If Benedetto is planning to let the Russians in, he'll need to come to one of us. And then we'll know."

His gut tightened at the words. There was no guarantee any of them would survive the next twenty-four hours.

CHAPTER 23

Enrico squeezed Kate's hand and brushed her hair back. "You are sure you want to come inside? I could say you have fallen ill."

She shook her head, her lovely auburn hair swishing over her neck and shoulders. "I'm sure. If I stay out here in the car listening in, I'll drive myself crazy worrying about you. Besides"—she patted her handbag and then her thigh—"I think I can take care of myself."

"I know you can. It is just—"

She placed a finger on his lips. "Hush. The baby and I will be fine. I have *two* guns, Rico. And if anything does happen, I'll head outside."

He studied her green eyes, looking for traces of fear, and tried to quell the flutters in his belly. *He* had to be there for Nick, but Kate did not. And yet she'd insisted on coming. He opened his mouth to object again, but she cut him off.

"I want to be with you. If something happened to you—" Her voice caught, then she continued. "Besides, if I'm not there, Dario will suspect something."

His throat grew strangled. *Dio,* if he lost her... He leaned forward, the leather seat creaking beneath him, and took her face in both hands. He kissed her softly, sweetly, as if he'd never kissed her before. As if this time might be the last. "*Ti amo, cara.*"

She placed her hands over his. "There is nowhere I would rather be than here with you. By your side."

He kissed her again, then smiled. *What a woman.* "You would not rather be in Capri with me?"

"Making love by the ocean?" She smiled. "Hmm... perhaps. I'll have to think about it."

He laughed. "I must work on my technique."

Her eyes went liquid and she leaned closer, her voice husky. "Let's get some practice in when this is over."

"Did I already mention how much I love you?"

"Too many times. I love you too, *caro.*"

One more quick kiss, then he said, "It is time."

As they walked up to the house, he made eye contact with Antonio and Ruggero and the other two guards, Claudio and Santino. Tommaso stayed back at the cars with three additional guards.

Each member of their party wore a bug and had at least one gun. The guards at the cars had receivers so they could listen in on what the bugs picked up. If things went south, their orders were to charge in with their Uzis at the ready.

Dario greeted them at the door. "My. Such a large party. And so many gifts."

Enrico smiled. "Of course. It is not every day my son gets engaged."

"Perhaps you are overcompensating?" Dario ushered them in.

Enrico ignored the jab and watched as the men carried stacks of elaborately wrapped presents to the designated table, careful to set them down without making noise. It wasn't easy when each package contained a cache of weapons.

Dario motioned over Flavio and another guard, who patted down Enrico and his men and took their weapons. "Is this truly necessary?" Enrico asked.

"This is a day of peace, yes?" Dario said. "Still, tempers may flare, and I would rather ensure everyone is safe. You understand."

Enrico shrugged. "Of course." He'd figured this would happen, though he'd hoped it wouldn't. But, as expected, they didn't pat down Kate or inspect the presents. They only searched the men. All according to plan, so far.

He surveyed the room, noting numerous bouquets on sideboards and tables. Delfina had promised to leave guns either in the bouquets or under them, or failing that, in the drawers below them. She hadn't been sure how many guns she could take without attracting notice, so she'd told him to keep searching if there wasn't one at a particular location.

If Dario were truly expecting trouble from Benedetto, he could hardly have picked a worse location to defend. They were in an oversized sitting room at the northwest corner of the house. Three large windows extended from the ceiling to window seats a couple feet off the floor. Even worse, glass-paned double doors led to a small terrace out back. The only point in the room's favor were the bulky chairs and sofas arranged in clusters. Not that the furniture would be impregnable shields against bullets, but it was better than nothing.

Enrico missed his gun. The muscles between his shoulder blades kept tensing and twitching, as though he felt a gun sight trained on his back. He leaned over to Kate. "Remember, if anything happens, stay with Ruggero or Antonio. *Not* me. I do not want you caught up in what happens to me."

"Stop it," she whispered. "I know what to do."

Delfina walked in, followed by her mother, Ilaria, and Giovanna d'Imperio. Benedetto and Lorenzo, deep in conversation, strolled in after them. Delfina's eyes seemed a little swollen, but her smile was radiant as she came over to greet him, Kate, and Antonio. She kissed Enrico on his left cheek and whispered, "Everything's in place." When she straightened, he asked about Nick. "He'll be along in a minute. He and Cris are still upstairs." She calmly moved on to Kate, then Antonio, as if Nick weren't being held prisoner. As if everything were okay. Only the slight tremor in her hands when she'd clasped Enrico's gave her away.

He'd hardly slept last night after her call. She'd been so upset and blamed herself for what had happened. But that was wrong, as he'd told her; the blame for everything rested squarely on Benedetto's head.

Talk of the devil... Benedetto placed a hand on his shoulder. "You have a moment?"

"Of course." He followed Benedetto over to the double doors that led outside. "What is it?"

"Do I have your support for the council? Will you head up Lombardy?"

"I need something from you."

Benedetto sighed. "Come, Don Lucchesi. It isn't like you to be greedy."

"But it *is* like you."

"So adversarial. Tell me what has you upset."

"My son believes you're unhappy with him and Cris. Perhaps unhappy enough to do them harm."

Spreading his hands wide, Benedetto smiled. "I admit I was angry at one point. But were you and I to be friends..."

"You could overlook it."

"I'd be a fool not to."

"And Cris as well?"

"Of course. Boys do get themselves into trouble from time to time, and I suppose I must learn to be more forgiving if I'm to understand this new generation."

"Then we see eye to eye on the council."

"And Lombardy?"

Enrico stuck his hands in his pockets. "I do not wish to start a war with Dario."

"Let me handle my nephew. He will have to accept my decision. And I will make it very clear that it was my decision. *I* sought you, and with good reason."

Enrico paused. If Delfina's suspicions about Benedetto were true, this whole discussion was moot. If she was wrong, trusting Benedetto could still prove dangerous. He studied Benedetto, noting the tension around the man's mouth, the way he fidgeted with a button on his jacket. He was desperate for Enrico to say yes, and that meant he needed Enrico, no matter what. "It is done then."

Benedetto beamed and clapped him on the back. "*Magnifico!*" He gave a sharp nod to Lorenzo, who was watching them and no doubt knew exactly what they were discussing. The old man caught Enrico's attention and smiled, a slow peeling back of his lips from long, yellowed teeth that did nothing to dispel the predatory glint in his eyes.

A flicker of movement to Enrico's left made him tense, but he relaxed when Nick and Cris walked in. Nick moved stiffly and he seemed tired, but otherwise okay. Enrico rushed to embrace him. As he leaned forward to kiss Nick's cheek, he whispered, "Delfina told me everything. We have done our best to prepare."

"She did?"

Enrico nodded. Nick's eyes sought her, and Enrico's chest constricted. He knew that look. His son could insist morning and night that he didn't love Delfina Andretti, but his face shouted out the exact opposite. And Enrico was going to do his damnedest to give his son the happiness he deserved. *Dio* knew it was the least he owed him.

———— ◆ ————

Did that mean Delfina still loved him? Or only that she felt bad for him? Nick tried to catch Delfina's eye, but she seemed to be looking everywhere other than at him. Or maybe it meant only that she wanted to protect his father. Well, if that was the case, so be it. Nick had brought this all upon himself; the fewer people who suffered because of him, the better. He leaned toward his father. "Don't get yourself or anyone else killed for me."

The face that stared back at him was hard as stone. "You are *my* son. I will not abandon you. Ever."

Nick's throat clamped shut. *Jesus.* Had he come all this way just to hear those words? It sure felt like it. He tried to speak, but he had to cough first. "*Mille grazie.*"

His father clasped his shoulder. "That is what a father *does*. You do not have to thank me for it."

"I've been such an idiot—"

His father's hand squeezed harder. "Enough. We have both made mistakes. We will do better in the future, yes?"

If they had a future. "Yes."

"Now go talk to that lovely woman of yours."

A school of leaping fish took up residence in Nick's belly. He fingered the ring in his pocket. What the hell could he possibly say to her? He'd been up all night, going over and over what he could say to prove himself to her, but all of it seemed inadequate. He had made some decisions, however. And the most important one was that if he lived, he'd give up all hope of justice or atonement for what he'd done. Making her happy, making sure she'd get to live the life she wanted, would be enough for him. If he managed that, he'd have done something worthwhile.

He scanned the room. The party was just close family. The fewer witnesses to what happened today, the better.

The gifts table was stacked to overflowing. Oddly, the majority of the presents had the same lavish wrapping. Who'd been the big spender? Probably his dad. Nick wasn't the only one with a guilt complex.

He walked over to the table and picked up one of the smaller boxes. The weight surprised him. What the hell was in there? He shifted the package and heard the clink of metal on metal. Gold bars? He looked up at his father, who was watching him. When their eyes met, his father nodded, a short, sharp bob of the head. A frisson rolled down Nick's back. Not gold bars.

Guns.

———— ◆ ————

Benedetto pulled Flavio aside, and gave him the prearranged signal. "I have a special gift for the happy couple. The delivery people need to come in through the side gate." Flavio nodded and gave him the new access code. *So easy.* Dario would never know what had happened. All Benedetto had to do was make sure Flavio died in the confusion, and Eusebio had his orders to take care of that.

With a smile, Benedetto patted Flavio on the back, then went outside and dialed a number he knew by rote. A number he couldn't store in his contacts.

When Ilya answered, Benedetto gave him the code. He glanced back inside, saw everyone gathering around the Lucchesi boy and Delfina, glasses of prosecco in their hands. "Wait five minutes. The boy is about to propose. Everyone will be distracted."

Ilya chuckled. "You are cold bastard, Andretti. I like you, almost."

The feeling wasn't mutual. But no matter. "Five minutes, *capisci?*"

Cris opened the outer door. "You're going to miss everything, Prozio."

Something about the boy's tone made Benedetto take another look at him, but Cris gave him an open grin. "Hurry."

Benedetto put the phone away and followed his grandnephew, pasting a smile on his face. He was getting paranoid. No one suspected a damn thing.

As usual.

CHAPTER 24

Why, why, why was Nick actually proposing to her in front of everyone? Delfina knew he was supposed to give her the ring, but here he was down on one knee in front of her, with everyone gathered around, ready to toast "the happy couple." What a farce!

But he looked so nervous and earnest. Why hadn't she trusted him? Why hadn't she asked him about the recordings first? Since she'd screwed everything else up, she'd at least give him the courtesy of her full attention and focus.

He held a ring box in his hand and gazed up at her. "Delfina, I've thought all night about what to say to you today. No doubt it shows," he said, gesturing to the dark circles under his eyes. He gave a nervous laugh that she echoed.

Nick reached for her left hand, and she squeezed his fingers. He smiled up at her and blew out quickly. "The thing is, I realize that maybe I wasn't your first choice. I want you to know that no matter what, *you* are *my* first choice."

A lump filled her throat and she raised her right hand to touch it. Did he truly mean it?

He let go of her hand for a moment and popped the ring box open and held it up for everyone to see. At the first glimpse of the marquise-cut solitaire, her eyes flew to her uncle Enrico. Gio was right—it was the famous Lucchesi ring. Nick's grandmother's ring, the one with the five-carat pink diamond and the scrollwork "L's" engraved on the sides of the platinum setting. Tears blurred her vision as she watched her uncle, looking for any regret on his face. "Are you sure?" she blurted.

Everyone's attention shifted to Enrico, the room utterly still. "I want you to have it, Delfina."

The tears started then, and she wiped them away as she glanced at her father and Cris, who both seemed stunned. Obviously Cris hadn't really looked at the ring yesterday, or hadn't absorbed its importance then. Her father was staring at Enrico openmouthed, and her mother was crying into a handkerchief. And Nick—Nick was watching her, seemingly oblivious to what else was happening around them. "Will you do me the honor of being my wife, Delfina?" His voice wavered with emotion, or perhaps nerves.

He took her hand again, ready to put the ring on her finger, waiting for her consent. She opened her mouth, but a blast of gunfire outside seized her attention. She turned toward the sound, saw a huge blond man crash through the glazed double doors, and then something slammed into her.

———————◦◆◦———————

Nick lunged forward, grabbing Delfina and almost knocking her off her feet, adrenaline and desperation making him clumsy. He thrust himself between her and the four Russians invading the room. *What the hell?* "Where the fuck are your guards?" he barked at Cris.

All of them were gone. The only ones in the room were his father's men, who were scrambling for the gifts table and tipping the lids off the wrapped boxes. Ruggero threw a large gun to Antonio and then armed himself.

Nick needed a weapon too. He pulled Delfina to the floor, trying to keep the furniture between them and the Russians, and scrambled over to the table, knocking discarded champagne flutes out of their way. She reached up past him and tipped over the bouquet of pink and white roses. A Beretta lay beneath it. "Take it!" she screamed. He grabbed it and whirled around to cover them, firing at the first Russian he saw.

The man went down with a wound in the right thigh, but raised his gun again, taking a bead on Nick. Nick fired and hit the man in the chest, but he barely grunted. *Fucking hell, he's wearing a vest.* "Here," Delfina said and shoved a mini Uzi into his hands.

The gun was set to full automatic, but there was nothing "mini" about it. He'd never fired anything so powerful; the bucking of the weapon made his first shots go wild. Grabbing on with both hands, he sighted at the man's head, which ripped apart like a melon as Nick held down the trigger. Bile rose in his throat, but this was no time to be sick. Scrambling forward, he upended a coffee table and dragged it back to Delfina. She picked up the Beretta he'd discarded and started firing, her shots deafening in his ear, nearly drowning out the general cacophony of gunfire, shouts, and breaking glass.

They weren't the only ones by the gifts table. His father and Kate had taken shelter behind a sideboard that someone had pushed out from the wall. His father's wife was a revelation, coolly aiming her Glock at their attackers. She took one down with a shot to the head, as if she did this all the time. Where had she learned to shoot like that? The rest of his father's men had spread out behind clumps of furniture and fired furiously as a half dozen more Russians breached the broken windows. How many men had Ilya brought? And where the fuck were the damned guards?

Cris dove down beside him, a Beretta in hand. "Cris, what's going on?"

"Don't know. All the guards are gone."

Nick scanned the room. "Where are Benedetto and Lorenzo?"

Cris shook his head. "Papà is searching for them. And Flavio."

A spray of automatic fire ripped up the center of the table they were hiding behind. Nick grabbed Delfina from her crouch and shoved her flat to the floor, gritting his teeth as bullets tore into the wood with solid thunks. Cris plastered himself to the floor beside them. Somehow the table held. Thank Christ the Andrettis didn't shop at IKEA.

"We have to get out of here," Nick said, twisting his head to look at Cris and raising his voice. There were too many windows in the room. Not to mention the broken double doors.

"There's a panic room off my father's study," Delfina said.

"Good. You take the women and barricade yourselves. Call the police," Nick said.

"No *polizia*," Cris said.

"We're fucking outnumbered here!"

"None of them live, hear me?" Cris said. "We don't call the *polizia* until this is settled."

Nick popped his head up and fired the Uzi at another man trying to crawl through a window. "I disagree."

Cris turned to Delfina. "Take Kate, Mamma, and Gio with you."

"Okay." She reached over, grabbing Kate's arm and shouting their destination over the din. The two women scurried over to Ilaria and Gio, who were huddled in the corner behind a large chair being defended by Antonio. He helped them up and took off with the women down the hall. With Delfina out of the line of fire, the tension in Nick's chest eased slightly.

"Do you have anyone outside?" Nick yelled to his father.

He nodded. "They should be helping us. I've tried calling Tommaso, but he's not answering."

Nick's gut compacted into a stone. Something must have gone horribly wrong. Someone had betrayed them. And it wasn't just Benedetto. He scanned the room. Why wasn't Dario back?

Gunfire erupted from the direction the women and Antonio had gone, and a fresh burst of adrenaline showered Nick in ice. Had the Russians infiltrated the entire house?

Delfina screamed. Antonio was hit, blood streaming down his side. His right arm hung useless. He shoved them all into the library and slumped down against the door. Just a few more meters, that's all it would have taken to get them to her father's study and its door to the panic room. But they hadn't made it. "Behind the furniture!" he shouted.

"Tonio, get away from the door," Kate hissed. "They'll kill you."

Antonio's blood, pouring bright crimson down his white shirt, made Delfina's stomach lurch. Her heart thudded in her chest and she gulped down air, trying to keep calm. But she couldn't. Benedetto and a massive Russian with a mane of steel-gray hair and a full beard were outside that door. The man who'd shot Antonio must be Ilya Vilanovich.

Bullets shredded the top half of the door, showering splinters of wood over

Antonio. He ducked, but didn't abandon his post. Something—probably a foot—pounded against the bottom of the door. "Open now, or we will blast in." Ilya, to judge by the accent.

Muffled gunfire came from the sitting room where Nick and Cris were. *Porca miseria*, Cris had her phone. She had to call the *polizia*, no matter what Cris said. They needed help.

She scrambled over to Gio. "You have your phone?"

"It's up in your room. Who was I going to call?"

"Kate?" Delfina asked.

Kate searched her bag, her mouth set in a thin line. "Got it," she finally said. She tossed the phone to Delfina, who dropped her gun to take it. Delfina pressed 112 and prayed someone would answer before Benedetto and Ilya broke in.

A fist thundered on the door. "You make me angry," Ilya bellowed. "Not good choice."

Silence for a moment as Delfina listened to the long-short *chirp-chirp* of the phone ringing. *Answer, per favore!*

Another blast of gunfire tore into the wood door, and more chunks of wood fell onto Antonio. She hunkered down behind a large overstuffed chair. *Answer, damn you!*

The ringing stopped and a woman's voice came on the line. "*Carabinieri*. You have an emergency?"

"Yes. Send someone to—"

Delfina's world went white as an explosion detonated in the middle of the room. Her head spun; she couldn't hear, couldn't see. She shouted at the *carabinieri* officer through the ringing in her ears, but couldn't make out the reply. After a few terrifying seconds, her vision came back, and she glanced toward the door, which rattled as Ilya and Benedetto battered against it. They must have tossed a flashbang grenade through the hole they'd made in the top panel.

Antonio rose and tried to hold them off by pressing his back to the failing door, but it was useless. The door splintered in half behind him and Ilya plowed through, knocking him down before kicking him in the head. "Tonio!" Kate and Gio both shrieked as he fell.

"Can you hear me?" Delfina screamed into the phone. "We're under attack!"

A muffled voice, as if Delfina were underwater. "Address, *signorina*?"

The phone flew from her hands as an arm jerked her up in the air. Ilya.

From her spot by the sofa, Kate fired at Benedetto but missed, and her gun stuck open, empty. She fumbled beneath her dress and pulled out a second gun, this one much smaller. Benedetto lunged forward and grabbed her wrist, pointing the weapon at the ceiling as she squeezed the trigger. Kate swung at him with a closed fist, but he blocked the blow and wrenched the gun from her and stuck it in his pocket. Then he took Kate by the arm.

Mamma and Gio cowered next to a bookcase, both of them crying. Benedetto pointed his gun at them. "Stay here, or you're dead." When they nodded, he turned away, and he and Ilya wrestled Kate and Delfina toward the doorway. Antonio staggered to his feet and blocked their path, his right eye swollen shut from Ilya's kick.

Delfina heard the rasp of metal clearing leather as Ilya pulled out a wicked-looking hunting knife and shoved it under her chin, pricking her skin. Her heart rate skyrocketed.

"Let them go," Antonio said. He sounded exhausted, his words a little slurred. Did he have a concussion?

"Move," Ilya yelled. He shoved her forward and she stumbled. "You want I should cut her, this beautiful girl?"

Antonio didn't move. Ilya pricked her skin again, and a second warm trickle started down her neck. She'd heard only horrible things about the Russians. Who knew what he'd do? "Tonio, *per favore,*" she whispered.

"Get down on the floor!" Benedetto shouted.

Antonio moved slowly and in obvious pain, but he obeyed and lay on his belly. Ilya pushed her toward him, then pulled a handgun and aimed at Antonio.

"No!" Delfina yelled and threw herself against Ilya's outstretched arm. The shot hit Antonio in the upper back, and she screamed in anguish. He lay still, too still. Ilya grabbed the back of Delfina's neck and forced her to look at Antonio. "Behave, or this happen to you."

Tonio must be dead. Delfina couldn't help her tears. He didn't deserve it; He was the kindest person she knew, kinder even than Nick. If only she hadn't abandoned her gun in favor of the phone.

Taking as deep a breath as she could manage, she stopped crying. She had to be strong, she had to keep thinking. She had to find a way to kill Benedetto and Ilya. Ilya yanked on her arm. She had only moments before it would be too late.

Turning to her mother and Gio in the corner, she said, "Gio, if I don't make it, please take care of Zeta." She hoped Gio got her message and had the courage to act on it.

Ilya propelled Delfina toward the door, Benedetto following with Kate. Only cowards would use women as shields. But it took a special kind of coward to turn against his family. Benedetto Andretti deserved to die.

For the first time, Delfina understood the burning hatred that fueled revenge.

CHAPTER 25

Multiple times Nick had tried to make his way out of the sitting room, but the onslaught from the Russians hadn't let up. Ruggero had been hit and so had Cris, but their wounds seemed superficial. Antonio and Dario hadn't come back—Nick could only assume they were dead or too badly hurt to move. He hadn't seen Benedetto or Lorenzo since the shooting had started, but that wasn't a surprise.

Based on the noises he'd heard coming from the main hall, the women were barricaded somewhere, but the splintering sound of wood breaking led him to believe the door to their refuge was about to fail. *Please let them be in the safe room.* That room would have a metal door. But what if they hadn't made it?

He and the men holding the sitting room were running out of fresh guns, which meant they'd soon have no ammunition. It was now or never.

An explosion from the main hall jacked his pulse into the stratosphere. *Delfina!*

Tossing his empty Glock, Nick grabbed a Beretta lying half under an empty gift box, and popped the clip. About a third full. Sod it, there was no time to find another. Yelling "Cover me!" at Cris, he belly crawled on his elbows and knees toward the doorway to the main hall. He was halfway there when he saw something that threatened to stop his heart: Delfina stepping through the entry, a knife at her throat, twin streams of blood running down her neck, a massive gray-haired Russian at the other end of the knife. Ilya Vilanovich.

Nick's lungs compressed up into his throat. He froze, flat on his belly. *Fucking hell.* Bloody Ilya Vilanovich had a knife to Delfina's throat, and here Nick was, in the worst possible position to save her. He looked up to his right at his father, who was firing across the room. "Nico?" his father asked, then followed Nick's gaze, letting out a curse when he saw Kate in Benedetto's grip, a gun to her temple.

Ilya bellowed a series of commands in Russian as he entered the sitting room. His men ceased firing, and soon the room was still, but no one lowered their guns. The acrid smell of gunpowder overlay everything. Smashed vases, scattered flowers, splinters of wood, and chunks of plaster littered the room, along with the bodies of a dozen Russians and two of his father's guards.

226

At least three Russians were still standing outside. He had no idea if Ilya and Benedetto had other men under their command. But all that was moot. With Kate and Delfina as hostages, Benedetto and Ilya had the upper hand.

"Where's Gio and my mother?" Cris asked.

Benedetto gestured with his gun. "Crying in the library."

"Where's Antonio?" Enrico asked.

"Dead," Ilya said.

Delfina's and Kate's eyes shimmered with tears. But neither one let them fall. *Jesus, they were strong.*

After a moment of silence, his father swallowed visibly. So Antonio's regard for Nick's father wasn't one-sided. "Let the women go," his father said.

Ilya laughed. "You must be the great Don Lucchesi."

"And you must be the dog Ilya Vilanovich."

Ilya growled and pulled Delfina closer. "You want her gutted?"

Nick's heart stuttered. "No," he said, hastening to his feet and stepping forward. He ignored the sound of Ilya's men climbing in through the windows behind his back. "I'm the one you came for. I killed your sons. Take me, and let the women go."

"Not enough," Ilya said.

"What else do you want?" Nick asked.

Ilya gestured to Cris. "That one. He is also responsible."

"I was the one who fired," Nick said.

"No matter."

"It matters to me. Those were my kills. He doesn't get credit." Nick prayed Cris would keep his mouth shut.

He didn't. "I got you into this, Nick."

"No. Benedetto's to blame." Nick glared at the man, but he held Nick's gaze, unashamed. "Why did you do it?" Nick asked.

"Do what?" Benedetto said.

Keep him talking. Maybe they'll get distracted. "Turn on your family."

"I haven't. Vilanovich has my father captive. I have no choice."

Was that true? "You're lying."

"No more talking," Ilya said, his gruff voice cutting through the room. He pointed the knife at Nick. "You, drop gun and kneel. You also," he said, motioning to Cris.

Fuck and double fuck. Nick dropped his gun.

"Now!" Ilya barked. "All guns down now!"

Nick swallowed hard, his stomach rebelling as he knelt on the carpet, bits of plaster and glass biting into his knees. They were surrounded, outmanned and outgunned, Kate and Delfina hostages. But it wasn't until this very moment that he lost all hope. Delfina was going to see him die.

"No." His father's voice rang out. "You kill my boy, you had better kill me. Because I will hunt you to the ends of the earth, Ilya Vilanovich."

"Then all of you die," Ilya said. He glanced at Benedetto. "I take Lucchesi territory and everything your nephew owns."

"You told me you only wanted revenge," Benedetto said.

"My plans changed."

"Mine haven't." Benedetto opened his mouth to say more, but turned and frowned, which was when Nick heard it—the scrabbling of paws on marble and the deep-throated growls of two very upset Rottweilers. Had Dario freed them from Cris's room?

Benedetto let out a howl of pain as Orfeo bit into his calf. He pushed Kate away while he tried to shoot the dog. She crashed into Ilya, who pushed her back into the hall, sending her flying. "Kate!" his father yelled.

Nick grabbed his gun and jumped up. This was his chance. Ilya stumbled backward, and Nick hurled himself at the big man, hoping to separate him from Delfina. Time stalled, slowed, lost all meaning as Nick's focus narrowed. Ilya pivoted and braced for Nick, pulling Delfina closer, the knife resting against her neck, and then Nick realized the error of his plan—if he slammed Ilya to the ground, there was every chance he'd kill Delfina by shoving Ilya's knife into her throat. Nick pulled up short, coming up on his toes as he struggled to stop his forward momentum. He caught himself with his gun hand on the entryway and had to drop the Beretta to keep from toppling into them.

Ilya smiled when he saw Nick's gun hit the carpet. "You lose," the Russian said.

The Swarovski crystals on Zeta's collar flashed as she launched herself at Ilya's back, the dog's snarls sending a shiver through Nick's belly. When Ilya swayed under the dog's assault, Nick saw his second chance and grabbed for the knife, twisting hard on the Russian's wrist, Ilya's arm feeling like it was made of living iron, not muscle and sinew. While Nick pried at Ilya's fingers, Delfina slipped downward in a graceful pivot that let her move an arm's length from Ilya. He still had hold of her left wrist. "Zeta!" Delfina yelled. "*Attacca!*"

The Rottweiler leapt in the air, going for Ilya's throat. Ilya dropped Delfina's hand and struck at the dog with his fist, slamming into her nose. Zeta yelped and thrashed.

With Ilya occupied, Nick grabbed Ilya's gun and wasted no time firing at the man, hitting him in the neck and just below the left ear. The Russian raised a hand to the wound, then fell back to the ground, Zeta leaping on his chest and tearing at his throat.

Nick pulled Delfina to him. As the room behind them erupted with gunfire, he yanked her into the hall, jumping over Ilya's body and shoving her to the floor behind the wall. "You okay?" he asked.

She nodded. "Cris. You've got to help him."

"I know." He kissed her cheek, then started back for the sitting room. His father was in the hall cradling Kate to his chest as the dogs tore into Benedetto and Ilya. Benedetto had his arms crossed over his head and was crying for someone to help him. *Not bloody likely.*

His gut tightened. Cris could very well be dead. Ruggero had been the only one still focused on Ilya's men, and even though the man knew his way around a gun, he was only one person. And there'd been three Russians left. So who was still shooting?

He crouched down by the entryway, feeling the slam of bullets higher up on the wall. Peering around the corner, he saw Ruggero crouched down firing at someone with a mini Uzi, his face blood streaked and grimmer than ever. Where was Cris?

He finally spotted him, behind the downed gifts table. He was picking up guns and discarding them, searching for one that wasn't empty.

One of the Russians pitched forward, and that's when Nick realized—someone was shooting *into* the room from outside.

Ruggero took aim at the remaining Russian and pulled the trigger, blowing the side of the man's head off. "*Basta!*" he yelled.

The firing outside ceased, and the only noise Nick still heard, apart from the ringing in his ears, was Benedetto's feeble cries for help. He looked across the sitting room, startled to see Dario and a gray-haired, somewhat heavyset man step into the room through the remnants of the double doors, both of them carrying Uzis. "Tommaso!" Ruggero shouted, then embraced the older man and slapped him on the back.

Dario ran toward Nick. "Cris? Delfina?" he asked.

"They're both okay."

Cris rose from behind the table. "Papà."

Dario embraced him. "*Grazie a Dio,*" he murmured into his son's hair.

"Help me!" Benedetto called again.

Dario, Nick, and Cris walked into the hall. Orfeo had clamped onto Benedetto's arm and was whipping his head back and forth, like he was trying to break the neck of a small animal.

"Orfeo," Cris called softly. "*Basta.*"

The dog stopped moving, but held Benedetto's arm clamped in his jaws, his teeth bared, a low growl rumbling from his chest. "Orfeo," Cris said again. This time the dog dropped the man's arm and backed away, then turned and went to Cris, licking his hand.

Delfina had an arm around Zeta, hugging the dog close as she lapped at the blood on Delfina's neck. Nick wanted to go to her, but he had unfinished business. Benedetto was still alive.

Nick glanced at his father and Kate. Relief washed over him when he saw Kate speaking to his father. Ruggero stepped into the hall and went over to them.

Turning away, Nick followed Cris over to Benedetto, who was cradling his arm. "What do we do with him?"

"I told you. No one lives," Cris said. "My gun is empty. He is yours."

Dario huffed with laughter. "Lucchesi doesn't have it in him."

When Benedetto struggled into a sitting position, Orfeo circled back, growling as Cris took hold of his collar. Benedetto looked up at Nick. "Can you murder me? Because that's what this would be."

Nick stared into the man's cold gray eyes, his gut churning. Who knew what would happen if Benedetto lived? He'd repeat that story about Ilya holding his father captive, and Lorenzo would probably back it. And then what? None of them would be able to rest easy.

Raising the gun, Nick said, "This isn't murder, Benedetto. It's justice." Then he pulled the trigger, sending a bullet into the man's throat. Benedetto fell backward, and Nick stepped toward him, firing once more, this time into Benedetto's forehead. It was done.

Dario clapped him on the shoulder. "You truly are an Andretti."

Nick turned. "I'm not. I'm a Lucchesi. I ask you to release me to my father's *cosca*."

"No," Dario said. "You took a vow to me."

"Papà," Cris said, putting his hand on his father's shoulder. "This family owes Nick a huge debt—he's saved both Delfina and me."

Dario's gaze darted from Nick to Cris, then back. "You cannot keep your vow to my son and be in another *cosca*."

"We are allying the families, yes?" Nick's father said. "If so, Nick can keep his vow to Cristoforo."

Dario muttered a curse, then nodded. "I release you."

Nick went to his father. He could hear sirens drawing close. He met his father's eyes and held out his right hand.

"I need a knife," his father said. Ruggero handed him a switchblade.

Flipping Nick's hand palm up, his father drew the tip of the knife in a short shallow cut across the center of Nick's palm. Then he startled Nick by doing the same to his own. What was this?

His father clasped their hands together, bloody palm to bloody palm, and he swiftly kissed Nick on both cheeks. "*Sangue del mio sangue*," he said, his voice thick with emotion. Blood of my blood.

"*Sangue del mio sangue*," Nick repeated, his voice likewise strangled by a lump in his throat.

Ruggero swore. "What?" Nick asked.

Ignoring him, Ruggero focused on Nick's father. "Will you bind him to the *cosca*?"

"No."

"I don't understand," Nick said.

His father held his eyes. "You are bound only to me, as father and son. When I die, you are free to choose another *capo*. Or not."

"I do not like this," Ruggero said.

His father turned to Ruggero, his face hard. "My son has proved himself."

Ruggero blew out noisily. "He is still with Interpol."

Was he? Nick wasn't so sure.

"He can be both. But above all, he is mine."

Nick nodded, the lump in his throat growing bigger. It was true. "Always."

"Very well, Don Lucchesi," Ruggero murmured, bowing his head.

They heard gruff cries from outside. "*Polizia! Carabinieri!* Drop your weapons and put your hands in the air!"

CHAPTER 26

It was nearly midnight by the time the *polizia* and *carabinieri* had left. Delfina felt near collapse. Antonio was still alive, though critically wounded. Her mother had bandaged his wounds while Gio—thank heaven—had gathered up the courage to sneak behind Benedetto and Ilya and free the dogs from Cris's room. She'd saved them all.

The *polizia* found Lorenzo locked in the pantry. He said the Russians had taken him captive. None of them could argue with his story, since it matched Benedetto's claim.

The *carabinieri* questioned them—particularly Nick—very closely regarding Benedetto's death. Nick maintained that he'd shot Benedetto in self-defense. The interrogation hadn't ended until a second lieutenant by the name of Fuente arrived. He'd vouched for Nick as a member of Interpol. This had raised a great many eyebrows, but the man had shut down the remaining questioning, saying that the situation was classified, per the DIA.

Flavio and nearly all of her father's guards were dead. After the police left, her father explained that someone—either Benedetto or Ilya—had bribed Flavio. He'd given the Andretti guards guns full of blanks. The only real resistance the Russians had met was from the handful of men her uncle had brought, all of them dead but Ruggero and Tommaso.

Numbness had settled over her like a blanket. She'd hardly spoken to Nick since the ordeal had begun. His proposal had seemed real, but now that she had time to reflect on it, she wasn't sure. Had he merely been trying to save himself? How would she ever know?

She lay curled up on her bed, Zeta by her side, the dog's broad head shoved under her hand. Zeta kept nuzzling and licking her, giving up the occasional soft whine. All Delfina wanted was to sleep. But that sort of peace eluded her.

Nick would be leaving soon, going off to his father's house, perhaps even, back to London. Why hadn't he spoken to her? Had he already left? Was this how it was going to end?

231

She heard the tread of footsteps outside her door, then a light rapping. "Delfina?" Her heart fluttered in her chest. Nick.

So he hadn't left. Maybe he was just coming to say goodbye, but maybe—hopefully—not. "Come in," she called.

He stepped inside. He'd washed his face and hands and combed his hair, even changed clothes, which made her realize she hadn't done the same. She glanced in the mirror over her vanity. *Dio mio,* she looked a wreck—her eyes and nose red from crying, her hair tangled, her beaded cream dress torn and filthy with plaster dust and blood.

But Nick was staring at her like she'd just stepped off the runway of a Gucci show. "I thought you'd left," she said, her voice rusty, even a bit accusatory. Not what she meant at all. "Forgive me, I—"

He cut her off. "I'm the one who should be begging for forgiveness." He came forward, and Zeta let out a warning growl. Delfina wrapped her hand around the dog's muzzle and forced the Rottweiler to focus on her. "Zeta, no. You know he's a friend. Stop it. Everything is okay now."

The dog whined and licked her fingers. Delfina released her muzzle and nudged the dog off the bed. "Lie down," she commanded her, and Zeta curled up beside the closet after licking the hand Nick offered her.

"Come here," Delfina said to Nick, tapping the bed beside her.

"You used the same tone with the dog," he said, amusement in his voice.

Her cheeks heated, and he laughed. "Sorry," she said.

He sat down beside her and took her hand. "I meant what I said earlier. When I proposed to you, I meant every word. And what I couldn't say then was that I'll quit Interpol and go anywhere you desire. I want you to have the career you want, wherever you want. You choose."

A great warmth filled her chest. Finally, someone—the man she loved—was putting her desires first, just like Aunt Toni had said should be the case. Except… "But you're still in the 'Ndrangheta."

"Yes, but my father has promised to let me do what I wish, provided I don't betray my vows." He interlaced his fingers with hers. "I was afraid to tell you how I felt before. I didn't see a future for us because we were on different sides. But now I do."

The warmth spread throughout her body. "So what you said to Benedetto and Antonio on those recordings—"

"Wasn't the full truth. Wasn't anywhere close." He pulled the ring out of his pocket and held it between his thumb and index finger. "It took me half an hour of searching, but I found it. Lucky thing Fuente shooed all those crime-scene techs out, or one of them might have pinched it." He grinned, then blew out hard. "Will you marry me, Delfina Andretti? Will you make me the happiest man alive?"

She could hardly breathe. He meant it. All of it. But he still hadn't said the words she longed to hear. And she didn't want to ask for them.

"What's wrong?" he asked, his grin fading.

She searched his face, not sure how to ask the question that plagued her. "Why do you want to marry me?"

"I thought it was obvious."

She shook her head. "It's not."

He frowned. "I'm not sure what you want me to say."

"I don't *want* you to say anything."

"Clearly you do."

A lump grew in her throat. She wasn't going to beg him to love her. She shrugged and turned away.

He took her hand. "Help me out, Delfi. What's bothering you?"

She looked at the corkboard above her vanity, at all the pictures she'd pulled from magazines of designs she loved, mixed in with some of her own. He was offering to make her dreams possible. Wasn't that enough?

It wasn't even close.

She'd give him one more hint. "Something's missing from your proposal."

His brows drew together as he mentally reviewed what he'd said. All at once, his face relaxed. "I'm an idiot," he said and grinned.

"You are?"

He nodded. "A big, sodding idiot of enormous proportions." He set the ring on the bed cover and took her face in both hands, his thumbs stroking her cheekbones. He took a deep breath. "I haven't been able to say this to anyone. Not for a long time." His voice thickened. "Not since my mum died." He paused, and her eyes grew hot with tears. He'd lost so much, too much, too young. "But it's time I got over myself." He pressed a kiss to her lips, then rested his forehead against hers. "I love you, Delfina Andretti." His voice was soft, just above a whisper.

A flood of warmth washed over her. She closed her eyes and put her hands over his. "One more time, *per favore*."

He let out a low chuckle. "I love you, Delfi."

A great thrill swooped through her. "Just once more."

He laughed this time. "You're getting me back for laughing at you when you said you loved me, yes?"

She nodded, still not opening her eyes.

"I love you, I love you, I love you," he said, his smile coloring his voice. "Would you like me to go downstairs and shout it out loud?"

Delfina pulled back and looked at him. "That won't be necessary."

He picked up the ring and gave her that devilish Lucchesi grin, the one she couldn't resist. "Will the third time be the charm, I wonder?"

She held out her hand, returning his grin with one of her own. "No need to ask again. I accept."

He started to put the ring on her finger, then stopped. "Just to be clear, you *do* love me, yes?"

She laughed. "Of course I do. I already told you so. A long time ago."

He cupped a hand to his ear as if he were hard of hearing. "Sorry, you'll have to speak up."

"I love you, Nick Clarkston."

"Lucchesi. Nick Lucchesi."

She smiled. "I love you, Niccolò Lucchesi."

He slipped the ring on her finger. Its weight surprised her. "Heavy little thing, no?" she said.

"I can get you something else if you want."

"No." She leaned forward and kissed him. "It's perfect."

He blew out. "Glad that's out of the way. I was starting to think you'd never say yes."

"I had to be sure. And I am." She stroked his cheek. "There is one thing we should settle though."

Nick's heartbeat ratcheted up. "What's bothering you?"

"What you said to Benedetto about him setting up the company for me."

"What about it?"

"If I'm going to be a designer, I have to do it on my own terms."

"I understand how you feel, but have you any idea how much Mafia money is in the fashion industry? You have an advantage—one you've already used once to get the interview with Morelli. Why not enjoy the benefits of what you have?"

"Do you plan to use your father's connections and influence to further your career?"

He sighed. "No. Though it may be beyond my control."

"Not if we leave here. You stay Nick Clarkston and we go to London. You go back to Interpol, and I start over with another designer. As Delfina Clarkston."

"You're sure?" He took her hand in his.

She nodded. "A fresh start is exactly what we need."

"Won't you miss everyone? Your family? Gio?"

"Of course. But it's only three hours by plane. We can come back on weekends."

"I hate to break this to you, but Interpol agents don't make much money."

"Neither do ex-Mafia princesses."

He chuckled. "You, love, will be a Mafia princess until the day you die."

"And you will always be Enrico Lucchesi's son."

"We all have our crosses to bear."

She leaned forward and kissed him. "Well, you're mine."

He burst into laughter, his chest full of bubbles. Leaning forward, he captured her lips in a kiss, and she let out a little moan and opened her mouth beneath his. What a delightful invitation.

Wrapping his arms around her, he slid his tongue into her mouth. Her tongue teased his, and his heart leapt. She loved him, he loved her, and he'd finally done something right. Right and true and wonderful.

She pulled back. "Lock the door," she whispered.

He swiftly took care of their privacy. When he turned back to her, she'd risen off the bed and held out a hand to him. He took it and followed her into the en suite bathroom.

She walked over to the glass-walled shower in the corner and turned on the taps to let it warm up. When she raised her hands to unhook the back of her dress, he hurried forward. "Allow me."

He unhooked the top and then slid the zipper down, baring her back to his gaze. Kissing the nape of her neck, he let the dress glide off her shoulders and pool at their feet. Then he unclasped the bra she was wearing. "Red again," he murmured.

She turned her head to look at him. "I can't seem to pick anything else."

He smiled. "I love you in any color, you know."

"I know." His chest felt full when he heard those words, the confidence behind them. She believed in him, trusted him. And he'd never break that trust again.

She let the bra join the dress on the marble floor, then bent over to unstrap one of her heels.

The sight of that tiny strip of red covering the place he most wanted to touch compelled him to pull her hips into the erection that strained at his zipper.

She pressed back against him, but kept at her task, stepping out of one shoe, then the other. With her out of the heels, his erection pressed into the small of her back instead of between the cheeks of her bum, and he felt the loss keenly.

Hooking her thumbs in the top of her tiny lacy knickers, she skinned them off and dropped them on top of the dress.

Good God, she was gorgeous, the perfect globes of her bum calling to his hands. He slid them over the cheeks, his thumbs stroking the dimples at the top.

Without looking at him, she stepped away from his touch and under the spray that had steamed up the glass walls of the shower. She turned to face him, then arched her back and closed her eyes, letting the water cascade through her hair and sluice down her back. He took in her high small breasts, the chocolatey nipples that turned up at the tips, the dark triangle between her legs.

She stepped out of the spray and stared right at him, pressing her hands against the glass, her dark eyes molten. "Are you going to stand there all day, or are you going to join me?"

His cock answered that question for him. He tore off his clothes, leaving them in a messy heap on the tiles.

Then he was in her arms, kissing down her neck to her breasts, taking the pebbles of her nipples in his mouth, one after the other, unsure which one he liked more. Her gasps and whimpers over the rush of the shower spray spurred him on, as did her fingers threading through his wet hair.

He cupped her bum again, pulling her hips to his, his cock pressing into her belly. She reached down and slid a hand around it, cupping the head, then with flicks of her wrist, wound a twisting path down to the root. He let out a moan, wanting her to do that again. After she obliged, he asked her where she learned that.

"Gio. Who else?"

"I owe her."

"We all do." She was referring to Gio letting the dogs loose.

"No argument here." He drew her into a kiss, his throat tight with emotion. "I almost lost you."

She brushed his wet hair off his face. "When Ilya ordered you to kneel down—" She stopped herself and pressed a trembling hand to her lips.

"I know, love, I know." He took that hand in his and kissed the tips of her fingers, then kissed her lips, pouring all his love into that soft yet hungry touch.

Wrapping her arms around his neck, she kissed him back, her mouth moving urgently against his. He met her fire with his own. He'd never wanted a woman this much, this fiercely.

Grabbing her under the buttocks, he parted her thighs and pressed her up against the marble wall. His cock nudged her tight entrance, and he was about to plunge in, when she placed a hand against his belly. "Don't you want a condom?"

"Do you? I mean, if you want to wait to have kids, that's fine by me." He grinned. "I guess I've turned right around on that issue. You do want to have them?"

"Of course." She smiled, tears glistening in her eyes. "I'm so happy you changed your mind."

He rubbed his cock against her clit, making her gasp. "You're happy I stopped being an arse, you mean."

She laughed and kissed him. When he started to push inside her, she reached down and took him by the root. "Can you pull out in time? I do want children, but not just yet. I want to work, get established first. You don't mind?"

His heart ached that she felt she had to ask. "Of course I don't." His cock throbbed in her hand. "I'll try to pull out in time, but you know it's a risk—"

"—that I'll gladly take. This time."

She let go, and he slid home with a groan. She felt so damn amazing—hot, wet, tight. It was going to be bloody difficult stopping in time.

The sensation of being inside her, of being gripped by a velvet fist, nearly overwhelmed him. He wasn't sure he could last long enough to please her. He wanted to touch her clit, but didn't think he could support her well enough with one arm in the slippery shower. Then he had an idea. A bloody brilliant one. He pulled out halfway. "Touch yourself," he said.

She hesitated, then reached a slender hand between them. His gaze followed her hand, watching her fingers parting the lips of her pussy, her middle finger making circles around her clit. She closed her eyes and moaned, and he almost came right then from watching her. He hitched her hips up higher and thrust into her, short rough strokes, careful to keep enough space for her hand to move.

His eyes were glued to what she was doing, his hips pumping against her, the muscles of his bum clenching and releasing, clenching and releasing, his cock sliding in and out, in and out as she started to keen, her fingers moving faster, her breath coming in high shallow gasps. Then her inner muscles clamped down on him hard and she cried his name. "Nico." He'd never heard anything so sexy.

Shuddering in his arms, she ground her hips against his, and it took everything he had to pull out when all he wanted to do was pound into her hard and fast. He came in a rush, his seed splashing over her stomach.

Letting go of her hips, he eased her to her feet, then braced his hands against the wet marble, blowing out and gulping down air while she did the same within the shelter of his arms.

She put her hands on his biceps and rose up on her toes to press a kiss against his mouth. He loved her, he loved her so damn much it hurt. And it drove him crazy.

And it made him so damn happy too.

"We're going to need more condoms," he said.

"Lots more," she said with a grin. "Until we don't."

He wrapped his arms around her. "You'd better become a famous designer right quick."

"That'll be my first order of business. Jacopo offered to write me a letter of recommendation to use in England, provided I promise to work with him again when I'm established in London."

He smiled. London. He'd finally be going home. And with a bride in tow.

Wouldn't his grandparents be pleased?

CHAPTER 27

Now that the *polizia* and *carabinieri* were finally gone—thanks to Fuente, something else he owed him for—Dario could finally relax.

Except that he couldn't. What had Benedetto meant when he'd said his plans hadn't changed?

Dario sat back in his desk chair, a glass of amaretto in his hand. He'd considered whiskey, but needed a clear head. The amaretto would take the edge off, but wouldn't blunt his thinking. He had to talk to Lucchesi. And Lorenzo. Though it would be hard—perhaps impossible—to get the truth out of either of them.

He picked up the phone to call Flavio, then remembered he was dead and set it down with a hard thunk on his desk. How could he have been duped by Flavio? The guard had never shown the slightest sign of ambition. Hell, he'd hardly shown a sign of independent thought. Clearly he'd underestimated the man.

So what else was he wrong about? And who could he trust?

He took a gulp of the liqueur and made a face. He really wanted the smoky bite of whiskey rolling over his tongue and down his throat instead of the slow sweet fire of the amaretto.

Damn it all.

He picked up the phone again and called Cris, asking him to find Lucchesi and Lorenzo. Lucchesi had wanted to let Kate rest for a bit, and Lorenzo had lain down somewhere, claiming he needed a rest too.

Unlikely. His grandfather had played confused and exhausted with the authorities, saying he was ignorant of what had happened between Benedetto and Ilya.

That was unlikely too.

Getting the truth out of him was just as unlikely. But he had to try.

A few minutes later, Lorenzo and Cris entered the study. As Dario had expected, Lorenzo seemed his usual self. He was getting old, but he was far from dead. Or from needing a nap.

Dario motioned them into the chairs in front of the desk. "Where's Lucchesi?"

he asked Cris.

"He'll be along in a minute. He wanted to wash up."

"Fine." He turned to Lorenzo. "Benedetto had something in mind for the aftermath of all this. When Ilya decided to kill us all, Benedetto told Ilya his plans hadn't changed. What did Benedetto mean by that?"

Lorenzo shrugged. "I can't read minds."

"I think it had something to do with Lucchesi."

Lorenzo leaned forward, tenting his gnarled fingers together. "If you hadn't been such a fool with the Lucchesi boy, none of this would have happened."

"Benedetto didn't like me having a pet in Interpol."

Lorenzo tapped his joined index fingers against his lips. "I thought he and I made that quite clear." His eyes bored into Dario's. "You may have Andretti blood in your veins, but that doesn't mean we"—he corrected himself—"*I* have to put up with your insolence. Someone else, another Andretti, can lead the northern branch of this family." Lorenzo looked at Cris. "For example, your son seems to have the loyalty you lack."

How he'd love to see the old man in his coffin. "So when Benedetto told me I'd be heading up Lombardy on the new council, that was a lie."

Lucchesi stepped inside the study. "It definitely was," Enrico said. "Benedetto offered it to me. And I accepted today." When Dario started to respond, Lucchesi held up a hand. "In exchange for Benedetto agreeing to leave Nico and Cris alone. Obviously, he lied about that as well."

Hmm... Benedetto hadn't been wearing the Patek Philippe today. There was no way to double-check Lucchesi's version of events. He studied his grandfather. "Is that true? Benedetto asked Lucchesi to head Lombardy?"

Lorenzo smiled with his mouth only. "I'll put you at ease on that point. Yes."

Dario felt as if he'd swallowed a box of razor blades. They had wanted him dead and out of the way. What a nest of vipers his family was. "So now what?"

Lorenzo sat back. "Now, you do what I say, Lucchesi runs Lombardy, and I let you live."

How nice for me. "And who succeeds Benedetto?"

"I haven't decided." Lorenzo's gaze slid to Cris for a second, then back to Dario.

Oh yes, you have. No doubt the old man thought Cris was malleable. And loyal to a fault.

Which he was. But Dario was certain he exerted far more influence over his son than Lorenzo ever would.

He took a deep breath. This could be to his advantage. If he could get Cris on the inside of Lorenzo's operation... Yes, that could be good for him and Cris both.

But if he truly was going to beat Lorenzo and save his own hide, he was going to need a strong ally. Gianluca d'Imperio was probably dead to him—unless Cris's idea of proposing to Giovanna worked. But that was a long shot at best. And more time needed to pass before they could even think of trying that tack. No, he needed someone else.

His eyes came to rest on Lucchesi. His stomach roiled. Lucchesi. Always, always, Lucchesi. Every time he thought the man was beaten, he landed on his feet like a goddamn cat.

He addressed Lorenzo. "Let me know when you've decided on a successor. I should like to meet the poor unfortunate bastard."

A slight smile tilted the corners of Lorenzo's lips. "I'll keep you informed, of course."

"Cris, would you show your grandfather to his room?" *Before I strangle him.*

Lucchesi rose to leave as well, but Dario stopped him. "I'd like a word." His gut continued to churn. How many times had he wanted to crush Enrico Lucchesi to a bloody pulp? More than he could count. He could pinpoint the exact moment he'd started hating him: it was the day in the schoolyard when Toni—his beautiful, wonderful twin sister, his best and only friend, the center of his world—turned to him after Enrico Lucchesi had stopped another boy from harassing them and said, "Isn't he amazing?"

Her admiration, and later her love, for Lucchesi grew to the point where Dario was quite shut out, losing his best friend, his confidante. Leaving him alone against their father and the world.

But he had one consolation. His sister had left him a legacy he could use to control Lucchesi.

Lucchesi may have given his precious family ring to Delfina—and even for a man of Lucchesi's wealth, it was a generous gesture—but he still deserved what was coming. It was so much less than what Dario had originally planned. But for now, he'd have to content himself with the one last weapon he had.

Lucchesi took a chair in front of Dario's desk, curiosity on his face.

He wouldn't like what he was going to hear.

———— ◆ ————

"How did you know to bring weapons today?" Dario asked Enrico.

No way was he going to betray Delfina. "Call me cautious."

Dario chuckled. "More likely my daughter called you. But I'm not upset. Seeing how everything turned out, it was fortunate."

Enrico sighed. The cat was out of the sack. "She mentioned something about some recordings of Benedetto?"

Dario nodded. "We haven't gone through them all yet."

"How did you get them?"

A smile spread across Dario's face. "My sister had a habit of going unnoticed. She planted bugs all over Benedetto's property."

Madonna. "She never told me this." *What else didn't I know about her?*

"Toni was always an Andretti to the core. You think because you were married to my sister that you knew her."

What was he driving at? "Of course I knew her."

"What did she make you swear to on her deathbed?"

"To keep the peace with your father."

Dario sat back in his chair, a smile once again on his lips. "In other words, not killing him. Why do you think my sister asked that of you?"

"To keep me safe."

The smile turned to laughter. "*Dio mio,* you never saw it, did you?"

"Saw what."

"She *denied* you your revenge for your family. Why?"

Enrico had no answer. A strange light came into Dario's eyes. "I'll tell you, Lucchesi. She loved our father more than she ever loved you."

"She loved me."

Dario shook his head. "She loved *me.* Why do you think she sacrificed herself in marriage to you? She wanted *me* safe, she wanted me out of your father's hands."

"But she—"

"Told you she fancied you, yes? That she thought you'd make a good husband, that you were a better man than her father. Isn't that what she said?"

Enrico's chest started to ache. That was almost *exactly* what she'd said to him.

"You're wondering how I know. I'll tell you—she confessed it all to me after you married. Her entire plan. Marrying you was the only way she could get me back—our father would never have conceded otherwise. She had to convince both families that this plan was in everyone's best interests. And for a time it was."

Enrico reeled inside, as if punch drunk. Was it true? Had Toni's love for him been an act? Had he sacrificed so much—had he abandoned his *son*—for a woman who'd never loved him? It couldn't be true. It couldn't. "I don't believe it." Except the catch in his voice gave him away.

Dario shrugged. "Love is blind. Weren't you recently taken in by your own cousin? He 'loved' you too."

If Dario was telling the truth… had she planted bugs in their home? "What else is on the recordings?"

"All sorts of interesting conversations." That slow smile crept across Dario's lips again. "Some of them might even be of great concern to you."

"What do you mean?"

"My father recorded all sorts of things. Many of his phone calls. I haven't reviewed everything of course, but I would wager that some of those calls might be from your late cousin Domenico." Dario paused and raised his eyebrows. "Might those recordings interest you?"

Enrico's heartbeat quickened. If such recordings existed, they would prove that Dom had betrayed him, that he'd schemed with Carlo. In the wrong hands, those recordings would portray Enrico as weak for having spared Dom's sons, when 'Ndrangheta law called for a traitor's family to die. In the wrong hands, those recordings would provoke Dom's sons into war. They'd want to avenge their father; it was only natural. Even if their father had betrayed his *capo,* his *cosca.* They could claim—not unjustifiably—that Dom had been acting in the *cosca's* best interests all along.

And if he couldn't repair the breach between the branches of the Lucchesi family, Enrico would be forced to shed more blood. To shed the blood of boys he'd soon take as sons through the vow of *comparaggio.*

His stomach sank to his shoes. Doing such a thing—killing more of his closest kin—he couldn't bear it. He had to have the recordings if they existed. Swallowing hard, he looked at Dario. "Yes, I want those recordings. What do you want of me?"

"An alliance. You and I against Lorenzo."

Enrico nodded. "Done. And the recordings?"

"They will be yours. When I find them."

Which most likely would be quite a while, provided that Dario made an honest effort and didn't hold on to them for his own purposes.

But what other choice did he have? He slumped back in his chair and pressed a fist against his teeth.

Had Toni ever loved him?

And did he dare trust her brother?

———————— ◆ ————————

One month later
London, England

Nick bounded up the steps to his flat, Delfina beside him, her nose and cheeks red from the December cold. He stuck the key in the lock and turned it, giving the door an experimental push. This time, no post blocked it. His grandparents had come by and taken care of it as they'd promised. Delfina was about to step past him and into the flat, but he stopped her. "Just a moment, love." He swung her up into his arms.

She laughed. "What are you doing?"

"Carrying my gorgeous wife across the threshold." He pushed the door open with his shoulder.

And looked at his flat through her eyes. Cramped, dingy, a bit of a mess—though his grandmother had obviously done some tidying up—his flat was the exact opposite of everything Delfina was used to. Heat crept up his neck. "I know it's not much—"

"It's perfect."

He set her on her feet. "You don't have to lie to me, Delfi. I know it's bloody awful."

"It just needs a woman's touch." She glanced around, then turned back to him and put her arms around his neck. "And it's what we can afford."

True that. If they were going to make it on their own, they needed to economize. He sighed. "I want to give you the best."

She gazed up into his eyes and grinned, her fingers playing with the hair at the base of his neck. "I have you. I already have the best."

"Did I ever tell you how wise you were?"

"No. But I like the sound of that."

He swung her up in his arms again. They had a bed to christen, and a life together to start.

EPILOGUE

Lorenzo Andretti strolled through the garden of his modest villa in Calabria, occasionally puffing on the one cigar he allowed himself a week in a concession to his doctor's concerns about his health.

He had fooled them all. For now.

But his grandson wasn't stupid. Lorenzo had seen it on Dario's face, the suspicion, the mistrust. Such a shame, but it was no surprise.

Benedetto's disloyalty had been a shock; he couldn't say the same for Dario's. The boy had been nothing but a thorn in Carlo's side since the day he was born. Stubborn, willful, intractable. An Andretti through and through.

Fortunately, Benedetto's betrayal had played into Lorenzo's larger plans; the families were in an uproar over a Russian attack on Italian soil, a Russian attack on two prominent families. All the talk was of a possible war.

Now was the time to strike, to take action. To put the Andrettis firmly in charge of the whole 'Ndrangheta.

But his years weighed upon him. Lorenzo needed a successor, someone he could be sure of. Someone who would do his bidding. Someone who would carry on his legacy.

Someone like Cristoforo Andretti.

He knew Dario had seen through him, knew Dario thought he'd win this battle. But Dario didn't trust in the one thing Lorenzo trusted above all else: everyone had a price. Even the loyal, even the incorruptible. The trick was finding their weakness.

Lucchesi's was family. D'Imperio's was money. Dario's was fear.

Cristoforo's was love.

Once he pulled the right levers, pushed the right buttons, Lorenzo would have them all in his fist. And when that happened, he would rain down the fires of hell upon any who dared oppose his rule.

243

AUTHOR'S NOTE

Due to the high level of secrecy maintained by the 'Ndrangheta (the Calabrian Mafia) and the relative scarcity of former members turned state's witnesses, there are few resources detailing the inner workings of the society. Therefore, I have used artistic license in portraying certain aspects of the 'Ndrangheta, particularly as regards La Provincia.

Until July 2010, it was widely believed that there was no overarching body in charge of the 'Ndrangheta. However, with the arrest of several prominent 'Ndranghetisti, it is now believed that there is a *capo di tutti capi* (boss of all bosses) who oversees a commission (La Provincia) with direct power over the individual families. *Retribution* does not reflect this type of organization, though the formation of such an organization comes into play in later books.

Additionally, to make this series easier to read for American readers, I have used the term *cosca* rather than *'ndrine* to indicate an individual crime family. I have also greatly simplified the organization of individual crime families and have chosen to name crime families after their *capo*'s blood family; in real life, a *cosca*'s name may consist of a region or place, or a hyphenated combination of the names of the two or three primary blood families that control the *cosca*.

In Italy, women typically don't take their husband's last name; for simplicity's sake, I have chosen to reflect the traditional American practice of taking the husband's last name upon marriage.

I have used some artistic license in portraying the workings of the Serious Organised Crime Agency (SOCA) and Interpol. Employees of SOCA may be loaned to Interpol from time to time, but those employees are not actually in the employ of Interpol. I chose to simplify this relationship because the distinction wasn't dramatically important.

Please note that where actual businesses or locations are mentioned, no real-life Mafia connection is alleged or intended, past or present. These businesses and locations are used in a strictly fictional sense.

All persons mentioned in this series are fictional; no resemblance to actual people, living or dead, is intended. The family names used in this series were deliberately chosen not to reflect names of actual crime families.

ABOUT THE AUTHOR

Dana Delamar is the author of erotic romance, LGBTQ romance, and the "Blood and Honor" Mafia romance series, which is set in Italy among the Calabrian Mafia. Her first book, *Revenge*, received 4 stars from *RT Book Reviews*, was a Top Pick at The Romance Reviews, and was a double-finalist for Best First Book and Best Romantic Suspense in the 2013 Booksellers Best Awards.

Her second book, *Retribution*, received 4 stars from *RT Book Reviews* and was a semi-finalist in the Kindle Book Review's 2013 Best Indie Book Awards. Her book *Malavita* was a quarter-finalist in the 2014 Amazon Breakthrough Novel Awards, and her book *Redemption* was a finalist in the 2014 Maggie Awards and a semi-finalist in the Kindle Book Review's 2014 Best Kindle Book Awards.

Dana is also an editor with over thirty years of editing experience in both fiction and nonfiction and has worked with everyone from newbie writers to experienced pros. The books she's edited have won numerous awards and critical acclaim, including two Top Picks from *RT Book Reviews*.

danadelamar.com

MORE BY THIS AUTHOR

Thank you for reading *Malavita*. I hope I have entertained you.

Writing a book is a rather crazy endeavor, similar to trying to put together a thousand-piece puzzle with no picture to guide you. When I started this series, it was going to be only one book. Then two. Then four. Now it's grown to five with more books in the "Blood and Honor" world on the way. I hope you're having as much fun as I am on this journey.

If you enjoyed *Malavita*, please consider writing a review to help others learn about the book. Every recommendation truly helps, and I appreciate anyone who takes the time to share their love of books and reading with others. (And feel free to friend me on Goodreads—I love seeing what everyone is reading!)

To hear about my new releases, you can sign up for my VIP Readers List at danadelamar.com.

Keep reading for a special preview of the next book in the series, *Redemption*, which is about someone very dear to my heart, Antonio. When he first walked onto the pages of *Revenge*, I began to wonder about him and how he came to work for Enrico. Despite Antonio's sunny, flirty nature, I knew there was a deep sadness in him, and I've wanted to give him his happy ever after for a long time.

A SPECIAL PREVIEW OF *REDEMPTION*
(Blood and Honor, Book 3)

Finalist, 2014 Maggie Awards for Excellence!
Semi-finalist, Kindle Book Review's 2014 Best Kindle Book Awards!

A mobster seeking redemption.
A woman on a mission.
A cunning enemy ready to pounce...

Antonio Legato has always been an outsider, even though he's moved up in the Lucchesi mob organization. When he falls in love with Bianca Lucchesi, Antonio may at last become part of the family, but he's hiding an ugly secret about her father's death. Telling Bianca the truth will pit blood against blood and annihilate the family he loves.

Bianca Lucchesi reluctantly agrees to help her brothers ruin Antonio so they can take their rightful place in the organization. As assistant to the don's wife, Bianca seduces Antonio while pursuing her brothers' revenge. But her loyalty is divided—she and Antonio share a secret that he's unaware of. She longs to tell him, but fears he can never forgive what she's done.

When Bianca and Antonio learn that her brothers have rashly allied with a cunning enemy who is plotting against the Lucchesis, can they heal the family's wounds before everyone they love is destroyed?

———— ♦ ————

Eleven years ago
Rome, Italy

On a day like this, the sun shouldn't be shining. Not when his parents were dead, his older brother dead. The sky should be weeping, like Antonio's little sister, Violetta, who clutched his hand in the hospital waiting room. "Hush," he whispered to her, stroking her hair, making his voice gentle, steady, even though he shivered inside. She was only six, not ten and a half like he was. She was still a baby.

"I want Mamma," Violetta said.

So do I. But he couldn't say that aloud. "Zio Gino is coming for us."

Her wailing increased, and the nurse behind the counter looked over at them. Antonio pulled his sister onto his lap, letting her wrap her skinny arms around his chest, her damp face burrowing into his shirt, despite the blood covering it. Blood from their parents, blood from their brother Aldo. He hadn't been able to do anything for them. All he'd been able to do was pull Violetta from the car wreck. Somehow, the two of them had escaped with only bruises and scrapes.

"Violetta." Their uncle crouched down in front of them and placed a hand on her knee. Relief swept through Antonio, and the shaking in his belly moved up into his chest, the sob that had been building for hours trying to escape. He wanted to let it out, but something in his uncle's face stopped him. He was looking anywhere but at Antonio.

"Zio!" Violetta launched herself from Antonio's grasp and into Uncle Gino's arms. "What's happened to Mamma and Papà and Aldo?"

"They're gone, *cara*. To heaven. With Nonna Clara and Nonno Ugo."

A fresh wail burst from Violetta's lips. "No!"

Frozen, Antonio watched his uncle comfort her. "Shh, *bambina*, it'll be all right." He was staring at Antonio as he said this, but his eyes flicked away again. What was wrong?

Antonio finally forced himself to speak. "Zio?"

A slight shake of his uncle's head, his frown stern, his gaze fixed on the floor. "We can afford only one child."

Antonio's stomach clenched into a ball. Only one of them? But there was no decision to make. "Take Violetta."

His uncle nodded. "That is what I thought to do."

"Will Nonna Agnese and Nonno Vitale take me?" Antonio asked.

Again, another slight shake. "They are too old, Tonio. They have to live with us now."

Tears blurred Antonio's vision, but he blinked them back. "Where will I go then?"

"The government will take care of you. They will find a home for you. Another family."

But I don't want another family. I don't want anyone else but you. He kept the words stuffed inside, lodged in his throat. At least Violetta would be taken care of. That much he could be thankful for.

He wanted to cry, to beg his uncle to take him too. But he had to be a man, not a boy. He had to be strong for his sister. Violetta leaned toward him, grabbing his hand, her big brown eyes wet with tears. "Tonio, I don't want you to go."

"It's just for a while." Focusing on his uncle, he asked, "You'll visit, yes?"

"Yes." But again he didn't meet Antonio's gaze.

Oh. Antonio swallowed hard, understanding in an instant. This was goodbye. Forever. They wouldn't come, wouldn't keep track of him. Maybe Violetta would try, but she was only six. In time she'd forget him. He would be just a dim memory to her, little more than a ghost, like his parents and Aldo.

"Be good and brave," Antonio said to her, giving her a quick hug.

"I will." She clutched his shirt and burst into tears again. "I'll miss you, Tonio," she choked out, her breath catching and hitching.

"I'll miss you too, Vee." His voice was so thick he wasn't sure she could understand him. "Take good care of her," he said to his uncle.

Zio Gino gently detached Violetta's hand from Antonio's shirt. "We'd best leave now."

Antonio nodded, unable to make a sound. When the social worker came for him a short time later, he still couldn't speak. He pretended to listen when she spoke, her words washing over him, none of them what he wanted to hear. Something about an orphanage in Rome. Something about how someday he'd have a new family.

None of it mattered anyway. The only people who mattered, the only things that mattered, were gone.

He was alone. A boy with no family. A boy with no home.

———— ◆ ————

Present day
Milan, Italy

Something was wrong, but figuring it out seemed beyond him at the moment. Slowly stretching his injured left shoulder, Antonio Legato slumped down in his office chair and closed his eyes, shutting out the spreadsheets he'd been staring at. His first day back at work at the Banca di Falcone, and he felt utterly lost. Not to mention more tired than usual. He'd never had to recover from a gunshot wound before—much less two of them—despite having worked for Don Enrico Lucchesi for coming up on two years. Although Antonio had been shot at several times, he'd never been seriously hurt. Up until the engagement party for the don's son, six weeks ago.

Pushing back from the desk, Antonio rose and paced over to the window, looking out at the beautiful park across the street. Leave it to Don Lucchesi to pick such a scenic spot for his bank.

With a sigh, Antonio pressed his forehead to the window. He really ought to try to make sense of the figures in La Provincia's account. Right now they didn't, and considering that the account was the repository of all the funds the various families in the 'Ndrangheta, the Calabrian Mafia, were contributing to the war effort against the Russian *Mafiya*, many powerful men had a keen interest in what happened to that money. The most powerful of those men being Don Lorenzo Andretti, the head of La Provincia—the quasi-ruling body of the 'Ndrangheta—and head of the Andretti family, until recently the bitter enemies of the Lucchesis.

Supposedly, with the marriage of Don Lucchesi's son Nick to Delfina Andretti, all that enmity was over. Supposedly the two families were united. Supposedly now they'd have peace and common cause against the same enemy: the Russians.

Antonio wasn't so sure though. If the figures he was seeing were any indication, Lorenzo Andretti was up to something. Something bad.

And as Lorenzo Andretti's banker, the Lucchesis were stuck in the middle of the mess—whatever it was. Tomorrow Antonio and Don Lucchesi were flying to Calabria for a meeting of La Provincia, and in case anyone asked, he needed to understand what had happened with the account.

He needed to talk to Don Lucchesi. Surely he'd be able to make sense of all this. Antonio printed out a copy of the last twenty transactions and headed to see the don, his footsteps echoing on the marble floors.

By the time Antonio reached the don's office at the end of the corridor, he had to stretch his shoulder again. The doctors said he'd been damn lucky. He could have been paralyzed or killed.

He hadn't felt lucky at first. He'd lain face down for weeks, too exhausted to move, too drugged up to care, his only bright points in each day the frequent appearances by Kate, Don Lucchesi's wife. She wasn't Antonio's—never would be Antonio's—but he'd caught himself repeatedly fantasizing about what could have been, had she not been in love with the don. The fact that she'd made a fuss over him on his twenty-second birthday, which he'd had to celebrate in bed, had only made it more difficult for him to stop his wayward desires.

Kate's pregnancy agreed with her—her auburn hair seemed thicker, lusher than ever, her creamy white skin aglow whenever she smiled at him and smoothed his unruly hair back. The fact that she was only twenty-nine, so close to him in age, didn't help matters.

When he'd first awakened to Kate's touch in the hospital, Antonio had flashed back to a horrible bout of the flu he'd had at age nine. The year before his parents had been killed. His mother had done the same thing then—brushed his hair out of his face, pressed the cool back of her hand to his cheek. Was it really so much that he desired Kate, or was it more that he enjoyed her loving touch?

He'd had his share of women, but after the first one had cut him to the bone, he'd never allowed any of them in, never given any of the rest the chance to reject him, to size him up and find him wanting. Kate was the first woman in a long, long time he'd let himself care for.

And he shouldn't have. It had been a mistake, and he wasn't sure how to fix it.

Taking a deep breath, he knocked on the don's door, waiting for the summons to enter. When he heard it, he pushed the door open. "Tonio," Don Lucchesi said, greeting him with a smile. "How does it feel to be back?"

Disorienting is what he wanted to say. "Wonderful" is what he said.

"*Bene*. What do you have there?"

"Something I wanted to ask you about."

The don motioned him to one of the chairs in front of his gleaming mahogany desk. "Before we talk about that, there's something we need to discuss."

A tingle started in Antonio's gut. Had he done something wrong? But that was foolish—he'd just come back today. If something was wrong, it couldn't be his fault. "What?" he asked.

Leaning back in his chair, Don Lucchesi crossed his arms. "I'm not quite sure how to say this, but it can't wait any longer." The don shifted in his chair, making the leather creak. He cleared his throat, then said, "I've bought you an apartment in Cernobbio. You'll have Raffaele and anyone else you care to choose as a guard. It's my present to you. For Natale." A chill swept across Antonio's back. If the apartment was a Christmas gift, why was the don's voice so flat?

"I don't understand. You want me to move out?"

"It's time. I need to start treating you like my second in command, not my bodyguard." The don wiped at a bit of dust on his desk, not meeting Antonio's gaze. "We need to strengthen our alliances, and you're going to need a wife and a home of your own. I'm thinking about Giovanna d'Imperio."

Where was all this coming from? This was the first time the don had mentioned Antonio marrying. And then it hit him. "Is this about Kate?"

The don said nothing, but the muscles in his jaw worked. When he spoke, his tone was clipped. "You used to call her *la signora*."

"She insisted on Kate."

The don waved his words away. "You have five days to move your things. The men will take care of it, of course. I want the move completed before Sandro and Matteo's *comparaggio* ceremony, which will be two days before Natale."

Antonio felt like he'd swallowed a stone. A big jagged one. "So you want me out of the way. Do you want me out of the *cosca* too?"

"Of course not. The situation is just tense at the moment."

That was a complete understatement. Ever since Don Lucchesi had been forced to kill Domenico Lucchesi, his first cousin and former *capo di società*, they'd done their damnedest to keep the secret of Don Domenico's treason from his family, from his remaining sons, Sandro and Matteo. Because Don Lucchesi didn't want to have to take their lives too. But the fact that he'd given Antonio the position that Sandro felt rightly belonged to him hadn't gone down well, and relations between the two branches of the family were still rocky, even after the don had taken Sandro into the bank. The *comparaggio* ceremony—whereby the don would recognize Sandro and Matteo as sons—was supposed to mend the rift.

"Should I leave my position here, then? So far today, I've avoided Sandro, and maybe he's been avoiding me too, but that isn't going to last."

"It's not that, Tonio, and you know it. If I'm to keep Sandro and Matteo in this family, if I'm to take them on as sons, I have to make some concessions. And one of them is treating you—"

"Like an employee?"

Don Lucchesi sighed. "'Differently' is what I was going to say."

"So this is just about Sandro and Matteo? Kate has nothing to do with it?"

"It's safer not to have the two of us in the same home."

"Is it? Is that what you would say to Nick if he were here? If he were your

251

capo di società?"

Another sigh. "There has been enough strife already. The last thing I want, or need, is to throw more wood on the fire. Dario Andretti has those recordings of Dom somewhere, and if he leaks them, if Sandro and Matteo hear them, they'll know what really happened that night."

The night two and a half months ago when Antonio had urged the don to put a bullet in his cousin Domenico's brain for his betrayal of the family. The night Antonio had learned that sometimes you couldn't trust your own blood.

But then again, he'd already known that, hadn't he? Zio Gino had proved it when he'd taken Violetta and left Antonio behind. Left him to fend for himself. Left him even after he'd known how horrible life was for Antonio in the orphanage.

What did he keep doing wrong? Zio Gino was only the first person to find Antonio wanting. He hadn't been the last. And now Don Lucchesi was turning his back on Antonio too.

"Tonio, I'm sorry," the don started to say when his secretary opened the door.

"Signorina Lucchesi to see you. Shall I send her in?"

A strange mixture of excitement and dread swirled through Antonio's belly. Had he heard correctly? Bianca was here? He barely had time to wipe the surprise off his face before she walked in. There was no mistaking her—the same rich flowing caramel brown hair, the same flashing green eyes, the same delicate face.

But Bianca was no longer fifteen. She'd filled out into lush curves, and he flashed back to their one and only night together—how she'd arched beneath him and called his name, her nails digging into his shoulders, her breathing ragged in his ears, her scent swirling in his nostrils, driving him to bury his face in her neck, her hair, as he'd groaned his release. She'd been his first. The one he'd given his heart to. The one he'd never forgotten. But she'd forgotten him all too easily, hadn't she?

He met her gaze head-on, hoping his face didn't betray his memories or the emotions they aroused. Alarm registered on her features for just the barest moment before she focused on Don Lucchesi instead.

What the *hell* was she doing here?

———— ◆ ————

Her heart pounding, Bianca Lucchesi smiled at the man she'd come to see while doing her best to ignore the one she'd never wanted to see again. Antonio Legato. She'd arranged to meet her uncle at the bank instead of at his home because she'd hoped to avoid Antonio. And here he was anyway.

Dio mio, would her heart never slow down? One glimpse of him had been enough to bring everything back. Everything she'd tried so damn hard to suppress. To forget.

She widened her smile. "Zio Enrico," she said as he came around the desk and embraced her, kissing her on both cheeks. Marriage had agreed with her godfather. He was still lean, still handsome as sin, with that black hair and those chocolate eyes. He looked happy again—not stricken, the way he'd been at the funerals for her father and her brother Fedele.

"Prego," he said, motioning to the chair beside Antonio. "I don't believe you've

met my *capo di società*, Antonio Legato."

Would Antonio say something about their past? She stuck out her hand and tried to appear mildly interested. Anything but infuriated. Or hurt. "Don Legato," she said.

Antonio rose and took her hand in his large one. *Cristo*, he'd grown. He was a man now—at least six feet, with the broad shoulders and slim hips of a male in his prime.

His blue eyes met hers, a shock of unruly blond hair falling just over them. Though he seemed a little pale, a wave of heat rolled through her. How many nights had she dreamed of him? How many times had she relived those moments they'd spent together?

He flashed her a casual smile, as if he were completely unaffected by her, and pressed a kiss to her knuckles, the light brush of his lips reminding her of other places he'd kissed.

"Signorina Lucchesi. It's a pleasure. I haven't seen you since secondary school."

"I wasn't aware you knew each other," Enrico said.

"We had a class together," Antonio said. "Chemistry, I believe."

Bianca wanted to kick him in the shin. Was he trying to *flirt* with her? Chemistry! Yes, they'd had it. But outside of class.

"You're mistaken, *signore*. It was biology, not chemistry."

"My error." He was still grinning at her—the arrogant bastard. Did he think she still wanted him? Well, if he did, he was wrong.

Antonio released her hand, and they retook their seats. Bianca's skin tingled where he had touched her, and she resisted the urge to press her hand to her mouth, to feel that tingling against her lips. *Damn him.* Antonio Legato was a hundred different kinds of infuriating.

And he knew it.

"What brings you here today?" Enrico asked her.

She took another breath, then delivered the lie she'd carefully rehearsed. "I'm a bit at loose ends, and I thought perhaps I could help out at the orphanage."

"Of course. I'm sure Dottor Laurio could find something for you to do."

"Perhaps your wife needs help with the records?"

"Perhaps." He smiled. "You'll have to ask her." He leaned forward. "Is that truly what brought you all the way to Milan?"

She'd been prepared for this too. This time she could tell the truth. "I'm concerned about Sandro." She shifted in her seat, all too aware of Antonio beside her. She hadn't counted on having this conversation in front of him. Especially since he was wrapped up in all of it. "Sandro's very upset." She glanced at Antonio. "He feels disrespected." And that was putting it mildly. Don Lucchesi had given Sandro's birthright to Antonio. And with absolutely no explanation.

Enrico's smile vanished. "I thought that might be the reason."

"You must address this soon," she said, then hastened to add, "Don Lucchesi."

"He is not happy about the *comparaggio*? He hasn't said anything to me about it."

Bianca shook her head. "He says you are toying with him. That the ceremony means nothing. That bringing him into the bank was nothing. Not when you also brought in Dario Andretti's son. He's almost as angry about that as he is about your picking Don Legato to be *capo di società*."

Enrico's face darkened, and the hand on his desk clenched into a fist. She risked a glance at Antonio and saw him stiffen. A look flashed between the two of them. Were they considering—

No, not yet. Not unless Sandro persisted. Not unless he made a move against the don.

Her belly tight with fear, she leaned forward, placing a hand on the edge of the desk. "Mamma is trying to get him to see reason. But he's got Papà's temper." She tried to smile, but it disappeared, and she wasn't going to force it. If only Papà hadn't been killed, if only Don Lucchesi hadn't put Antonio in her father's place, things would be different. They'd still be one big happy family, Uncle Enrico and his wife visiting for leisurely suppers.

Except that was a lie. Her family hadn't been happy since Bianca's mistake. Her shame. At least *she* hadn't been. *Dio* knew what had happened during the six years since her father had sent her away.

At least Don Lucchesi didn't know of her shame. Only two people outside her immediate family knew. One of them was Giovanna d'Imperio, but Gio would never breathe a word. She'd sworn it.

The other was Antonio. Bianca's face heated. How could he sit there, how could he flirt with her, how could he act as if they didn't have a *child* together? He truly was as callous as Papà had said. He'd told Antonio about the baby, had given him a choice, and Antonio had said to get rid of the child. As if she could ever do that. Giving up their son for adoption had nearly killed her. But the alternative—what a cold *figlio di puttana*. That made him well-suited to the 'Ndrangheta, didn't it? She shouldn't have been surprised to hear that he'd joined, but she'd fallen for his act when they'd been in school. She should've known better. Antonio was an orphan, a tough streetwise boy. Not the gentle soul that she'd thought. Not that boy at all.

Her uncle spoke, pulling her out of her reverie. "Bianca, I'm at a bit of a loss with your brother. I don't want to remind him of what he owes me, but perhaps I must." She swallowed hard. Yes, Sandro needed to remember what he owed the don. His loyalty, his fealty. Utter and complete. Anything less was mutiny, betrayal. Treason.

Her brother walked a tightrope. The don would give him a touch more tolerance, because he was family, because he was blood, because he was his godson. But even blood went only so far.

If Sandro didn't come back into the fold, if he didn't stop railing against his *capo*, he'd end up dead.

"Mamma and I are trying. Perhaps if you offer him something—"

"*He* does not make demands of me. He is my blood, yes, but he needs to remember his place."

"Which should be at your side," she said, keeping her voice soft. Antonio shifted in the seat beside her, but said nothing.

"I have my reasons. It is not your place *or* his to question them."

She lowered her gaze. "Have we displeased you in some way? I thought you and Papà—"

"We were close. I miss him very much."

"Then why?"

"Bianca, do not push me." His tone was a warning. One she'd heed. She nodded, but still she wondered, her eyes sliding to Antonio. His face was carefully blank. Just what role had he played in all this dissension in her family? Once again, her family was at odds, and once again, Antonio Legato was at the heart of the conflict.

Bianca Lucchesi. She'd come and gone, and Antonio had reeled back to his office, thoroughly undone. The last time he'd seen her, a few weeks before she'd left for boarding school, she'd told him, with absolutely no sugar to coat it, that her family would never accept an orphan, that he should put any notion of them as a couple entirely out of his head. That he was nothing. Worthless. That their time together had been a lark for her. "A nice memory," that's what she'd said.

He slammed his fist onto his desk. "Nice" is not how he would have ever described their time together. Amazing. Hot. Overwhelming. Those were the words he would've used. But not "nice."

He thought he'd gotten over her. But he hadn't. He'd even made up an excuse to avoid the funerals for her father and her brother. He'd told Don Lucchesi that her brothers were likely to be upset, that he hadn't wanted to cause any additional drama at a time when the focus should have been on Don Domenico's and Fedele's deaths. And while that was true, the real reason had been *her*. He'd hoped to avoid Bianca. Preferably forever.

Damn. He'd reacted just the way he'd hoped he wouldn't. He'd even—*Dio* help him—he'd even *flirted* with her! Why? Why on earth couldn't he have just ignored her? Been as chilly, as polite, as she had?

Because she'd always been special to him. Apparently much more so than he'd been to her. Until Kate, Bianca had been the only person outside his family that he'd ever felt connected to. She'd cared about him when he'd been so alone.

And if he was honest, she'd hurt his pride. Bianca had been a challenge. She'd been asked out many times, but she'd never dated a single boy in their school. Until him. He'd persisted to the point where she'd jokingly called him "mosquito," but she'd finally agreed to see him, though she'd said they had to keep it quiet. Her father didn't want her dating anyone.

Turned out, her father didn't want her dating *him*.

A sharp rap on his office door shook him out of his thoughts. He'd been so rattled, he hadn't even asked Don Lucchesi about La Provincia's account. Perhaps the don had remembered. "Come in," Antonio called.

But it wasn't his *capo*. Sandro Lucchesi, eyes blazing, charged in and right up to Antonio's desk. Placing two meaty hands on the polished mahogany, Sandro leaned forward, his black curls falling over his forehead. "You think you're so clever, but I've caught you."

Adrenaline rocketed Antonio to his feet and he balled his fists. "*You* don't address me that way," he barked. Sandro was a few centimeters shorter, but very nearly matched him in weight. And he had the Lucchesi name. But Antonio was *capo di società*, and Sandro had to respect that.

"I've been checking around, *capo*"—Sandro put as much sarcasm into the title as he could—"and I've just finished talking to Cesare Palumbo. He saw you with my father. About four hours before Papà's body was found. Cesare said that you both were acting strangely. Really tense."

Fuck, fuck, and double fuck. Had Cesare seen the gun Antonio had been pressing into Don Domenico's back? Probably not, or he'd have done something about it. Antonio had thought they'd been unobserved. How the hell had Cesare seen them? Fuck! He needed to talk to Don Lucchesi. If the truth got out—if Sandro learned how his father had truly died—there'd be no hope for the Lucchesi family. Sandro and Matteo—maybe even Francesca and Bianca—would have to die like their traitorous patriarch. Like Don Domenico.

Those were the rules they lived by. A traitor's family died along with him.

But Don Lucchesi hadn't had the heart to condemn them along with Don Domenico. They were all the family he had left. The last of the Lucchesis.

Antonio took a breath. He needed to stay calm. To think. "Of course we were tense. Carlo Andretti had kidnapped Don Lucchesi's wife. I was sent to guard your father."

"Then why is he dead?"

Antonio groaned inwardly. He'd said too much. "He refused the escort. Said he could get home by himself."

The look on Sandro's face couldn't have been more skeptical. "My father refused a guard? On *that* night, of all nights?"

Antonio shrugged. It was all he could do. "He didn't explain himself to me."

"Of course not. He didn't have to explain himself to a mere *guard*."

"I'm no longer a guard." He tried to keep his voice as even as possible.

"I am well aware of that. So just how did a *guard* become *capo di società*?"

Again, Antonio shrugged. "Don Lucchesi has his reasons."

"And what reasons are those?"

"You'll have to ask him."

Sandro leaned closer to Antonio. "I will. I will get to the bottom of this. And I will have what is mine." Sandro rapped his knuckles on Antonio's desk, then he jabbed a finger at Antonio. "You'd best watch your back, Legato. When I prove that you killed my father, I won't hesitate to cut you down. In fact, I'll relish the opportunity."

"You cannot threaten your *capo di società* and not expect to answer for it."

Sandro laughed. "Do your worst. You think my *padrino* will make me lick your boots? I'm like a son to him. And soon I will *be* his son. And you? You will still be street trash."

Antonio didn't even think. He just threw the punch, his fist connecting with Sandro's jaw in a quick uppercut that threw Sandro off-balance. Antonio followed with a blow from his left. Agony seared across his upper back as the shot connected.

Not. A. Good. Idea.

Sandro staggered back and Antonio inhaled against the pain, rounding his desk in an instant, shoving his body into Sandro's. They were so close he could smell the espresso on Sandro's breath. "Insult me again, and I will discipline you in front of the *cosca*. Don Lucchesi doesn't like to take fingers. But the idea doesn't bother me."

Sandro wiped at the blood trickling from his nose and sniffed. "Peasants do fight with their fists, don't they?"

"I was going to start with one finger. Would you like it to be two?" Part of him hoped Sandro would keep pushing. He'd love to show Sandro a thing or two he'd learned on the streets.

The door banged back on its hinges and Cris Andretti walked in. He took in Sandro's bloody nose, then addressed Antonio. "I heard you out in the hall. Need help?"

"Fuck you, Andretti," Sandro said. "Like you could even touch me."

Cris crossed his arms, and the movement made his broad chest and shoulders even more impressive. "Try it."

Sandro looked from Cris to Antonio. "Well, now I *know* you killed my father. Your friend here is a fucking Andretti, if you haven't noticed."

"They're our allies."

"*Your* allies, maybe." After a pause, Sandro shook his head and smirked. "You don't get it. Cesare Palumbo is only *one* of the men who doesn't trust you or my uncle. He's willing to follow me. There are others. I wonder how many?"

Antonio's stomach turned to stone. Sandro was talking about an out-and-out mutiny. A catastrophe for the *cosca*, and annihilation for the Lucchesi family. "You're bluffing."

"Maybe you bluff, Legato. I never do." With that, Sandro stomped out and Cris followed him. Which left Antonio to contemplate the huge hole he'd dug for himself.

What was he going to tell Don Lucchesi? He'd let his temper get away from him, and instead of defusing tensions with Sandro, he'd inflamed them. He'd even stupidly threatened to take two of Sandro's fingers! The don would never stand for that.

Antonio plopped onto the top of the desk with a thump and rubbed his left shoulder. When he shifted his weight, papers crunched beneath him, and he stood up and discovered what he'd sat on. The statement for La Provincia's account. On top of everything else he'd fucked up, was he going to tell the don he couldn't figure this out either? Was he going to give Don Lucchesi another reason to question his choice of Antonio as *capo di società*? No. No he wasn't. He was going to solve that problem himself.

And somehow, he'd figure out how to bring Sandro Lucchesi to heel.

Preferably without a bullet.

END OF SPECIAL PREVIEW

Print and Ebook

www.danadelamar.com

Continue reading for a special preview of Kristine Cayne's second Deadly Vices novel

DEADLY ADDICTION

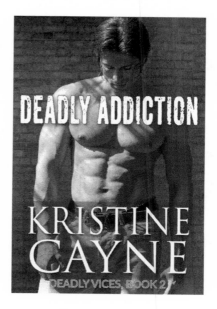

A proud people. A nation divided.

Rémi Whitedeer, police officer turned substance-abuse counselor, dreams of restoring order to his tribe. Violence and crime are rampant throughout the unpoliced Iroquois reserve, and a civil war is brewing between the Guardians, a militant traditionalist group, and other tribal factions. As the mixed-race cousin of the Guardians' leader, Rémi is caught in a no-man's land—several groups lay claim to him, but all want him to deny his white blood.

A maverick cop on an anti-drug crusade.

When she infiltrated the Vipers to take down the leader of the outlaw biker gang responsible for her brother's death, police sergeant Alyssa Morgan got her man. But her superiors think she went too far. Her disregard for protocol and her ends-justify-the-means ethics have branded her an unreliable maverick. To salvage her career, she accepts an assignment to set up a squad of native provincial officers on a reserve.

A radical sovereigntist bent on freeing a nation.

Decades of government oppression threaten the existence of the Iroquois Nation. But one man, Chaz Whitedeer, is determined to save his people no matter what the price, even if it means delving into the shadowy world of organized crime.

When Rémi and Alyssa uncover the Guardians' drug-fueled scheme to fund their fight for true autonomy—a scheme involving the Vipers—Rémi must choose between loyalty to family and tribe or his growing love for Alyssa.

Can Rémi and Alyssa leave everything behind—even their very identities—for a future together?

An excerpt from *Deadly Addiction*

Eyes closed, Alyssa pressed the glass of water to her neck. "I can do the talking if that makes you feel any better."

Although Rémi heard the words, it would have taken an act of Parliament to get him to respond.

The heat of her skin caused the condensation on the glass to liquefy. Like a tractor-beam, his gaze followed a drop of water as it slid down the long pale column of her neck, followed the curve of her right breast and slipped under the collar of her blue cotton T-shirt into the V of her cleavage. Oh fuck. He wanted to be that drop of water. He wanted to be snuggled between her warm ripe breasts. His cock swelled and lengthened, letting him know that it wanted to be there too.

He squeezed his eyes shut and willed his hard-on away. This wasn't the time and certainly not the place for Mr. Happy to make an appearance. But the more he tried not to think about where the drop had gone, the more he did. He'd thought he was a leg man, but he knew the truth now. It had slapped him in the face. He was a breast man. An "Alyssa's breasts" man, and he fucking wanted to see them, to feel them, to taste them. Right now.

Print and Ebook

www.kristinecayne.com

Made in the USA
Middletown, DE
17 September 2019